Give Me What You Can't

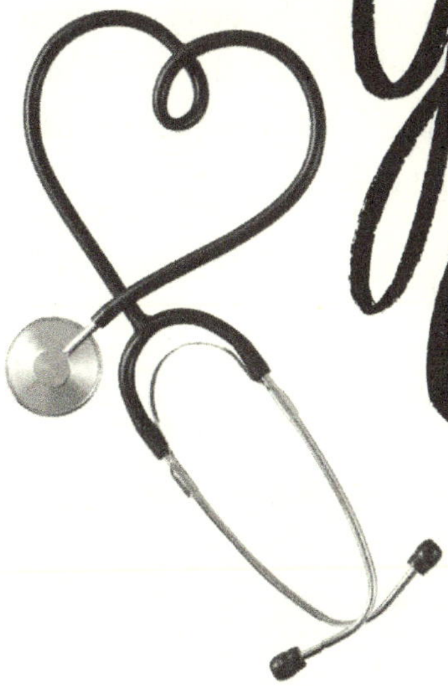

Give Me What You Can't

Published by AB Publishing

Cover illustrated by Aleksandra Czerw

Edited by Mandy Tayian

June 2026

Paperback: 979-8-9963640-0-8

Epub: 979-8-9926695-7-2

Audiobook: 979-8-9926695-8-9

This book is for those who give a little too much and forget themselves along the way. Remember darling, there is no age requirement for self-discovery. So don't be afraid to explore the marvelous frontier that you are. You might find exactly what you need on the other side. Like a cowboy who needs to take care of ya.

Hello, my darling baddies,

Welcome to Saint Sierra Hospital in inner-city LA. For those who wish to go in blind, please keep in mind that this MM romance is a work of fiction. This is an interconnected, standalone, fighting-feelings, age-gap romance with a happily-ever-after

Also, I'm not a doctor, I just write about them. Please don't take this medically seriously!

Now off you go—we've got a needy cowboy and his bearded daddy waiting for you.

Mental Health Disclaimer:

This book includes mention of sibling suicide, burnout, depression, physical manifestation of stress/trauma, dementia, divorce, violence, death, and topics related to trauma and mental health, as well as explicit sex between two men.

Terms:

Highly Sensitive Person (HSP): Someone who feels everything deeply, all the way down to their nervous system. Often called empaths, HSPs are intuitive, creative, and empathic deep thinkers who are often incredibly giving and perceptive.

Shame: Believing we are not good enough, or bad. We attempt to control our shame through perfectionism, never showing our true emotional selves. Shame can be an emotional reaction to little (or big) mistakes, flaws, or negative beliefs we have about ourselves. Shame is the toxic ex in the backseat of your car, slapping you every time you make a mistake while driving through life. Shame makes us believe that we aren't worthy of belonging to anything/anyone, ruins our connections, and can blind us to love.

Vulnerability: Vulnerability is GETTING THE FUCK BACK UP despite what happened to us, despite potential risk, uncertainty, and emotional exposure. Vulnerability is courage and incredibly hard, but worth it. It is bravery and strength in their highest, purest forms, and the most essential emotion for living a true, authentic life. Being vulnerable is fucking powerful, even if it hurts. It is choosing love over fear. ***It is magic made real, and the spell is our hearts' spoken truth.***

THE PLAYLIST

After Midnight—Dorothy

Don't Fear The Reaper—AMAZONICA

For Whom the Bells Tolls—Metallica

Spitting Off the Edge of the World—Yeah Yeah Yeahs

Inner City Blues—Marvin Gaye

Damn Right, I've Got The Blues—Buddy Guy

Closer to Home (I'm Your Captain)—Grand Funk Railroad

I Know You're Hurting. -RAYE

Youth—Daughter

Mustang Sally—Wilson Pickett

Revolution—Bishop Briggs

Sayin' What I'm Thinkin'—Lainey Wilson

Closer—Nine Inch Nails

Save a Horse (Ride a Cowboy)—Big & Rich

Set It Off—Audioslave

If I Can't Have You—Shawn Mendes

And Love—Florence + the Machine

Country Boy—Muddy Waters

Effortlessly, I feel everything—The Man The Myth The Meatslab

Lose Control-Teddy Swims

Chapter 1

John

The tension pressing against his skull seemed unrelentingly endless.

He knew perfectly well that nothing he did would make it go away, either. No amount of medicine, massage, whiskey, dark rooms, or a complete eight hours of uninterrupted sleep.

Nothing would help.

Not this damn headache.

This was his stress, manifesting into a big ball of fuck-you pain that rested right behind the eyelids. Not to mention the throbbing ache in his shoulder. His self-diagnosis was a frozen shoulder. Which, at least for the moment, wasn't as noticeable as the headache.

"Do you think your body is trying to tell you something, John?" the therapist asked, referring to the headache John had complained about before taking a seat on his couch.

John had chosen this therapist specifically because he worked with first-responders—doctors. He needed someone who understood, not just sympathized.

John's issues with trusting others to help him were limited, if non-existent.

"Oh, probably," John had replied with a forced tug of his lips, not bothering with an actual attempt at a smile.

"What do you think it's trying to tell you?" the therapist asked.

John sucked in an impatient breath, his chest expanding, leaning back into the cream white couch. "Probably a lot, if I chose to listen."

The therapist, an older man with light brown skin, graying stubble on his cheeks, and direct dark eyes beneath simple black glasses, shifted in his seat, seeming to contemplate before saying, "I'm getting the impression you don't want to be here."

John actually smiled this time, shaking his head, "No. I don't."

The therapist didn't look the least bit offended. "Then why are you?"

John let out a reluctant sigh. "My charge nurse threatened to have the nurses ignore me for the rest of the month if I didn't talk to someone."

The therapist, Miles something, chuckled. "A serious threat, then."

"Very serious," John replied coolly. Any doctor worth their salt knew they couldn't do their job without the nurses, especially in his department.

"What type of medicine do you practice?" Miles asked.

"Emergency. Trauma medicine."

"An expertise and a trauma, in and of itself."

John swallowed, giving a short nod. "Yeah, sure. But the rewards are there, too."

Right, the rewards, he thought bitterly, and what are they, John?

When was the last time you actually felt something for a patient? For anything?

"Tell me about them," Miles said.

John's throat tightened. His patience had quickly zeroed out for this conversation. He leaned forward on his elbows, rubbing his forehead. "Look, I came here because a friend suggested it… and honestly, I'm questioning my decision. No disrespect for you, I just don't think this is what I need."

Miles nodded, "What do you think you need?"

He paused, wondering when the last time he asked himself that question was—outside the basics such as food, sleep, and coffee. Usually in that order.

"I dunno," John replied. "I used to think it was family, playing house..." he hesitated, working the muscles at the back of his neck and shoulder. "But when all that ended, I realized I was..."

Lost.

So fucking lost.

Guilt washed over him, followed quickly by anger. He should've wanted the same things Melissa had wanted. His ex-wife. He should've wanted the life she offered him, and yet... he didn't. No matter how many times he tried to convince himself otherwise, and how much easier his life might've been if he had.

Or worse, his mind whispered.

"My ex and I separated a while ago," John explained. "It was best for both of us. We recognized we couldn't give each other what we wanted. She's now happily remarried, adopting her second kid."

John felt a wave of shame as he thought about how much Melissa had accomplished once she had finally left him.

Maybe if he slowed down with work? Maybe if he listened...?

He shook his head, refusing to get sucked back into that spiral.

What was done was done. He couldn't go back and fix their marriage. And if he were honest with himself, he didn't want to.

He had been so focused on meeting his family's expectations: college, relationship, career, family, that one day he woke up, five years married and drifting through his relationship with his wife and with himself.

He'd lost touch with what he wanted, and then Melissa began to push for a baby and everything in his world came crashing down.

Love was not what he thought it was.

Love eventually led to something he couldn't give.

So, he ran to the only place that felt familiar.

His job.

And he worked a lot. He was the type of doctor who valued staying up to date with the latest medical journals and research papers. He thrived on knowledge and learning, which made him a better leader and a better attendant to his residents-in-training. The problem was that the politics of the hospital environment were becoming more convoluted under the constant pressure from higher-ups and insurance companies, who seemed to be more in charge of his job than he was half the time.

His job was hard enough without the constant red tape, making it difficult to find it a refuge from his mind lately.

"Do you want to talk about it?" Miles asked curiously, patiently coaxing John to peel back the layers of his life.

John's throat closed, his stiff shoulder inching closer to his ear, and he rolled it, attempting to make it settle.

Do I really want this?

To purge myself on someone's couch?

Is this really going to help me?

John opened his mouth to reply when his phone dinged.

"Excuse me," he murmured, pulling it out from his back pocket. He was about to turn it off when he glimpsed the number and quickly opened it.

We still on?

A flutter of excitement rushed over him. Feeling the unexpected tremble in his hands, John texted back quickly.

Yes.

He clicked off his phone and leaned back. Relief swirled at the base of his spine, all the way up to his shitty headache, which surprised him. All because Ben had texted him.

The young man had been sucking his dick for the past couple of months, and he, in return, had gotten to do the same. And it had been exhilarating, if not fundamentally life altering. Not for Ben himself, but for the sex. It had been fucking bliss, and exactly what he'd been missing in his forty-plus years of life on this spinning globe in the vast universe.

John's awakening to his sexuality had been painfully slow.

It wasn't until Melissa had left him and he had crawled long enough out of his pain that he began to recognize certain things about others… specifically men. He noticed he looked a little longer at attractive men, far more often than he did at attractive women. It was merely a suspicion at first that seemed to grow louder every day, making it impossible for him to continue to ignore. He explored gay porn first, in the privacy and comfort of his home, and watched it only a handful of times. He was unable to look away at certain men in those videos—the handsome, virile, and strong young men, who were so confident, so claiming of their desires that it left him breathless and harder than a damn sledgehammer.

He felt ashamed the first few times he watched. But the release and the relief he experienced afterward washed away some of the shame, leaving behind only faint traces.

It wasn't until he met Ben, a young, handsome paramedic who liked to brush shoulders with John a little too often and hold his gaze for a little too long. One night, Ben made a direct pass at him, right outside the med bay with no one else around, and John, terrified, said yes.

And thank God he had.

The last few weeks had confirmed the theory that he desired men, even though he was initially awkward and nervous with Ben, feeling like a teenager all over again in that vulnerable phase of self-discovery. John wasn't interested in Ben beyond sexual exploration, and Ben wasn't interested in commitment either, so it worked out well for them.

The problem was their schedules, which were getting busier and harder to pin down for the night of mutual relief.

Ben missed the last one, and John was growing restless.

God, I am so fucking ready.

He nearly smiled. His stomach tingled in anticipation and his cock twitched eagerly to life at the mere thought of having sex with a man.

Because this would be his first time taking that next step beyond foreplay.

Ben would pop his gay cherry, and John couldn't fucking wait.

"I appreciate you taking the time to see me, Miles," John said, deciding in that instant that he'd rather go home and get ready for his hook-up later tonight than spend another twenty minutes talking about nothing important.

"I don't know if I'm ready for therapy yet," he said, and stood. "Bill me for the full hour, please."

Miles also got to his feet, a cool understanding in his gaze.

Every good physician knows, just like a therapist, you can't force treatment onto an unwilling patient.

Miles paused, hand on the doorknob of his office door. "Can I say something, just an observation…?"John stiffened, chin lifting, and nodded.

"Our professions, that of healers and givers, can be demanding work. We're not supermen, nor are we perfect by any means. I can only imagine the truly incredible burden you feel with literal lives on the line. The pressure from others to perform and to give. I suppose I simply want to say, we are not limitless creatures, we're not supposed to be. It is okay to stop every once in a while."

John nodded politely. "I'll take that under consideration. Thank you again for your time."

"Another?"

"Yeah, but only if you make it as good as the last one."

The bartender, a handsome twenty-something man with a pretty smile, gave him a flippant smirk, "I'll do my best."

John paused, thinking about those words and how often he said them to his own patients.

And on some days, like today, it didn't matter if he did his best.

It didn't matter if he was the most skilled doctor in the emergency department.

It didn't matter if he had unlimited resources, time, and energy.

It didn't matter if he had the best intentions.

It just simply didn't matter because days like these were impossible to get out from under. And lately, John wasn't sure he could ever shake the feeling.

He raked a hand through his short, dark, salt-and-pepper beard and up to his neck, tempted to work the muscles of his right shoulder but knowing it probably wouldn't look too polite doing arm stretches at this posh, overly pricey bar. So instead, he leaned forward on the bar counter, kneading the tight muscles at the back of his neck. The bartender returned with his drink, slipping it between his elbows.

John glanced up and smiled thinly at the young man.

"Hope you like this one, too," the bartender said.

John noted the flash of a flirtatious smile before he sauntered off to help the couple that had just approached the end of the bar.

Sighing, John released his neck and took a sip from the crystal glass. He let the sweet whiskey sit on his tongue before swallowing it, letting it burn down into his lungs and through his chest. The sultry croon of the blues band playing in the corner on stage filtered over him, but he barely heard it, lost in his thoughts, which was the last place he wanted to be.

His mind of late had been an inhospitable place, if not, at times, a truly dangerous place.

Taking another sip, he ruminated on the losses that happened today, yesterday—hell, this whole damned month. It had been rough, rougher than usual. Or maybe it had been exactly the same, but his tolerance for it was lowering.

Fuck, he thought bitterly. He hated to think that. He loved his job.

It was exciting, thrilling, even when he made a major save. Except, all he could remember were the bad days, and they were stacking up in his soul like an avalanche ready to cave in and crush him.

John pinched the brim of his nose, refusing to see the faces of the patients who had died or their grief-stricken families, sobbing, wailing, or worse, just staring at him, vacant and empty—like him.

Stop it, John. Just fucking stop.

He pleaded with his mind to be quiet.

If it gets too bad, I can always quit. Set up a small, boring family practice somewhere just like Dr. Seevers did…

His mentor, Dr. Seevers, retired and set up his own practice, stepping away from the chaos of the emergency department and the bullshit bureaucracy of hospital work. John wanted to talk to him, but he was worried that if he did, he'd end up quitting, and he wasn't ready to do that. Not yet. The difference was that Dr. Seevers was in his late fifties when he left the hospital. John was only 46 years old, and yet he felt like the oldest person in the department lately. Maybe it was because of the fresh litter of residents he had filling his hallways that made him feel ancient with their youthful, hopeful glow, so eager and optimistic. He cringed, rubbing his temple. They were naive and had no idea what this life meant. What it would cost them to dedicate their lives to being doctors, especially in emergency medicine.

Because eventually, it would take everything.

Or maybe just a shoulder.

John leaned back in his seat and rolled his shoulder, attempting to relieve the knot in the muscle. He tried to stretch his shoulder, knowing he needed to see a chiropractor, or at least a physical therapist. Except, when would he have time for that? When he wasn't working, he was sleeping. So he did what most busy physicians did: he relegated his physical health to convenience, settling for ice packs and a heating pad. He tried cold plunges, steam rooms, and massages, but they were essentially useless. The shoulder felt permanently stuck. Frozen in place like a crippling iceberg that wasn't melting or yielding in the slightest. It was moderately painful, but mostly irritating. If he moved his arm in the wrong direction or tried to lift a patient, then it hurt, and he was fucked.

Like today.

God, what a fucking mess…

He scrubbed a hand over his face, feeling the flush of embarrassment and shame. John was the head of the department, the senior leading resident on his shifts, and the captain of the ship. So when he couldn't perform, people noticed and grew concerned, and he couldn't afford for anyone on his team to see that.

But Lawson had seen him crumble.

Fucking Lawson.

If it had been anyone else, he would've maybe tolerated it. But it was the new resident, who had been there for less than six months, who saw it.

Lawson saw him hesitate, filled with doubt and pain...

Lawson, who stepped in and took over.

A kid!

Regret washed over him, and John's thoughts returned to the day with a vengeance.

The first mistake was the bodybuilder patient. The overly large man, wearing a paper-thin black t-shirt and bright green shorts with flashy sneakers, stumbled into the ED from the lobby with one of the nurses, and when he couldn't make it to the stretcher, he collapsed in a mass of muscles, nearly taking the nurse down with him. He was pale and shaking, and John was the first to reach him, followed by the closest available doctor-in-training, Lawson.

The nurses brought over a gurney and lowered it as much as possible to lift the man onto it. Forgetting all about his shoulder, John knelt with Lawson and two other nurses and attempted to lift the oversized man. The pain had been instant and he jerked, but he managed to maintain his grip, refusing to drop the patient on the floor in the middle of the goddamned ED.

Once they were able to transfer him, John let go and nearly stumbled back, pain etched in his features, which Lawson saw.

"Are you okay?" Lawson took a step toward him, his eyes darting over John's body and leveling on his shoulder, seeing him roll it and trying desperately to release the muscle that refused to give.

"I'm fine," John replied sharply. Too sharply, causing the heads of the two nurses to turn toward him, surprised. Because John was always the calm, cool, collected captain. And that reputation was something he strove to maintain no matter what.

They had taken the man into the first available room, and as the nurses were hooking him up, the patient revived. In a panic, he shot up, his large arm swiping at one of John's nurses. John had reached out instinctively, catching the arm and firmly but gently guiding it back down while calmly informing the patient where he was and what John and his team were doing.

His shoulder burned in protest the entire time, but there wasn't a damn thing he could do about it until the patient was controlled.

He finally left the room a few minutes later, heading toward his locker to take something for the pain and, maybe if he had time, which he knew damn well he didn't, put an ice pack on his shoulder.

Unbeknownst to him, Lawson had followed him.

"Excuse me, um...Dr. Donnelly?" Lawson asked tentatively from behind him.

John continued in his clipped pace down the hallway. "Good job in there."

"Thanks," the young doctor said, still following him.

"What do you need, Lawson?" John asked shortly.

"Are you... okay?"

John's teeth mashed together, and he stopped abruptly, causing the young resident to collide into his back before quickly side-stepping around him to face him.

"Sorry," Lawson fumbled, wiping his nervous palms onto his dark gray scrubs.

"I'm fine," John repeated, attempting a bland smile of reassurance.

Lawson hesitated, eyes darting once more to John's shoulder. "Do you need anything?"

John sucked in a tight breath, trying his best not to show his impatience. "That's usually my question."

Lawson was overstepping. John was in charge. Lawson was simply a crewmate. He wasn't supposed to question his captain.

Lawson flushed, his cheeks reddening the longer they stood there, and he nervously took another step back. "Right, yeah. Okay, sorry..."

Lawson finally tucked tail and returned to the nurse station to take another patient. John had hoped that would be the end of it. But somehow, Lawson was everywhere he turned today. And by the end of the shift, John's shoulder was throbbing.

The last patient of the day was a homeless man found unconscious outside a gas station. The paramedics wheeled him in on a gurney and transferred him to a hospital bed. Lawson and another junior resident, Reyes, came in to assist.

But as the paramedics were transferring the patient to the bed, the man reared to life, bucking wildly. Usually, John was the first to jump in and attempt to restrain, but with his aching shoulder, he hesitated. And Lawson saw it. In a flash, Lawson shouldered past John, forcing him to take a step back as the young doctor took over.

John watched closely, eyes fixed on Lawson's strong arms as they bunched and tensed as he gripped down, pressing the homeless man down onto the bed as Reyes attempted to inform the man where he was and how he had been found. The patient proceeded to be hostile, forcing the staff to administer a sedation shot. Less than two minutes later, the patient was sufficiently subdued.

John praised the team for their good work and quickly left, feeling utterly useless and desperately wanting to go home and stew in a big glass of whiskey. But he couldn't because he had booked his therapist appointment for right after his shift.

He was cursing under his breath when he heard Lawson. "Dr. Donnelly…"

Before John could give another placating answer, the young resident rushed out, surprising him. "You're in pain."

John stilled, glancing around to see if anyone had overheard that. No one did.

"I can tell," Lawson said knowingly. "I used to work with horses that would do the same thing when they had a cramp or were in pain."

John tilted his chin, curious. "Horses?"

They were deep in the city, and there weren't any horses for at least twenty miles or more in almost every direction.

"My dad runs a dude ranch in Arizona," Lawson informed him, and despite his nerves about approaching John, his eyes were locked with his.

Jesus, his eyes were blue, John thought, unable to look away from the stunning color, a mixture of blue and gray.

"A dude ranch?" John stared, slightly dumbfounded, and realized then that he knew absolutely nothing about Lawson, which was pretty normal under their circumstances. Choosing to work in the emergency department meant nonstop action most days and very little time to socialize. And even if John did talk to someone, it was either his second-in-command, Dr. Samuels, or the charge nurse, Steph.

Lawson was low on the conversation list.

"Horse ranch for tourists," Lawson said, his full lips thinning into a tight line. "But also for people who just need to get away from places like this—busy cities or jobs. Get back to nature."

He nodded, thinking he probably could use a bit of relaxing nature himself. He wondered when the last time was that he was outside long enough to notice it, let alone appreciate it. Standing on the medical tarmac of the hospital's roof waiting for a helicopter to land didn't count.

"Anyway," Lawson shifted. "I, uh, just wanted to see if I can do anything to help?"

"You already did. And it's nothing to be concerned about, all right? Just a frozen shoulder. I'm working on it with *my* doctor." He lied, not really caring. He didn't have a doctor helping him with his damn shoulder because he didn't want to be told what it meant.

That he was old. That he needed to slow down. Retire. Maybe see a therapist, which he was doing today, and he hoped like hell that didn't make him an idiot.

Lawson's eyes narrowed, taking in the information, "Frozen shoulder? For how long?"

John hesitated, face pinched in mild disapproval of the question.

Lawson's chin tilted back in sudden understanding that he had overstepped the line again. "Sorry, I didn't mean…"

John cut him off by dropping a firm hand on Lawson's shoulder, squeezing, "It's fine. You're allowed to be concerned. But know I've got it handled, all right?" John noticed the hard muscle beneath Lawson's scrubs, which he had no right to be noticing, and quickly snatched his hand back. "It's time to get outta here anyway. Go ahead and head to the nurses' station for a debrief."

"Okay," Lawson said, eyes flickering over him once more before sliding away.

John took another sip, letting his second glass of whiskey at the hotel bar soothe his frustration. He knew he was a bit old-school in refusing to show any vulnerability at work. This job took everything from the doctors, staff, and nurses. And he wasn't going to make anyone else's job harder because he was struggling.

He supposed Lawson was trying to be nice, but still, it drew unnecessary attention to him. He had to maintain composure when everyone else broke down or when chaos ensued, as it did nearly daily in his job. It was his duty to be unflappable and maintain course.

So then why did he feel so lost?

Why was his shoulder getting worse, not better?

And how come this aching hole swirled in his chest that he couldn't seem to fucking shake?

Maybe he needed to escape to Lawson's dad's dude ranch for a long weekend and get lost on a trail with a horse. He snorted. Justine, his sister, would keel over in shock if she saw him on a horse. They were city kids, with no concept of animals outside the dead ones on their plates. Their parents wouldn't even allow them a family dog growing up.

Maybe I could get a dog? Right—and when would I have time to take care of a dog?

John glanced at his phone, noticing an unread text message. He stilled, disappointment already rising in his chest. He knew what this meant. He recognized the number with no name and opened it.

> I'm really sorry. I can't make it tonight. Working a double...

Fuck.

John stared numbly at the text message.

This was supposed to be the night he'd been leading up to with Ben. It had been his night to let go of the control he held so firmly on his life, to find release and pleasure in someone else—to not give to anyone or anything—just take.

Take everything.

Greedily, hungrily, desperately.

His throat clenched and he clicked the screen off, tossing the phone onto the hard marble bar top, his frustration peaking.

He *needed* this tonight.

He needed to forget about the pain in his shoulder, to forget about these past few months, and feel the weight of a muscled, toned body pressing him down into his hotel bed, pounding into him with the sweet, tantalizing feeling of an orgasm pulsating through every fiber of his being. He needed for one goddamned second not to feel so alone.

John was supposed to be everyone else's container, and that meant he couldn't break—he couldn't lose his shit.

Hold it together.

Push through.

Don't show them how weak you fucking are…

John felt his chest ache and a throbbing burn behind his eyelids. He sucked in a controlled breath, commanding his body to hold it together.

I cannot have a fucking breakdown in public. Not in the middle of the bar like a sad, pathetic old man.

Dammit.

John pressed his fingers into the glass, hating how dependent he had become on his fling. Seeing Ben, bent on his knees, feeding his cock into his mouth one inch at a time, had been exactly what he needed. John had climaxed those first few times very quickly because it had been so new, so thrilling, so liberating. He hadn't realized how much he needed the touch—the sensation of being held.

He raked his fingers through his beard.

Fuck. Fuck. Fuck.

John would once again be alone tonight, stranded on the edge of a vast cliff, with nothing but his thoughts for company. And he never felt this dangerously close before. The emptiness burned through him, and he closed his eyes, vaguely wondering what it would be like to surrender to it.

Stop, John.

Just fucking stop.

You can't think like this.

This was the second time Ben had stood him up.

John was particular about his home and didn't like bringing anyone there. It felt too intimate. Too personal. He preferred the autonomy of a hotel room, with room service and a full bar. He barely had time to take care of himself these days, let alone have clean sheets or food in his fridge. He hadn't even finished unpacking the boxes from his divorce several years ago in the spare bedroom yet.

John's life and his mess were for his eyes only. He didn't need the scrutiny, or worse, the concern from someone else.

His phone vibrated. He swallowed the lump in his throat.

Maybe next week...?

No, there would be no other chance with Ben. He couldn't keep getting his hopes up when he was this fragile. This weak. It felt crushing to admit it to himself, but here he was, aching and alone and so fucking disappointed he wanted to scream and cry and…

John typed his reply.

Have a safe night.

Bubbles. Stop. Then nothing. Ben was smart enough to realize the second missed night would be their last. Both understood the arrangement. No talking, no intimacy. It was easy, fun, and no one got hurt. No emotions, just a release. Because that's all John could handle at the moment.

Needing a distraction, John opened the last text message from his sister.

Talked to mom. She mentioned the garage door is stalling. Can you fix that? Dad shouldn't be climbing ladders. Mom bitched about your beard again. I told her you're going through a midlife crisis and to expect a flashy red sports car next time she sees you.

He smiled at the text and his response.

I'll come by this weekend and take a look. The beard is a statement piece for the depressed and nearly middle aged. So yeah, I'm keeping it. As for the sports car, I already have two. I was thinking about a motorcycle next. Where are my pictures of Olive and Johnny?

He opened the dozen photos that followed, all of his ridiculously cute five-year-old niece and newborn nephew and smiled.

The dark, bottomless cliff inched out a little further, giving him room to breathe again and permission to step back in his mind.

If you get a motorcycle, Mom will have a stroke.

Good thing her son's a doctor then.

Ha ha.

He closed the text thread and turned the phone around so he wouldn't see any more notifications. Something he'd been doing more often. He had been on a few dating apps and struggled to dedicate any real time to them. He had been lucky when he met Ben, and the timing of it was convenient. And it helped that Ben was exactly his type.

Young, handsome, brimming with vitality and sex.

John had been initially surprised to discover he even had a type, but Ben told him briefly that it was normal and not taboo in the gay community to date people of different ages.

His mind flashed briefly to the moment he touched Lawson's shoulder today—the hard feel of muscles and natural strength beneath his scrubs. His brilliant pale, almost gray blue eyes searched John's body before awkwardly fumbling away, with a bright blush on his cheeks after John had touched him…

Stop it.

Hooking up with a resident under your watch is out of the question.

Ben was different because I rarely saw him.

I see Lawson every damned day.

He knocked back the rest of the contents of his whiskey, squashing all thoughts of Lawson.

He waved down the bartender for another drink, deciding to get drunk at the bar. When he was ready, he would head up to his hotel room, alone, jerk off into his fist under the hot spray of the luxurious hotel shower, and pass out.

His shoulder ticked.

Sounds like a great fucking night.

Chapter 2

Wyatt

The club lights sparkled and bounced off the crowded dance floor, and the music pulsed with a steady beat, but Wyatt heard none of it.

He really, really didn't want to be here.

He wanted to be in his dark room, finishing off a beer before promptly passing out.

Today was a long day.

He had been training as a junior resident emergency medicine doctor for the past six months at Saint Sierra hospital, alongside some of the most qualified and insanely skilled doctors in all of LA. He had transferred from a slower rural hospital, fearing that his skills as a doctor were stagnating. So, when he was accepted as a transfer to this hospital, he was both terrified and excited.

And he loved every minute of it.

Well, almost.

The projectile vomiting was never fun. Or the deaths, which came often despite how much he tried to save his patients. He was slowly becoming less uncomfortable with death, but it didn't make it any less difficult to bear, depending on the patient.

"Approximately seven to eight thousand people die in the US daily, Lawson. You are inevitably a part of that cycle in that your job is to save lives. So, try not to take it personally when the statistic, or God, or the universe does what it inevitably does. And if you do, well, remember, you're doing the best you can, and in the end, sometimes that's all that matters." Dr. Donnelly had reassured him six months ago.

Preacher don't fear the Reaper.

Come on baby, don't fear the Reaper...

Wyatt hummed the tune in his mind, thinking back to the day he first arrived at Saint Serria Hospital. Dr. Donnelly's hand had captured his shoulder firmly, the way he would often do now in passing, as if his touch was a way to check on his residents, followed by direct, almost penetrating eye contact, assessing them quickly as he moved through the ED.

That day, Dr. Donnelly's deep blue eyes were brimming with compassion for not only the deceased patient, whom they stood vigilantly over, but also for Wyatt because he couldn't save them.

"You are enough even when you think you aren't. Death can remind us of our mortality, and as a doctor, our flaws. Compassion for yourself, too, is necessary," Dr. Donnelly had said to him softly. Gently even.

Wyatt had experienced plenty of egotistical, dickhead doctors and professors as a student and now as a resident. He had assumed it was simply part of the profession. Empathy and the grueling work of being a doctor could, at times, be a hard line to straddle. He understood why a lot of assholes chose this job, they saw people as machines rather than human beings.

So, when Dr. Donnelly met him that day with kindness and compassion, Wyatt nearly gaped in surprise at the older man.

He hadn't anticipated a senior emergency medicine doctor being so... sensitive.

"Keep doing good work," Dr. Donnelly had continued to say, smiling warmly at Wyatt, the crinkles around his eyes deepening as he brushed a hand onto his back.

And that, right there, was the start of Wyatt's mild obsession with his captain. But unfortunately for him, Wyatt made a lot of mistakes, especially in those first few months. He suspected Dr. Donnelly hadn't thought he was much of a doctor yet, given his rural hospital transfer.

Donnelly was a hardened inner-city doctor who saw gunshot wounds and stabbings as common occurrences, while prior to coming to this hospital, the most Wyatt had seen was the occasional farming accident that resulted in some sort of bodily injury.

Whatever Dr. John-handsome-as-hell-Donnelly thought of Wyatt, he never showed it, maintaining professionalism and respect regardless of opinion. In fact, he was the epitome of a great fucking teacher. Never once crossing those sacred lines.

But whenever Wyatt did do something right in front of his captain, and Dr. Donnelly's firm grasp came down on his shoulder, followed by that half-hearted smile, it felt like all the blood in his body went straight to his cheeks, flushing at his praise.

Because he loved that man's praise.

The thought had initially mortified Wyatt, but the longer he worked with his captain, the more he craved it. He melted like hot butter in a skillet every time he got it, even though Dr. Donnelly praised everyone all the time.

There was nothing special about Wyatt to Dr. Donnelly.

The club music, pulsing with heavy bass, cut to another song, and Wyatt was pulled from his thoughts, sighing and dragging a hand through his hair. His roommate and best friend, Jin, stood at the bar ordering them drinks. Wyatt had promised to go out after skipping the last two Friday nights, and he was trying hard not to think about how comfy his bed sounded right now.

His eyes slid over the overly crowded dance floor as he watched from the corner table they had managed to grab, when he noticed a tall dark-haired man with a beard swaying with a male couple. Their bodies were sliding off one another, joined in a tandem of rhythm and something else—something sensual and hot.

Wyatt frowned when the flash of the club lights illuminated the dark bearded man's face, realizing he was young, mistaking the beard for age.

Jin appeared a moment later, his face pinched in suspicion as he handed Wyatt his milky green cocktail, tracking his line of sight. "Dude, you are a heat-seeking missile."

"What?" Wyatt asked, pretending not to know what he was referring to.

"You somehow manage to find every bearded man within twenty yards of you."

Wyatt rolled his eyes.

"It's true!" Jin teased.

He sighed, "I just like..."

"Beards all of a sudden?"

"I'm allowed to have a type," Wyatt replied, feeling oddly defensive.

"Yes, queen, you are," Jin drawled. "But you're looking a little too hard."

"What's that supposed to mean?"

"I think you're looking for *him*."

Wyatt's heart flopped over, and he frowned hard into his cocktail, taking a sip of the minty green flavor Jin had ordered for him, cringing. He should've ordered for himself.

"I'm not stupid, you know," Jin remarked. "I know when you're crushing. And honey, you're crushing hard for a certain doctor..."

Heat raced to his cheeks, and he attempted to cover it by turning away, casually slipping his hand into his front sweater pocket. "I don't have a crush."

"Oh, baby, you *so* do. You talk about him constantly. I swear, if I hear Dr. Donnelly's name one more time..." Jin's eyes widened in sudden epiphany. "He's got a beard, doesn't he?"

Wyatt's flush deepened, rising up his neck now.

Jin let out a hooting sound, whipped out his phone, and began speed typing into his phone. "I'm googling him."

Alarmed, Wyatt reached for him.

Jin ducked out of the way.

"Dude—don't!" Wyatt knew he couldn't die from embarrassment, and yet he sort of wanted to.

"I have to know!" Jin shrieked, drawing the attention of the passersby and forcing Wyatt to shove his hands back into his sweater, knowing it was pointless trying to stop his bestie. Jin was as ferocious as an attack dog in a junkyard when he wanted something.

And Wyatt had figured out early in their friendship to never try to stop Jin from what he wanted, or risk getting his head bitten off. They had met in undergrad as roommates in UCLA's dorms. Wyatt was a country boy with a little too much twang for Jin, who immediately helped him adapt to city life and introduced him to the world beyond the ranch. He had been achingly naive when he moved away from his father's ranch in Arizona and was lucky to have found Jin. Though radically different from him in almost every way, they somehow worked as best friends.

Jin had been making waves in the LA art community and had even co-hosted gallery openings and showcases over the last few years. His charming, no-holds-barred conversations with people and confident levity were what drew Wyatt to him and kept him there.

Jin also never shamed him for his sexuality because he, too, was gay.

Their roommate situation was convenient for them as both were constantly working these days. It was nice to have a friend at home when they were actually both home at the same time. He knew it wouldn't last forever, Jin seemed more determined than ever to find himself a steady partner.

Wyatt had dated a lot in college, gaining confidence and more certainty about what he wanted in the bedroom. But the rigorous demands of being a med student, and now a junior resident, left him little time to date, let alone have a relationship other than with his pillow.

In fact, he hadn't gotten laid in…

Wyatt paused, doing the math in his head, and nearly went slack-jawed at the year-long sexual drought he had unknowingly been in.

"Jesus Christ on toast," Jin exclaimed, eyes widening beneath the bright pink glasses. "Please tell me this is him?"

He flashed him a picture of Jonathan Donnelly, MD, from his profile picture on the hospital website. The image was updated, too. His thick, full beard had hints of gray sprinkled through the dark brown layers. His short-cropped brown hair was ruffled as though he had run his hand through it right before the picture was taken. The crinkled lines around his eyes were deep from his warm smile, and that kindness—that goodness, reflected in the depths of those dark blue eyes was evident even in the staff picture.

"Oh my," Jin drawled. "I didn't realize he was actually *hot*. You made him sound like Mr. Rogers."

He snorted, "I did not."

"This man is not made of Care Bear DNA, darling. This man screams sex. Look at that beard! I couldn't grow something like that if I were held at gunpoint."

"He's not like that." Wyatt couldn't explain it, but he felt a sudden protectiveness for his captain. Maybe because Wyatt had never met anyone like him. Dr. Donnelly was a man who led with compassion over confidence, and that was something of a rarity in their profession.

"Yes, he is." Jin smirked, "I can always tell."

Wyatt hesitated, recalling the surprisingly accurate number of times Jin had predicted such things about a person over the course of their friendship.

His heart fluttered again, wondering if that was true... that Dr. Donnelly was more than just the best teacher he ever had. That he was more than just kind and considerate, with the patience of a saint.

Maybe he was capable of other things...

Dirty, naughty things...

Unexpected heat flushed through his entire body. Wyatt was suddenly rooted to the spot as images came to him of Dr. Donnelly naked on all fours, sweat beading his brow, grunting and cursing as his perfect, tight ass got gloriously fucked. And he knew Dr. Donnelly could definitely take a good pounding because his body was built for it, all thick muscle and masculine. Wyatt's imagination tortured him some more by adding some sexy whimpering praise out of that mouth of his. Because Dr. Donnelly always praised.

Always.

Oh fuck.

He felt his cock twitch and stiffen uncomfortably in his tight jeans. Thank God for thick denim.

Jin arched both eyebrows, "You look like you're about to stroke out on me."

"I think I am."

Jin pivoted on his booted heel, assessing him. "What's happening?"

"I just never—" he swallowed, shifting on his feet to alleviate the strain between his legs. "I never thought about him that way."

"Really? Why not? He's hot."

Wyatt puffed out a breath, "Stop saying that."

"Well… if the heel fits."

"He's my attending. My captain—boss—whatever. I can't think about him like that."

Jin chuckled, "Sometimes I forget that the square country boy is still in there."

"Shut up."

"Do you know if he's…?" Jin gestured with his cocktail to the gay club.

He tensed. "I don't know. We don't exactly have time to talk about our personal lives."

Jin looked disappointed and made a pouty, irritable face, carefully making a show of sipping his cocktail. He had something to say and was clearly biting his tongue. Wyatt nearly growled in frustration at him.

"Just say it," he bit out.

Jin side-eyed him. "Do you want it rough or do you want me to spit on it?"

Normally, Wyatt would've laughed at the crude statement, but his heart was racing too quickly, and he impatiently shot Jin a stern look.

"Do you remember Professor Lewis?" Jin asked.

He stilled, unsure what point Jin was trying to make by bringing up their old English professor. "Yeah."

"Do you remember how hard you worked in that class?"

Wyatt shifted on the balls of his feet. "Yeah. So?"

"There's brown-nosing, and then there's what you did. You got a little obsessed, honey. Working yourself to the bone to get him to notice how *good* of a student you were..." Jin hummed. "Sound familiar?"

Wyatt sucked in a breath and let it out steadily.

Shit.

"Dr. Donnelly is your new Professor Lewis. Do you remember what happened after your precious Professor praised you after our final?" Jin snorted. "I do. You were a walking hard-on for an entire weekend. I don't think I ever partied that hard in my life, trying to keep up with you. You fucked half the basketball team... and I fucked the other half! I thought I was going to die in the arms of muscles. It was heaven." Wyatt slunk onto the high-top table, grasping the horrendous cocktail and swallowing the entire contents in one gulp, hoping to avoid tasting it.

This all felt so glaringly obvious.

Why hadn't he put this together himself? Probably because he spent the last several years in the torturous throes of medical school, then his internship, followed by working his ass off for the last three years at the rural community hospital, and now at one of the toughest hospitals in the city. Coming up for air and having fun felt self-indulgent, if not impossible.

But this was more than that.

This was basic self-reflection, which apparently he wasn't doing.

"Honey, you got a kink. A couple, actually. Praise, but only from men you want to razzle-dazzle. Key word: men, not boys."

Wyatt had been hung up on earning Dr. Donnelly's praise every day for the last six months, and it also explained why he was such an awkward mess whenever he was near, which was a lot. They were sometimes rubbing shoulders while working on a patient, or Dr. Donnelly would watch him perform a procedure with his concentrated, steady gaze.

Wyatt suddenly imagined himself in bed, those penetrating dark blue eyes on his cock while he stroked himself into fucking oblivion.

His entire body shivered, followed by an irritable curse at himself for allowing this to happen.

How could I have been so fucking blind?

I can't have a crush on my senior attending.

Wyatt thumped his head on the table. "Fuck," he groaned. "I'm so fucked."

"I'm sorry," Jin finally said. "I didn't mean to go for the jugular."

He straightened, scrubbing a hand over his stubbled jaw and cheeks, trying hard to get that image of sweaty, ruggedly handsome Dr. Donnelly out of his head.

Fuck. Shit. Piss.

He let out a stream of curses. "God, I feel so stupid."

"Why?"

"You figured this out about me before I did."

Jin snorted, "Please. We're complicated beings, and surprisingly easy to please when we finally figure out what we like. Don't be embarrassed or ashamed about that. We gays must battle extra hard not to allow the shame closet to eat us alive when it comes to our spicy delights." He shot him a playful smile. "And you happen to like sexy daddies—welcome to the club—half of us here want that, and the other half just claim to like Pedro Pascal. It's the lucky few who actually get to fuck Pedro that leaves us all wet with envy."

Wyatt balked. Dr. Donnelly certainly was daddy material. Compassionate, hard working, strong values, generous, older, incredibly fucking sexy...

Stop!

He cursed again, raking his finger through his hair, pulling at the roots.

Dr. Donnelly even had a dad-bod, all broad shoulders and a thick waist, reminding him of old school boxers, with more meat than muscle, which was exactly the type of men Wyatt liked to manhandle and get pinned by, feeling the solidness and weight of them over him, or even better, more body for Wyatt to straddle while he fucked them into oblivion.

"Shit." He buried his face in his hand. "I'm already a nervous wreck when he's watching me at work. Now that I know I wanna…"

He couldn't even say the words out loud.

How could he?

He had to somehow function at work with him. He couldn't think about all the dirty things he wanted to do to his captain.

Jin seemed to sense this and finished the statement for him. "Fuck him? Or be fucked? Either way would be hot."

"Stop talking," Wyatt moaned.

"First step is admitting you have a problem."

"This totally *is* a problem—"

"Next step," Jin cut in. "Is figuring out how to fix it," he said with a mischievous twinkle in his gaze. "And if I know you, you always have a plan to relieve pain."

Wyatt snorted, pinching the brim of his nose. "You are the worst."

"I know. It's why you love me. I'm always good at giving you permission to get into a little trouble."

Except there was no way in hell he could get into trouble even if he wanted to.

Because Dr. Donnelly would never cross that line between them.

Ever.

For one simple reason alone: he was a good man. And good men like him didn't do stupid, reckless things like fuck their residents.

Chapter 3

Wyatt

The chilly fall air nipped at his ears, and the fresh smell of rain coating the pavement filled his nostrils as Wyatt gratefully left the stuffy club behind him.

Luckily, Jin met a couple and was immersed in heavy flirting and petting, giving Wyatt the go-ahead to finally leave.

He wasn't exactly in the party mood, especially after that conversation. He was too restless to sit in an Uber, so he decided to walk back to their apartment. The light misting of rain dusted his worn UCLA sweater, but he didn't mind it. He lifted his head to greet it and exhaled heavily.

Aside from the revelation that he may want more from Dr. Donnelly than for his coveted praise, Wyatt thought about their brief interactions today and his vulnerable admission about his shoulder. A frozen shoulder could be painful and last a long time if not treated properly.

Wyatt couldn't help but think of his old horse, Roxeanne, who had had something similar. The shoulder issue went undiagnosed despite the number of vets his dad had brought in trying to figure it out. Wyatt had a theory about what was behind it, but his dad dismissed it. She had had a stillborn baby earlier that year, and her mood had seemed more despondent ever since. Then, on one of the rides with a tourist group, she nearly slipped off a cliffside due to improper handling of the tourist riding her, causing her to sprain her ankle. It didn't help that his dad's grueling work schedule for all his horses had left her with little time to recover.

Wyatt had hated seeing her suffer, so after all the other horses were tended to and bedded down for the night, he stayed up late in the barn, working on her shoulder, massaging the tight muscles, stretching her leg, and grooming her.

She had been a good horse, and Wyatt missed her.

Thinking about her now and how she had died always made his stomach tighten.

He refused to let his mind wander, instead focusing on his booted heels striking the pavement as he walked. The one thing about Roxeanne and his father's horses that he appreciated was that they led him to discover something about himself: he really liked being needed.

It was different in the emergency department, where he was constantly needed for his skills. With the horses, he was needed because he was wanted.

It was a quiet need. A soft one that didn't demand or take anything from him.

If anything, it gave him purpose and meaning.

He wondered if Dr. Donnelly had anyone outside of the hospital who took care of him the way he did with everyone else.

Wyatt sighed, chastising himself for the thought, knowing that it wasn't appropriate.

But still, he liked that Dr. Donnelly told him the truth. He had worked with him for six months, studying him, watching him work with such practiced ease amidst the madness of the emergency department, and Wyatt prided himself on someday being like him.

He couldn't believe he thought it was just hero worship.

More like daddy worship, he thought with a derisive snort.

Blushing, Wyatt raked his fingers through his sandy brown hair, pulling the long waves on top and out of his face. Now he knew the truth. He wanted to fuck his senior attending, and there was no way in hell he would be able to see Dr. Donnelly as just his captain anymore, but also as a man with sexual needs. And if Jin's theory was true, Dr. Donnelly had hungry, voracious, sensual needs, and that thought alone made Wyatt's pulse skip.

Fuck.

I need to get laid. That'll get Dr. Donnelly out of my head, at least for a little while.

Jin wasn't wrong that Wyatt was a bit of a player in college. Once he was free from his dad's strict regime, he was finally liberated to do whatever he wanted. And that meant sex. Lots of it. It was the one arena in his life where he was surprisingly confident, outside of working with horses.

Maybe that's what he needed, he thought, a confidence boost, anything but to think about a certain doctor for the weekend. The problem was, he just left the club and really didn't want to go back.

He heard the soft croon of a blues band outside a very posh bar and lounge, and he paused, the rain slicking his face, his eyes flickering down the dark street heading back to his apartment. The warm lights of the bar lounge beckoned him inside.

Moving on instinct, Wyatt pulled his wallet out and handed his ID to the bouncer at the door. They always asked for it. He blamed it on his boyish face, even though he was 26.

"Forty-dollar entry," the bouncer informed him.

"Forty?" Wyatt asked incredulously.

He had student loans coming out of his ears. There was no way he could shell out money at the door and then another twenty or more at the bar. He hated being this broke. It would be at least another six more months before he was actually making money as a doctor.

"Sorry, I'm—" He glanced through the large windows of the lounge, seeing the sparkling candlelight and band. The bar had only a few people, and his eyes narrowed half an inch and then widened. He recognized the lone man sitting at the end of the bar, and his heart slammed into the bones of his chest.

He quickly reached for his credit card and handed it to the bouncer.

"Have a good night," the bouncer said, removing the black velvet rope and allowing him entry.

The warmth from inside the bar greeted him, and Wyatt stared, suspended in shock.

Dr. John-haunt-my-sex-dreams-Donnelly was here.

He had never seen Dr. Donnelly outside of work. Hell, he didn't see any of his fellow doctors or nurses once their shift was over.

Dr. Donnelly, with all his confidence, all his knowledge and wisdom, was the epitome of a great—no, fantastic doctor, and possibly the best in the city. So, the idea that he was alone, sitting at this posh bar on a Friday night, felt wrong.

Wyatt took this rare, unexpected opportunity to study Dr. Donnelly as he tugged off his rain-dampened sweater, racing a hand through the damp waves, swallowing down the nervous butterflies creeping up his throat.

Dr. Donnelly's hands were clasped around a glass of whiskey as he leaned against the bar top, an achingly sad expression on his face. Wyatt took an instinctive step forward, recognizing the emotion instantly: loneliness. And that surprised him, because he was attractive with the hint of gray peppering his dark brown hair and beard, and the sexiest crinkles around his piercing blue eyes. He was especially handsome when he smiled. The older doctor was tall, at least 6'3, but his height never felt imposing. His broad shoulders were typically donned in the dark gray scrubs and the occasional sweater these days.

Tonight, he wore a white button-up that molded to his thick, brutish body, the sleeves rolled up past his elbows, with a silver watch glinting on his wrist. His strong forearms were sprinkled with rich, dark hair as he sipped his drink. Wyatt's gaze fixed on his hands. They were aged with experience and life. Hands that brushed behind Wyatt's neck on occasion, clasping roughly and then affectionately. Hands that he could easily imagine grasping him between the legs, taking control, demanding him with touch alone…

Collaring him while he sucked his cock.

Jesus, I can't be thinking this.

He swallowed, wondering if the minty drink from the club was finally catching up with him.

This is stupid.

I should leave.

The nerves of this moment suddenly slammed into him like a bullet through the chest.

What the hell am I doing? Am I really going to—what? Join my lonely-looking attending at a bar and have a drink?

Inhaling an unsteady breath, Wyatt, deciding to man up, strode forward and maneuvered past a few candlelit tables, all preoccupied with lovey-dovey couples. The nervous energy increased the closer he got to the bar—to him.

I've literally inserted tubes down windpipes, removed bullets, been vomited on more times than I can count, and mended gushing wounds.

I can say 'hi' to Dr. Donnelly outside of work.

I'm not doing anything wrong…

So why did it feel like he was?

Wyatt's foot caught the edge of the sleeve of his sweater that he was carrying, and he stumbled into the barstool next to Dr. Donnelly, face flushed and nervously grasping the edge of the bar to steady himself.

Shit. What am I doing?!

Dr. Donnelly glanced up immediately, and his dark blue eyes widened in surprise.

"Lawson?" he asked, the same surprise reflected in his gaze.

"Yes," was all Wyatt could think to say, followed quickly by a stammering. "Sorry… sorry. I don't mean to intrude. It's just—well—I…"

Mercifully, the bartender interrupted his humiliation and asked him if he wanted a drink.

Yes, definitely, yes.

"Uh, yeah," he managed out in a rush. "Whiskey."

The bartender succinctly slipped away, preparing the drink.

He returned his gaze to Dr. Donnelly and saw him smiling gently, and somewhat incredulously. "Whiskey?"

Wyatt sucked in a breath, trying hard to calm the fuck down. "I don't really drink, but when I do it's usually just whiskey or beer," he said with a slight shrug, trying to look casual and not flustered and heart-poundingly nervous.

"Same," Dr. Donnelly said and gestured to the barstool Wyatt was practically straddling. "Well, if you ordered a drink, you might as well stay awhile." He paused and glanced behind him, as though looking for a date or friends. "Unless there's someone here with you?"

"No, and thanks. I would love to join you." He tried not to flinch at how eager he sounded. "Sorry again, I didn't mean to interrupt your evening. I really just wanted to come over and say hi."

"You didn't interrupt anything," Dr. Donnelly replied coolly and seemed to mean it, a genuineness in his gaze that made the storming butterflies in Wyatt's stomach ease a little. "I'm surprised to see you here, I will admit."

"Really? How come?"

"This place doesn't seem like your style." Dr. Donnelly cringed with a half-hearted smile. "Though that doesn't seem fair when I can't say I know much about you."

"I've never been here. My roommate said they have good drinks, so I decided to try it." Which was partially true, until he saw Dr. Donnelly by himself. Wyatt glanced down at the closeness of their knees beneath the dimly lit bar, and he sat back. "Do you come here often?"

Oh God, did I just use the most generic pick-up line ever?

Fuck.

Dr. Donnelly continued to smile, a slight laugh slipping from his chest. "A few times."

Wyatt nodded, swallowing down the mortification as the bartender returned with his drink and Dr. Donnelly indicated for another one for himself.

Wyatt immediately lifted the fancy glass to his lips and took a long gulp, needing to create space between himself and his ridiculous nerves. A wall of alcohol might do the trick, he thought, letting the burn of the whiskey slide down his throat.

He returned his gaze to Dr. Donnelly's and saw that his eyes were fixed on his throat before carefully averting them, the jaw muscle beneath his beard twitching. "Shouldn't you be at a pub, or club, or something? God, that made me sound old."

Wyatt felt his lips pull into an easy smile. "I was at the club a few blocks from here. I owed my bestie a night out. But the clubs not really my thing."

Dr. Donnelly smirked, the lines deepening around his eyes.

Wyatt felt mesmerized, wondering if he had ever let himself look this long at his captain.

"Not really my thing either," Dr. Donnelly said. "Though I'm sure there's an age limit to those sorts of places."

"Are you saying you're too old to club?" Wyatt asked, relaxing slightly.

Dr. Donnelly snorted, "Maybe. I dunno, I suppose clubs really weren't my thing when I was younger, anyway. I was more inclined to smoke pot and listen to blues in my parents' garage, that kind of thing."

Wyatt glanced at the blues band behind them. "You must like this then."

Dr. Donnelly hummed, "Yeah, minus the pot. But yeah. I love live music, especially the blues. Makes you feel..." he abruptly cut himself off, sitting back and clearing his throat.

Before Wyatt could press, the bartender reappeared with Dr. Donnelly's drink and he thanked him, taking a long sip.

"You're not that old, by the way," Wyatt heard himself say out loud and immediately hid the rising flush of embarrassment by taking another drink of his whiskey.

Dr. Donnelly didn't seem to notice as a wistful sigh escaped his lips. "Some days, I feel ancient."

He wanted to ask, and in a way, he supposed he knew. He was their captain and knew it probably took a lot out of him. It was an impossible task to be responsible for others in life-or-death situations, and yet Dr. Donnelly did it. He showed up every day, managing to hold it all together, especially at times the crew, and kept the ship sailing.

"Are you here alone?" Wyatt asked.

"Yeah," Dr. Donnelly replied, rubbing his large hand through his thick beard.

Wyatt noticed how well-groomed Dr. Donnelly looked. His beard neatly trimmed, his clothes ironed, and his shoes polished to a shine on Italian leather. He narrowed his eyes, knowingly. "You were stood up."

Dr. Donnelly's eyes jerked back to his, "How could you possibly tell that?"

"I've been you," Wyatt admitted. "I know the feeling. So, I'm... sorry." Except he wasn't, not in the slightest.

"You're perceptive, or maybe assuming," Dr. Donnelly retorted, assessing him. "It's twice in one day you've called me out on pure assumption alone. In the ED, that could be dangerous if wrong, Lawson."

Wyatt flushed, slipping a hand through his hair. "Shit, I didn't..."

"I'm giving you a hard time," Dr. Donnelly replied gently. "You're good at reading people. I hadn't realized, though maybe I should've."

Wyatt heard the praise, but it was mixed with Dr. Donnelly's own negative self-assessment, which bothered him. He frowned, noticing the faint lines of emotion strained on the doctor's lips and the dark bags under his eyes. He was tired—they all were. But there was something else there, something deeper and unspoken that Wyatt could sense. More than the loneliness he had seen earlier. This undercurrent of emotion felt raw, almost delicate.

Surprised, Wyatt continued to stare, wondering if this was from his shoulder or something else.

"How's the shoulder?" he asked cautiously, trying not to overstep.

"Sore," Dr. Donnelly clipped out, chin down as though not to let Wyatt look too closely at him.

"Do you take anything for the pain?"

"Not if I can help it."

"What do you do to treat it?"

Dr. Donnelly shot him a hard look, despite the smile on his face. "Are you my doctor now, Lawson?"

"No. I'm..." he stopped himself. He wouldn't apologize. He didn't want to. "I'm just concerned about my captain, that's all."

Dr. Donnelly's eyes turned to stone, his smile falling. "I'm fine."

"You say that a lot," Wyatt murmured and closed his eyes, suddenly wishing he could vanish in his seat.

That was a blatant overstep.

"It's just a frozen shoulder, Lawson. I can handle it."

He nodded, returning to his place in the ranking against his captain. And yet, he bristled with irritation. It reminded him briefly of Roxeanne and how she bucked and reared her head when he first attempted to get close while she was on the verge of collapse. Why did this feel so similar?

"Forgive me," Dr. Donnelly said after a moment. "It's been a long week."

Wyatt was fully aware of how awful this week at work had been.

He heard Steph, the head nurse, blame it on the full moon and the Santa Ana winds, saying that city people tend to go a little mad this time of year. Shorter tempers, bad decisions, explosive behavior, and sometimes violence. And it always ended up in the emergency department, his team having to deal with the aftermath. The winds had finally brought in the rain, washing the city clean of the turmoil.

"And, you were right, it doesn't help that I was stood up on Friday night," Dr. Donnelly admitted softly.

"She couldn't make it?" Wyatt asked.

Dr. Donnelly let out a tight laugh, hands clamped firmly around the glass, his gaze locked to the amber liquid rolling inside. "No, he could not."

He?!

Jealousy, like a fist to the gut, knocked the wind out of him while Wyatt simultaneously rejoiced in the possible fact that Dr. Donnelly was gay or bisexual.

Stop—don't.

Don't think about that.

Dr. Donnelly was off-limits. It didn't matter that he was like him. But it did matter—a lot.

"He was called in," Dr. Donnelly continued.

"Called in? Is he a doctor?" Wyatt asked, noticing the slight strain in his voice and clearing it quickly. He hoped to hell that his date wasn't Dr. Samuels, because if it was, Wyatt didn't stand a chance against that stupidly handsome ED Viking. Or Dr. Walsh, who was handsome in his own pale, scary sort of way, but he didn't seem to be Dr. Donnelly's type. He needed someone…

Protective.

Wyatt paused, wondering where that thought had come from.

"Paramedic," Dr. Donnelly clarified. "He's young—" he stopped himself abruptly, busily taking a careful sip of whiskey, curtailing his words.

"So, he's like us," Wyatt replied. "Makes sense, we have odd hours."

Dr. Donnelly's averted gaze flickered to his face. "Right."

Wyatt attempted an assured smile. "I'm sure you guys will find the time to meet up again."

"I don't think so."

Surprised, Wyatt asked, "How come?"

Dr. Donnelly's eyebrows arched, and he cocked his head to the side, seeming to consider. "I think that's a bit personal…"

Wyatt stifled the disappointment and was surprised when Dr. Donnelly continued, "Or maybe we're just two people who happen to know each other, sitting at the same bar. After all, we're not at work."

Yes, fucking, please.

He wanted to know everything about this man—everything.

Wyatt shivered, racing a sweaty palm over his leg.

"We have an arrangement." Dr. Donnelly let out a soft sigh. "We meet once a month at a bar with a hotel, and I book us a room… well, you can figure out the rest."

Wyatt felt the heat flush the back of his neck, and he nodded stiffly.

Sex. They had sex.

His cock twitched, wondering if he had ever met the young paramedic who got to fuck or be fucked by Dr. Donnelly in hotels once a month. The swift sting of jealousy reared its head again, and he gritted his teeth, refusing to show how much he didn't like knowing this information.

"Your silence is really comforting," Dr. Donnelly remarked with a slight tease.

Wyatt jerked, "Sorry, I'm not judging you, I swear. I just—um, I didn't know you were…"

Stop talking right now, Lawson.

"It's all right. All cards on the table?" He glanced at him, and Wyatt quickly nodded, knowing he was being a little too eager. "I actually didn't know I was gay until about a few years ago. I suppose you can say I've got the stereotypical overachiever storyline. Golden child through high school, honor student in college, overly pedigreed med school. Lost in the scramble of becoming great, drifting through my personal life. My ex would hate hearing that. But it's unfortunately true, I wasted her time not knowing myself. It took me figuring out what I didn't want—to see what I actually wanted. Not the best strategy, but it's how it happened."

Donnelly seemed to age right before his eyes. He looked so vulnerable, so helpless.

Wyatt felt himself sway a little closer.

"I realized tonight that when he canceled, I…" He paused, shaking his head. "Sorry, that was a lot," he said, clearly self-conscious now.

"It wasn't," Wyatt reassured. "It's not."

Donnelly hesitated, fingers rubbing the ridges of the whiskey glass in his hands, looking so damned exposed that Wyatt couldn't stand it. He knew that feeling. Knew what it was like to open up and not know how the other person would receive it.

"I just realized tonight that I haven't had sex in almost a year," Wyatt blurted out and immediately flushed in embarrassment, raking his fingers through his hair. "That I've been so busy with finishing my last year as a resident, that I don't do anything other than sleep, shower, and work."

Donnelly cursed in surprise, smiling broadly at him. "I don't think I could survive."

Something shifted in the air between them, crackling with an energy Wyatt hadn't felt in a long time. The inside of his stomach heated and fluttered with excitement.

Fuck, Jin was right.

Goddamn it! And thank fuckin' God!

His blood pounded in his ears as he nervously took a quick sip of whiskey.

"Are you seeing anyone now? You and Emily seem close..." Donnelly said casually.

Wyatt breathed in through his nose, catching the faint scent of his cologne. Donnelly didn't wear anything fancy like this at work, and if Wyatt were honest with himself, he preferred his natural, musky scent. Because there had been times when the nerves were high, the adrenaline pumping, and Dr. Donnelly's larger frame overshadowed Wyatt's, pushing into his back or side, his scent engulfing him.

He swallowed. "Who?"

"Dr. Sawyer."

Wyatt blinked and shook his head, "No. She's incredible, but we're just friends."

He sat forward, deciding to be brave for five fucking seconds and just tell Donnelly the truth. After all, he had been honest with him. "I um… prefer… men."

Donnelly stared for half a second longer than usual, and Wyatt saw his eyes darken before sliding down to glance at his lips, chest exhaling before he immediately drew back, pushing his forearms off the bar top, creating space between them.

Wyatt noted his knee hadn't moved, though.

Not yet.

All he had to do was widen his legs another inch, and they would be touching.

Because Dr. Donnelly—in that split second—had considered kissing him, and Wyatt saw it like an exposed vein. Real and pulsing, and full of life.

Fuck me.

Gasoline pouring rapidly into his bloodstream, Wyatt's voice grated as he said, "I, uh, figured it out when I was a teen on my father's ranch. I grew up on a dude ranch, surrounded by desert and mountains, horses and cowboys. Lots and lots of cowboys." He glanced sideways at Donnelly and saw that he had leaned forward again, that half-hearted smile dancing on his lips, appearing relaxed once more.

Feeling braver, Wyatt continued. "I had plenty of crushes, but none of the cowboys stayed too long—a season or two at most. Probably because my dad is such a hard ass. But, one day, when I had just turned nineteen, I…" he cleared his throat, stunned he was admitting this story, but it felt right. Easy even—with him. "I seduced one of my dad's ranch hands."

Donnelly's jaw unhinged, and he covered it quickly with a hand, looking amused.

Wyatt smirked, "What?"

He shrugged, looking thoughtful, "You don't seem the type."

"To seduce ranch hands?"

He nodded, revealing his smile as he laughed.

"I couldn't stop myself," Wyatt admitted. "I used to think all these handsome cowboys coming in and out of my dad's ranch had turned me gay. Their uncompromising work ethics, their values, the way they used their hands..." his eyes, unable to resist the temptation, looked at Dr. Donnelly's hands. Strong, sure hands that grew steadier under pressure.

He wondered how they would feel on his body, tracing over the seam of his lips, the groove of his backside, the length of his cock...

He glanced up and stilled, their eyes colliding.

"I figured out that I had a type..." Wyatt drawled, intentionally dropping his tone into a seductive rasp. "Cowboys, much older cowboys, that had hands of steel and beards that I could sink my fingers into."

Donnelly made a sound from the back of his throat, his nostrils releasing a hard breath, as he quickly looked away. He knew he was treading a fine line, but at that moment, Wyatt didn't care. He liked seeing the faint blush on his captain's cheeks.

"My dad found me in the barn with one of his seasonal cowboys," he continued, tone lightening, wanting to relax Donnelly again. He had to take this slow, he thought. He didn't want to spook his controlled, tightly wound captain. "It was my first time, and I was butt ass naked, and a happy, ruined mess. Right then and there, my dad disowned me. Kicked me out. My aunts let me stay with them until I got accepted into UCLA. I've been doing everything on my own ever since."

"I'm sorry," Donnelly said.

"It's all right. I still love my dad even though he's—well, an asshole."

"Not everyone could do that," Donnelly breathed quietly, and as if seeing him for the first time, he said, "You're a good man, Lawson."

Donnelly's hand casually grasped the back of Wyatt's shoulder, fingers brushing along his neck. Wyatt closed his eyes, arms braced on the cool marble bar top. His entire body, every fiber, every muscle, heated under the simple touch. He felt the vibrating awareness pulsating between them and knew, with absolute certainty, that he would be replacing the paramedic who was supposed to be in Dr. Donnelly's bed tonight. That thought alone stirred something inside him. Unable to deny himself any longer, he leaned into Donnelly's touch, the bottom of his chin grazing his strong fingers, and he melted into him.

Donnelly let out a strained breath, and Wyatt's eyes shot open and saw the desire—the lust etched in the lines of his face.

Wyatt trembled, feeling Donnelly's fingers slip upwards, capturing his jaw, and the rough pad of his thumb grazing tantalizingly close to his lips.

Oh, fuck yes.

He stopped breathing, waiting for more, needing more. Feeling his stomach clench, Wyatt leaned even deeper into the touch and dipped his chin downward, forcing Donnelly's thumb over his lips. Heat flooded his limbs as his tongue slipped out, licking the pad of his thumb, desperate to take it fully into his mouth and suck.

And damn, did he want to suck this man down until there was nothing but grunting, gasping curses. Wyatt couldn't stop the weak noise that escaped from the back of his throat, which Donnelly heard, and he quickly snatched his hand back, eyes fully dilated with the same scorching lust that rippled through Wyatt's body. Both men breathed heavily, knowing they were inches away from crossing the line.

"That was wrong," Donnelly said, his voice hardening. "I'm sorry, I shouldn't have touched you."

"You always touch me," Wyatt replied, letting his leg drop and brush against his beneath the bar top. The older man stiffened but didn't retract. "I like it…"

Donnelly scrubbed a hand over his lips, unable to keep his gaze away, seeming just as transfixed as Wyatt felt.

"I want you to touch me every time you walk by," Wyatt admitted. "I—I ache for it."

Donnelly let out a shaky groan, laced with the same desperation Wyatt felt coursing through his body.

That simple, breathy groan unraveled whatever last resistance he had left to reason.

Maybe it was the whiskey, maybe it was the clear, stark hunger reflected in Donnelly's face. Maybe it was this reckless, vulnerable moment. It didn't matter. All that mattered was that Wyatt was ready to worship at the altar of his captain and take more than his thumb deeper into his mouth if he'd let him.

Wyatt, feeling bold, slipped his hand beneath the bar, clasping Donnelly's thigh, squeezing through the layer of material. Donnelly stiffened instantly as though he'd burned him, but he didn't jerk away. Instead, without looking, he firmly grasped Wyatt's hand. He waited for Donnelly to fling him away, but was surprised when he squeezed him.

Was he giving in?

Or fighting it? Wyatt couldn't tell, and it bothered the hell out of him.

"No one has to know," Wyatt murmured.

Donnelly closed his eyes, conflict tightening around his lips, his jaw clenching.

Say yes.

Don't think about how wrong this is for both of us.

Don't think—just say yes and give us both what we want.

"Thanks for the offer, Lawson, but we both know that's not possible." He released him, shifted fully away, and signaled for the bartender. "Put our drinks on my room, please," Donnelly instructed the bartender, smoothly getting to his feet. "Have a good night, Lawson."

The dismissal was so casual, yet so dispassionate, that it left him confused.

Wyatt watched as Donnelly headed toward the hotel lobby elevators, his heart pounding.

No fucking way. He was not ending the night getting rejected by a man who clearly wanted the same thing he did. And if Wyatt was good at anything, he was good at chasing after what he wanted.

He slammed down the rest of his whiskey, preparing for the chase. Maybe it was insanity. Whatever it was, he was going to try again because images of Dr. Donnelly sitting alone at the bar, and then sitting alone in the hotel room, would not be tolerated.

Wyatt was on his feet in an instant, running after him.

Donnelly slammed his finger into the elevator button, the only person in the hotel hallway this late at night.

"Wait," Wyatt said, breathing fast from the adrenaline pooling in his chest.

Donnelly shook his head, "I'm not interested, Lawson. Besides, it crosses so many ethical boundaries..."

The elevator dinged, and Donnelly quickly stepped inside, hitting the button for his floor. This was it, he thought. Now or never. Once Donnelly was in that elevator, this opportunity would never come again.

Fuck it.

Wyatt rushed inside, the elevator doors sliding closed behind him.

"What are you doing?" Donnelly snapped, sounding frayed and unexpectedly emotional.

Wyatt had sensed the undercurrent of emotion from Donnelly at the bar, but had been distracted by his desire to explore it further. But now, it was here again, brimming and cracking beneath his carefully controlled façade. Donnelly's shoulder was ridged and cramped against his neck, his posture stiff, and he appeared more vulnerable than ever in the tight confines of the elevator.

He thought of his old horse Roxeanne.

He thought of the pain and weight his captain carried.

And all Wyatt wanted to do was soothe him—take it and carry it for a night. Anything to see him smiling and at ease with himself as he had been at the bar a moment ago. That was the Donnelly he wanted. This one felt like a wounded wolf, scared and hostile, ready to attack rather than give.

"I..." Wyatt sucked in a breath.

Donnelly shook his head, staring up at the digital numbers leading them up to his hotel room.

Wyatt, biting his inner lip, stepped forward, drawing his attention, feeling the weight of his gaze and the tight cord in his own body as he exhaled. "I just want..."

You.

The tension in Donnelly's expression broke like an explosion as he suddenly grabbed Wyatt by the front of his shirt with both hands and slammed him against the wall, rocking the elevator. "I have no intention of ruining my career for this, Lawson. Back off."

Except Wyatt wasn't the one pinning the other to the side of the elevator.

His actions and his words didn't match, and they both knew it. They both felt the undeniable spark between them.

Wyatt's hands reached upwards, clasping Donnelly's, his fingers bunched and digging into his shirt.

"I can't do this…" The vulnerability lacing Donnelly's voice broke open, and Wyatt couldn't help but sway closer, feeling Donnelly's hot breath on his face.

"I won't say anything," Wyatt husked. "This stays between us…"

"Stop," Donnelly commanded roughly and pushed back, untangling them. Wyatt stepped back only a few feet, careful not to touch.

"Let me take care of you," Wyatt heard himself say. The exact words he'd said to the horses on the ranch over the years. The ones that fought and bucked and needed the most attention and care. "Please…"

Donnelly let out a strangled gasp as though he were drowning.

And at that moment, Wyatt realized that he was.

He was breaking, crumbling right in front of him, and all Wyatt wanted to do was soothe and touch and give. Give this man everything he had given Wyatt for the past six months—kindness, compassion, strength.

Donnelly's eyes locked with his, scared and yet aroused. Unable to see anything else but that needy desire, Wyatt reached for him, fingers digging into his thick beard, feeling the coarse yet soft hair and yearning for more. "This stays here. You can trust me."

Wyatt's cock, hardening between his legs, brushed against Donnelly's body, whose lips had parted with a soft groan as his eyes shut in resistance.

He was more than ready to plunge off this cliff and straight into Donnelly. Free-fall into oblivion with him.

But only if he'd let him.

He would not force him to do anything he didn't want to.

Before either of them could do anything, the elevator door rang, and the doors silently slid open.

Chapter 4

John

John's heart was ticking so fast he wondered if he was having a heart attack.

Because this was wrong, so fucking wrong, and he couldn't stop it. He felt like he was swan diving out of a plane without a parachute. Lawson was brushing his gloriously hard cock against him, and all he could think was… *more.*

Please, fucking please, more.

But they had to stop. He couldn't let this happen. John was supposed to be the responsible one, not Lawson. He was supposed to steer this ship and make smarter decisions than this.

Lawson was off limits.

He shouldn't be touching him, he shouldn't know what the imprint of his cock felt like against the straining of his own, and—fuck, he felt so Goddamned good that his vision blurred.

This is a heart attack, John.

You're dying.

Lawson's hot breath warmed his lips, and everything in his body told him to take—take what was being so easily offered. Not only was it offered, but Lawson *wanted* to take care of him. Jesus Christ, the mere thought had him shivering.

Take it, you stubborn old bastard.

The elevator slid open, and the resounding ding alerted him that they had reached his floor. He stilled, hating himself. He wasn't sure if he was a coward or a fool. A coward for wanting to run, or a fool for wanting to take.

He pushed Lawson away, raking his fingers through his hair. Unable to speak because of the achy desire that was pulsing through every part of his body, he practically stumbled out of the elevator, and once more he felt the younger man chase after him. His heart, still thumping, began to stutter. Lawson had demonstrated tremendous tenacity in the ED, especially after he had failed or made a mistake. It was as if he were a man possessed to redeem himself. He knew this about him, and knew he would pursue John to the end of the world if he had to.

Fuck. I'm so fucked.

He strode down the hallway, managing to stay upright despite the throbbing cock-stand that pushed against his slacks and painfully dug into the zipper.

"Dr. Donnelly," Lawson persisted, right on his heels.

With a trembling hand, John dug out his room key, pressed it on the keypad, and the door clicked open. All he saw was a dark, empty room, and his chest burned. He felt the swoosh of the edge, that empty place, that void of nothingness, and he stilled.

Another dark night alone.

I can't...

Swallowing hard, he turned to see Lawson, who jerked back at his abrupt turn. They stared at one another, both waiting for the other to move or run. Lawson looked so fucking... bright. His skin still seemed to glow with the warmth of sunshine from weeks ago, and his gaze leveled his own as an equal, not his resident.

"This is it, Lawson. End of the line," John said as firmly as he could muster, knowing perfectly well that he was a damned liar.

Lawson, so observant, so damned good at reading him, narrowed his pretty pale blue eyes a mere fraction before he tilted his head. "You want me to go?"

No. Fuck no.

John's jaw clenched.

"Tell me that you don't want me and I will," Lawson breathed, standing to his full height, taking up the space of the doorway as alarm slid down John's back.

Lawson was much bigger than he had realized. He wasn't as tall as himself, but he was broader in the shoulders and had incredibly muscular arms that he'd seen more than once easily lift or restrain patients.

John closed his eyes, feeling the resistance fall away brick by brick, weakening his resolve, and they both knew it.

Unexpectedly, he heard a rustle of clothing and his eyes sprang open. Lawson, standing brazenly in front of him, chest heaving, reached for the belt at his waist and unclasped it slowly, his stiff erection pushing against the jeans. John sucked in a breath, mesmerized. He moved with such confidence, such bold authority over this moment—over John, that he could only stare and marvel at the transformation of this young man.

Lawson's eyes were hooded and intent, heavy with desire, and he unbuttoned the top button of his jeans. "Tell me to stop."

Jesus Christ.

Pulse roaring in his ears, John's tongue was glued to the roof of his mouth.

Lawson continued, unzipping his pants, loosening them, dragging his other hand up to reveal the sharp, smooth lines of his abs, the perfect, strong V-lines of his hips, sloping downward beneath the hemline of his jeans.

Fuuuck.

Fuck.

He watched the display of raw, masculine power, offering him the feast he was ravenous for. He was completely buzzed, and blamed his limited self-control at this moment on several very strong drinks. John's fingers curled into his palms, refusing to reach for him.

"Tell me you don't want me," Lawson challenged, dragging out each word like a heated threat as his hand slipped beneath his jeans, cupping himself.

John let out a harsh curse.

A door down the hall opened, and Lawson stepped forward, pushing them both inside the room, and John went, heart hammering. He touched the firm wall of Lawson's chest, digging his fingers into the muscle around his heart, not sure whether to push or pull. Lawson kicked the door closed with his boot, and it shut with a resounding click.

This is wrong.

This is so fucking wrong.

"Lawson…" John murmured warningly, pushing him against the door, not sure what the hell to do. He couldn't give in. He knew he couldn't. Yet his body and mind weren't working together because his cock was thickening between his legs, causing him to let out a strangled moan of frustration.

"Tell me to fuck off," Wyatt teased, biting his lower lip.

"Fuck off."

Wyatt grinned, eyes dancing with seduction. "Tell me you don't want this."

"That's not fair."

"I know."

Something passed over Lawson's handsome face. Being this close to him, he could see the same bags under his eyes that were beneath John's. And yet, the heat behind his gaze packed a punch to his gut.

John studied the usually smooth, chiseled outline of Lawson's jawline that was already forming whiskered sprinkles of hair from his last shave.

He remembered how the nurses in the ED giggled excitedly over Lawson when he first started. Blue eyes, classic, strikingly good looks, charming, and most of all, polite as hell. He had the best bedside manner among his new team of residents and went above and beyond for every patient in his care. The nurses were in love with the kid. If only he had a Southern accent and they knew he was actually a cowboy, he'd have nurses actively swooning whenever Lawson walked by or smiled.

Because, fuck, his smile was blindingly handsome. Boyish and sexy all at once.

And now, this cowboy, soon-to-be-doctor, with the most perceptive gaze he'd ever seen, wanted to take care of *him*...

John shivered.

Lawson pushed him deeper into the room, flipping on the lamp, which illuminated the youthful beauty of his face, making John suddenly feel self-conscious about his age.

"I can keep a secret," Lawson breathed.

Fear and excitement bubbled up in his chest as he let Lawson crowd him, the back of his knees hitting the edge of the bed. The sudden reality of them doing this hit him hard in the gut, and he stiffened. Lawson didn't know that John had never had sex with a man other than with his hands and mouth. So if Lawson stayed—if he consented to this—he would be surrendering more to him than he would ever know.

Because he didn't want his sexual inexperience to affect this moment.

This rare, wonderful, stupidly impulsive moment.

"No one can know," John said in a dry croak.

Lawson's eyes darkened as though the hunter had just been given permission to kill. Except that wasn't it at all. Lawson was offering to give, not to take.

"I know," Lawson murmured. "Can I kiss you now?"

Buzzed, reckless, and wanting to forget the tension in his shoulder, to forget the dark, empty void in his soul, John moved, capturing the strong, stubbled jawline with his fingers and tilting him upward into a crushing kiss.

Lawson let out the sexiest goddamned moan he had ever heard, and his cock responded painfully, pushing with such demand his knees nearly buckled. He forced open Lawson's mouth, slipping his tongue inside, tasting the whiskey and fiery need that was burning him alive—and fuck—fuck! He tasted too good, and it was his turn to groan.

John hadn't been unaffected by Lawson's presence in the ED.

He'd seen how handsome he was, how natural he was at soothing certain patients. He was talented when he was confident, and a bit of a mess when the spotlight was on him. His nerves sometimes got the best of him, and John had seen it often. It was why he pushed Lawson, why he was at his side, encouraging him to take more risks. And Lawson responded eagerly, almost hungrily, to John's praise. He saw it but ignored it. He'd had plenty of teacher-pet types try to get on his good side, but this—this was something else entirely.

Something more.

Goosebumps erupted down his back, and his hands went to work, capturing Lawson behind the neck, holding him close while he greedily took from his soft lips and hot mouth.

Lawson's hands were busy as well, fastening themselves to his hips, locking them together as the young man arched into him, chasing the sensation and friction of their hard cocks against one another beneath their clothing.

Another reason he had been craving tonight with paramedic Ben was that John didn't want to bear the weight of responsibility. Not in the bedroom, at least. He was looking for someone else to take control—to lead him. To give him the permission and freedom to lose control, just here in the sanctity of bed play. Because he needed somewhere in his life where he wasn't there to *give* but to *receive*, and better yet, be taken care of.

Withdrawing from the kiss, he tilted his forehead into Lawson's, breathing hard and catching his breath.

"Are you going to tell me to leave now?" Lawson teased once more, yet his voice was rough, his body arching against his.

"I should," he muttered.

Lawson stepped back and provocatively slid his fingers up the sides of his stomach as he tugged off his thin black shirt, deliberately tossing it to the floor, revealing the well-built muscles and perfectly smooth flesh that beckoned to be touched.

Jesus fuck, this kid was hot.

He was a living, breathing Adonis, come to life to tempt him.

"You should," Lawson agreed with a nod, his fingers slowly tracing over the buttons of John's shirt, working them free one flick at a time, giving John plenty of opportunity to say no.

"Why did you come to me at the bar?" John bit out, trying hard to reason his way out of this and remind himself that this was a colossal fucking mistake. Because it was. He just couldn't stop it.

"You looked lonely," Lawson admitted softly, opening his shirt, letting his fingers slide over John's stomach, over the contours of his chest, through the brown hair that curled and lined the planes of his torso. Lawson's fingers found his nipples and tantalizingly twirled over the flesh, lavishing attention on each nipple until they peaked and strained under his touch.

He swallowed, liking a little too much the bold way Lawson was touching him, as if he had every right to do so.

"I wanted..." Lawson licked his lower lip, seeming to want to take one of his nipples into his mouth. Something John wouldn't protest.

"The last six months, you've taught me more than med school. You're incredible. And I'm a nervous wreck whenever you're around. I want to impress you all the time and not fuck up. I want to... fuck..."

John's lips parted in surprise, and before Lawson finished his confession, he dropped to his knees and reached for the clasp of John's slacks, unbuttoning them. He watched as this bold young man took complete control.

It seemed so easy for him. And John couldn't look away.

Lawson expertly pulled down his pants and boxer briefs, eyes still holding his, licking his lips, pupils dilated. He felt his cock spring free, relieved from the restraints of his clothes, the tip of his sex already leaking with precum. Without breaking eye contact, he lifted John's ankle one at a time, helping him step out of his clothes. The excitement, the adrenaline, the thrill of this moment astounded him.

It had never been like this with Ben.

It had never been this intense. This real.

He swallowed hard as Lawson slowly dragged his eyes over John's naked body. This past year, he had put on a little more weight due to his stiff shoulder and his inability to take care of his body as he normally did at the gym. He wasn't overweight, just thicker around the hips and chest. If John went back to his boxing club, the weight would transform once more into hardened muscle.

And yet, Lawson didn't seem to mind. In fact, he seemed to marvel at him from on his knees, as though looking up in a longing worship as Lawson reached for his hips, squeezing his flesh. Lawson positioned himself closer, his rich golden hair shining in the soft glow of the lamplight in the bedroom. Sighing, he bit his lip in greedy anticipation, and didn't ask permission for what he did next.

Lawson opened his mouth over John's sex, sucking it into his mouth, rolling his tongue over his sensitive leaking tip.

The rush of sensation had John cursing. The wet heat from the velvety sheath of Lawson's mouth made his head spin as he reached for the back of his head and held him, trembling as he watched the way his cock slid in and out of those gorgeous damn lips. And Lawson knew what he was doing. His cheeks inhaled with each suck, taking him all the way down to the root and dragging back up, licking and sucking. His tongue slid over his tip and underside, making sure to taste and take every inch of him.

"Jesus, Lawson," John gasped, watching the young man bob up and down on his dick. His cock was somehow getting harder under his tongue, and he decided to tell him, because he knew how much Lawson liked his praise.

Gently scraping his fingers through Lawson's thick honey-colored hair, John leaned back to see more of Lawson's face as he rasped, "Fuck... You're good at this. Really good..." He gasped when Lawson sucked harder, more frenzied. His balls tightened and tingled, the orgasm tantalizingly close. "That's it. Oh fuck, you're too good... stop, stop..."

Lawson stilled, listening to his command and carefully lifting off his cock. Seductive pale blue eyes met his. John cupped the side of his face and dragged him upward.

"I wasn't expecting that," John whispered, rubbing the lips that devoured him with his thumb. "I wasn't expecting you."

Lawson let out a sexy moan and slipped John's thumb into the seam of his lips and sucked.

John's cock twitched, leaking between them with unmet need.

It didn't matter that Lawson was his responsibility at work, that he was off-limits in so many ways.

Tonight would be the one and only night they did this. He would make sure of that.

One night of pleasure.

One night, and they would never speak of this again.

One night, when he was just John.

Just himself. The man who could make mistakes, have faults and flaws, and be vulnerable. Scared even. Because this was a mistake. He shouldn't be so weak. So weak for this man that he didn't even know but wanted more than his next fucking breath.

John reached between them and unbuttoned Lawson's jeans, their hungry eyes locked on each other, both unable to look away as though pulled by a magnetic string.

Lawson stepped out of his pants and boxers, kicking off his shoes and socks, standing naked and blindingly beautiful before him. Lawson was fucking gorgeous, and all John could do was look, and look greedily over the sharp contours of his body.

"Fuck," Lawson breathed. John hadn't even touched him yet, and his eyes leaped back to Lawson's, confused.

"What?" John asked curiously, unable to breathe properly.

Apparently, Lawson was having the same reaction to the sight of his naked form as he was. Lawson reached for him, their bodies brushing, causing both men to groan at the sensation.

Lawson tilted his head upward and roughly kissed him. It was a collision of mouths, and John's legs trembled, barely holding himself upright as they fought with lips and tongues. John instinctively undulated forward, his cock sliding against Lawson's, and he moaned into his mouth.

Lawson gently but firmly pushed John back onto the bed, and he went, but his shoulder pinched beneath him unexpectedly, drawing out a curse.

Fuck, he didn't want to be dealing with his shoulder right now. Not when he had this glorious stallion, hard and ready for him. Lawson abruptly stilled and pulled away, and without a word, headed toward the bathroom, the light flicking on for a brief second before turning off.

Lawson reappeared with the hotel's small, individually sized bottle of lotion, his expression tight. "Lie on your stomach."

John froze, unsure.

Lawson's tone softened, "Please. Just trust me."

He nodded, tossing the excess pillows onto the floor and sliding onto the cool bedding, letting out a breath as he stretched out. John, hyperaware of every movement, felt Lawson's knee on the bed next to his hip before he felt the weighted feel of his body straddling his waist. The warm heat of his naked body pressing against him made the fire in his veins rip through him. Lawson felt so fucking good and strong and…

John gulped, his cock straining into the mattress, as he listened to the sound of the bottle being opened. Was Lawson really about to give him a massage?He was about to protest when he felt strong, calloused hands descend over his shoulder and he tensed, the pain forcing his eyes to shut and his back to arch.

"You're all right," Lawson murmured in the huskiest voice John had ever heard. "Just relax…"

John couldn't, not when his dick and shoulder were throbbing.

"Breathe, Donnelly…"

Slick fingers expertly slid over the muscles of his back and up to his shoulder, and John let out a whooshing breath into the pillow.

"That's it," Lawson crooned. "Keeping breathing like that…"

Lawson's incredible hands worked the muscles of his shoulder, over and over, sliding and pushing, going from soft to firm, stretching the muscles out.

This went on for what felt like an eternity, and all he could do was wordlessly obey.

"Jesus, Lawson," John finally said after several minutes.

"I'm good at this, too," Lawson said, and he could hear the smile in his voice.

"Took the words right out of my mouth."

Lawson hummed, his body inching closer now, letting John feel the thickness of his manhood pressing into his backside, but his hands never once stopped, working their magic. "I wanted to do this when you first told me today," Lawson admitted in that deep, richly timbered voice. "I wanted to drag you into an empty room and take care of you."

John let out a nervous breath.

Lawson's hands slid downward, chasing the muscle from his shoulder to his back. "I see how hard you work for us. How much you give to every single person, and you never quit. It's incredible. *You're* incredible," Lawson murmured, and paused, sliding his dick between his cheeks, letting him feel him, all of him. John gripped the sheets beneath his hands, nearly humping into the firm mattress beneath him.

Lawson's hands moved down his lower back and over his hips, gripping him before moving up his sides, continuing to stroke, touch, and massage. Fuck, it felt so good.

"That's it," Lawson drawled.

He was surrendering one muscle at a time to the young cowboy, and he was surprised by how little he minded. He trusted Lawson.

His hands slid once more to his hips, "Get on your knees…"

John did, his heart beginning to race.

Lawson applied more lotion to his calloused, strong hands and began to work the backs of his thighs, then upward, climbing higher and higher. John saw stars by the time Lawson reached over and grasped his dick between his legs, stroking it firmly in a tight grip. His moan was weak and breathy. Lawson let out his own breath, fingering the tip of his wetness.

"You're so sexy," Lawson whispered against his side, his cock brushing against his ass, pumping against him slowly and methodically. "Do you know how hard I work to earn your praise every single fucking day?"

He shivered, unable to move as Lawson's other hand slid between his cheeks, sliding his lotioned finger over his entrance, causing John to jerk and nearly buck.

"All I want is your eyes on me, telling me how good I am..." Lawson admitted in a rush, fingering the tight hole.

John barely contained the moan as Lawson's finger edged around the rim of his hole, slowly inching inside, widening him, preparing him. He cursed himself for not being brave enough to admit to Lawson that this was his first time. It felt too vulnerable, too exposed—that he was so far gone from knowing himself that it had taken him until nearly middle-age to figure out that he liked men.

His face flushed with embarrassment and shame.

He refused to let it ruin this perfect moment with Lawson.

He wouldn't regret this now. That was for later.

John pushed backward onto his hand, and Lawson cursed in a hot breath against his skin, shoving another finger inside him and causing him to finally buck, fingers grazing that euphoric spot that caused shivers to erupt all over his body.

"I want you to feel as good as I do when you praise me, Donnelly."

Oh. Fuck.

Lawson slid in and out of his tight hole, and Donnelly's head dropped into the pillow, his ass in the air as Lawson fucked him with his fingers. It was intrusive and filling, and he couldn't wait for more. He was so relaxed, so ready, because Lawson had warmed up every part of his body.

"Condom?" Lawson asked in a tight breath.

John slowly eased himself off his hand and reached for the nightstand drawer, opening it to reveal the lube and condom he had intended for another person as he handed it to him.

Lawson's hands were on his body a second later, working his hole with slippery lube and his other hand racing up and down his back before clasping his hip, adjusting himself behind John on his knees.

"Fuck," Lawson murmured. "I never thought this would happen..."

His strained confession startled him, and yet aroused him more. Lawson wanted him, and that felt selfishly good. He liked that this young man wanted to fuck him. Being wanted was a powerful thing that he now truly understood as he chased Lawson's fingers over his entrance, needing more. So much more.

He had seen how large Lawson was and wasn't surprised by how beautiful his dick was, too. Every inch of this young man's body was breathtaking, and he wanted to see it, but he also wanted to be fucked, exactly like this.

"I didn't think I could actually sneak into my captain's quarters and fuck him," Lawson rasped, and his body thrummed with a sudden rush for how forbidden this was, how taboo, and how deliciously hot.

He swallowed, his dick pulsating with need, his blood roaring in his ears as Lawson tilted his hips toward him, feeling the thick press of his cock into his tight virgin hole.

How many times had he fantasized about this with a man?

How many times had he wished for this very thing?

He would never have imagined it would be Wyatt Lawson fulfilling this fantasy for him.

Lawson pushed slowly in as he let out a gasping noise. John felt himself stretch around Lawson's thick, hard cock. He almost felt too big, and John tensed, which Lawson felt, and he began massaging him again, touching everywhere, all at once.

"Relax… breathe…" Lawson said in that sexy goddamned voice that made John's tip leak. "I'm not gonna hurt you… unless you want me to."

*Jesus Christ, this kid!*The feel of his heavy cock pushing into him made the stars return behind John's closed eyes as he pushed himself backward onto him, forcing himself to relax.

"That's it," Lawson whispered, inching slowly into him.

He tried hard to stay relaxed, feeling the invasive sensation of Lawson filling him. When the cowboy was fully sheathed inside him, John realized that Lawson was much bigger than he had realized, and it took a moment for his body to accommodate his size. He trembled, fingers gripping the sheets, stuffed to the brim with Lawson's dick.

It was sublime.

It was perfect.

It was everything he needed.

Everything.

Lawson's body shook against him. "I need to move."

"Yeah…" John rasped.

Lawson's magical hands were once more stroking him as he slid his impossibly hard erection out slowly and thrusted forward all the way in. John gasped. Lawson did it again and again, hitting his prostate, sending shockwaves of pleasure through his bloodstream, sizzling him from the inside out.

"Oh fuck, Lawson," John moaned, head hanging, arms braced, body tense as Lawson groaned, hands gripping his hips, picking up speed. John's cock was leaking everywhere, his balls tingling and tightening against his body.

He was so close. Too close. He didn't want it to be over so soon.

It felt so fucking good.

Lawson let out a strained breath and began to fuck him. Each thrust, each pounding tempo of his hips, unlocked something deep and raw inside him. John's jaw clenched as the burning tension of his headache vanished, replaced by a tidal wave of emotion bristling at the corners of his eyes, and he tensed.

Lawson immediately stilled, panting. "You okay?"

"Yeah. Don't stop."

Lawson hesitated, unsure.

John cursed, blinking away the moisture, grateful Lawson couldn't see it. "Lawson, Jesus Christ, keep fucking me."

Lawson's fingers reached between his legs, tightened painfully around his cock, and slipped over the tip, "Fuck… Yes, sir."

John's brain exploded.

Yes, sir.

Oh no.

Oh God.

He liked that far too much. He shivered and began to shake. He never remembered sex feeling this fucking good. Never this good with a woman. And never this good with Ben, even though it never got this far.

Where Lawson was unsure and nervous in the ED, he was confident, if not utterly magnificent, in the bedroom.

Fuck, it was almost too much.

Lawson's hand pumped him one more time before sliding away and returning to his shoulder, and he, unexpectedly, pushed hard onto the frozen muscle, dick buried deep inside him. John grunted and then groaned as Lawson dug into the muscle and carefully lifted his arm backward, forcing John to arch his back as Lawson stretched his arm and shoulder. Lawson kept stretching, pushing him so far back that he was fully impaled on Lawson's cock, causing John to nearly cum. And then Lawson maneuvered his hips, sliding in and out, holding his arm behind him, fucking him slowly—thoroughly.

"Holy shit," he gasped out into a breathy sob.

Lawson held his arm like a rein and rode him like a stallion, picking up the pace, fucking him with a pounding wildness, galloping together to the edge.

His cock was leaking so much that he knew he could cum just like this.

His sex spasmed, tip filling with the scorching need to release.

John didn't have to chase the orgasm building. It was already there, desperate and needy. Lawson let go of his arm, positioning John's hands into the bedframe and holding them both together as he rutted into him. John felt Lawson's face bury into his shoulder, groaning.

"Your ass is so fucking tight," Lawson growled. "You feel so good. I don't want to stop. I don't wanna cum yet."

John moaned. It was loud and thoroughly embarrassing, but he didn't fucking care. He was all sensation now. All thought, all reason, had fled him the moment Lawson's dick entered him.

Lawson's hand reached once more between his legs and grasped him fully, tightly. All it took was a few pumps and John's entire body tightened, bracing himself.

"Fuck..." Lawson hissed against his shoulder. "You're close."

"Yes," John panted.

"Cum for me, Dr. Donnelly," Lawson husked into the shell of his ear, and that was all he needed to be pushed over the edge as he gasped and came, spewing hot, thick ribbons of cum all over Lawson's fist and the bed.

"Oh god..." John whimpered, cheeks tightening around Lawson's thick cock. "I can't stop."

Lawson let out a stream of muffled curses and pounded so hard that John nearly buckled under his powerful thrusts, and that's when Lawson stiffened and unloaded inside him. He loved the sensation of it and would have loved it more without the barrier of a condom. He wanted to feel the warmth of his cum deep inside his ass, stuffing him full to the brim.

Lawson held John against him as he climaxed ruthlessly, shaking as he finished. John continued to squeeze him, milking out every drop, enjoying every jerky flare of his hips as he seemed to sink further into him.

Panting hard, Lawson didn't release him right away, continuing to hold him, brushing light kisses over his shoulder, murmuring incoherently in hot breaths.

He loved the sensation of being this ruined.

His legs shook beneath him, but he continued to hold himself up for Lawson's affectionate petting, as though he, too, didn't want this to be over. Because fuck, it was good. It was too damned good.

Lawson humped a little more, his dick softening, and he was too weak from pleasure and euphoria to stop him from taking whatever liberties he wanted with his body.

"Donnelly," Lawson marveled, "Fuck..."

The young cowboy finally eased out of him, and John collapsed into the bed, uncaring of the sticky sheet beneath him. Lawson's hands were on his body again, stroking and palming his cheeks, up his lower back.

John smiled into the pillow, humming and feeling so fucking blissed out he couldn't move.

Finally, after several long minutes of massaging and kissing, Lawson stopped and climbed off of him, walking back to the bathroom to clean up.

John managed to sit up, sinking against the bedframe, thoroughly and utterly relaxed, and downright amazed. He hadn't expected that from Lawson. He never would've thought the quiet, mild-mannered resident could fuck like that. Or that John would like it that much. Because he did.

Lawson strode out, looking devastatingly handsome. His dark sandy blond hair was sex-tousled, his skin radiated a post-orgasmic glow, his sharp pale eyes were heated, and his lips danced upward with an arrogant smirk as he gazed over John's wrecked body.

"How's the shoulder?" Lawson asked.

"Better. A lot better," he admitted. "Thank you."

Lawson nodded, picking up his jeans and looking ridiculously pleased with himself. "Good."

John shifted, grabbing the edge of the sheet and pulling it over his lap. A sudden fatigue washed over him as the drain from the long week finally caught up to him, as well as the annihilating orgasm he had just experienced. He yawned and contentedly slid down into the bed, his shoulder feeling fantastic and his ass a bit sore from being ridden so roughly toward the end.

"I should go," Lawson said, still holding his jeans and watching him.

John hesitated. Having him stay meant Lawson getting back in bed, which also meant the possibility of more sex, and they both knew that would be treading too close to the line they just crossed.

They couldn't let this happen again, and they both understood that. A relationship with an attendee and his resident was heavily frowned upon, if not a fireable offense, depending on the hospital. And it wouldn't affect just him. Lawson could be transferred out, or worse, possibly repeat his last year of residency.

"Yeah, it's probably for the best," John replied.

Lawson slid into his boxers and jeans, then his socks and worn-down black leather cowboy boots.

John arched his eyebrows in surprise, smiling. Lawson caught his smile, hand hesitating on his black T-shirt. "What?"

"Cowboy boots?" he asked.

Lawson shot him a roguish grin, "If you like these, you should see my hat."

He chuckled, ignoring how easy it was to picture Lawson wearing nothing but a cowboy hat, cock hard and ready for him. "You really are a cowboy, aren't ya kid?"

Lawson tugged on his UCLA sweater. "I was on a horse before I could crawl," he said, his hair ruffled, which he smoothed down with another careless brush of his hand.

He couldn't help but feel a twinge of envy. Oh, how the youth was wasted on the young, he thought. He was just like Lawson not too long ago, but it all felt so damned far away. He was lucky if he wasn't waking up to the sight of more gray appearing in his hair, let alone his beard. He was almost tempted to shave the damn thing off because of it. John wasn't afraid of aging, but considering he just spent the last twenty-something years in the closet, he wanted to enjoy the sex he could have with the men who may still want him. Men like Lawson. Because he liked this. And he wanted more.

But it couldn't be with Lawson.

Lawson, once fully clothed, shifted nervously, returning to the familiar version of himself that John was used to, maybe even better equipped to handle. Because whatever version of Lawson he experienced in bed made him want more. A hell of a lot more.

Lawson must have seen something in his face and smirked again. "Thanks. This was…"

John sucked in a breath, then exhaled slowly, suddenly feeling apprehensive.

Please don't say fun.

Sure, it was fun, but John didn't want to hear that his first time was just 'fun'. It meant more to John than that, and he intended to keep this information to himself. Lawson had simply been the means to an end. John now knew, for a fact, that he was unequivocally gay, having never orgasmed that intensely in his entire life. Sex with women was enjoyable, and he found release almost every time. But this—this was different.

"I won't say anything," Lawson reassured, then shifted again. "I really liked this, just so you know."

John swallowed hard, refusing to say anything, not wanting to give Lawson or himself hope of this happening again.

"See you Monday, Dr. Donnelly." His blue eyes sparkled with a confidence that John couldn't look away from.

Who the hell was this man, and what happened to the fumbling Lawson he knew?

Christ, please leave this room before I ask you to stay and fuck me again.

He scrubbed a hand over his jaw in mild shock and watched Lawson leave.

Once the door was firmly shut behind him, John climbed out of bed, turned on the bathroom's shower, and stepped beneath the hot spray. His body, like a tightly wound knot, was unraveling the longer he stood there. An incredulous smile tugged at the corner of his mouth, thinking of Lawson… thinking how quickly the night had possibly become the best one he'd had in months.

Maybe even years.

After showering, John returned to bed, darkness descending on him as he waited for the thoughts that always came in the silent stillness of night. But instead, his mind was blissfully empty.

The cliff, where he usually stood so precariously close, had vanished.

Relief dropped into his belly and he sighed, drifting off to sleep, hearing the deep timber of Lawson's calm, soothing voice and the feel of soft kisses fluttering over his frozen shoulder.

Chapter 5

Wyatt

One week later

Wyatt tried to keep his gaze fixed on the patient board, which was already lit up this morning with plenty of red. There were still overnight patients who needed to be seen, and the lobby was packed. He knew they had a full load today, and he needed to be efficient and quick. When the ED got swamped like this, it meant everyone became more focused, more intentional with their treatment. And Dr. Donnelly became the tip of the spear, leading them through, steady and reassuring. This was when he was at his absolute finest as a leader.

And irresistibly fucking sexy.

Wyatt's eyes flicked over to the man now, who was consoling an elderly woman in a gurney in the hallway, while her adult daughter cried, restlessly shifting from foot to foot.

Dr. Donnelly's beard was tidier today than it had been in a while, his short dark brown hair tousled, sprinkled with the attractive hints of gray. His hands were secured to the stethoscope around his neck as he patiently listened to the elderly woman, who had a bruised jawline and bleeding ear.

Dr. Donnelly's warm gaze was understanding and patient, never looking away, listening to every word. There was something about having Donnelly's full attention that seemed to still a person. He'd felt it the other night in the hotel room, as though the universe had stopped and all there was was his fixed, mesmeric gaze. Clearly, Wyatt wasn't the only one effected by this, as the woman beside Dr. Donnelly began crying harder, and he signaled to a passing nurse. "Could you help Mrs. Mayner get a cup of tea or coffee from the kitchen, Liz?"

His tone was kind, without a hint of judgment. Even though everyone in the ED suspected this was an elder abuse case, and it was only a matter of time before he called for Jasmine, their hospital social worker.

The nurse nodded at once and gestured toward the elevator, leading Mrs. Mayner up to the hospital cafeteria.

Reyes was working with Dr. Donnelly on the case, and Wyatt felt his fingers tap impatiently against the nurses' station barrier, trying not to feel ridiculously jealous of Reyes.

Steph, the head nurse of the ED, caught his attention by tapping the end of her digital tablet over his drumming fingers. "Eyes up, Lawson. We've got a full board. I need you focused."

Wyatt immediately jerked his gaze away from Dr. Donnelly. "Sorry, yeah."

"Room two needs to be discharged, and we've got a metal head in room five that needs a fractured nose popped back in," Steph informed.

Wyatt sucked in a breath, steeling himself for another round of patients, his eyes flicking back to Dr. Donnelly, unable to stop himself even if he tried.

Ever since their secret night together, Dr. Donnelly had seemed lighter, not as moody or tense. And it fucking thrilled Wyatt to think that he had a hand in that. The only problem was that Dr. Donnelly had been ignoring him the entire week. A price to fucking the captain, he supposed.

Steph leaned forward and tapped him firmly on the top of the head with the tablet.

Wyatt jumped and was about to dart away when she shook her head and beckoned him closer with a parental finger. He obeyed, knowing that one did not disrespect the nurses in the ED, or else it was hell trying to get back into their good graces.

"Lawson, could I give you some advice?" Steph asked, though Wyatt had a feeling he had no choice but to accept it.

"Sure."

"I know you got a crush."

Wyatt stiffened, alarm spreading through his limbs like wildfire. He was careful to keep his gaze away from Dr. Donnelly and hoped to hell his flushed cheeks wouldn't give him away.

"Most of the nurses here think you're cute and want your number. I, on the other hand, figured you had other priorities," Steph tilted her head toward Dr. Donnelly. "It's normal, I've seen it before. Plenty of residents tripping over themselves tryin' to impress him. I get it. He's something special, our Johnny, and we've never had a senior resident like him..." Steph hesitated, looking stern. "And if you keep lookin' at him like that, he's gonna notice, and so will the rest of the team. So, eyes down and chin up. Whatever you're feelin', I suggest you let it pass, all right?"

Wyatt was about to apologize, which would be somewhat of an admission, and stopped himself. He didn't want there to be a whisper of anything connecting them because he couldn't—wouldn't—jeopardize Dr. Donnelly's career.

Dr. Donnelly, too, had carefully evaded him all week and was only in the room long enough to make sure Wyatt wasn't royally fucking up. In fact, he was giving him so much space that Reyes asked if they had a beef. Before, Wyatt had walked on pins and needles whenever he got too close to Dr. Donnelly. Now, he ached.

He pined like a kid at prom, hoping his crush would ask him out on the dance floor. Because, fuck, he couldn't get their night together out of his head. All he wanted was for Dr. Donnelly to look at him longer than two seconds, but he intentionally kept an invisible wall between them.

Most of the time, Wyatt didn't mind a one-and-done scenario, especially when he was in college. He had more time to explore, taste, sample, and take risks. Hookups were common, and forgetting names the next morning was normal. Now, it was taking everything in his power to keep himself away from the handsome older doctor with the sexiest crinkles around his eyes and the sluttiest glasses that he left at his workstation for paperwork.

And, fuck me, the sounds Donnelly made!

Wyatt couldn't unhear it, letting it play on repeat in his head.

And the times he had to be close to Donnelly this week in the ED had been an unbearably sweet torture. Bumping shoulders with him, catching that faint musky scent, and hearing him reluctantly acknowledge his good work. He was even more addicted to Dr. Donnelly now, and it was getting damn near crippling how hard he sometimes got, having to run to the bathroom, hating how thin his scrubs were.

Every day after his shift this week, Wyatt would try to convince himself that the shower would scorch away remnants of his day and of Donnelly, but it never worked. He would usually end up masturbating under the hot spray, hearing those ragged, cock-inflating moans, and climaxing all over his fist within seconds, gasping under the water, needy for more.

He felt so fucking restless. Like a horse that needed a good hard run.

Wyatt wondered how many other residents had become ensnared by Donnelly's soothing warmth as he had, and the only person who knew that was the short, curvy woman before him, her curly black hair pulled back in a thick ponytail, her face etched with the unbothered expression she wore daily.

"How many others?" Wyatt asked.

She smirked, "Oh, at least a couple dozen over the years."

"Really?" he asked, surprised and yet not.

"Someone in each new rotation," Steph drawled, glancing at the patient board, chewing the end of her pen cap.

"That's..."

"...a lot of crushes," she finished, eyes sparkling with amusement. "The nurses have a whole betting pool on it. Donnelly doesn't know, or Samuels. Walsh figured it out last year and started betting on it, too, the devil. The nurses were too scared to tell him no."

Wyatt nearly laughed. He'd only ever met the night doctor, Dr. Walsh, once in passing. He had heard the rumors, though, that he was a bit unhinged, unfiltered. He figured someone would have to be a bit mad to work the night shift in the emergency department.

"Like I said, it's normal," Steph said with a shrug. "Donnelly sometimes figures it out, sometimes he doesn't."

"What happens when he figures it out?" Wyatt asked, throat tightening.

"They get rotated to the night shift with Walsh, or to a different hospital." Her eyebrows arched at his expression, which he couldn't hide unless he covered himself with his hoodie. "Don't worry, hon. Your secret is safe with me, handsome. Besides, I always thought betting on impressionable young pups was wrong."

She tapped her flashy red-painted nails on her digital black tablet, letting the phone at her desk ring. "Hey, I forgot to mention, it's Dr. Williams's retirement party tomorrow. The whole crew is invited. We're meeting at the Hot Dog Palace. It's a place we sometimes go for happy hour—well, more like midnight hour."

"Dr. Williams?" Wyatt asked.

"Cardiology. Rarely comes by these days, and now even more so with the whole retirement thing. Starts at eight sharp, kid. Bring Reyes, or better yet, bring a date."

Wyatt studied himself in the mirror for the millionth time before letting out a frustrated sigh. He was going to be late. This was his tenth outfit change before settling on his nicest pair of dark blue denim jeans, his worn but comfortable black cowboy boots (the same ones Donnelly had commented on), a plain white undershirt, and his favorite tanned leather jacket. He even put some of Jin's fancy hair product in and slicked his hair back a bit. He got a haircut after his shift, trimming the sides and top.

He closed the door to his room, hoping to sneak out before Jin saw him, but halted with his hand on the front door of their apartment when he heard a low, catcalling whistle.

"You can salt and burn my ashes any day, Dean Winchester," Jin drawled.

Wyatt pivoted on his boot heel, exhaling slowly. Jin had been walking from the kitchen to the living room when he spotted Wyatt in the hallway. He was cradling a large bowl of popcorn, wearing a blue silk kimono, and the sounds of people laughing from the television in the living room told him Jin was having a movie night instead of going out.

"Where the hell are you going looking like that?" Jin asked, almost offended.

"It's a work thing," Wyatt said in a rush. "A retirement party."

"Please tell me it's Donnelly's party and you're his Dean Winchester candygram?"

He snorted out a laugh, "No. Do I really look that generic?"

"Maybe add a bit of flair?"

"Flair…?"

The bar door swung open, and the scent of beer and hot dogs wafted over him. He heard the boisterous laughter and classic rock drifting over the packed bar. The red, green, and yellow glow of last year's Christmas lights adorned the stained-glass windows. The Hot Dog Palace slogan was painted in slanting white block letters, on a forest-green wall above the bar: *Fresh beer, booze, and hot dogs! Come and get it!*

He smiled, charmed by this oddball place.

"Hey! You made it!"

Wyatt turned and saw Reyes coming at him for a bear hug, holding a beer. Wyatt gave him a one-armed shoulder hug and patted his back before motioning to the bar, needing alcohol to take the edge off. He was nervous as a new pony, and he blamed it entirely on letting Jin convince him to wear his cowboy hat. Normally, he tried to blend in with the LA crowd, especially amongst his peers. But Jin, as always, managed to talk him into questionable things.

"Damn, Lawson, you clean up good. I should introduce you to my sister. She needs to date someone that doesn't suck," Reyes teased, taking a long swig of his beer.

"Thanks, but uh," Wyatt hesitated, and shook his head, deciding he wasn't about to tell a half-drunk Reyes that he was gay in a public bar, filled with their co-workers. Some other time, he thought and patted his back. "I'm gonna grab a beer, you want another?"

"Damn straight," Reyes pointed to the back of the bar. "I got a table with Emily and Ava in the back."

Wyatt hid his cringe. Ava was the last person he wanted to be sharing a table with. She was in her first year of residency and was the biggest gossip in the ED. Ava was the type of person to see a hornet's nest, kick it, film it, and share it with everyone. He despised people like that. Luckily for her, she was a good doctor, and so far her antics on the team had gone unnoticed. But it was only a matter of time before her true colors showed.

Emily was cool, though. He really enjoyed working with her and Reyes.

A few people from the emergency department recognized him on the way to the bar, and he stopped to say hi before pushing through the crowd, barely untangling himself from the nurses' table.

He exhaled a nervous breath once his hands reached for the sticky bar top, and the bartenders, two middle-aged women sporting tattoos and rocker vibes, were busy taking orders.

"Man, I swear if Tanya doesn't get off my ass, I'm gonna have to switch back to night shift."

He heard Dr. Samuels's familiar tone, which at times held a hint of a Boston accent, and saw Donnelly sitting next to him, unaware that Wyatt was a mere foot away from him. Wyatt tried to rein in his fluttery nerves, but it was no fucking use when he was next to Donnelly.

"Oh, bureaucracy at its finest," Donnelly said, taking a sip from his beer. "You haven't been here long enough for her to already be hounding you. It must be your charm."

"Must be."

"Walsh would be thrilled to have you back on his night shift," Donnelly commented drily.

Samuels snorted. "Key word—*his*. That man is terrifying. I swear he enjoys chaos—like, *likes* it. The crazy bastard wants the blood, guts, and gore."

"C'mon, weren't we all like that at one point in our careers?" Donnelly challenged with a smirk.

"He's our fuckin' age. Grow up, man. Find a hobby—somethin'. Don't let your life be the ED. I've only seen him one time here, and he's—he's fuckin' mean, man."

Donnely snorted a delicious laugh, his large hand clasping the amber bottle as he tilted it up by the neck and took another sip. "He's not that bad. I like his company. Sometimes. Just gotta know how to work around the frayed, slightly crazy edges."

"You say that like it's easy. Which makes sense, because it's you."

"Meaning what, exactly?" Donnelly asked.

"I think you know."

"I don't," Donnely replied, his tone shifting to an unexpected defensiveness.

"Look, man, I ain't sayin' this to be mean, I'm sayin' it outta love. But you gotta know when to quit. You spend too much time on lost causes and not enough on the lives that can be saved. It's gonna catch up, and when it does, it's gonna hurt. I feel like every time I turn around, you're in the grief room because of it."

"I'm the senior attending, Sam. That's what we do."

"No," Samuels said firmly. "You don't delegate. You take on too much when you have me and a dozen other fully capable doctors who can be the bearer of bad news. It doesn't have to be you every time, brother."

Donnelly's hand reached for the back of his neck, gripping and rubbing, his right shoulder slightly higher than the other, and Wyatt's eyes sharpened over him.

"Some of the residents aren't ready for that," Donnelly replied coolly.

"Bullshit."

Donnelly stiffened.

"That's just an excuse to not ask for help."

"I don't need help," Donnelly retorted. "I'm fine."

Samuels paused, assessing him with those cool, dark green eyes. "Yeah, I know."

Something passed between the two older doctors that Wyatt couldn't see, and for a split second, he thought they were maybe having a moment. Was it a romantic moment? Wyatt nearly leaned over the bar to look, but forced himself to keep his boots firmly planted on the damned floor.

"I'm done hounding you," Samuels patted Donnelly affectionately on the back. "I'm glad you finally decided to join us tonight. It's nice seeing you in the land of the living."

Donnelly scoffed, "I came out last month."

"No, you didn't. We've hung out approximately five times outside the ED since I moved out here eight months ago."

Wyatt frowned at not being able to read Donnelly's expression. He was always better at reading between the lines and seeing what people said with their bodies rather than their words. It annoyed Wyatt that he hadn't figured out Donnelly yet, but he knew it was only a matter of time before he did.

He had seen a few things. The first thing Wyatt noticed was his shoulder. The next was seared into his brain like a cattle brand. Donnelly, sprawled out on the king-size hotel bed, looking like the most delicious midnight snack Wyatt could've ever asked for. Blissed out of his mind, sedated in his orgasmic glow, utterly fucking glorious.

Donnelly was the epitome of a masculine old-school man, with a thickly built physique that could easily pack on muscle, rich, furry chest hair that trailed all the way down the flat planes of his stomach, and that impressive, mouth-watering cock.

Wyatt licked his lips, breathing hard through his nose, thinking about how he had briefly felt that dick in his mouth, and how much he needed to feel it again, and soon.

Stay fuckin' cool, cowboy.

"What would you like, handsome?" asked the bartender, startling Wyatt out of his thoughts.

"Whiskey and a pitcher of beer, please."

"Comin' right up."

"Christ, Lawson, is that you?" Samuels said, causing Wyatt to turn in time to see Donnelly's shoulders tense at the sound of his name.

Wyatt tipped the brim of his hat to the doctor. He liked Dr. Samuels. He was like the cool uncle everyone liked hanging out with. He was around Donnelly's age, maybe younger, with curly dark brown hair that was graying at the roots, and currently intent on growing a mustache. He was also stupidly handsome. Wyatt heard Ava complaining about how hard it was to keep her focus while they were both working the same shift, because they were both distractingly hot.

And now, a possible threat to making moves on his captain.

His captain?

Get a grip, Lawson.

"Why on earth are you trying to be a doctor?" Samuels asked almost accusingly. "You should be on a commercial or television show somewhere. Not in this old guy's ED."

Donnelly slowly turned on his barstool with a firm grip on his beer, careful to glance only briefly and politely in Wyatt's direction, and taking another sip of his beer.

Acknowledge, but don't absorb, Wyatt thought, knowing precisely what Donnelly was attempting to do.

Keep it professional—keep it neutral.

Don't think about the sounds their bodies made fucking, or how hard Donnelly came in Wyatt's fist. His hand tingled afterward at the mere thought.

He swallowed thickly, heat flooding his body at how close Donnelly was to him now that he had turned in his seat. Wyatt couldn't help but notice how handsome he looked in his worn jeans, long-sleeved dark gray overshirt, and black undershirt.

Wyatt came to the bar tonight with two things in mind: look as good as humanly possible and make Donnelly notice him, and then ignore *him*. It was petty and low, but it was the only way he could enjoy this night without sulking in possible defeat. Because Donnelly wasn't breaking, and maybe never would.

Maybe their sinful night of pleasure was a one-off, and he needed to accept it.

Except, he couldn't. He had fucked plenty of men in his life, but Donnelly had surrendered everything. Giving everything over to Wyatt in a way he had never, ever felt.

It was invigorating and addictive.

And he wasn't going to admit defeat until the bitter damned end.

"Who says I didn't try?" Wyatt countered smoothly.

"Bullshit," Samuels shot back over the noisy bar.

He shrugged, playing it off, but unable to stop the smile dancing on his lips.

"You serious?" Samuels asked, slightly impressed.

Wyatt never talked about this blip in his life, but it happened. One day, he was riding a horse; the next, he was riding a horse on a commercial for a major car company, all because the right producer came to his dad's dude ranch with her girlfriends and hired Wyatt after watching him on a horse all weekend.

"A couple of years back, there was a Ford commercial for the latest truck. The one shot in the Arizona desert…"

He paused when Donnelly, for the first time all week, finally looked at him, his dark blue eyes riveted to his face.

Wyatt licked his lips, clearing his throat. "The one where the cowboy races on horseback with the truck. They ride up to the edge of a cliff and stop. The commercial was a whole production. It aired for the Super Bowl."

"No shit," Samuels said incredulously.

"Is it on YouTube?" Steph materialized out of nowhere, her phone out, already searching for the commercial.

Wyatt flushed, and the bartender appeared in time with his shot of whiskey and pitcher of beer for the table.

"Yeah, I think so." Wyatt slammed back the shot of whiskey, the burning relief filling his mouth and slipping down his throat. He let out a hard breath from his chest and heard the song 'For Whom the Bell Tolls' on Steph's phone as Samuels, Donnelly, and her crowded around the phone.

"You can stream that if you want," the bartender said and pointed to the TV behind her.

Oh shit.

Steph pushed a couple of buttons, and the large bar screen lit up with a dusty picture of the Arizona desert and a beautiful all-black mustang horse. The horse's muscles rippled in the orange glow of the dying sunlight. The song was slowly building as the camera zoomed in on a cowboy's hands gripping the leather straps of her reins and straddling the horse. His legs strained against his black jeans as he squeezed his legs around her, securing himself in the saddle beneath the restless beast, while simultaneously a black Ford truck revved to life beside them.

"That's not you," Samuels baited, but none of them looked away, except Donnelly, whose eyebrows arched in surprised amazement at him, before quickly returning to look at the screen.

A massive formation of thick gray storm clouds hung over the canyon, lightning flashing and sparkling in the distance, as the camera zoomed in on the truck and the cowboy, the cinematic picture depicting a race to the edge of the cliff. The camera then focused on the cowboy, revealing Wyatt, his black cowboy hat tilted low, sweat already beading on his brow, and dust on his all-black outfit.

"Holy shit," Samuels whistled.

"Well hell, kid," Steph murmured.

Donnelly was quiet, and he tried his damnest not to look at him.

The mustang reared back on its hind legs and then galloped at full speed, not once jostling Wyatt on the saddle, who, with practiced ease, managed to hang on and hunker low on the horse, speeding straight toward the cliff. The truck roared to life and chased after them. They were neck-and-neck as the music amped up.

"Jesus, Lawson," Donnelly breathed low and...

Fuck.

Wyatt's belly clenched, instantly transported to their night together, feeling the way Donnelly's ass clenched around him like a fucking fist as he thrusted wildly into him.

Fire ignited in his blood, and his cock twitched to life. Wyatt jerked off his beige cowboy hat, raking his fingers through his hair and steeling himself, trying to focus on the commercial.

The music and cinematography added drama as the truck suddenly skidded to a halt. Dust billowed out beneath the black tires, spraying him and the horse from view. Wyatt emerged from the cloud of brown and orange dust, and at the last minute, he came to a careening halt at the edge of the steep canyon cliffside, the dust from the hooves and the truck spilling around them, the lighting flashing.

Then the famous actor narrator says, "We build them fearless. We build them tough. Ford."

The camera zoomed in on Wyatt as he led the horse back, covered in dust, passing the truck and tipping the brim of his black hat in appreciation for the race. Sweat glistened on his face as he smiled confidently and trotted off frame.

"Did you really do that?" Donnelly asked, stunned.

"The commercial?" he asked, unable to keep the teasing from his tone.

"The race…!" Steph cut in.

"If you're asking if there was a stunt cowboy on set, no, there wasn't. Just me."

"Jesus Christ, kid. Bartender, I need a round of shots. Right now," Samuels pressed. "That was by far the coolest shit I've seen all month. Possibly the best thing all year."

"I don't believe it," Steph said with a dismissive wave. "Movie magic and special effects. That's all. Besides, real cowboys don't wear all black in Arizona. Heat strokes would be through the roof."

Wyatt snorted and agreed with the last half of her statement. It was true, no sane cowboy would wear all black in the dry heat of the desert.

The movie magic part, she was wrong, because that was all his ability on horseback that created that shot. But he decided it was better just to let her believe that, rather than challenge her.

He had discovered over the years that no matter how much evidence he had, or how he said it, people believed what they wanted to believe.

He saw it constantly in the ED. Patients stubbornly believe in whatever the internet tells them rather than the living, breathing, skilled experts in the room.

"I don't care," Samuels declared. "It looked cool. You want another whiskey, cowboy?"

He nodded as the bartender lined up the shots. Steph and Samuels were busy bickering about what to order Williams when Donnelly casually leaned toward Wyatt, voice low and directed only to him. "You actually rode that horse to the edge of the cliff, didn't you?"

He swayed a little bit closer, voice equally low. "What do you think?"

Donnelly's eyes darkened, searching his face, before dipping briefly to his lips.

Wyatt licked his bottom lip, stomach tightening in anticipation. Donnelly let out a hard breath from his nose and abruptly sat up, creating distance between them just in time for Samuels to line up two shots in front of Wyatt and Donnelly.

Samuels proceeded to shove two shots in front of Donnelly.

"Two?" Donnelly asked, face pinched in a frown.

"Aw, c'mon, live a little. Besides, it's not like any of us are working tomorrow."

"I am," Steph said, and knocked on the bar top with her knuckles. "Don't care. Let's drink."

"Somebody hand these to Williams!" Samuels shouted and passed the two shots of whiskey through the crowded bar.

This caught a few people's attention, and Samuels raised a loud "congratulations" over the crowd, which was met with a shout of appreciation.

Samuels took his first shot, followed quickly by the second. Steph mimicked him and Donnelly hesitated, but not Wyatt. He knocked the two shots back and felt the warmth heat his insides and calm his nerves as he let his knee brush against Donnelly's beneath the bar top.

Donnelly's shoulders stiffened.

"C'mon, Donnelly!" Samuels yelled.

Donnelly's jaw twitched beneath his brown, gray-speckled beard, and finally downed the first shot. Wyatt watched his throat work as he swallowed, his knee rubbing against his. He waited for him to move away, but he didn't. He shot back the final shot and sighed, hand scrubbing over his lips and beard, looking almost resigned. Defeated even.

Wyatt, blaming it on the heady warm bar and the buzz filtering through his system, reached beneath the bar top, making sure no one was watching as he slowly slid his hand down his own leg, before reaching for Donnelly's, his fingers gripping his upper thigh. The muscle was strong and hard beneath his touch, and he released a breath.

Fuck, it felt good touching him again.

Donnelly briefly closed his eyes, his elbow on the counter. One hand rubbed his face while the other cradled his beer.

"How did you do it?" Donnelly asked, his voice rough and laced with something… needy.

Sweet Jesus.

Wyatt slowly moved his fingers in a swirling pattern on the inner lining of Donnelly's jeans, head tilting to the side. "Do what?"

"Riding to the edge like that…" Donnelly's strained tone was music to his ears. He was getting to him.

Thank fuck.

"Plenty of years of practice."

"But that was dangerous."

Wyatt nodded, "That horse and I worked together a lot. She was one of my dad's staple horses for the ranch. It's trust that makes somethin' like that work. She trusted me, and I trusted her. That's why we caught each other at the very end."

He watched the tension around Donnelly's shoulders and felt the weight he carried, wondering how his shoulder was doing.

"It helped that the horse was older," Wyatt continued, letting his voice drop. "More sure of herself, confident. Had I chosen a younger one, we would've gone flying off into that fuckin' canyon. Riding a horse like that—more mature, more experienced, but still willing to take a risk occasionally—is my favorite kind of ride. Addicting, even."

Donnelly's jaw clenched fiercely, and Wyatt flicked his fingers upward, touching the stiffness trapped against the denim of his jeans. His pulse slammed to a halt. He was as hard as a cinderblock.

It took everything not to lean forward and rake his hands through that beard and capture those delicious lips one more time. Wyatt's cock was damn near leaking in his jeans.

"You were movin' really well the first half of the week," Wyatt breathed. "You weren't in as much pain. But you are now. I can..." his fingers opened up and over the tented bulge, "...take care of you. All you gotta do is ask."

Donnelly's face hardened in an instant. "Let go," he murmured.

The rejection was swift and stinging, more so than he cared to admit. Wyatt hesitated and then nodded, leaning back into his barstool and retracting his hand discreetly.

The bartender was in front of Wyatt then, "How many glasses for your pitcher, cowboy?"

He swallowed down his hurt pride and pulled out his wallet, "Four, please."

She nodded and reached beneath the counter, pulling out the glasses as he placed the cash on the counter and stood. He could withstand a horse bucking away his hand or a patient flinching at his treatment. But Donnelly knew what he could give him, and he still retreated.

Frustrated, he grabbed the pitcher and the stacked glasses and was walking away when Donnelly's voice stopped him.

"Lawson," he said firmly.

He stopped, eyes locked with his.

Donnelly hesitated, looking surprisingly uncertain.

Wyatt smiled blandly. "You have a good night, Dr. Donnelly."

He spotted Steph watching them, sipping a beer, eyebrows arched at Wyatt. He shrugged innocently and strolled over to the booth where Reyes and the others were, reminding himself of his place in the hierarchy. Making passes at his captain, after a night that he clearly regretted, was a mistake. It didn't matter that his body responded differently.

Except it *did* matter.

And Wyatt could think of nothing else the rest of the night.

Chapter 6

John

One month later

John braced his arm against the bathroom stall, breathing through the pain. Tears clouded his vision as he sucked in breath after breath, trying to calm down.

God, I'm such a fucking idiot. I should've seen that coming…!

His arm practically dangled at his side, while his shoulder throbbed and burned.

"John?" Steph's voice echoed through the empty men's bathroom.

"Yeah," he managed to say between clenched teeth.

"Tanya is on her way down," Steph said gently. "She heard about what happened."

"Fuck," he bit out. "I'm fine!"

"Tell that to her," she said. "You know she'll want a full evaluation done with a write-up. You should take the day. Come back tomorrow, or don't. But you should head home. I already called Walsh to come in early."

He thumped his head against the cool steel, wanting to vanish into the floor. "You didn't have to do that."

When she didn't answer, he sighed, "Anything else?"

"That's it. Nothing I can't handle till you're back on the floor. I'll get you an ice pack and something for the pain."

He knew she was just being nice, and the offer was sincere. He didn't need to rip her head off. "Give me two minutes."

"I can give you five." He heard the door open and close once more, and he was peacefully alone with his miserable, aching shoulder.

It happened fast.

One minute he was working on a GSW, gun-shot-wound patient, who was unconscious, when the large man abruptly awoke, flailing around like he was still in the gun battle. He kicked John hard in the chest. He had stumbled back but held his ground, knowing how to take the occasional hit. The patient flailed desperately, slamming his massive fist into his shoulder and neck, attacking anywhere he could out of adrenaline-fueled survival mode.

If it hadn't been for Lawson, he would've taken a fist to the face next. Lawson stepped in, grabbed the large patient and tackled him back down onto the gurney, followed by Reyes, a couple of nurses, and the security officer. But the damage was already done. John could barely lift his arm, and the other doctors in the department were forced to take over.

John pressed a hand to his chest, knowing he was probably going to have a good-sized bruise come morning. But that wasn't what was worrying him. His shoulder had shown slow progress over the past month, and he'd finally been able to stretch it over his head, but this… this was bad.

And he had to get back to work.

He couldn't take time off for something like this.

The door opened, and he wondered if it was Steph with the ice pack. The door closed, and he heard footsteps approach the handicapped stall John had locked himself in.

"Donnelly," Lawson's voice came through the gray steel wall. "Open up."

He hesitated, gritting his back molars, sweat beading his brow from pain. He opened the door and was greeted by cool, impenetrable pale blue eyes.

Lawson didn't ask as he stepped in, pushing John back, then he closed and locked the door behind him.

John swallowed, shaking. "I'm fine."

Lawson looked unconvinced, taking up far too much space in the small confines of the hospital bathroom.

"Let me see," Lawson commanded without a hint of reservation.

"Are you serious?"

"Take your shirt off, let me see."

"This is so unnecessary and out of bounds, Lawson. I don't…"

Lawson was on him in an instant, his firm hand touching the injured neck and shoulder, and John let out a hiss of pain.

"Your shoulder is stuck." Lawson carefully touched the shoulder now, stroking it. "It's locked in."

He cursed, leaning back against the cool tile, feeling Lawson's touch like a calming balm, and hating how easily his body betrayed him. He closed his eyes, resisting as long as he could. He'd gone an entire month, almost nearly forgiving himself for doing something so catastrophically stupid with Lawson.

But having him this close, feeling the heat of his breath on his skin, the press of his fingers gently rolling out the muscle on his neck… He released a sigh and dropped his head forward into Lawson's chest.

The younger man hesitated only a second before continuing to work his shoulder, humming smoothly from the back of his throat at John's submission. The shooting tension in his neck and shoulder relaxed enough for him to breathe again.

This went on for several wonderful seconds, until Lawson guided him back against the wall and lifted his shirt. John didn't resist as Lawson revealed the white shirt beneath his dark gray scrub shirt, before peeling that off next. Both men assessed the damage on his chest. The red imprint of a boot heel was already forming a purple-black bruise, and his neck and shoulder seemed locked together as though by an invisible band.

Lawson's eyes flashed with an anger John had never seen before, and before he could say anything, the young doctor led him to the toilet, slamming the seat cover down, instructing him to sit. John complied like a docile child.

Lawson positioned himself over him, straddling his legs, and went to work on his neck and shoulder, massaging the tendons with both hands. John tried to stifle the groan, but the more Lawson rubbed and soothed, the harder it was to control his body's reaction. He moaned weakly, letting the pain retreat, replaced by relief.

"Fuck," John said with a surprised gasp. His shoulder and neck finally dropped apart. His neck straightened naturally and was able to move again, while his shoulder, still frozen, didn't hurt as much. Lawson wasn't done, though, and continued to massage his shoulder, aggressively now, pushing hard into the muscle and down his bare arm.

Christ, it felt so good...

John was hypnotized by the young man's bold, confident hands. Rubbing and soothing. Touching and gripping. He studied Lawson's focused expression and saw the lines around his lips and the intentionality in his gaze. Lawson's dirty blonde hair swept over his forehead, his cheeks were cleanly shaven, and his jawline was sharp, almost chiseled from granite. He was reminded of those classic, handsome Hollywood actors from the 1940s, who were almost too handsome to be real.

John felt his cock thicken between his legs, and his shoulders tensed. Lawson greeted the tension with a strong, unrelenting push, forcing them back down. He sighed, releasing the rigid control and relaxing under his ministrations.

And to think, I only had one night with him and saw nothing of how truly beautiful he was.

One night, John had allowed himself to be weak.

To give in to temptation and lose himself entirely.

To not, for one second of his life, have to be responsible.

To be, instead, recklessly wild.

John had thought about that night constantly and held onto it, trying his best not to shame himself for it. Because that night was more than a loss of control, it was deeper than that. And he still was grappling with the effect it had on him. Something he would never admit to himself, and certainly not Lawson. But seeing him now, so close, touching him almost the same way, giving to him the way he had that night, was overwhelming him.

"Lawson…" he rasped, resisting the urge to pull him close.

Lawson's blue eyes met his.

John wasn't sure what he wanted—what he needed.

Lawson seemed to know, and without hesitating, slipped his hand beneath his jaw, fingers raking through his beard. John reached instantly, wrapping his arm around Lawson's waist, dragging him closer, dropping his forehead into his stomach, not sure how to give anymore, when all he wanted to do was take. And it felt selfish to do that to him, especially after ignoring him and his advances for an entire month. For pretending that their night never happened.

Lawson's hand was suddenly in his hair, gripping his head with both hands and dragging him back, forcing John to look at him. Lawson's jaw clenched for a mere second, as though deciding. Deciding his fate, because the truth was, he couldn't deny him again.

Lawson leaned down and kissed him.

Shit.

Yes.

John felt the urgency with Lawson's kiss and matched it. Their lips clashed with such force, such horrible need, he choked out a groan.

Lawson devoured him, angrily, hungrily, conqueringly.

The heated passion between them burst into millions of stars, pulling him up and out of the darkness of this moment, out of his fucking life. And he wanted to drown in this kiss. Lawson's intensity wouldn't be outmatched, and John could feel it as their tongues mated and battled, their teeth scraped and grazed over lips.

He clung to the stronger, younger man, feeling like a vine caught in a storm and only Lawson's hungry kisses anchoring him to something better—something real.

John got to his feet and pushed Lawson back against the tile wall, pressing himself against him, unable to stop himself from taking… and taking…

He felt Lawson's cock push and grind against his.

"Fuck," Lawson gasped against his lips as they dry-humped one another, both needing the same release and chasing it with fumbling, urgent hands.

"John!" Steph's voice echoed off the walls of the bathroom, and John yanked back, panting. "Five minutes are up. Tanya's here." The door slammed shut behind her.

Lawson, panting, dropped the back of his head against the tile, his lips red and almost bruised from John's kisses. Unable to stop touching him, he reached up to drag a thumb over Lawson's reddened lips, sucking in a breath. Lawson's eyes were fully dilated and watching, waiting.

John closed his eyes, unable to see the consequences of his impulsiveness, and snapped his fingers back. "That can't happen again."

Lawson was quiet for a moment before finally saying, "I know."

He opened his eyes, and he saw a calmness on Lawson's face that he wasn't expecting. The young doctor picked up John's undershirt and scrub shirt and handed them to him.

Feeling oddly nervous, John hurriedly dressed, not even thinking about his neck and shoulder, and when the uniform was back on, he stilled. Stunned.

"Holy shit," he said in awe, rotating his shoulder and even cracking his neck. The pain was almost gone. His shoulder still ached, but it wasn't half as bad. And his chest felt like it got stomped on, but he could handle that.

Lawson was watching him closely and smirked in pleasure at the way he was moving.

"Thank you," John said, clearing his throat, trying his hardest to maintain some sort of fucking professionalism after such a heady make-out session. "It feels better already."

Lawson nodded, opened the bathroom stall, and without another word, left.

Regret flooded him, but not in the way he had anticipated. Regret that he didn't say more. Only that Lawson didn't fight him and didn't press for more.

John's lips thinned into an impatient line and he raked both hands through his hair. He took another deep, lung-clearing breath and opened the bathroom door.

The bright fluorescent lights of the ED greeted him, along with the hustle and bustle, the noise, and the smell.

Time to work.

He showed up the following day despite Tanya's insistence that he take the rest of the week off after the incident.

"No rest for the wicked," he told Steph upon arriving, coffee cup in hand and sunglasses still on, already heading toward the lockers to drop off his bag.

"No kidding," Steph replied, scrutinizing him as he walked by. "You're movin' all right. That's good."

Yeah, all thanks to the resident whose magic hands worked my body like a fucking fiddle.

And damn him to hell, that's all he thought about when he finally made it home last night and under the spray of a hot shower, urgently masturbated, still able to feel the press of wet, hungry lips and Lawson's hard cock pressed against him, with only the barrier of their thin scrubs holding them back. The moment had been undeniably hot. Everything John had been needing the last month.

If only they had a few more minutes alone, John would've dropped to his knees and taken Lawson's dick into his mouth, and that thought alone had him spiraling into an orgasm, which was swift and destroying. Thick ribbons of bliss streamed out of him for so long that his knees buckled. By the time he dragged his weary, tired ass to bed, he pictured piercing blue eyes and heard two little words: "I know".

He slept like the dead. In fact, he hadn't slept that well since the night at the hotel with Lawson.

John punched the keycode to his locker and heard footsteps behind him. He recognized Lawson's UCLA hoodie as he entered the hallway, carrying his backpack over his shoulder.

"Good morning, Lawson," he said politely, deciding to no longer ignore him. That had been his rationale for acting like a starving man presented with a feast the day before, and maybe small interactions would help him build a fortified tolerance toward him instead.

"Good morning, Dr. Donnelly," Lawson said in a slow, deliberate tone.

John frowned, glancing over his shoulder and noticing there was no one around but them. And the way Lawson was looking at him now...

Fuck.

He shivered and ignored the reaction, turning to put his backpack and sunglasses into the locker and slamming it shut. Before he could turn, Lawson's hand was on his shoulder, kneading the muscle into relaxed compliance, and John's knees went weak, his body instantly responding in a way that he didn't fucking understand.

"We have two minutes before Reyes gets here," Lawson whispered, and then his other hand descended on him, working the tight muscles over his sweater and scrubs.

He tensed, trying to shift away, but Lawson moved, pushing him against the lockers and insistently working his hands over his body. John melted against the wall of lockers, letting out a trembling breath.

"That's it," Lawson murmured.

He felt his cheeks flush. Was he seriously blushing? He nearly moaned in mortification.

This is so wrong.

Just tell him to stop, John.

It's not that fuckin' hard!

It was hard because whatever Lawson was doing to his frozen shoulder was cowboy voodoo magic that apparently caused John's prefrontal cortex to shut down. No one had ever cared so much to do this for him, let alone know exactly how to massage his frozen shoulder. He'd gone to a dozen massage therapists, trying to recreate what Lawson had done to him since that night, and no one could replicate him.

"I need my captain in good spirits today." Lawson's husky, low tone sent shockwaves through his body, and straight to his cock. He stifled a groan the best he could, and it came out in a weak whimper at the back of his throat, which was way worse.

Lawson seemed to like it as his touch grew more intense, digging almost painfully into his shoulder before releasing, dragging it out.

"Lawson…" John croaked. "This isn't…"

"I know. I know."

More massaging, more soft, panting breaths.

"I take a break between two and three," Lawson whispered. "Meet me in the break room today. Give me another two minutes."

He thumped his forehead against the locker, "Lawson. That's not a good idea."

Lawson's hands withdrew, and John could finally breathe again. He turned and saw Lawson stripping off his hoodie, the brief outline of his abs and that sharp V-line of his hips, and the telling signs of an erection. John flushed again, quickly retrieving his coffee from the bench. Once Lawson's head cleared the sweater, he glanced toward him and then downward. Lawson didn't even blink, his expression perfectly neutral, and yet his eyes… Something flashed there for the briefest of seconds, seeing his own telling signs of John's semi-hard dick.

The young man kept his eyes locked with his as he casually slid his hand beneath his scrubs, adjusted his erection upward, discreetly snapping the waistband of his briefs and scrubs over himself.

John wondered if he should do the same.

"Yo, yo, yo," Reyes chimed down the hallway. "Dr. D! You're alive. I thought you'd want the day off."

"Good morning to you too, Reyes," John said politely, smiling half-heartedly at the young doctor, shifting his stance to alleviate the pressure that had built there. "I'm tougher than I look."

"Yeah, we know," Reyes said, punching in the locker code. "You're the toughest son of a bitch in the ED, next to Samuels. The only difference between the two of you is that you smile on occasion."

"Well, Samuels has that ability, too," John replied. "I just think he forgets how to do it sometimes."

Lawson frowned considerably at him for some reason, making him hesitate, wondering what shifted the younger man's mood, before nodding briefly at the two men and heading toward the central station to Steph. Lawson and Reyes reminded him of the younger days when he and other young doctors were battling for dominance in the ED. All ego-driven, trying to outsmart and outdo one another.

Lawson and Reyes seemed almost indifferent to competition and were more like teammates, wanting to support rather than stifle with judgment or rivalry. He supposed it was a generational difference. And the thought suddenly made him feel old.

He instinctively rolled his shoulder and sighed. Damn it, Lawson had the magic touch. His shoulder had never felt so loose. Maybe he'd take him up on the offer to meet in the break room.

Just two minutes.

It couldn't hurt.

That's it, and that would have to be enough.

Chapter 7

Wyatt

Pride welled in him at the sight of how well Donnelly moved through his morning, his shoulder pain undetectable from what Wyatt could see. And he couldn't stop the small victory smile whenever he noticed it, whenever he noticed *him*.

After that moment of raw vulnerability from Donnelly in the bathroom stall yesterday, Wyatt felt like he was falling rapidly without a parachute. His mind went back to that moment again and again, the way Donnelly's body released, relaxing and surrendering—finally—under his touch. But when he had tilted his head into his stomach, relief etched on his features rather than pain, entirely at his mercy, vulnerable and needy, Wyatt had rushed to greet him. He had thrown himself headlong over the cliff and into his own canyon, labeled: John Fucking Donnelly.

When Donnelly's arm had wrapped around his waist, tugging him in closer, he dug in, knowing that it wouldn't last long, and he'd have to take what he could before his captain slammed the door in his face again.

He kissed him like the ship was sinking, battling him with tongue and lips, kissing the hell out of him. And fuck, every time he thought about it, he nearly got hard again.

There were kisses, and then there were *kisses.*

That one left him edgy and desperate for more.

More. More. Goddammit, more, please, Dr. Fuckin' MD.

So, when he saw Donnelly alone in the hallway by the lockers, and he actually greeted him instead of ignoring him as he had been, Wyatt pounced like a hungry lion. And his prey let him take. He knew when he told Donnelly to come to the break room, he would. He knew in his bones and blood that the older doctor wasn't done with him yet, either.

Breathless with anticipation, Wyatt finally managed to sneak off around 2:45, while the ED seemed calmer, and headed for the break room. The staff avoided the break room like the plague, saying it was haunted by the tears of fallen med students who couldn't quite hack it. It also had the worst coffee maker, producing liquid sludge instead of coffee.

He opened the door and froze.

Dr. Ava Taschen was passed out on the small kitchenette table, drooling into the crook of her arm. Her unruly brown ponytail flopped over her shoulder, and her scrubs were wrinkled.

Wyatt glowered.

Ava had yet to earn his respect as a fellow resident. She slacked off, showed up late and left early, and, worst of all, pretended to be competent in critical moments, sometimes harming patients in the process, which luckily for the patients, Donnelly or Samuels always caught. He couldn't wait for her day of reckoning. But until then, he had to tolerate her like the wart she was.

He made himself busy washing out the leftover coffee sludge, prepping the coffee maker, and clearing his throat loudly.

Ava jerked awake, her pale, pasty face crinkled in disgust as she wiped the saliva off her lip. "Shit, I must have dozed off."

He noisily washed the cups in the sink while the water heated for the coffee maker. "Rough night?"

"Yeah," she muttered, getting to her feet and tugging at her dirty scrubs. "My roommate decided to host a party in our apartment last night without telling me. I maybe got an hour of sleep and grabbed the wrong scrubs."

"Sucks," he said, trying hard not to sound that indifferent. "Coffee?"

"Christ, no. I'd rather be stuck in the eye with a needle than drink that."

"Suit yourself." He placed a clean mug on the counter and poured the first bit of coffee, watching it splash thickly into his cup.

"How can you drink that?" Ava asked, cringing.

"Grew up on a horse ranch. I've endured far worse."

Ava quickly retied her hair into a fresh ponytail and headed for the door, which almost opened onto her face as Donnelly stepped in.

"Aw, Taschen, I was wondering where you were," Donnelly said smoothly, slipping his reading glasses off and sliding them onto the hem of his scrubs.

"Sorry, Dr. Donnelly. I—uh—" She glanced imploringly at Wyatt as though he'd save her. He merely leaned against the kitchen counter indifferently. She rolled her eyes. "Just needed a minute. Sorry."

"It's alright. Next time, just let me know if you need some extra rest, I'll be happy to send you home early… again." His tone was impeccably polite, making Wyatt laugh, which he unsuccessfully covered with a cough.

She flushed, gave them both a bland smile, and hurried out the door.

Donnelly pivoted on his heel, shooting Wyatt a knowing look. "That wasn't very nice."

"She's not very nice," Wyatt drawled. "Coffee?"

"Absolutely not. That stuff tastes like tar."

"You'd think a hospital this good would have a nicer coffee maker."

"I'll work on getting us a new one," Donnelly replied, and for a moment, they simply stared at one another. Donnelly scrubbed a hand at the back of his neck, looking adorably bashful.

Wyatt stared, thunderstruck. Was Dr. Donnelly nervous? Of him?!

Holy fucking shit.

Heart racing with excitement, Wyatt went to him. Donnelly shifted slightly, stiffening. He was taller, but Wyatt was slightly more muscular. He could smell the musky scent of Donnelly and nearly sighed. He liked his natural scent so much. It was stupid and nonsensical, but there was something oddly arousing about it. Sweet, spicy, male.

"How's the shoulder?" Wyatt asked quietly.

"Good. Could be better." He said it in his Dr. Donnelly tone, and Wyatt couldn't stop the smile.

"So, let's make it better then." He reached for him, and Donnelly sucked in a wavering breath.

Facing him, Wyatt began to work the tight muscles, feeling the knot bunch beneath the layers of clothes and skin. He worked his hands and fingers into the tense muscles, and within seconds, Donnelly relaxed, swaying toward him but not into him—not yet.

His head lowered, giving Wyatt easy access to the side of his neck. Access for his lips to take… to suck…

"Better?" Wyatt husked into the shell of Donnelly's ear.

He answered with that moaning sound again, which was weak, raspy, and so fuckin' hot he couldn't stand it.

Wyatt hummed, placing his free hand on the opposite side of Donnelly's neck, holding him in place as he dragged his knuckles up his neck. It was risky being this close. They both knew it, and yet whenever Wyatt touched him like this, Donnelly became compliant and subdued.

He wondered if he were to drop to his knees right now and take his cock into his mouth, if Donnelly would let him. The mere thought had his dick hardening.

"It's been two minutes," Donnelly murmured in a shaky breath.

Wyatt's fingers inched into his hair at the base of his neck, deliberating on leaning over and licking the taste off the side of his captain's throat. Instead, he released him, taking a giant step backward and returning to his coffee mug.

Donnelly's head snapped up, as though waking from a hazy dream, eyes clouded as he blinked rapidly.

"I..." Donnelly started and then stopped, confused. "I, uh—thank you."

He nodded, sipping the motor oil coffee. "You're welcome."

They stared for a long time before Donnelly nervously glanced away and headed for the door.

"Dr. Donnelly," Wyatt said, halting the doctor in his tracks, his hand on the doorknob.

The tension in Donnelly's shoulder was already beginning to form upon returning to the ED. Wyatt frowned, and in a reckless impulse he rarely ever experienced, except whenever he was around this man, said, "Give me another night."

Donnelly's eyes widened, and his lips parted, about to protest.

Wyatt continued quickly. "Give me as many nights as it takes to heal your shoulder. No strings. No attachment. Just... enough time to rub you down thoroughly. And then we'll stop."

"Lawson..."

"It doesn't have to mean anything. Just relief."

"And what do you get out of it?"

"The same thing."

This was true. Wyatt would finally get to have another night with Donnelly, and if he had to present it to him in terms of convenience with no strings attached, maybe the older man would feel more in control about crossing the line—again.

Donnelly scrubbed a hand over the back of his neck and then his jawline. "I don't think this is a good idea."

"Agreed. But sometimes the best ideas are the worst ones. Kinda like riding to the edge of the cliff just for the view."

"Or for a car commercial," Donnelly's smile was slow and genuine, filling up the forgotten space in Wyatt's soul.

"So?" Wyatt asked gruffly, trying hard to hide his need to keep doing this. He needed it far too much, and he knew this was dangerous, considering Donnelly was more interested in following the rules than breaking them. But with the way Donnelly was looking at him now, he didn't give a flying fuck.

"So..." Donnelly drawled, eyes slipping back to the door and hesitating.

"Think about it."

"I already have."

Surprised, Wyatt stood on the balls of his feet, waiting.

"Meet me at the Four Seasons. I'll text you the room number."

Excitement thrummed in his veins, heart skipping like he just won the biggest prize at the fair. "You don't have my number."

Donnelly put his slutty black rimmed glasses back on, letting them perch low on the bridge of his nose, his eyebrows high. "I have all your pertinent information on file, Lawson. I'll see you tonight at 9pm sharp. Don't be late."

CHAPTER 8

John

I'm late.

"Tanya," John glanced at his wristwatch, patience zapping to a hard zero. It was 8:45 pm. He was going to be late with Lawson.

He rubbed his temple, feeling the brewing of a headache. "I submitted the form this morning. Getting HR involved is merely going to make this situation bigger than it needs to be."

They had been going back and forth for the last hour. The shift had already gone into overtime after a city bus accident on the freeway, which had filled their ED with crash victims.

"John, I understand, but I need you to look at this from my viewpoint—" Tanya began.

"I've been trying for the past hour, and frankly…" he shook his head, exasperated. "I can't."

Tanya's dark brown eyes widened, and her back straightened indignantly. Tanya was his boss, the director of the entire hospital. John was forced to deal with her or Sean, her boss, on almost a daily basis these days. The bureaucracy of the hospital was beginning to bleed into his ED, and it was getting ridiculous. The politics of the business side of running a major city hospital was his concern to some extent, but right now, he didn't fucking care.

"You're wanting me to jump through extra hoops because you're afraid I might sue," John said sharply.

Tanya blanched.

"That's exactly it, isn't it? You're afraid I'm gonna sue on the grounds that after months—no, years—of complaints, I've personally taken to HR about my concerns, I might actually have a case now. Jesus Christ, Tanya, this could've been prevented had you listened to me—to us. Instead, more nurses are quitting because they know this hospital doesn't protect them. More violence is happening in the lobby because we're short-staffed, and not only violence, but deaths. Preventable deaths, because we can't keep functioning on a skeleton crew. And you're more concerned about fucking paperwork. That's your concern? We don't have enough beds, nurses, or security. The attack is not the issue here! It's about the systematic fucking failure of this hospital, and your leadership that borders on negligent indifference."

Slow, loud clapping erupted from behind him, and he realized he had laid into Tanya, in public at his workstation, for the whole night crew to hear. He glanced up and saw Dr. Walsh leaning forward on his elbows on the workstation only a few feet away, wearing his all-black scrubs and a long-sleeved shirt beneath, which made his pale skin look even whiter under the glow of the fluorescent light. The only color on his body was from his reddish-brown hair. And he was wearing his sunglasses still, sliding them off to look directly at John, and then back up to Tanya, an insolent smirk dangling from his lips.

"What he said," Dr. Walsh said, with a faint hint of his original Irish home.

Samuels cleared his throat, and John turned to see that he hadn't left his shift yet either, and had intentionally placed himself at the central station, eavesdropping on Tanya's conversation with him, while the rest of the day shift had gone home.

John suddenly felt very proud of his crew—especially the two men who led when he couldn't.

His gaze flickered over to Samuels, whose gruff face was handsomely sporting a now fully matured, ridiculously bushy mustache, and maybe because he was tired, or fed up with talking in circles and just wanted a hot shower and the firm press of Lawson's hands on his body, John began to laugh. It sounded hysterical, and he didn't care. Because clearly he had lost his damned mind, having impulsively agreed to another night with Lawson.

What the hell was I thinking?

This is so stupid.

Fuck.

More weak hysterical laughter bubbled out of him like an uncontrollable creature.

Samuels and Tanya watched him in mild alarm as tears formed in his eyes, holding a hand over his face, trying not to look at Samuels's ridiculous Tom Selleck mustache.

"Is this conversation amusing, Dr. Donnelly?" Tanya snapped.

"Yes—no," he said, smothering his laughter. "Shit, I'm sorry, Tanya, it's been a long day." He shook his head, eyebrows furrowed, yet an exhausted smile tightened his lips. "Can we pick this up tomorrow? Let me sleep on it, okay?"

Tanya looked like she was about to protest when Dr. Walsh interrupted.

"I'd listen to our cap," Walsh drawled darkly. "I wouldn't want to be on this man's bad side."

"He doesn't have a bad side," Samuels retorted irritably.

Walsh cocked his head to the side, his dark brown, nearly black eyes narrowed over John. "The nice ones always have the biggest snap, and it's mighty marvelous to behold. I've always prided myself on being able to tell when someone's a breath away from snapping."

Samuels snorted, "Only because you've got a screw loose."

Walsh seemed to consider this and gave a slight nod. "I think we all do. I just don't hide it behind a mustache or kindness." He glanced between the two men and winked, and strolled off to his night nurse, ready to take command.

Tanya's rigid stance softened, and she stood, gathering the infamous zipped binder she carried everywhere, its digital tablet filled with notes, constantly dinging with updates or emails.

"Yes, of course. I've held you over long enough. Have a good night," she said with a clipped tone, and promptly left. John wondered if it was what he had said—or what Walsh had said.

"Walsh is looking extra vampiric tonight," Samuels muttered, before casually side-eyeing John. "So, how's things?"

John sighed, still feeling the silly urge to laugh again. "Better now that that conversation has ended."

"Yeah, Tanya's been on a rampage lately. Better you than me."

He raced a hand through his hair. "I need to get outta here. So should you."

Samuels nodded and gave him a dismissive wave, "On it, captain, just finishing my notes."

He retrieved his backpack from his locker and slipped on his black zip-up hoodie.

Backpack slung over his good shoulder, John began to walk out the front just to say goodbye to Samuels. "By the way, nice stash, Selleck. It's getting bigger."

Samuels beamed proudly at him. "You grew the beard three months ago. This ED couldn't handle two bearded daddies."

John snorted a laugh, the giggles emerging once more, a sign that he was beyond tired. Maybe meeting with Lawson was a mistake tonight.

The right thing to do was to text him and cancel.

The right thing to do wasn't to have made plans in the first place.

The doors to the lobby opened to a packed house. He shook his head, more than ready to get the hell out of there. He waved to the security team before leaving, and was greeted by the brisk night air.

He inhaled in relief and exhaled slowly, taking a moment to appreciate the darkness, before he headed toward the employee parking lot. He made it to the gated entrance when he noted a motorcyclist, dressed in jeans, black cowboy boots, a worn brown leather jacket, and an all-black helmet. He hesitated, unable to take his eyes off those familiar-looking boots.

Upon John's appearance, the motorcyclist slipped off the helmet, and his heart stuttered to a halt.

"You're kidding me," John said incredulously to him, another burst of laughter coming from his chest.

Lawson ran a hand through his thick dirty blond hair, the waves breaking beneath his fingers. "What? You don't like it? It's my dad's old bike. He said if I could fix it, I could keep it."

"Horses, motorcycle, doctor…" John drawled, stepping up to him. "Is there anything you can't do?"

Lawson's pale blue eyes were oddly calm despite the heat reflected in them. "For a while there, you."

His smile froze on his face, and Lawson hummed in that sultry, low tone of his. "But my default state is persistence and patience. My Aunt Carol once told me that the best things in life are worth waiting for."

"Wise woman," John murmured. "Are you flirting with me, Lawson?"

"Yes," he said quickly, unabashedly. "Always, if I could."

He felt the ridiculous blush stain his cheeks. He sucked in a breath, "Sorry I'm late. I don't know if tonight's a good night. I'm tired..."

"I know," Lawson said gently. "That's why I'm here to pick you up."

"On that?"

Lawson reached for a spare black helmet and handed it to him.

"Not a chance, Lawson," he retorted. He had been teasing his sister when he said he was thinking about a motorcycle, because as an emergency doctor, he had seen the devastating toll they took on the human body. And he wasn't interested in actually losing a foot or leg tonight.

"I booked us a room," Lawson said, surprising him.

Heat instantly flooded his body. The hard, uncompromising glint in Lawson's expression suspended him. "I have every intention of taking care of you tonight, Donnelly. Starting right now. So, get on the damned bike and let's go. The sooner this starts, the sooner both of us feel good."

The heat turned into molten lava at his words. He took the helmet and slid it on. Lawson reached for him, strapping the lower chin strap on over his beard, his fingers quick and efficient.

"Have you ridden a bike before?" he asked.

"A bike? Yes. This? No," John replied through the helmet.

Lawson smirked. "Lean with me, keep your arms around my waist the whole time, and trust me."

Lawson pulled on his helmet, buckled it, and straddled the bike. His jeans pulled tight against his lean legs. John followed suit, positioning himself behind Lawson on the bike and feeling his body brush against his back and his legs push into his thighs. Lawson reached around and adjusted John on both sides, sliding him deeper into the seat. He was fully wrapped around Lawson now, but it didn't stop there. Lawson grabbed John's hand and guided it around his waist, followed by the other. A flash of the other day popped into his brain of how he had wrapped his arms around Lawson's waist, dragging him closer. Very similar to this.

The motorcycle's engine roared to life and started forward. John's arms tightened around him instinctively, and Lawson navigated them onto the busy LA streets. The streetlights illuminated the dark roads. The vibrations of the bike between his legs and its power were incredible. He was lost in the experience, and so absorbed by the ride that he hadn't noticed Lawson's hand move over his until he squeezed and moved it toward the inside of his thigh. He suddenly couldn't breathe, feeling only the way Lawson's leg muscle strained while he drove them through the backroads to the hotel.

John, deciding to take a page out of Lawson's book, slid his hand further upward and intimately brushed his fingers over him, feeling the young man's back shudder and cock press hard against the thick denim.

Lawson let him touch him for the next few minutes, his body straining under his touch the longer it went on. John braced his other hand against his chest, feeling the firm muscles there as his own cock filled with blood and throbbed. By the time they reached the hotel, his heart was racing like a jackhammer as Lawson pulled into the dark parking structure and into the designated motorcycle spot. It was the same hotel from their first night together, which pleased John for some reason.

Lawson turned off the bike, yanked off his helmet, and jumped off, reaching for the strap at John's chin before yanking his helmet off, too. Before he could react, Lawson's lips descended on him, hard and heady, fast and rough. He hadn't expected the onslaught, but maybe he should've. After all, he had been teasing him for almost ten minutes of the ride.

Lawson pulled angrily back from the kiss, cursing and adjusting his jeans to accommodate the bulge. John let out another tired laugh, which caught Lawson's attention, his eyes flashing at him.

"Sorry," he said, sliding off the bike. "I—uh—laugh when I'm tired."

Lawson tilted his head and unexpectedly smiled. "That's fucking adorable. I'm a cranky old bitch when I get that tired. Now, c'mon."

Laughter spilled out of him again, and he followed Lawson through the parking lot and into the side entrance of the hotel. He was suddenly grateful Lawson had already booked the room. The thought of interacting with any more people tonight sounded exhausting.

They walked through the lobby and to the elevators. It was blissfully empty. The low-key vibe, mixed with minimalist aesthetics and expensive décor, had appealed to him when he first came here. The elevator doors slid open, and they stepped inside. He carefully positioned himself on the opposite side, creating space. Lawson noticed but didn't comment.

"We should talk first," John said, clearing his throat of the sudden rush of nerves. He wasn't sure why Lawson evoked this reaction from him.

"About?" Lawson asked.

"We need to establish some ground rules."

Lawson watched the digital numbers tick upward. "Is this how you normally do this?"

The elevator pinged onto their floor, the doors sliding open. "Do what?"

Lawson pulled the room key card out of his front pocket and glanced at the number. Once they found their room, Lawson flipped on a lamp as John let the door shut firmly behind him.

"With the others," Lawson finally said, setting the motorcycle helmets down on the table at the far end of the room.

He scrubbed a hand over the back of his neck, confused.

The others?

Lawson had assumed that he did this often. Just not with his own residents.

"I've actually never done this," John admitted, too tired to care about perception.

Lawson's head jerked toward him, "I thought..."

"Look, it's complicated enough doing this again with you. I think by setting some ground rules we can know what to expect..." He hesitated. "I love my job and my hospital, even if it pisses me off like it did tonight." He sighed, "I'm not risking that for a hook-up."

Lawson nodded thoughtfully, sliding off his leather jacket and then working on his boots. John swallowed hard, watching the display of raw masculinity as Lawson began to strip before him.

John set his backpack down, "I need to shower and..."

Lawson smirked, "Yeah, I figured I'd join you."

Oh. Fuck.

His heart skipped as Lawson walked forward, tossing his jacket and shirt onto the chair and unbuckling his jeans. "It'll be easier in the shower to massage your shoulder. And then when we're done, you can go over your rules."

The flutter of nerves slipped low in his belly. "I, uh... might not last long," John admitted.

"Have you...?" Lawson asked slowly.

"Been with anyone else since you?" John asked, knowingly.

"Yeah."

"No," he replied, not sure why that made him feel nervous again.

Lawson's eyes darkened, and he reached for the zipper on John's sweater, slowly pulling it down off his shoulders and arms. He wasn't used to someone undressing him or wanting to take care of him, yet Lawson insisted, even moving John's hands away to pull his shirt off and toss it into the pile of clothes at the foot of the bed. He was a shivering mess by the time Lawson was done.

His pale eyes assessed the dark purple bruise on his chest, frowning. "Does it hurt?"

"Not so much," he admitted. "Maybe just don't jump on it."

Lawson smiled, "You're funny when you're tired."

He fucking shivered again and sighed.

Lawson led him into the fancy bathroom in their room. It had a large, luxurious shower with granite marble tiles, a black showerhead, and see-through glass doors. It was more than spacious enough for both men. He was looking forward to the shower, but especially now with Lawson.

He watched as the young man slipped out of his jeans and boxers, gloriously naked under the soft glow of the bathroom light.

Last time, John didn't get to appreciate his body as much as he would've liked. Now, he took his fill, gaze sweeping over the rippling muscles of his chest and abdomen. Lawson clearly worked out, and his body was proof of his discipline. He was stunning, especially the sharp lines that descended to the apex of his sex. His skin was pale but not overly so, as though it still managed to cling to the summer rays it had gotten months ago.

Lawson was beautiful, with riveting blue eyes that were far too perceptive at times. His lips were pouty, soft, and perfect. John felt self-conscious about his body by comparison. And seeing Lawson in all his virile athletic glory was really inspiring him to get his tired ass back into the gym.

Lawson was catnip to everyone who fell under his spell at work with his easy charm, polite manners, and boyishly handsome good looks. But he wasn't a hot head ego-manic like some of the other residents he'd had been forced to endure over the years. Lawson was humble, kind, and comfortable enough to ask for help.

So, why the hell is he interested in me?

"Have you?" John asked, tongue sticking to the roof of his mouth.

"Have I been with anyone else since you?" Lawson reached for him again, bringing John's hands to his flat stomach, feeling the hot skin beneath his fingers as Lawson proceeded to untie John's scrubs from around his waist.

"You know what, never mind," John muttered in a rush. "I don't want to know."

"I haven't," Lawson replied gently. "Just you."

Just you.

Goosebumps erupted over his arms, and an odd tingling washed over his chest, but he ignored his body's reactions, letting his hands explore what his eyes already had, traveling upward over Lawson's chest. "Why not? You know every nurse and some doctors have the hots for you."

Lawson seemed uninterested in this conversation and leaned in to kiss John's neck, releasing a sigh as he did so, as though he had been holding himself back this entire time from doing it. "So...?"

"So..." He felt Lawson's lips begin to suck the sensitive place beneath his ear. "You can have anyone. Be with anyone."

Lawson pulled back from his slow, hungry kiss at his neck. "Are you saying you'd prefer me sucking on Dr. Samuels's neck?"

He released a strangled laugh, refusing to imagine that as he shook his head, "No."

Fuck, he wasn't prepared for Lawson.

He wasn't prepared for any of this.

Something felt different with him than from last time. Everything about Lawson was different for him, and he wasn't sure he could handle it.

He could barely handle his own emotions lately. He thought about how easy it had been for him to have a complete breakdown at the drop of a hat, or to stand numbly in the shower at home for over an hour, dissociating, before dragging himself to bed and passing out. He had stopped drinking, thinking that would help. But it didn't. His emotions were on high alert, crippling him in unexpected moments, and he didn't understand why.

Well, he did.

He just didn't want to admit he was burnt out. Or maybe it was depression. Probably both. Whatever it was, he was fucking angry and stressed, and that cycle spun him out daily.

So to have Lawson, this incredible man with magical hands, slowly getting to his knees, helping him out of his pants and boxers, fingers skimming over the back of John's legs and over his ass, face nuzzling his cock before…

"Fuck…" he groaned.

Lawson's hot wet mouth enveloped him, sucking him down lazily, dragging his mouth over him and grazing his head with his teeth. He didn't have to ask, Lawson just gave. He wanted to give, and that was utterly foreign to John.

John gave everything to everyone all the time.

And some days, it was never enough. And those days were the hardest of all.

Lawson was so damned good at giving effortlessly.

His mouth…

Oh. Fuck.

"Lawson," John exhaled a long breath, already panting, feeling the swirl of emotion battling for release in his chest. "You're… oh fuck… you're so good…"

The intensity of Lawson's gaze and the sudden wave of unexpected emotion slammed into him.

No, not now!

He reached blindly over to the shower knob and turned it on. He lifted Lawson upward, dragging them into the shower together, the water slicking and heating their bodies. Lawson's piercing gaze surveyed him, as though looking for something. John intentionally ignored the concern reflected there and kissed him, hard. Lawson hesitated a mere second before giving in, and they greedily took what they both wanted from each other. John moved his hands over his jawline and neck, tracing the layered slopes of his defined back, loving the way their bodies seemed to fit together.

Lawson pushed his tongue inside John's mouth, caging him against the wall of the shower. Their tongues clashed and battled. His cock hardened painfully between his legs at the torrid, wild kissing. Lawson tasted like whiskey, smoke, and apple. He wanted to taste more. So much more.

John began to move to his knees when Lawson shook his head, pinning him to the wall. He shot him a questioning look, and Lawson licked over his lower lip, sucking it in. "If you get down on your knees and I see my cock in your mouth…" Lawson groaned, pushing his demanding cock into John's stomach, "I will come in two seconds."

John let out a whooshing breath and nodded, unable to form words.

"I need to touch you," Lawson said, reaching for the hotel shampoo and massaging it into John's chest, careful of the bruise as he worked his way up to his shoulders.

His body responded the way it did every time Lawson touched him—subdued and compliant, surrendering one muscle at a time. Lawson hummed low from the back of his throat, looking incredibly pleased, even smiling. "I love watching you do that."

John's eyes blinked open, head tilted back against the shower, letting Lawson go to work on him. "Do what?"

"Give me everything you can't. But you fight it."

John was surprised, and yet he knew he shouldn't be.

Lawson, from day one, saw things about others—understood patients without words.

"How do you do that?" John heard himself ask.

Lawson seemed to understand the question and stroked his fingers up and down his neck, moving over the sensitive tendons. "I spent my whole life around horses. Creatures that only communicated through nonverbal cues. People are very similar. We say more with our faces and our bodies than we sometimes do with our words. Especially you."

He swallowed, and Lawson watched his throat bob and felt his shoulders tense.

"Want me to tell you what I see when I look at you?" Lawson asked.

"Fuck, probably not."

Lawson smirked, "You've been a bit of a challenge, Dr. Donnelly." He rubbed and soothed the frozen shoulder as he spoke. "I know you want me. I saw it that night, but you denied me. I watch your shoulders tense whenever you walk into the ED, but you never seem to take a day off. I know you're tired and… raw, like an open wound."

He clenched his jaw, refusing to show how close Lawson was to the truth.

"And you do that when you're fighting with yourself," Lawson commented, eyeing his jawline. "You have something to say, but you're holding back—why? What are you afraid of?"

The nerve Lawson had been dancing around finally struck, and the steel wall inside John came down with a swift bang. He grabbed his wrist, squeezing him. "First rule, none of this."

"What?"

"We're here for one thing, let's keep it that way. Keep it simple. I don't wanna talk…"

Lawson's eyebrows shot upward, the hot spray of the shower wetting and darkening his dirty blond hair. "I don't know if I like that rule."

"Then this stops now."

Lawson reached for the hand gripping his wrist, eyes locked with his. "I don't think I can."

"Lawson," John attempted, but the young man continued to rub, pressing him against the wall, the shower slickening them. "I need..."

"Control?" he offered flippantly, flicking his wrist downward and off him, arching his hips into him, making John feel everything. Lawson's hard, smooth body and thick, wonderful cock spearing into him. He nearly whimpered.

God, I'm pathetic.

I can't say no.

I'm weak for how good this feels.

For his touch…

"Order," John croaked, attempting in vain to control this situation.

"Same thing," Lawson retorted.

"It's not," he snapped, and sighed, scrubbing a hand over his wet beard. "I'm not ruining my reputation for a fling, Lawson. So, if you can't respect what I'm asking for—"

Lawson's fingers were rubbing so deeply that he winced, and his chin jerked out, sucking a hard breath.

"I'll respect your damn rules, Donnelly," Lawson's grip eased over the sensitive tendon. "But on two conditions."

Relief clutched in his chest, watching the water trickle over Lawson's freshly shaved cheeks, down his tanned neck. All he wanted to do was forget this conversation and trace the water running down the cowboy's body with his tongue. The pulse between his legs flared and he licked his lips, fighting himself, demanding discipline and patience. Something he was normally good at, but right now, with Lawson's cock sliding against his, he was slowly losing control.

And a part of him wanted to. To surrender to the tension between them and be absolutely fucking reckless. To explode in passion and desire.

"I want more than tonight," Lawson whispered, the shower steam rising between them, surrounding them in a hazy wall of heat. "And no one else fucks you but me."

John stared, stunned by the avalanche of his words crashing over him.

Fuck.

The possessiveness in his tone unhinged something primal inside him. Almost animalistic. Except that more nights like this were dangerous. He couldn't afford to get close to someone else. It took too much from him. It hurt too much when they left. Because everyone who ever mattered to him left in the end. He watched countless souls over the course of his career say goodbye too soon. And he already said goodbye to his best friend, his brother, and now his father…

He wasn't interested in experiencing more pain.

Besides, Lawson was young, practically screaming with sexual prowess and virility. He'd have his fun and fill with him and be done in a few weeks, maybe a month. And John would be left with nothing, right back where he started, and maybe even worse off.

He felt the door open in his soul once more, the empty void.

He shivered despite the heat from the shower and the feel of Lawson against him.

"Can you give me that?" Lawson asked quietly, his fingers reaching for his jawline, tracing through his beard, watching him consider his answer.

"I'll think about it," he said, closing the door mentally, returning to this moment.

"You asked me to follow your rules, Donnelly. I need your answer by tonight."

"I can't give you that."

Lawson searched his face, frowning, and pushed John's shoulder back down, not realizing it had stiffened and inched upward again.

"I wanna try something with you," Lawson murmured, intently eying his shoulder.

"Is it going to hurt?"

"In a way, yeah. But you'll feel better afterward."

He hesitated, and Lawson kissed him, "Trust me."

Heart racing, he nodded. "Don't make me regret this."

"You won't. Turn around."

He did, feeling the heat of the water slide down his backside, followed by Lawson's hands palming him. "Damn, I love your ass. Your scrubs don't do you justice."

John chuckled out a moan, letting Lawson massage his cheeks, fingers slipping into the crevice, making him stiffen. "There are condoms in my bag..."

"I'm clean, I tested last week. You?" Lawson asked, his magical fucking fingers grazing over his hole, causing John to buck backward, breathing hard into the wet tile.

"Yeah, I'm clean. Tested a few weeks ago."

Lawson let out a grunt and kissed his shoulder, "Can I fuck you raw? Or do you want me to wrap it?"

He moaned at the idea of feeling Lawson—all of him inside him—and filling him with his hot cum. Why did that idea turn him on so much?

Fuck. Fuck. I am so fucked.

"Jesus," John muttered. "Yeah, we can..." He couldn't even say the word; it felt too intimate somehow, but it was just sex.

Just sex.

Right, keep telling yourself that, old man.

Lawson let out a breathy moan and continued to graze over John's hole, a little more urgently now, his hand reaching out to get more soap, working his shoulder again. This time, it was painfully deep. He let out a surprised gasp and tried to relax, but it was hard to do.

Lawson's fingers began to edge inside around the tight rim. He bit his lower lip, eyes shutting, feeling the sensations all over his body. Lawson widened John's stance, angling his hips out to accommodate his own aching dick as it throbbed between his legs, desperate for Lawson's touch. But he was busy painfully working his shoulder, tirelessly pushing on the same spot, digging deeper and harder. John's jaw clenched and he fisted his cock, already leaking as Lawson fingered around his hole, which he finally withdrew, replaced by the tip of his cock.

Lawson released the grip on his shoulder and spat into his hand, lubing his dick, and once more returned to John's entrance, slicker now. He was barely breathing, waiting in anticipation for the feel of Lawson inside him again. The young man pushed slowly forward through the tight rim, and John sighed, his body sucking him in and then…

Lawson's voice changed, becoming that deep timber, low and so unbelievably sexy. "Take a deep breath…"

Fuuuck.

Where did this man come from?

Lawson speared forward, slamming into him. John let out a cry of pain and pleasure, knees trembling. This was only his second time doing this, and he was still getting used to the sensation of being fucked.

Lawson's hand returned aggressively to his shoulder, digging once more at his muscle. With the other hand, he pushed John's hips out, reaching around and tugging firmly on his dick. His calloused hand went to work on his cock, and John felt his body sway against him, relaxing once more, despite the tingling already starting in his balls.

"That's it," Lawson murmured against the shell of his ear, surrounding him, engulfing him. "You feel so goddamned good."

Lawson released his shoulder, positioning his hands on his hips, and he began to move, thrusting in and out, a tight groan echoing from his chest, sending bolts of lightning through John's bloodstream, forcing him to brace himself with a hand against the wet shower tile.

The sensations were too much and too slow. Lawson was taking his time, driving John insane as he felt every inch of his delicious hard cock slide in and out, hitting that sweet spot every damn time.

"Christ," Lawson cursed breathlessly. "I wanna fuck you like this forever..."

The sound that came out of John was unexpected and humiliating—he whimpered. Shame flooded him, followed quickly by a blush that he was grateful Lawson couldn't see. He rolled his head down, letting the water cascade over the back of his neck and over his jaw, his body moving in tandem with Lawon's slow, methodical pace. The tightening in his lower belly began to unravel, his body relaxing with each thrust, the tension moving solely to his aching cock and balls now.

John groaned, feeling the release of his shoulder for the first time in months. That's when he felt Lawson slip out of him, and suddenly, he impaled him so hard John wasn't ready for it. His back arched from the impact. His hand slipped up the shower wall, bracing himself. Lawson then did it again, pounding into him, sending a shockwave of tremors through every limb of John's body.

"Fuuuck," Lawson gasped, hands fastened to his hips. "Yes... that's it..."

He steadily fucked him like that—out fast, in hard. Over and over. John placed both hands on the wall, stars blinking across his eyelids as Lawson fucked him at a blindingly brutal pace. So much so that he knew he would be sore tomorrow. And that thought made his dick leak. He wanted to hurt. Wanted to feel Lawson's branding touch all over his body—deep inside him—marking him.

He wanted it all.

Lawson cursed again, feeling John continuing to give himself over and take the furious fucking. Lawson's movements were becoming wilder and jerkier. He was close. And so was John. He reached for his own dick, stroking himself and tensing again.

"No," Lawson gruffed out and reached for his shoulder. With both hands, he dug into the muscles so hard that John nearly yelled.

The intense touch stopped at his shoulder and was immediately replaced by Lawson's hand over his cock, stroking him vigorously, forcefully.

Pain and pleasure. The combination was almost too much. Too overwhelming. Breaking through his body, his tendons, his muscles—pushing past reason and sanity. Breaking him open wide and without warning. Lawson relentlessly did it again, impossibly breaking him further down, until he was an open wound, bleeding out on the gurney, unable to stop the free flow of emotion and pleasure dumping out of him.

"*Fuck-fuck-fuck…!*" John gasped.

He was about to burst, his balls tingled painfully, and his tip was leaking all over Lawson's fist.

All the tension, all the stress over the last few months—maybe longer—burst from his body, and Lawson grabbed him once more, fisting hard over his cock and forcing him to climax painfully into his hand. He let out a sobbing cry, his body shaking, his climax spewing violently out of his dick, coating the shower wall and Lawson's hand.

It went on and on.

Hot, thick cum pulsed out of his dick like an explosion. He felt Lawson thrust again inside him, filling him to the brim, and his cock spasmed in another wave.

It's too much.

It's all too much.

I can't!

Tears burned at the corners of his eyes, and his whole body surrendered.

Lawson must have felt it and let out a groan of praise that John couldn't understand; he was pure sensation.

Lawson barreled into him only a few more times, his magnificent thick cock spearing into his tight hole, before unloading deep into his ass. John was too weak to appreciate the feeling of Lawson's climax, and wobbled on his feet. With Lawson's dick still fully seated inside him, he grabbed his shoulder once more and, using his knuckles, jammed into the frozen muscle.

John collapsed into the tile. Lawson held onto him, digging ruthlessly.

Tears streamed down John's face, and a gasping sound escaped from his chest like a dying animal. He'd never heard himself make that sound—well, actually, he had. Only once before, when he was a teen and his mother had told him that his brother had committed suicide. He broke that day and had rebuilt himself into the trophy kid, pleasing everyone around him, taking care of everyone else's needs so that they never had to feel what he felt.

Everything he'd been holding together the past year finally broke open, and John fell headlong over the cliff into sweet oblivion.

Chapter 9

Wyatt

Wyatt stared at Donnelly, who seemed to be in a coma, and wondered if he should wake him.

No, let him sleep. He needs it after what I fucking did to him.

He raked his fingers through his hair, knowing he had pushed Donnelly too hard, and felt like an asshole for it. He had warned him it would hurt. But he hadn't expected what happened after they orgasmed.

Donnelly had slid away from him, falling to his knees and crying. It was the most painful sound Lawson had ever heard, and all he wanted to do was hold him. Instead, he turned off the shower, bundled Donnelly into a thick white hotel towel, and led him to bed. He hiccupped and sobbed, sitting on the edge of the bed, shaking his head as though he didn't want Wyatt to witness him being emotional.

Donnelly confirmed it by saying, "Don't. Don't stay for this. Go home."

"Not a fucking chance," Wyatt retorted, quickly toweling off and climbing into the bed behind Donnelly. He wrapped his arms around him, dragging him into the wall of his chest and holding him, letting him cry.

Guilt ripped at his insides. He didn't mean to push Donnelly this far. He fucked up.

"I'm sorry," Wyatt whispered, burying his face against the back of his neck, closing his eyes at the pain that seemed to tear through Donnelly as he cried into his own arm, shielding Wyatt from himself, from his emotions.

Wyatt let him, not wanting Donnelly to feel any more exposed than he already must have felt. They didn't really know each other. And he didn't want Donnelly to feel ashamed of his feelings.

"It's not your fault," Donnelly wheezed, chest heaving for air as he cried, shoulders shaking. "Fuck. I'm sorry."

"No. Don't apologize."

He held him for a long time, heart breaking in his chest, and not understanding why. Donnelly was his captain, and they had great fucking sex, but seeing him in pain, seeing him struggle with his emotion, unlocked something in Wyatt that he didn't understand. All he knew was that it hurt, and he wanted to make it better somehow.

He wanted to soothe him, hold him, kiss every inch of his body until whatever it was he was crying about was forgotten.

Donnelly eventually stopped crying and to his surprise, fell quiet—too quiet.

Wyatt waited, his fingers swirling in Donnelly's thick chest hair, incapable of letting go. Luckily, Donnelly was still okay with him touching him.

"I haven't cried like that since…" Donnelly stopped short, his voice gravelly from emotion. "Jesus," he sighed, rubbing a hand over his face. "I feel ridiculous."

"Don't," Wyatt whispered. "Don't be."

"I—I don't know what to say."

"You don't have to say anything."

Donnelly reached for Wyatt's hand that was still wrapped around his waist, his fingers threading with his. It felt intimate. It felt good. So fucking good that it hurt a little. Wyatt swallowed.

"It's been a hard year," Donnelly admitted. "Possibly the hardest year I've had as a doctor. The politics, the trauma, the loss... all of it just hit so much harder for some reason."

Wyatt understood, thinking about the highs and lows of ranch work, knowing how some seasons felt more painful than others. And he was young in his career as a doctor compared to Donnelly. He didn't have the same responsibilities as him, nor did he really understand the weight he carried.

"I did all the wrong things to try to cope. I drank more, slept less, worked more..." Donnelly continued softly. "None of it helped. So, I just kept working, kept moving—thinking it would pass. That one day I'd wake up and feel better." He wiped more tears from his cheeks, scrubbing a hand over his beard. "Fuck, I've been so lost. I hadn't realized it until..."

He abruptly pulled away, dropping his face into his hands. "Christ, this is embarrassing."

Wyatt wanted to reach out to him, wanted to soothe the ache deep in Donnelly's soul.

"This job catches up to you," Donnelly murmured. "It can break you if you let it. For a while there, I never thought it would. But it did. Then this stupid frozen shoulder happened..." He snorted a bitter laugh. "Oh, and let's not forget I crossed a very real line and had sex with one of my residents."

Wyatt flinched but said nothing. The power dynamics alone were questionable—Donnelly, the attending senior resident, and Wyatt, the fourth-year resident on the cusp of becoming a fully licensed doctor.

On the most basic level, it was teacher fucking his student—well, Wyatt corrected, student fucking his teacher.

"I'm sorry, I should go." Donnelly got to his feet suddenly, towel still around his waist as he reached for his clothes.

Wyatt climbed out of bed naked and touched the spot where Donnelly carried all his pain, all his stress, and pushed it.

Donnelly buckled and cursed. "What the fuck?!"

"You're not leaving like this," he declared firmly. "Get back in bed, let me make this better."

"You already did enough," he snapped, but it held little venom.

"I didn't."

Wyatt dropped to his knees and yanked Donnelly's towel away, deciding to use his body rather than words to convey how much he needed to take care of him. To fix what he had done to him. Anything but to see him leave in such a state of emotional turmoil.

"Wait..!"

He didn't listen to the older man's weak protest and simply took Donnelly's dick into his mouth, determinedly sucking it back to life. Donnelly let out a whimpering groan, stumbling into him. Wyatt held him upright and devoured his cock, sucking him furiously and bobbing over him, taking him deep into his throat.

"Fuck, Lawson," Donnelly whimpered.

His gasping moans were a symphony to his ears as he greedily consumed him, pushing past his own gag reflex to take his thickening erection into his throat, burying his nose into the hair of his pelvis, throat muscles contracting around his cock, inhaling his musky scent and fucking loving it.

He loved his smell. His taste. His moans. It was alluring and intoxicating. Addictive.

"Shit..." Donnelly's hands were in his hair, raking his scalp, slowly rocking his hips, his cock sliding in and out between his lips. Wyatt's dick grew painfully hard, letting Donnelly use his mouth like this. His personal, free-use cowboy. Here to suck his cock and clear his mind of thought. And holy hell, was that thought tantalizing.

Shaking with need, Wyatt reached for Donnelly's perfect globe ass cheeks, palming and squeezing appreciatively before pushing him deeper into his mouth.

Donnelly sucked in a breath, hips jerking against him. "Oh... fuck... I'm going to..."

Dear Christ, the groaning sounds of his pleasure were too much. Wyatt doubled down on his efforts, stroking, tonguing, and sucking so hard he stopped breathing. He felt the stiffening tension of the thick, veined cock in his mouth, pushing him deeper down his throat and needing him to come.

And Donnelly did, trembling and moaning and chanting his name like the sexiest, most dire and sinful prayer ever spoken aloud.

Donnelly's cock spurted against his tongue, stretching further down his throat, and Wyatt swallowed several times to take it all, greedily milking every drop from his captain. Donnelly's climax tasted salty and male, and fuck, he wanted more. So much more. Adrenaline, coated in gasoline, coursed through his entire body.

Wyatt loved sucking cock. It was kind of his thing. So, the fact that he enjoyed the taste of Donnelly and the sensation of his thick cock filling his mouth elated him. Because that meant he enjoyed this as much as Donnelly clearly did. And he planned on sucking this man's cock any chance he could fucking get because hearing him unravel, unglue, unhinge was the most exhilarating part of it all.

Donnelly stared dazedly down at him, panting. Wyatt got to his feet, touching his body along the way, unable to stop. And Donnelly, in his drunken orgasmic haze, wasn't resisting him. Wyatt kissed him roughly before pushing him back into the bed, licking the tips of his fingers with his saliva and Donnelly's cum, and reaching between his own legs, stroking his throbbing sex.

Donnelly let out a strangled breath, gaze traveling over the tight contours of Wyatt's body, moving from his face to his lips, down his chest, and finally to his throbbing cock, fisted in his palm. His pulse skipped, the gasoline lit by the glint in Donnelly's gaze, as though he were a marvel. A god. A king.

Goddamn this man.

Wyatt's cock shuddered in his hand, and he stood over Donnelly's naked, spent body.

"Can I cum on you?" Wyatt asked, his cock demanding release and knowing that Donnelly would not be able to take another rough pounding after everything that he just endured less than twenty minutes ago, as well as the emotional crash out that followed.

Wyatt couldn't do that to him.

He wouldn't.

So, he'd settle for making a delicious mess all over this man's large, brawny body that was covered in hair and taut meat.

Donnelly nodded, and Wyatt fisted his hand over his cock, dragging down smeared precum over his shaft to the base, stroking into a hard line and repeating it. It wasn't as good as the sensation of breaching Donnelly's tight ass as he had done earlier, but it was still incredibly sexy getting to do this under his salacious, heady gaze.

"You like what you see?" Wyatt drawled darkly.

Donnelly let out a needy sigh, "Yes. You're beautiful, Lawson."

He shuddered, feeling the tingling around his balls as they tightened against him, ready to unleash. It felt so damned good. This was all too good, and it was terrifying.

Donnelly didn't want more than just sex.

But Wyatt did. He wanted everything. He wanted all.

He slowed his pace as much as he could, despite the tightness in his belly, demanding release. "I want more than tonight."

Donnelly's eyes shot to his and held.

"I need to feel that tight ass of yours again," Wyatt murmured. "I wanna gag on that cock of yours until you come down my throat again. I want more. I fucking need more."

Donnelly cursed, breathing hard, jaw clenching.

"Say yes," Wyatt commanded, stroking himself out, barely hanging on to his sanity, needing Donnelly to stop denying the sparks that were ricocheting off them.

Donnelly's tongue slipped out of his parted lips. Panting, he gave a slight jerk of his head, indicating yes.

Thank fuck!

Wyatt growled in triumph, practically jumping on top of him, pinning him to the bed and furiously fucking his fist. Donnelly gasped, mouth open and… waiting.

Oh-fucking-yes.

He maneuvered his hips upward, and the orgasm slammed into his back and out his dick like a fucking rocket, spewing messily all over Donnelly's lips, beard, and neck. The sight of his captain's face covered in cum only unhinged him more as he chased the second wave of his climax, demanding more from his body and smearing his pulsating red tip over those slutty fucking lips.

"Fuck," Wyatt breathed as he watched Donnelly suck in the tip of his messy cock, licking him clean.

His entire body trembled and he could barely hold himself above him. He felt a sweat break out on his brow as he watched Donnelly's tongue slowly, lazily lick his sex like the tastiest lollipop imaginable.

"Fuucck..." he said again, this time dragging the underside of his cock over Donnelly's bearded chin, intentionally making more of a mess for his captain to lick up. Which he did, all the way down to his balls.

Both of them were breathing hard, staring at one another, and Wyatt wanted to capture this moment—to remember every line of Donnelly's face and the way he looked, soaked in his cum. It was the sexiest fucking thing he'd ever seen.

Wyatt dropped down and kissed him thoroughly. Tonguing his bliss into Donnelly's wet lips and feeling their tongues clash. He clasped his hand over his sticky beard, digging in the moisture, wanting to somehow mark him—claim him like a fucking dog.

Donnelly moaned into his mouth, and after several long, glorious minutes of kissing, he finally broke away. Donnelly's lips were red and bruised from his rough kisses, and he smiled down at him.

"So... what are you doin' tomorrow?" Wyatt drawled huskily.

Donnelly blushed. He fucking *blushed.* It was adorable.

He was tempted to kiss him again but resisted, waiting for his answer.

Donnelly paused, searching his face, "You're serious?"

"Absolutely."

"I just—" Donnelly stopped short, looking self-conscious.

"What?"

"I just had an existential breakdown in front of you, and you want to see me again?"

Wyatt smirked, leaned down to his neck, licking the cum off with the slow trace of his tongue. "Fuck yes."

Donnelly sighed, and after a long minute finally pushed him away, slipping off the bed looking thoroughly ruined as he stumbled to the bathroom to clean up. When he returned, dark bags hung beneath his eyes and Wyatt knew that there was no way they could continue this conversation in the exhausted state he was in.

"I need sleep," Donnelly gruffed out before climbing into bed and practically collapsing.

Wyatt went to rinse off in the bathroom next, and when he came back, Donnelly was asleep. He hesitated, wondering if he should leave, but he didn't want to. Not yet. He climbed back into bed beside Donnelly and within minutes, fell asleep too.

The early morning sunlight streamed through the curtain windows, illuminating the handsome contours of Donnelly's face. Wyatt, now fully dressed and sitting in the chair by the window sipping on hotel coffee, couldn't take his eyes off him. His dark brown beard matched the thick hair on his chest, which Wyatt was mildly obsessed with, wanting to rub his face in it like a cat. But he didn't want to wake him.

The smattering of rich chest hair traveled down his stomach and over his navel to the epitome of his masculinity, which was an impressive fucking dick in his opinion. He wondered if he'd ever get a chance to ride it, because Wyatt enjoyed it both ways—top and bottom.

He liked Donnelly's body, liked even more how perfectly they seemed to fit together. He swallowed, imagining all the ways he'd like to taste, take, and ride this man… because last night wasn't nearly enough, and a part of him feared it would never be enough. That he would always want more from this vulnerable, strong man.

But he could sense that Donnelly was guarded. Last night proved it. He refused to show his emotions, even when he was sobbing. Some men were like this, he understood that. And yet, he hadn't expected Donnelly to be ashamed of his sensitivity. It was what made him such a good doctor.

"I never did ask you…" Donnelly's groggy voice said, cutting through his thoughts. "Do you prefer Lawson or your first name?"

Wyatt's eyes shot to his, and he saw that Donnelly's dark blue eyes were focused on him, the tangle of white bedding hiding half his face. Donnelly had complimented him last night, but the truth was, he thought Donnelly was the sexier one.

"Honestly, I don't mind it," he admitted. "Friends call me Wyatt—you can call me Lawson."

Donnelly perched his head on his hand, lying on his side, "Lawson it is, then."

"What about you, Dr. Donnelly?" Lawson said in a light tone, sipping his coffee.

"John," he answered. "Donnelly reminds me of work. My parents and sister call me Johnny—you can call me John."

Wyatt's throat bunched for some reason, and he cleared it. "John it is, then."

The sound of his name said out loud in the space between them felt even more intimate than taking his glorious cock down his throat.

Fuck, everything felt good with John.

John.

"Did you make me any?" John asked, tilting his chin to the coffee mug.

"I did. Don't know how you take it, though. How do you like it?"

"Dark and black like my soul."

"You're certainly not that." He stood and handed him the paper cup of coffee in bed.

John pulled himself upright and took it, eyeing him self-consciously. "I'm sorry again for…"

Wyatt shook his head, deciding to play it off, knowing that it would be safer for John than admitting the truth. "Don't. I did that to you. I sliced open that wound, and I should've known better. I knew you were in pain with your shoulder, I just hadn't realized how much."

John nodded, keeping his gaze averted, which bothered him. He reached down and clasped his fingers under his chin, fingering the beard as he tilted him upward, needing to see his eyes. "You have nothing to be ashamed about."

John blinked, shifting uncomfortably, and Wyatt let go, deciding not to push it. He returned to his chair across from him, propping his feet up on the edge of the bed. "We were supposed to have that talk about your rules."

"Right. I forgot. I thought about them last night before everything went to hell at work," he scrubbed the back of his neck, and Wyatt couldn't help but imagine a stethoscope there, loving the way his big hands would constantly be touching his neck, beard, or face...

Wyatt felt the lightbulb go off in his head and leaned forward in realization. Dr. John Donnelly kept a hell of a lot to himself, and whenever he struggled to suppress it, he rubbed his neck, fingered his beard, or scrubbed a hand over his face.

That was his tell. It was right there all along, and Wyatt never saw it.

Fuck, I'm finally figuring him out.

It's a start.

A start to what, he had no fucking clue. But he liked that he was slowly peeling back the layers to this man who clearly didn't want to be seen beneath his steel armor.

"Well, we already broke two rules," John muttered, sipping his coffee.

"Really?" he asked, feeling oddly pleased.

"Condoms, always. And no sleeping over."

He hummed, unable to suppress a smile.

"I suppose we can adjust it," John said, pulling the bedding over his waist, his naked back leaning against the headboard. "We can continue to not use condoms if we—uh—stay exclusive, as you asked."

Wyatt certainly planned to, and now, hearing that John did too, he tried to smother his elation. He didn't want another cute paramedic riding his Dr. Donnelly.

His? Where the fuck did that come from?

"Sleeping—well, considering we're both ED doctors," John drawled. "We may accidentally fall asleep on each other from time to time."

"So, there'll be a next time?" he asked.

John's dark gaze met his, vulnerably exposed. "Do you really want there to be?"

He knew what he was referring to—and it wasn't the sex from last night, or their positions at work. It was about his breakdown last night.

"Yes," Wyatt breathed, without hesitation.

Something flashed over John's expression, but he hid it behind his coffee mug as he carefully took another sip.

"What else?" he asked impatiently, irritated that John was determined to hide from him. He didn't like it. He wanted to know what was going on in his head. After his emotional display last night, he wanted nothing less.

Emotion was what made them all human, flawed and connected.

He couldn't unsee that—couldn't run from it like John clearly wanted to. He supposed he could be patient with that, waiting for him to trust Wyatt enough to share his emotions, rather than having them spill out uncontrollably. John didn't seem to like being a man with a deep well of feeling. And this man ran deep. Deeper than anyone he knew, besides himself.

"No attachments, no emotion," John's voice was rough when he said it, and Wyatt arched his eyebrows in surprise. "Minus what happened last night."

"And what happens if feelings get caught?" Wyatt asked, unable to keep the edge to his tone.

"We'll have to end it."

Wyatt pressed him with a questioning look.

"We work together, Lawson. It's complicated already. It was a mistake the first time..."

"I know, you already said that last night," he cut in, irritated.

John tilted his head to the side, lips pursed, "Sorry."

"Stop it."

John raised his hands in defense and set his coffee mug down. "You're right. Stopping."

"I have a question..." Wyatt began.

"Shoot," Dr. Donnelly answered, making him cringe and give an apologetic look. Wyatt narrowed his eyes, waiting for another stupid apology, but John shook his head. "I will resist the urge."

He couldn't help but chuckle, "Good. Is talking allowed?"

"You mean, you want to talk to me, other than fuck me?" he asked, the tension in his shoulder easing.

"Yeah," Wyatt said, grinning now.

John returned the smile with his own, dropping the back of his head into the headboard of the bed, looking possibly the most relaxed he had ever seen him. "Yeah, of course."

His chest filled with an inexplicable warmth, and he licked his lower lip. "Kissing?"

John swallowed, "Yeah."

"I wanna kiss you," Wyatt admitted with a shallow breath.

John's eyes darkened, "I wanna kiss you, too."

He felt his cock stir and dropped his feet onto the floor, leaning forward. "Any other rules?"

John hesitated, clearing his throat. "I prefer hotels. Coming over to my place feels too..."

"Intimate."

"Yeah." John sighed. "And the obvious rule, no one can know about this. At least no one at work."

"What about Samuels? He's like us." He said, referring to his sexuality.

"Yeah, well, he's more of a stickler for the rules than I am about certain things."

"I have a hard time believing that," Wyatt countered.

"Samuels is more comfortable taking orders than I am."

"I noticed you have a bit of an issue with authority."

John snorted, "How could you tell?"

He knew it was a sarcastic statement and asked, "How come you don't leave? Set up a practice somewhere?"

John reached for his coffee mug. "And what? Grow old and stale in some dungeon of my own making? No, thank you. I like my high-functioning depression, PTSD, and early-onset graying."

He laughed, biting his lower lip. "Have I mentioned I like your gray?"

John let out a breath, scrubbing his beard, his voice oddly rough. "How old are you?"

"Does it matter?"

"Yes."

"27… this year."

"Jesus."

"How old are you?" Wyatt countered.

"47… this year."

Wyatt whistled but continued to smile.

"Shut up," John shot back.

"You ride like you're in your prime," he drawled huskily. "Because you are. And I like riding you… a lot."

John puffed out an exhale, once more blushing. "You're going to kill me at this rate."

"I don't mind being rode either, just in case you need a break," Wyatt said slyly, watching the blush turn bright red and his chest heave. Apparently, the good doctor was excited by the idea.

"This can't happen more than once a week," John declared abruptly, as though trying to squash the mood.

"Yeah, I get that. My wallet took a beating with this room." Though he complained about the cost, he couldn't imagine kissing, tasting, and tonguing John in anything less than expensive sheets and luxuriously large showers.

"I'm paying from here on out," John said in a non-negotiable tone.

"I can manage."

"I don't care. My student loans are practically non-existent, yours aren't. And I make more than you, so I'll take care of this. Besides, this is my decision for hotels—not yours. You shouldn't have to pay for it."

Wyatt liked this side of John. It was the fiery, take-charge one who came out fairly often in the ED, especially when he could no longer stand back and watch, taking over because of his greater skill and experience.

"Anything else, Dr. Donnelly?" he teased.

John smiled, softening. "Not at the moment."

"Give me your number," Wyatt instructed, grabbing his phone off the charger.

John paused, and he arched his eyebrows. "You're not allowed to stress about this," he said forcefully. "I know how to keep a secret. I was a gay boy raised in a conservative household on a fucking horse ranch. Now, c'mon."

John gave him his number, and he saved his contact name as "JD".

"Give me your phone," he ordered. John gave him a reserved look, grabbed his backpack that was by the bed and unlocked his phone, tossing the hunk of metal at him.

John had his number, but no contact name associated with it. Wyatt saved his name as Sally with the cowboy emoji.

When he tossed back the phone, John frowned at the name.

"Mustang Sally. You said you like the blues."

"That I did," John drawled, impressed.

"So how about that ride?" Wyatt murmured.

"I've gotta be at work in a couple of hours. Don't you need to go home?"

"Do you?"

John shook his head, "I always pack an extra pair of scrubs just in case I work a double."

"Good habit, I'm stealing that." Wyatt glanced at him, waiting. "So?"

John flushed, "Christ, I don't know if I can…"

"I was talking about me," Wyatt breathed, sliding his fingers over his pants. "I wanna feel you today, even if I can't touch you."

John sucked in a harsh breath, his voice raspy as he said, "Come here."

Wyatt shook his head. "I think I wanna do it—right here," he said, indicating the perfect armless, cushioned seat. Perfect for riding.

John got out of bed, his body relaxed and rested after a night of brutal releases. His shoulder was level with the other one, and his walk was tight. Wyatt smirked, licking his lower lip as John stood before him, naked, his cock already in the early stages of erection.

Dear God, this man was sexy with his tousled bed hair, sexy half-smile, and the crinkles around his eyes. Wyatt quickly took a seat on the chair, grabbing Donnelly by the waist and taking him eagerly into his mouth again, tasting precum on his tongue and lapping it up. John sighed, raking his fingers through his hair, guiding him up and over his erection. Wyatt intentionally gagged and coated John's dick with his saliva before drawing away and putting John in the seat.

John watched him with a hungry gaze as he stripped out of his boxers and black T-shirt, dick hardening under his gaze. His heart skipped and he tried hard to ignore it as he straddled him, feeling his naked legs brush against John's thighs, his butt cradled in his lap. Wyatt was more muscular than John, but John was strong and took his weight easily, shifting under him. Wyatt leaned forward and kissed him.

John let out another soft moan into his mouth, sucking his tongue into his wet heat. Their kiss went on and on, leaving both leaking and gloriously hard. John pulled back and pushed his fingers into Wyatt's mouth, wetting them. Excitement spilled into his veins as Wyatt watched Dr. Donnelly take charge—his captain—his new lover.

John reached behind him, slipping those wet fingers over his hole, causing Wyatt to shudder and arch his hips in greeting.

"I've…got a confession," John murmured.

Wyatt grated his teeth over his beard, "I'm listening."

"I've never actually done this."

He pulled back, surprised. "Done—what?"

"Been with a man," John rushed out, cringing.

Wyatt leaned back, eyes widening, searching for the truth.

"That night we hooked up was my first time," John confessed, surprising the hell out of him.

"Are you serious?"

"Very."

Astounded, he glared at him. "Why didn't you tell me?"

John tilted his head to the side, eyebrows raising. "I'm telling you now."

Wyatt resisted the urge to sigh out his frustration and nodded patiently instead. "You still wanna do this?"

"Jesus fuck, yes."

Relief eased the tension in Wyatt's body as John bit sexily on his lower lip, slipping his finger inside him, and then another. Wyatt's entire being lit up in flames, slowly sinking himself deeper into his hand, riding him.

"Fuck, Lawson..." John marveled, his eyes cutting across his body, clearly turned on by the display on his lap. Wyatt's blood thickened, and so did his cock.

John slowly withdrew and took his cheeks in hand, guiding himself over his entrance. John's dick pushed through the outer ring and into him, edging in achingly slow, which Wyatt appreciated. John's cock was a bit of a sledgehammer, and it had been a while since he'd done this. Wyatt clenched his jaw and lowered himself onto the impossibly hard cock, feeling his body meld and mold around him.

John's head tilted back, panting. "You feel incredible."

Wyatt leaned down and kissed him, feeling the scrape of soft beard and lips, and without waiting any longer, dropped himself into his lap, becoming fully speared by him. Both men groaned and cursed.

Wyatt lifted himself up and down, John moving in slow tandem rhythm with him. His legs didn't feel the strain of the position; in fact, it reminded him of horse riding, and it felt natural. Everything with John felt natural—easy.

Stop, Wyatt.

Don't think like that.

Not now.

Wyatt dropped down again, fully seating himself and shivering, his cock leaking messily between them, his heart hammering wildly in his chest. His feet pushed off the ground and he lifted, ass cheeks clenching, sucking him further in as he moved upward.

"Fuck," John muttered. "You're doing so good, Lawson," he said with a hint of his Donnelly tone, causing Wyatt to fling his gaze onto his, see the glint of praise and… need. "I need you to pick up the pace."

He gasped, pulse stuttering, and did as demanded. John's hands went to his ass and they both rocked against one another. John shivered, groaning, "That's it… just like that, Lawson. Keep going…"

Wyatt fucked himself on John's dick, his own cock aching and throbbing, and yet, it didn't matter that John wasn't touching him; he was already so close and started thrusting down on him harder and harder.

"You ride me so fucking good," John praised, sending electrical currents through his veins.

"Oh…fuck…" Wyatt groaned, addicted to anything this man would give him.

"Do you know how many times I've fucked my fist, thinking about what you did to me that night—about all the things I want you to do to me?" John rasped.

He trembled, his legs beginning to shake.

"That fuckin' commercial…" he gutted out. "I envied the fucking horse…"

Wyatt sunk his hands into his beard, framing his face, needing more words. Needing more!

John seemed to understand and whispered, "I imagined this, too. Riding me—fucking me—using me for your pleasure."

Wyatt moaned, wildly thrusting, hips undulating, and riding him just like he imagined—giving him that reality and creating a fantasy for himself. John's rapture was his. Watching him watch him was intoxicating. Wyatt reached between his legs, finally granting himself the merciful relief of touch and palming his hard sex, stroking it upward using the precum as lube to fuck his fist.

"That's it, cowboy," John husked, panting and shivering beneath him, watching him stroke himself. "Fuck, yes...! God, look at you..."

Wyatt sucked in a breath, belly tightening with need and cock quivering. His orgasm was peaking, his body clenching around John, who let out a gasping sound, mixed with a long, drawn-out moan.

He sounded like pure fucking sex.

Wyatt grabbed the back of John's neck, hanging on as he made one final push, and his cock burst with his seed, spewing hot, uncontrollable ribbons of cum onto John's chest.

John gasped and leaned forward, face buried into Wyatt's chest, about to climax. But he refused to let him hide his face, his hand still around his neck and dragging him backward.

"I wanna see you..." Wyatt pleaded through panted breaths. "Cum for me, John..."

He shuddered and did, his lips parting and hips driving upwards, impaling Wyatt so deeply. He cursed, and his cock leaked a little more.

The sound of John's orgasm ripped through him, vibrating him through his core and sending another heavenly blissful wave through him, cock spurting again. Wyatt held on tight, not realizing his body could do that—keep climaxing even after he thought he had finished.

"*Fuck* me, that was hot," Wyatt panted, taking his mouth into his, kissing him thoroughly. John, breathing hard through his nose, returned the kiss, his body trembling.

He never thought sex could feel *this* good.

"I'm gonna need a nap or a double espresso to get me to work," John grumbled, but smiled.

"You could just have a cup of hot motor oil from the break room. That'll get your juices going," Wyatt suggested teasingly.

"I need to buy us a new one," John muttered. "Especially if you plan on killing me the night before."

Wyatt laughed now, chest rumbling. He liked the feeling of John relaxing against him, holding him close. There was something so secure about it. John rested his temple against his chest as he caught his breath.

"Or the morning of..." Wyatt whispered, gently raking his fingers through his hair.

"That would be close to breaking a rule." John kissed the base of his throat, his sexy beard brushing against his skin, affection sparkling in his blue eyes.

"Yeah, it would be." Wyatt's heart was practically beating out of his chest at the way John was looking at him.

Oh shit.

I think I just caught a feeling.

Chapter 10

John

John sat at the bar with Samuels and Steph at the Hot Dog Palace, classic rock playing in the background as the noise of Friday night filled the hole-in-the-wall dive bar.

"What a fuckin' week," Samuels grumbled, signaling the bartender for another round of beers.

"I don't know who I hate more—Tanya or Sean," Steph complained, finishing the last dregs of her beer before plopping it angrily down. "No one cares about her bottom line if she doesn't care about security. Max pulled a gun off a homeboy right outside the damned door. The place is turning into a circus. We need more staff to handle the overflow."

John listened with one ear, knowing this was the same old gripes and complaints as before. And lately, he hadn't been as bothered by the usual stressors at work.

Probably because I'm being pounded into oblivion by a cowboy every Saturday night until the sun comes up for the last two weeks.

And fuck, it was incredible. The best sex of his entire life. Lawson felt like an infection—or an addiction.

The second the hotel door swung closed behind them, they collided like the force of stars merging, passionate, brilliant, and bursting with pure, unfiltered need. Work had somehow become their foreplay—guarded glances, brief touches, fingers grazing, and lots and lots of praise. Lawson responded every single time to it, either with a quick inhale of breath, a darkening in his eyes, or even a stumble, which happened today, over his own feet, while leaving the exam room. He liked making Lawson squirm.

Because the reward was Lawson making him squirm in the bedroom. Jumping his bones with punishing, unmet need. And fuck, it was hot.

Lawson's body seemed constantly full of energy, and John had made the executive decision last Saturday to go back to the gym just to keep up with him. He returned to his old boxing club, his shoulder feeling almost fully back to normal due to Lawson's magic touch, in more ways than one.

His old coach, Arnold, was excited to see him return, and they immediately went back into training mode. It felt good—no, better than good, it felt fucking rewarding to hit a heavy bag again. He'd gone three times this week before work, getting up early to get in some much needed conditioning and training.

But since John hadn't been working out, other than with Lawson in the bedroom, he was currently sore, which he didn't mind. Though he'd have to ask Lawson to be a bit more gentle with him tomorrow night.

He stretched his back, feeling the deadlifts he had done at the club creep up on him as he sat on the barstool.

"Sore, old man?" Samuels teased.

"I'm two years older than you, asshole."

"And I'm ten years older than both of you jackasses," Steph chided. "But seriously, how's the shoulder?"

"Better," John admitted, taking a sip of fresh cold beer. "I went back to my old boxing club this week."

"Good for you," Steph said, smiling happily at him, her warm brown eyes holding him. "It's been a while since you've done that."

He cocked his head to the side, surprised. "You can tell?"

"I see everything, honey. When will you two knuckleheads figure that out?"

He sincerely hoped she didn't see everything, because he may have let his hands linger a little too long on Lawson's shoulders when he passed him in the hallway today.

"Well, then you would've noticed I wasn't wearing any boxers last Tuesday, and got laid on Thursday, 'cause I had a pep in my step," Samuels said flippantly, eyes on the football game playing on the screen above the bar.

John laughed, and Steph swiped a hand at the back of his head. "Gross."

"Speaking of pep," Samuels turned in his stool, dark green eyes riveted on him. "I've noticed you're awfully peppy lately."

He shrugged, swallowing down a large gulp of beer and hoping to hell his blush wasn't showing. "I don't know what you're talking about."

Steph hummed suspiciously. "We've all noticed, John. You're more patient with Samuels's bullshit, and even Tanya's. I don't think I've ever heard you say to that woman, 'I appreciate your feedback and will take it under consideration'."

Samuels gasped dramatically, "You did not!?"

John rolled his head to the side and sent him a bland smile.

"You traitor!" Samuels exclaimed. "I can't believe you caved!" "I did no such thing. Being civil to her a few times a week gets her off my floor and out of my department a hell of a lot faster than challenging her, and also less time with her floating around, critiquing my team or me at every turn, which is not something I care to endure anymore," John said reasonably.

"Jamie," Samuels said to the bartender, "Hand me back that beer I just bought him."

John swiped the beer off the counter, chuckling. His eye caught the front door of the bar as it opened to reveal a striking black cowboy hat, followed by a line of cowboy hats. He turned quickly in his seat and saw Lawson stride in with Ava, Emily, and Reyes at his heels.

Lawson glanced toward the bar, and their eyes collided with the same force as one of their fantastic, knee-melting kisses, and John's heart nearly stopped.

Fuck, this kid is ruining me.

Lawson was the epitome of a cowboy tonight, wearing almost the same outfit from the truck commercial, all black, down to his boots, except the outfit looked worn and molded to his figure like a second skin. And he had the inexplicable urge to slowly strip him with his teeth. He'd have him keep the hat on, though. Maybe the boots, too.

He flushed at the thought, and Lawson's eyes darkened hungrily over him, licking his thick lower lip before strolling casually to the bar, the others behind him, laughing and clicking their boots. They, on the other hand, looked like something out of the play *Oklahoma*. John would've laughed if the blood hadn't been roaring in his ears as his cowboy approached.

His cowboy.

Fuck. Fuck. Fuck.

Stop, John. He's not yours. He's a fling.

It's not gonna last. It's not supposed to last.

It was only Friday night, and they had agreed to Saturdays only. But Jesus, Lawson looked good enough to drag into the dirty bar bathroom and...

He cleared his throat, rubbing a hand at the back of his neck and attempting to duck away from Lawson's scrutinizing gaze.

"Well, fuck me sideways, you guys just come from a rodeo? Do they even have rodeos in LA?" Samuels asked loudly, getting to his feet and clamping a hand on Lawson's shoulder. "Dude, you need to stop putting the rest of us to shame. It's starting to hurt my feelings."

Lawson chuckled, and Reyes tilted his fancy, very clean white cowboy hat up at Samuels. "Lawson took us line dancing."

John snorted a laugh into his bottle of beer.

Lawson shot him a hard look, a playful smile creeping up on his lips. "What? We can't go line dancing?"

"No, sorry," he said, quickly. "You guys know you look, well…"

"Amazing!" Emily beamed proudly. "I always wanted a cowboy hat!"

Steph signaled Jamie, the bartender, for another round of beers. "We need to get a table with these cowfolk, 'cause I need to hear all about line dancing."

An hour later, Reyes, Ava, and Emily were thoroughly bombed, getting louder and more chaotic as Samuels continued to reload pitcher after pitcher of beer. Steph, too, was getting a little red in the cheeks and giggling more easily. The only sober people at the table were John and Lawson, who were both intentionally drinking their beers slowly, knowing exactly what kind of fun they wanted to have when the rest stumbled out of the bar and called for their rides home.

It took everything not to look at Lawson, who had intentionally picked the chair right next to his but hadn't looked at him the entire fucking evening since walking into the bar. John's palm itched beneath the table as he smoothed them over his jeans, his patience for the drunken frolic wearing thin, especially being this close to temptation and not being able to do a damned thing about it.

It also proved that Lawson had more restraint than he did, and this bothered the hell out of him because he sat there perfectly relaxed, his lips slipping over the rim of his beer, causing excess blood to shoot to John's cock.

Christ, what was wrong with him? He was acting like a schoolboy with his crush sitting next to him. Wyatt, on the other hand, was the epitome of unbothered, sitting next to him for the last few hours. And it bothered him.

Had he met someone line dancing? Because according to Ava, every short-shorts-wearing cowgirl in the bar had gawked, flirted, or worse, had the audacity to rub against Lawson on the dance floor.

Was Lawson already getting bored with their hotel rendezvous?

Bored with *him*?

A nervous insecurity unlike anything he'd felt before slid into his stomach, making a nest of his insides, and his shoulders began to tense. In the last few weeks, John had learned that his shoulders were a sign of his stress, and he needed to be mindful of relaxing them after a long, grueling shift.

John sat back in his seat attempting to relax, but it was no use. Images assailed him of Lawson on the dance floor with booty-shorts-wearing cowgirls, or worse, another cowboy just like him, young and hot, grinding into his crotch—taking what was his.

Shit.

Lawson is not mine.

He's not, John. Stop acting like a jealous boyfriend.

John swiped a hand over the back of his neck, wondering if he should just get drunk and call it a night. Anything would be better than stewing in this self-induced misery.

He felt Lawson's subtle shift beside him and glanced in his direction. Lawson's jaw was clenched tight, his hat low on his eyes. His black boot slowly crept out, widening his legs, as his heel touched John's beneath the table.

Sudden relief flooded his lungs, all from a simple touch, and he could breathe again. John reached for his beer and took a long gulp from the glass. Jesus, this was bad. He shouldn't be reacting this strongly to Lawson. Maybe he should end it now before it becomes any more complicated.

He'd already proven to Lawson he was broken. That he had trauma from his job that had built up in his body like an overflowing lake, until finally the dam had burst and driven him into a full-on collapse after shower sex. It was something that he still felt immensely ashamed about, and the young cowboy seemed careful not to bring it up again.

Lawson was better off far, far away from him. He should be doing things like this—out with friends, line dancing, having flings, having fun.

He felt another touch, a knee brushing against his beneath the table, and he resisted the urge to close his eyes and savor the reassuring feel of Lawson.

This was so fucking wrong.

John, unable to stand the self-loathing and pity anymore, abruptly got to his feet and headed over to the bar to close out. He knew he was running away, but he also knew he couldn't stay.

His phone dinged in his back pocket, and he withdrew it with his wallet.

It was Lawson, aka Sally. He fought the temptation to glance over his shoulder at him and opened the message instead:

You're upset.

Jamie took his card, and he typed back a quick reply.

I'm fine.

I do love it when you say that.

He sighed, and Jamie handed him the bill. He signed it, paying for tonight's fun, knowing Samuels and Steph were always good at footing the bill next time. His phone vibrated again. He checked it.

Are you leaving?

Yeah. Long day.

Wait 10 mins out back behind the bar.

He didn't reply, tucking his phone away and returning to the table, noting the steely glint in Lawson's gaze as he sipped his beer looking—angry?

"All right, kids," John began in a long sigh. "It's time for me to head out for the evening. It was fun," he said to the younger doctors, and patting Samuels on the shoulder. "You can get the bill next time."

Samuels's grin was lopsided and his eyelids at half-mast, clearly drunk. "Aw, you shouldn't have, buddy."

"Yeah, I did," he replied, ruffling his curly hair. "Hope all of you have rides."

Reyes and Emily waved their goodbyes happily. Ava had promptly taken John's vacated seat beside Lawson and was leaning provocatively into him, playfully fingering the brim of his hat in a flirtatious way that set John's teeth on edge.

Fuck, I need air.

"I'll walk you out," Steph said, getting to her feet and slinging her purse over her shoulder. John opened the door for her, the crisp scent of fresh fallen leaves and damp pavement filling his nostrils. He let out a long breath.

"I love this time of year," Steph said, pulling out her car keys.

"You okay to drive?" he asked.

She waved a dismissive hand and paused, "Well, now that you say that... Probably not. Wait with me till my Uber gets here?"

"Of course," he said as she ordered her car via app. He leaned against the red brick building, listening to the commotion within and trying not to think about the way Ava was looking at Lawson.

"God, to be a kid again, with all that damned energy. I don't remember how we did it," Steph drawled, joining him against the wall, wrapping her arms around her waist to keep warm. John slipped his arm over her shoulders and drew her into his side. They had been friends since day one. Years of going through hell together had bonded them.

Steph was his rock, his navigator, and in many ways, his best friend.

"I don't remember either, if that makes you feel better," John said with a gentle smile.

She snorted. "We had fun times, though."

"We still do."

"You say that, but all we do is come here. And then go back to work. Rinse and repeat."

"True, but I like it here."

Steph returned the smile, burrowing into him. "Me too."

"We could always go line dancing," he teased.

Steph barked out a rich laugh, and they watched the light mist of rain and the twinkle of city lights. Finally, Steph said, "I'm glad you're doing better."

He stiffened.

Steph glanced at him with that knowing expression. "I'm not stupid, you know."

"Never said you were."

"I know you weren't doing well there for a minute, Johnny. You know you can always come to me, right?" she murmured. "You're my best friend—hell, possibly my only friend, outside of Samuels and my husband."

Overwhelmed with the tenderness of her statement, John kissed the side of her temple, squeezing her shoulders. "I appreciate that."

"And if he gives you any trouble, just send him my way."

He hesitated, breath hitching in his chest. "Who?"

Steph elbowed him hard in the side. "You know who. You guys remind me of high schoolers, can't keep your hands off each other."

John swallowed, unable to speak.

"Though I think he's hung up on someone back home. Doesn't talk about it, but I think it's love. Only love can make someone that crazy," Steph said, her phone dinging in her hand. "Driver's around the corner."

John frowned, wondering if she was talking about Lawson—or Samuels. Both men had homes outside of California and had good relationships with Steph, though Samuels was closer with her…

"Samuels?" he finally asked, tilting his head down to look at her.

Her pretty brown eyes snapped to him, confused, "Yeah."

He couldn't help but laugh, "Not in a million years."

"What? Really? How come?! He's so fucking—difficult."

They both laughed now, holding each other as they did. Tears sprang to the corner of his eyes, and he couldn't remember the last time he laughed this hard.

"Shit," Steph sighed. Phone dinging once more as headlights turned from the road into the parking lot. "I need to get my Cupid arrow tuned, or something, 'cause I swear I thought you and…" the bar door swung open, and Lawson stepped out, alone.

John's heart hammered, and he made sure to keep his face neutral as Steph released him and kissed the side of his cheek. "Watch out for that one," she murmured firmly.

He eyed her questioningly.

"The cowboy's got a crush the size of Mount Rushmore on you," Steph hiccupped, and quickly covered her mouth. "Shit, I didn't say that. Nor did you hear it. I told him last month he needed to rein it in. He's a good kid, John. Let him down nicely, okay?"

He nodded, pulse ticking so loudly at her words that he barely noticed as she slipped into her Uber and waved from the back passenger window, the car returning to the road and disappearing out of sight.

Was that true? Did Lawson have a crush on him, or was it just their subtle change in relationship in the last few weeks she saw? No, Steph said she talked to Lawson last month about him. He sucked in a breath, realizing then that Lawson had been the one who pursued him, not the other way around.

Lawson's pale blue eyes were on him now, searching, waiting.

John swallowed and nodded, tilting his head to the side alley behind the bar and heading there first.

He barely made it a few feet into the alley when he felt Lawson's hands on his body, pushing him against the brick building of the bar and kissing him hungrily. Devouringly.

Jesus fuck.

John's body reacted instantly, grabbing the collar of his shirt and dragging him closer, their bodies pressed together as he kissed back.

Lawson let out a harsh breath against his lips, pulling back to kiss a hot, urgent trail down his jawline and to his neck.

"Fuck, I've wanted to do this all evening," Lawson murmured, his mouth opening over John's raging pulse and feeling him roughly suck on his neck. John's gasp turned into a moan as Lawson's teeth grazed the spot he was sucking beneath his ear before soothing the pain with his tongue. His cock undulated impatiently against John, grinding him into the wall.

Lawson was marking him—branding him—claiming him.

Yes!

John's cock leaked with such raging need that he reached between them and grabbed the hard denim of Lawson's jeans, panting.

"I want you here," Lawson whispered.

John trembled, and before he could react, Lawson dropped to his knees in the dirty, rain-soaked alleyway and opened his jeans, unfastening his belt with quick, sure hands.

Before he could stop him, Lawson reached inside, pulled out his cock and straight into the hot sheath of his mouth.

"Fuck, Lawson..." he gasped.

He pumped forward into his wet mouth, feeling the stretch of his lips around his grith and the touch of his tip at the back of his throat. "You're such a good..."

Lover? Boyfriend? Fling? None of those worked.

The base of his balls began to tingle and he closed his eyes, all thoughts vanishing into sensation and this moment. This stolen moment.

Lawson reached between his own legs, pulling out his cock and unexpectedly releasing John from his mouth. He stood, wrapping his hand around the back of John's neck, his other free hand pushing their cocks together, letting them slide and pulsate as one. Lawson's dick was longer, while John's was a bit thicker. And yet, they seemed to fit perfectly together beneath Lawson's hand as he fisted over them and began to pump, rocking his hips back and forth. But it wasn't enough friction. He needed more. John moved, capturing their cocks, and together Lawson and he pumped and thrusted against each other.

Thoughts of where Lawson had been and of other people ogling him pierced his mind like a splinter. He gritted his teeth, pivoted on his heel, and with years of maneuvering people onto gurneys, flipped positions with him, pushing his back against the wall and crowding him. Lawson let out a whoosh of breath from his lips, eyes dancing with pleasure at being manhandled.

The orgasm chased through his bloodstream, shooting shockwaves over his tip, ready to spew at any second. Their eyes briefly met before returning to their cocks being stroked in their hands.

It was a dirty, glorious sight.

Lawson's cock was leaking all over them.

"Make a mess of me, cowboy," John growled, the words tumbling out of his mouth.

Lawson let out a loud moan, so loudly that John was surprised. Lawson never made that sound before as it tore from his throat. He fucking needed more. He wanted to hear it again, and again.

He fisted and jerked them off, breathing hard. "You were thinking about this all night, weren't you, Lawson? Wanting to cum for me... Please me..."

Lawson jerked, jaw slack and eyes glazed, close to coming.

"You wanna take care of me?" John husked out.

"Yes, yes..." Lawson's panted plea was music to his ears.

"Cum on my dick, baby."

Lawson's eyes flew to his, and in that instant, his cock spasmed in John's hand, drenching him with hot, pulsing streams of creamy bliss.

His pulse shuddered at the sight, reaching to grab Lawson by the throat, still thrusting into his palm, thumb sliding over his soaked tip. "Good fucking boy..."

Lawson made that sound again, this time whimpering as he jerked into John's hand, his cock rearing up as another wave of his climax spurted from his messy red tip.

Fuck.

John groaned, feeling his own orgasm finally slam into him, and he dragged Lawson into a searing kiss, unloading against him, wanting to paint his perfect black shirt and pants with his cum. And Lawson, his pulse frantic against John's fingertips at his throat, let him. Lawson's kiss was pure heat and intensity. Suddenly, the young cowboy dropped once more to his knees and cleaned John's dick with his tongue, lapping up their spent bliss.

He gasped, watching in amazement as his cowboy sucked his limp dick into his mouth as though worshiping him, and not wanting to let this moment go.

Or maybe he wanted more praise.

Lawson's tongue slid underneath his cock, licking his balls.

"Fuck… baby…" John whispered.

Lawson pushed his entire face into him now, hat falling off the back of his head, tongue and mouth sucking his sacks.

"Is this what you want?" John asked, something opening inside him. Something forbidden and extraordinary. Exciting, new, and fucking thrilling.

Lawson hummed, desperate eyes flashing upward.

"Get up," John commanded breathlessly.

Lawson did, and they kissed, long and hard.

"We're still meeting tomorrow?" Lawson asked, a hint of anxiousness in his tone that surprised John yet again. The power between them shifted, and he still wasn't sure what to make of it.

"Once a week," John said licking his lips, hands all over Lawson's body. Something dark filled his stomach at the sight of his cum, a stained mess on his black shirt.

They had both marked each other.

"I need you," Lawson grated out, kissing him along the edge of his neck again. "Fuck, that was so fuckin' hot. I need more..."

The desperation in his tone was so sexy, so needy. John hummed, greeting his lips with his own, tonguing him into submission.

"Tomorrow night," John muttered between their lips. "I'll text you the hotel."

"Thank god," Lawson whimpered. "Sunday, too."

John smiled, "You're pushing it."

"Do you have any idea the crazy amount of gay or bi-men who would climb over hot coals just to hear you call them 'baby'? Fuck, John. You are a daddy-wet-dream."

John leaned back, tensing. "Daddy?"

Lawson's hands moved up and down his chest, breathing hard, sucking on his bottom lip, and John couldn't help but reach out and place his thumb there instead. Lawson moaned, sucking in the pad of his thumb.

"Has no one called you that before?" Lawson asked, astounded.

He shook his head, thoroughly confused, and yet the way Lawson was looking at him seemed to short-circuit a part of his brain that logically told him that they were both actively, if not aggressively, crossing the lines and making plans to cross them again. It was electrifying and terrifying all at once.

"I can't imagine taking you to the gay club by my apartment, you'd be mauled. Daddies in our world are older men who date younger men—they're more dominant, powerful, sometimes mentors, and usually cooler. *You*, in every, single, fucking, way." Lawson sighed, taking his thumb and opening his palm over his mouth, kissing the heartlines. "Daddy is praise in the highest form."

John suddenly laughed and released him. "I need to get out more."

"Only after you're done with me," Lawson whispered, gaze averted.

His stomach clenched. "Done with you?"

"I think we both know that those rules you made were to keep people away, John," Lawson unexpectedly blushed. "Especially someone like me."

"What do you mean?" he asked, tone unexpectedly gravelly.

Lawson's eyes softened and he stepped back, looking more like a man to him than ever before, capable, sure and strong, even with the vulnerability reflected on his face. He picked up his hat and brushed off the rain and leaves on his jeans, raking his fingers through the gorgeous dirty blond locks before slipping it back on. "I'm just a page in your book. Not a chapter of any meaning. And when you're done having fun with me, I just hope to hell that I can let go, too."

Lawson had just admitted to what John had been worried about almost the entire evening. The only difference between them was that John was too afraid to say it in return.

Chapter 11

Wyatt

The monitors beeped incessantly, drilling into his skull like needles in his brain. Wyatt's gaze was riveted to the little girl's face. Black ash and soot covered her pale lips. Her skin was gray and turning whiter by the second. She wasn't breathing, and her heartbeats were stuttering to a stop. Everyone in the room seemed to be holding the same collective breath every time Wyatt stopped chest compressions.

The monitor blinked and then flatlined.

She had been alert for less than a minute when she was wheeled into the ED.

But sometimes it happens that fast.

Sometimes they're here.

And then gone.

Trembling, forehead slick with sweat-induced adrenaline, Wyatt resumed compressions.

An old movie theater had caught fire during a movie, trapping at least two dozen people inside. The fire spread so quickly that most people didn't have time to get out. Including her, the six-year-old little girl in a pale pink dress with blue leggings. One of her pink rainbow boots was missing and her hair was tangled with the pink bow someone had put in it earlier that morning. Her big brown eyes were open and scared when she came in. She looked so damned scared, and when Wyatt saw her, everything in his body compelled him to move—to act—to save. To do everything in his power to save her life.

She blinked, tears dried on her face and mouth gaping open like a fish drowning. Their eyes locked and held, and everything stopped.

Wyatt had experienced loss plenty of times. But it never, ever got easier.

Trauma was still fucking trauma, even when it happened to doctors. Her dark brown eyes reminded him of his horses, of how they would sometimes look at him for the last time, knowing…

Something in Wyatt broke. He fisted his hand and pushed into her chest, sweat trickling down his back and panic setting in.

"Hold compressions," John's voice came through, and Wyatt stilled, trying not to notice how fragile she felt beneath his hands.

"Reyes, take over for Lawson," John said.

"No!" He nearly shouted, "No. I can keep going."

He glanced up, seeing the concern tighten around the corners of John's lips, his stance rigid, and yet he nodded. "All right. Resume compressions."

Relieved that his captain trusted him, Wyatt continued.

One more minute.

"Hold compressions," John said, once more breaking through Wyatt's motion.

He kept his hands over her chest, ready to start again, ears tuned solely to the monitors, but he still heard it.

The telling sound of a flatline. No change. The chest compressions weren't working because she was…

Wyatt sucked in a breath, arms shaking.

"Lawson," John murmured, a slight edge to his tone, yet gentle. So fucking gentle. "You've done enough."

No, I haven't.

A nurse stated the time of death. The finality of it didn't register in his mind.

This isn't real.

This can't be happening.

He felt Reyes's hand on his shoulder, indicating to let go. Wyatt swallowed the thick lump forming in his throat, legs shaking beneath him as he stared down at the little girl in the pink dress, her face etched like a sizzling brand in his mind. He'd never lost a child patient before. This felt different than the others.

It felt wrong.

"Are her parents here yet?" John asked.

"Yeah," Steph rushed in, "they just got here—" she stilled, seeing the girl and cursed under her breath, shaking her head. "Want me to send them in?"

"Yeah," John nodded. "Any word on the aunt and uncle she came in with?"

"Aunt's in surgery and uncle is stable. Smoke inhalation did some respiratory damage. It's gonna be a long recovery."

"For everyone," John finished and nodded to the team of nurses and doctors in the room. "We'll take a moment of silence."

Wyatt's spine shivered with the sudden weight of her death as he stumbled backward against the wall, barely holding himself up. He was transported back to his father's ranch, looking at his childhood horse gasp her last breaths, feeling the hole opening in his heart like a dagger.

Unable to look at his patient anymore, Wyatt braced himself against the wall, fighting the urge to flee. The moment of silence felt like an eternity and somehow, despite the ravaging pain inside him, he was still alive.

He was still fucking standing. And he didn't understand how.

"Okay, thank you, go ahead and bring her parents in," John said softly.

Wyatt, unable and unwilling to see this child's parents' grief, raced out of the room and was surprised to feel the comforting hand of Reyes on his back, leading him to the staff break room. "C'mon, man."

Disoriented, the room opened to the smell of fresh coffee and sanitizer. A wave of nausea rolled through him. Reyes led him to the couch on the far wall. "Sit down before you fall down, dude."

He did, collapsing into the hard cushions.

"You need anything?" Reyes asked.

All Wyatt could manage was a small shake of his head as he leaned forward, head between his legs and elbows digging into his knees, wanting to vomit—scream—cry.

He wasn't sure how long he had been there until he heard the door open again followed by John's voice. "Do you mind giving us a minute?" John said to Reyes.

"Yeah, yeah, of course. I'm here if you need me, Lawson," Reyes said kindly and left.

Wyatt lifted his head from his hands and was met with warm, tender blue eyes that he wanted to sink and vanish into completely.

So, he did. Wyatt reached for him at the same exact time John did, wrapping his arms around his shoulders and head, cradling Wyatt against his stomach. And for the first time in his career, he broke.

The tears came fast and hard.

His fingers dug into John's waist, clinging to him. He remembered briefly the moment John had done the same thing to him, holding him the same way but in reverse. They had come full circle.

"You did everything you could," John murmured gruffly, emotion lacing his voice. "There was nothing you could do."

"It shouldn't have been me," he cried, clutching John. "Her parents were coming... to see her one last time... not fucking me."

John dropped to his knees shaking his head, "But it *was* you. And that's okay. It's okay..."

"It's not!"

John framed his face with his hands, forcing Wyatt to meet his unyielding gaze. "Hating yourself right now is not the answer. You chose this job, or maybe it chose you. Just like she did. She needed someone to see her, and that's what you do, Lawson. That's what makes you so incredible. She managed to find the one doctor in this hospital who could give her peace right at the end. And that's what you did—I saw it."

His throat bunched and his heart, whose shattered pieces had sliced through his body, began to warm and melt back together. He swayed against John, their temples touching, and both breathed through the emotion, the pain, the grief.

"Thanks," Wyatt croaked out.

John nodded, leaning back and kissing his forehead before sitting back on his heels, taking his hands into his and squeezing, holding tight. "I want you to come to my house tonight. I'll cook us dinner, open a bottle of wine, light some romantic fucking candles..."

Wyatt sucked in a breath, the warmth now spreading everywhere, to every limb. John wanted him to come to his home. Not a hotel. Somewhere personal, intimate, and real. It had been a glorious month of hotel rendezvous, escaping, and getting lost in each other and the intimacy of their bodies.

And the open, vulnerable look on John's face told him that he was scared—that they both knew this was a risk. "Let me take care of you for a change, yeah?"

He hesitated, unsure.

John paused, too, and stood, scrubbing a nervous hand over the back of his neck. "Sorry, that's not fair. You're vulnerable, and I just put that on you. Let's forget I said it, all right?"

Wyatt stood. "John…"

The door to the break room opened and Steph walked in, expression tense, eyes immediately finding John's. "We've got more theater victims comin' in. All hands on deck, cap."

He nodded, heading for the door, and stilled. "You are what this hospital—these patients—need, Lawson. Exactly who you are today. Not the doctor you think you should be or want to be. But the one you are right now. That's the man they need—who I need."

They stared at one another for a long heartbeat, and John tilted his head to the ED, "Let's go save some lives."

He punched the gate code John had texted him, and the large iron gate came to life, slowly swinging back to let him in. A nervous energy brewed low in his belly as he rode his motorcycle into the long driveway and parked his bike next to the front of the house. The house was tucked away in the LA hills, out of the city noise and some of the traffic. It was a cool spot, and an even cooler house. Modern design with sleek black metal and large windows overlooking the sprawling city. Lush greenery was layered around the front of the house to keep it secluded and tucked away.

He pulled off his helmet, legs still straddling the motorcycle, and felt his phone buzz in his front pocket. He resisted the urge to curse as he checked it, already knowing who it was.

> We need to talk.

He read the text and closed it.

For the last few days, his Aunt Carol and Aunt Nancy had been texting him, asking him to call them.

Wyatt gritted his teeth, putting his phone on silent. He would not allow his night with John to be interrupted by them, especially after he had repeatedly told them to stop texting and calling. He had nothing else to say or do when it came to his father. His father hadn't spoken to him since he left eight years ago. Wyatt had called on his birthday and during the holidays, and the man never answered the phone or returned his calls. So eventually he stopped trying. His father didn't want anything to do with his gay son and made his disapproval loud and clear with his continued silence.

He climbed off the bike and took a long, deep breath, clearing his lungs and his mind of his father and his persistent aunts.

His phone vibrated again, and Wyatt let out a stream of curses, debating whether or not to block his aunts for the evening. But it wasn't them, it was Jin.

> Sent you the tickets via email. You'd better be there, cowboy! You have 2 tickets because I have every intention of meeting this mystery man you've been sneaking around with. Bring him, or don't. Either way, you're coming???

He smirked and texted his reply.

> Thanks, I'll be there. Wouldn't miss it.

> Good! Bringing him?!

Maybe.

Wyatt was pretty sure he would be breaking one of John's rules by asking him to come to his friend's art show. Granted, they were breaking a rule tonight, too.

I'll see you tomorrow night. Btw—it's a dressy affair.

He hesitated. He had only one suit. And the one and only time he had worn it was for a funeral…

His chest tightened with grief and he pushed the phone back in his pocket, refusing to go there. Not tonight. It had already been a hard day. He didn't want to think about his past or his family. All of that could wait.

Shoving his emotions down, he walked up the front porch steps to John's house and pushed the doorbell button. He swallowed, raking his fingers through his hair and shifting back and forth. Before the low-level anxiety had time to work its way up to panic, the large, heavy wooden door opened.

John's hair was damp and tousled from a shower, and he wore casual gray sweatpants and a form-fitting black T-shirt. His beard was cleaned up around the edges, and he was barefoot. Wyatt decided right then and there that he was madly in love with John's beard and how it framed his face, seemingly blending from his jawline into his hair, with a sprinkle of gray.

John looked so fucking good it hurt to look at him.

After possibly the hardest shift of his career, all Wyatt wanted to do was go to him.

It was silly and terrifying. He needed John more than this man needed him, and he wasn't sure if tonight was a good idea because of it.

The last couple of weeks of hot and heavy sex had rattled his comfortable little life. The anticipation of waiting all week to taste him, along with the tease of being close to him at work but never getting to touch him, tormented him. And when their one night of the week finally came, Wyatt was a wreck of pure need and they went at it like starving, desperate men.

And fuck, it was good. So damned good that Wyatt wasn't sure if he could handle only once a week anymore. He needed more. More time, more nights, more everything.

Before John could even say a nervous greeting, his telling hand scrubbed the back of his neck, eyebrows raised with that adorable fucking half-hearted smile of his. Wyatt, nerves forgotten, stepped forward and kissed him urgently, putting everything he wanted to say into his kiss, instead.

John swayed against him, wrapping his arms around him, and they made out on his doorstep for the best minute of Wyatt's night. His mouth opened for him, giving Wyatt what he needed, and he took, gripping his sexy fucking bearded jaw, digging his fingers through the thick hair and sucking his tongue into his mouth. John let out a delicious groaning sigh before he dragged them inside and closed the door firmly behind him.

Wyatt proceeded to push John against the door and ravish him some more, and the older man hummed. He gripped his helmet, wanting to use both hands and escape into this moment. But he knew that he couldn't. He was in John's home, and he was a respectful country boy, and he could resist the urge to devour this man in his own home, at least until after dinner.

He finally broke the kiss and straightened, reigning in his cockstand.

"Well, hello to you, too." John smiled at him, flushed.

"Sorry," he breathed, inhaling and exhaling steadily. "I needed…"

I needed you.

Just you.

The thought startled him, and Wyatt stepped back. John seemed to understand and reached for him, cupping his cheek, "That's what this evening is for. Whatever *you* need."

John kissed him this time. It was slow and tender, something they rarely, if ever, did. John was the first to pull back, something flickering in his gaze, but he concealed it just as quickly. "You okay?"

"I will be," he replied thickly, smelling the food John had been cooking and suddenly realizing he hadn't eaten anything since breakfast.

"I have dinner on the stove. Here, let me take this." He took his helmet and placed it on the hallway table, which also had a fashionable shoe rack.

Without asking, Wyatt peeled off his black leather cowboy boots and set them beside John's. He stared at the image of their shoes side by side and slowly looked away.

"I can give you a grand tour after dinner," John said, already heading to the kitchen.

He followed him through the long hallway, into a sizeable living room, and then into the kitchen. It was an open-space design, with no walls blocking the view of the windows or of what was happening in the living room. It made the space feel cozier and more spacious.

"Your home is incredible," Wyatt marveled, peeling off his jacket and setting it on the couch, noting the wall of records and books. The record player was on, and the crooning sounds of blues drifted through the house.

"Thanks," John said with a hint of pride. "Designed a lot of it myself. With the help of the architect, of course. Walking into rooms all day long made me want something…" he trailed off, searching for the word.

"Freer."

John shot him one of those kind, sexy smiles. "Exactly."

Heart swooping, Wyatt nervously licked his lips and walked up to the marble granite island in his fancy kitchen. "What are you making?"

"Pasta. Pairs well with wine." John turned, bottle of wine in hand, and poured Wyatt a full glass of red wine. "I've only seen you drink whiskey or beer."

"I like wine," he replied, taking a sip. "It's good."

"Good," he said, the crinkles around his eyes drawing in Wyatt's gaze. He loved those crinkles a little too much, wondering if they were possibly the handsomest part of John's face, outside his lips… or eyes… or beard.

Stop, man.

You're pining.

He took a long sip of his wine this time, hoping it would take the edge off his nerves. "I wanted to thank you for what you said today."

John glanced up from the chopping board and nodded. "I meant every word."

"I know."

He tossed the veggies into the sauce, glancing over his shoulder. "I know you know."

Wyatt stared, unable to look away, unable to speak. It hadn't been that long since their relationship became sexual, and yet, everything had changed. Everything. And he wasn't sure, in this moment, he would ever be the same again. That he could ever look at another man the same way—see the same things that he saw with John.

Feeling bold, Wyatt walked around the island, deciding to let his body speak everything that was trapped in his heart, kicking and screaming to come out, and to let tonight be what they had agreed upon between them. Physical. No attachment. But he feared he wouldn't be able to resist the affectionate part.

He slid behind John as he stirred the pasta sauce over the stove and wrapped his arms around his waist, resting the side of his face into his shoulder.

They swayed, holding one another, listening to the blues guitar and piano in the background.

"Did you always want to be a doctor?" Wyatt asked, brushing his lips across his shoulder.

"I think I always gravitated toward helping people. But with different ages and phases, I would go back and forth."

"With what?"

He shrugged, "Oh, you know, the normal stuff. Be a doctor or an astronaut. Police officer or professional baseball player. Firefighter or the world's best guitar player since Stevie Ray Vaughan."

Wyatt smiled, "Sensible choices."

"Every last one of them," John said without a hint of sarcasm. "But ultimately, I decided on medicine. I saw the power of it. My mom had breast cancer when I was a kid and managed to beat it. That stayed with me. Influenced me, I suppose."

He nodded, releasing him, but not before sliding a hand over the shoulder that had once been frozen, locking John in and crippling him.

"How's your shoulder?" he asked, leaning backward across the marble island for his glass of wine.

"Good—really good, thanks to you." John turned, his gaze falling to where Wyatt's shirt rode up over his belt, exposing the skin and muscle of his stomach. His eyebrows lifted and he sighed, "You're making me regret not having dinner ready before you got here."

Wyatt settled, placing himself directly in front of him, stance widening and eyes teasing him as he sipped his wine. The need reflected in John's expression was his, and his stomach fluttered.

John's gaze traveled over his body slowly, and he shook his head, "I've never been one to have dessert first, but if you keep looking at me that way, I might have to."

As if on cue, Wyatt's stomach rumbled, and he chuckled, "Maybe next time, because I'm starving."

John's smile faltered, a vulnerability flashing across his face. "Do you want there to be a next time? Here?"

"Only if you want to."

"That wasn't the question."

Wyatt tilted his head and nodded, "Yeah. I like seeing you like this."

"Like what?"

"Relaxed."

John scoffed playfully, "What, I'm not relaxed at the hotels?"

"It takes an orgasm or two, but yeah, eventually."

John stepped forward and reached for the bottle of wine behind him, his arm brushing his as he leaned over, his scent engulfing him like a hit to the gut. Wyatt dropped his forehead once more into John's shoulder before kissing his neck and spotting the hickey he had intentionally left the last time they were together.

Heat spilled into his veins as he thumbed the spot.

John sighed, but his mouth continued to quirk up, "I considered wearing a turtleneck to work this week."

"What? Worried you'd have to explain to Steph you're having fun?"

John chuckled, "She thought I was interested in Samuels. That we were..."

Wyatt growled, unable to hide his irritation, "I thought the same thing for a while."

"Really?" he asked, handing him the bread knife, the cutting board, and a fresh loaf. "Cut this for us, will ya?"

"Yes, sir."

"So, why did you think Samuels and I were—God, I can't even say the word," John said, shaking his head.

"Fucking? Probably because I never met two out gay men in command. I thought it made sense y'all would wanna battle dicks, too."

"Ugh, gross."

Wyatt enjoyed John's reaction, the ridiculous jealousy knot in his belly released as he sliced into the soft focaccia bread. "I eventually realized you guys would never work."

"Not that I actually want to know or have ever considered this, but why not?"

"He's got a lot of anger, deep bottled anger that needs to be contained by someone like him. Someone not afraid of it, meeting it with something entirely more powerful."

John glanced up from the stove curiously.

"Love," Wyatt finished.

He arched his eyebrows, "You saying I can't love?"

"I'm saying that Samuels needs a hard ass like him."

"Now I'm not a hard ass?"

"Your ass is possibly the best thing I've seen all year, but no, John, you are not a hard ass. It's why we work so well together." He stilled, hand on the knife, wanting to bite off his tongue.

Fuck.

Wyatt was too afraid to turn to face him and instead, busily finished cutting the loaf.

"I'm listening," John said quietly.

He blinked, wondering if it would be safer to make something up. Not tell him what he'd been thinking about for the last month…

"You're a storm," he heard himself say, knowing he was taking a big risk admitting this. "The quiet ones that come at night. You soak the earth, give it everything it needs to grow and flourish. You crackle a bit, light up the sky, but you never hit—never strike. Sometimes you give too much and vanish. But then all of a sudden you're back, giving again, even though a little bit of you vanishes each time."

John's silence forced him to turn and look at him, and he saw that his back was to him, standing by the stove, unmoving.

"And I'm the horse that chases you through the dark," Wyatt murmured. "I wanna see everything you got, marvel at it, watch it, dance in it. And I want you to see me, too."

John's dark blue gaze flickered to his, raw and powerful emotion brimming beneath the surface, unspoken but there.

"I want you to remember who you do this for," Wyatt breathed. "That you're wanted for more than what you give."

Tears filled John's eyes as he turned away, jaw clenching fiercely. He always turned away when his emotions stirred, and Wyatt, in this moment, couldn't stand it any longer. He moved, turning John in his arms and cradling his face in his hands, heart hammering in his ears.

"Whatever happens, promise me something?" Wyatt said, holding him, feeling his emotion as though it were his own. "Don't vanish. And if you have to, find another horse—find something to anchor yourself to. Anything. Because this world is so much better with you in it than without."

It took him some time to unpack their first night, and then their second, before Wyatt finally understood what was happening to John. He knew it because he had felt it himself briefly before in his life—after his father had rejected him, and…

His throat clenched and he leveled a steady gaze at him, wanting John to feel safe with him and wishing he did.

Tears brimmed behind John's eyes and he tried to look away, "Lawson…"

"I ain't gonna push you," Wyatt reassured gently. "I'm here if you ever wanna tell me."

John nodded, blinking away the tears, and kissed him.

Wyatt stilled.

This wasn't John's usual kiss, hurried, hard, and hungry. This was achingly slow and affectionate. There was a tenderness that left him breathless and scared. He wanted exactly this from John. He wanted him to let go of his armor and know that he was safe to hold his emotions—that he could handle it. And if it started with a kiss, he'd take it.

John pulled back, resting his temple on his. "You figured me out..."

He smiled lazily, kissing him again just as lazily, heart fucking glowing. "Yeah, I'm getting there."

He searched his face, "I think I'm okay with that."

John kissed him again, and it was so fucking affectionate that Wyatt gasped into his mouth, feeling the weight of his emotions swirling and building.

He had just broken John's rule. Wyatt, without a doubt, was falling fast and hard for his captain—for John.

And he wasn't surprised in the least. In fact, he marveled at how quickly it was happening and how natural it felt. But he couldn't say any of this. Not tonight. Because tonight, he wanted nothing more than to have dinner, talk, drink wine, and make love.

He withdrew from the kiss first, trembling. John studied him, and with another light-hearted smile and deep exhale, he returned to the stove.

After dinner, Wyatt took another lazy sip of his wine, perusing John's album collection.

"See anything you like?" John asked, wiping his hands on a kitchen towel.

"A few things," he replied, sliding his eyes over his body. "Gray, extra-tall, thin cotton."

John chuckled, shaking his head. "Not so fast, Lawson. We have plenty of night left for that."

"I thought we said no sleepovers."

"There's an exception for every rule. You had a tough day, and you're not leaving until you feel better."

He already did. Just being around John was enough.

He never wanted to leave. But he figured he'd keep that thought to himself. He'd already revealed enough, and the last thing he wanted was to scare John away.

"We certainly do make a lot of exceptions to your rules," Wyatt drawled, pulling out one of the albums.

John tossed the kitchen towel onto the island, refilled his glass, and strolled over to Wyatt's unattended glass, topping it off. "I never heard your reason for becoming a doctor."

He hummed and then sighed.

"That doesn't sound good," John remarked, eyebrows arched.

"It's not as good as yours."

"We don't compare in this house," he said evenly, and took a seat on his plush couch, legs pushed out in front of him and crossing at the ankles. He sipped his wine, resting the stemless glass on his stomach, hands folded around it, patiently waiting.

"I sorta fell into it," Wyatt admitted with a shrug.

"Fell into it?" John asked curiously, without an ounce of judgment.

"It's a long story."

"And as I said, we have all night." John patted the couch. "Come here."

He did, sliding into the firm comfy couch beside him, setting his wine glass on the wooden coffee table. John rotated to face him but maintained the distance, clearly wanting to hear his story. Wyatt didn't like that they weren't touching, so he pulled his leg up on the couch, brushing his knee against his. It wasn't hard to imagine a Sunday morning curled up on this couch, cuddling with him.

He let out another sigh, focusing. "I told you about the dude ranch. The men I worked with were mostly ranch hands and handymen to get through the season. Good ones would come back. Bad ones would drift onto other ranches that didn't know them. My dad preferred hiring the same ones. You remember that story of the man my dad found me with?"

John nodded, "It was pretty unforgettable."

"His name was Mateo. Strong, silent type, and really good with the horses. He had a way with them. He'd talk to them at the end of the day, his voice drifting them off to sleep most nights." Wyatt hesitated, flushing. "He was the first man I ever fell in love with. I was nineteen. Fuck, I've never told anyone that."

John's fingers squeezed his knee, his soft gaze holding him.

"The first time he touched me was out on a trail that we were prepping for the new season of tourists and visitors. He kissed me right here," he placed two fingers on the back of his neck behind his ear. "I remember it was soft, and then his hands were on my body, everywhere, touching me as though he had every right to, and it was so..." He drifted off, remembering the smell of the dirt, sweat, musk, horses, Mateo. "...hot. It didn't feel wrong. I felt safe with him, and I had never been so aroused in my life. I wasn't experienced like he was."

"Was he older?"

"Early thirties."

John nodded, smiling. "So, is that where your thing for older guys started?"

He considered this and shook his head. "After him, I went off to college and had sex with guys my age. It was different. It was more just to get off, and it felt a bit selfish. Don't get me wrong, I had fun, but the sex wasn't as exciting. Then med school happened, and I kinda got lost for a while. And then I came to your hospital and realized the senior resident with the gray in his beard and kind eyes was someone I desperately wanted to hear cum for me."

John's cheeks flushed, and he pinched his inner thigh. "You're getting off topic."

"Sorry," he tossed him a cool smile. "So, Mateo and I had a good season. A really good season. And then it ended, pretty abruptly after my dad found us. I left the ranch and stayed with my aunts for a while, trying to figure out my life. One day, I got word that a ranch hand and a horse had gotten hurt." A wave of emotion washed over him like it always did when he told this story. "It was Mateo. The horse got spooked on a tough trail up a mountain pass, fell, and crushed him. Broke his spine and right leg. The horse had to be put down on the trail—they couldn't save her."

"Jesus. I'm so sorry," John murmured.

"I visited him a few times in the hospital. His doctor..." Wyatt shook his head, anger filtering through his bloodstream. "His doctor told him he'd probably never ride a horse again, and something broke in Mateo. He went into surgery and never came out."

John reached for him, a soft curse under his breath.

"That doctor stole his hope. And sometimes, that's all we've got," his throat bunched. "I realized that if I had been Mateo's doctor, I would've given him hope, given him something to fight for. That's when I knew what I needed to do, and I haven't looked back since."

John pulled Wyatt's hand from his lap. He hadn't realized his fingers had balled into a tight fist until he gently pushed his fingers through, drawing them up to his lips and kissing him. "You're a good man."

Needing more than words, he leaned forward and captured his lips, tasting the wine off his lips. "So are you."

John deepened the kiss, fingers grasping the back of his head, and they fell into one another. Wyatt was on top of him, straddling him on the wide couch, feeling their bodies brush and burn together.

He trembled.

Mateo had opened him to the possibility of something more during a time in his life when he didn't have much. John gave him something else entirely—the space to make mistakes and, in the same breath, be forgiven, and the courage to be more vulnerable, the permission and reassurance to stay the course even when everything looked bleak.

John, without saying it, gave him love.

Because that had to be love.

He grasped John's bearded jaw, opening it to slide his tongue inside as his hips undulated into him, the couch dipping beneath their combined weight.

John arched into him, his cock straining against him from beneath the thin fabric of his sweatpants. Thank God for easy access, Wyatt thought wickedly, as he reached between their bodies and pulled John's erection free, sliding his hand down the elongated, throbbing cock and stroking it root to stem. John's face pinched with desire, lips parting and back arching once more off the couch.

"Fuck, you are so goddamned sexy," Wyatt hissed, doing the same motion again and watching nearly the same reaction from John, but this time his dark gaze locked with his.

"So are you..." John whispered breathlessly.

His jaw clenched and he sat back, quickly tugging off his shirt and tossing it to the floor. John did the same thing with Wyatt's help. Their naked chests touched, and Wyatt raked his fingers through his glorious chest hair and over his nipples. They hardened, and Wyatt grazed his lips over one, sucking it into his mouth and biting, drawing it upward to a pointed peak.

John let out a long breath, rubbing against him. "Fuck… your mouth feels so good, baby."

Baby.

That word again. He used it in the alleyway behind the Hot Dog Palace, and they never talked about it. And they certainly never brought up 'good boy'.

Wyatt's cock hardened ruthlessly between his legs, and he yanked his belt off and opened the button and fly to his jeans, granting himself relief from the strain of the material over him.

He then went to work on the other nipple, doing the same thing, hand stroking between John's legs. "Tell me what you want…" he demanded, pressing the pad of his thumb over John's leaking cock.

John bucked wildly beneath him, shuddering.

"Tell me what you want, daddy…"

John gasped, staring right through him and into his soul.

"Suck my cock," he rasped. "I wanna see me in your mouth."

Trembling, Wyatt moved down his body and between his legs, licking his lips before drawing the tight, hard flesh into his mouth, tonguing the precum off his tip.

John watched him work his shaft with his hand and mouth, his dark gaze on his mouth bobbing up and down over him. He quickened the pace, heat spilling in his veins at the angry, almost hungry way John was looking at him.

"That's it. Suck me down your throat, let me feel how much you want me."

Wyatt smothered a wet moan over his cock, so hard he thought he would burst. Instead, he took all of John's lengthy member down his throat, his muscles convulsing and tightening around him. John cursed, grabbing him with both hands at the back of the head and arching upward, spearing into his mouth.

Wyatt choked, gagged, and swallowed, his own cock spurting more precum, making a mess on John's nice couch. He liked the mess. The chaos. The authority. The power. All of it.

"Uh..." John gasped, hips bucking beneath Wyatt, fucking his mouth. "Good... fucking... boy...!"

Wyatt felt his release coming and wanted more—wanted total fucking annihilation. He pulled back, eyes locked with his. "Fuck my face until you come, and when you're about to, sit up."

John shuddered, lips parted as he whimpered a glorious, sexy fucking moan and dragged Wyatt back down on him, all restraint gone, replaced by utter carnal lust. John's hips pounded upward, spearing into Wyatt's throat, and he took it, saliva dripping out of his mouth, the sounds of his grunting need with John's flesh driving into him. He raked his fingers through Wyatt's scalp and pushed himself so deep that his nose and chin were in John's pubic hair, and he forced himself to breathe through the nose, taking in his musk, his cock twitching in painful need.

Oh god, he was going to come without touching himself. All from the dirtiest blow job he'd ever given.

"Fuuuck...!" John nearly shouted, a sound of utter abandonment rippling from his throat. "Lawson... God—fuck..."

John suddenly sat up, and Wyatt braced himself, exhaling a deep breath, knowing he was about to be smothered, and fucking needing it.

John pushed further down over him as his cock heated and pulsed in Wyatt's mouth, down his throat, unloading everything—hot, sticky, and wet. He clasped his hands onto John's waist as John simultaneously pushed Wyatt's head down, smothering him completely into his lap. John began to uncontrollably shiver, his cock continuing to spasm.

He swallowed him, his throat contracting around him, his breath held in his chest, lungs burning, and cock so painfully swollen, he knew one touch would send him spiraling.

John released him, and Wyatt came up for air, gasping. John stared at him in shock, eyes fully dilated, almost black. "Wyatt…"

He heard his name, breathy and in reverence, and he couldn't wait. He couldn't. He shoved John back down on the couch, lifted his hips, spread his cheeks, and licked and spat into his tight hole. He pushed his face between John's legs, tonguing his entrance. John groaned, gripping the couch and levitating upward in his grasp. Wyatt did it again and again, ruthlessly driving his tongue into his hole.

"Jesus, Wyatt!"

He said his name again.

Fuck!

Wyatt devoured his asshole, brutally digging into him with his tongue, needing to climax, delusional for it. He abruptly sat up, straddled John, and without even taking off his jeans, because there wasn't time for that, shoved his aching cock into him. Both men moaned together, and Wyatt, knowing it wasn't going to take much, pumped into him three quick thrusts. He knew he was rough and also knew John liked rough rides. A lot.

He saw the evidence of it, as John's deflated cock started to stiffen again.

Wyatt shoved John's legs up and around his waist, burying himself deep into his asshole, nearly coming at the feel of being fully sheathed inside him.

John bucked, cheeks clenching around him, tightening his hold.

"Fuck," Wyatt breathed.

John's blue eyes flew to his. "Ride me hard, baby."

Wyatt's groan was low and rumbling, knowing what he was asking, and he wrapped his hand around John's throat, pounding into his tightness, a wild madness taking hold.

He maneuvered one of John's legs down so he could lean in closer to him, their breaths mingling with the same heat in their gazes. Hand still collaring John's throat and hips thrusting, the orgasm closed in on him. He grasped John's cock and tugged, milking him for another orgasm.

John clung to him, shivering violently. He speared into him, hitting that sweet heavenly spot inside John. He could feel the man unhinging beneath him. His body had completely surrendered over to Wyatt's whim and will, and he never wanted to leave the tight sheath of John's perfect fucking body.

Wyatt licked John's lips, deepening his tone into a low, gravely husk, "Give your good boy another orgasm, daddy…"

A guttural cry tore through John's parted lips and his cock spasmed in Wyatt's hand for a second orgasm.

"That's it," Wyatt ground out, fisting his cock. "God, you ride so fucking good."

"Yes, yes!"

He thrusted hard, panting between each pound and slamming home. "The best fucking ride I've ever had…" he admitted hoarsely. "I don't ever want to stop."

John whimpered, eyes locked with his.

He broke. The orgasm whooshed through his body like the thundering gallop of a thousand horses, and he unleashed his hot seed inside him.

The roaring in his ears finally subsided after what felt like the longest minute of unloading in his life. John's shivering, quaking body bore the mess of his orgasm, and he looked so blissfully spent and utterly relaxed, panting.

But Wyatt wasn't through.

He slipped down John's body once more, lifting his hips and, with the skill of someone who knew how to flip a patient, did so to John's body. John let out a surprised gasp, flopping onto his stomach and smearing his rapture onto his nice couch, which made Wyatt smile as he then forced John onto his knees, baring his perfect fucking ass for him.

"Wyatt..." John warned.

"This ass belongs to me," he heard himself say, his orgasmic bliss making him feral—wild—mad. He spread John's cheeks and licked his cum back into his tight hold. John's words were garbled and strained, whimpering. "No one else calls you daddy but me."

He licked, sucked, and tongued.

"No one," Wyatt declared. "You're mine."

John's body relaxed even further, melting into Wyatt's face as he ate his ass. He loved the taste of his cum in his body. It was primal and animalistic. And he didn't fucking care.

Wyatt reached between John's spread open legs, grasping his soft dick and beginning to gently tug it back to life.

"Lawson—fuck... I don't think I can..." John murmured weakly.

"I've been good to you, haven't I, daddy?"

"Oh, fuck. Yes."

"Your good boy...?"

John moaned, hardening in his hand.

"I'm gonna eat your ass and milk your cock until you ruin this fucking couch."

The sound John made almost sounded like a cry, and yet he nodded, already beginning to leak into Wyatt's hand.

"That's it," Wyatt drawled, pushing open his cheeks with his face, and went to work, taking what was his like a fucking feast.

This went on for a long time, his hand slowly jerking him off while his tongue lazily stroked and entered, sucking on the slick entrance. He pushed his entire face into his ass now, using his chin and stroking him stem to root and over his balls.

John's breathing was erratic, and he suddenly thrust back onto Wyatt's tongue, fucking himself on his face. He hummed approvingly, picking up the pace with his cock in his hand, until John was mercilessly grinding into him, letting out the sexiest fucking sounds of pain and pleasure.

Wyatt smothered his face into him and with one final suck of his puckered hole, he pushed his tongue inside him. John let out a cry and miraculously climaxed again, spewing messily all over his fancy couch cushion and onto Wyatt's fist.

He released him, and John fell into a heap on the ruined couch, looking thoroughly destroyed, and he had never felt prouder in his whole damned life at the glorious sight. Wyatt sat back on his shaking legs, breathing hard, enjoying the view of his work.

"You killed me," John breathed with a sigh.

"I know. It looks fucking good on you, daddy."

"Oh God, why does that turn me on so much?" He cringed. "It's not normal."

"It is normal," Wyatt stated, slipping out of his jeans and socks. "Where's your bathroom?"

John sighed and pointed toward the hallway.

"Do you need help?" Wyatt teased, biting his lower lip.

"Yes," John said without skipping a beat. He sat up, and Wyatt helped him stand, leaning him against his side as they walked toward the master bedroom.

John's bathroom was bigger than Wyatt's room in his apartment. He flipped on the shower and led John inside, letting the warm water soak him before stepping in, grabbing the luxurious bar soap that smelled like John, and working it all over his body, massaging as he went. John braced his hands against the wet tile, letting Wyatt take care of him. He knew John was fading, and quickly went through his aftercare ministrations, wishing he had more time to dedicate to it, but not wanting John to pass out in the shower, either.

Flipping off the water, they toweled off and tumbled together into the king-size bed with navy blue silk sheets. It was rich and soft and cozy. John rolled onto his back, dazedly looking at him from his pillow, eyes already at half-mast and closing.

Wyatt kissed his lips affectionately, a calming peace washing over him.

John, without another word, fell asleep.

He slept beside him for a couple of hours, then woke early and kissed John's temple, letting his heart whisper the words he wanted to say, and left. He knew staying any longer wasn't a good idea simply because he needed time to think about how he was feeling.

Because he was feeling a lot.

Too much.

And he was terrified of losing John because of it. This situationship was becoming too much of a real relationship, and he knew that was not something John wanted. But that's all Wyatt wanted. He wanted to wake up in bed with him without feeling like he didn't belong there. He wanted John to choose him—see him—share with him.

But he was afraid that this was all John was willing to give him, and it was only a matter of time before it wasn't enough for Wyatt anymore.

He scrubbed a hand through his hair and shook his head. The truth was, this situationship was doomed from the very beginning, because Wyatt already knew exactly what he needed.

Everything.

Every. Fucking. Thing. From John. And most importantly, his sensitive damn heart.

Fuck. I am so fucked.

Chapter 12

John

He woke from the deepest sleep of his life, his body thoroughly sedated and well-fucked. He smiled lazily, remembering Lawson's hands and tongue on his body, sinking into the pillow. Last night was a sexual revelation. The things Lawson…

No, his mind whispered, *Wyatt*.

He shuddered.

The things Wyatt did to him last night, pushing him to the brink and pulling him back, had been incredible. He'd never had sex like that before. Never thought he could. And yet Wyatt, the skilled lover that he was, somehow managed to get not two, but three orgasms out of him. John bit his lower lip, skin tingling and body vibrating with a delicious warmth. Sunlight streamed through the thick blackout curtains over his bedroom window and he blinked, rolling over. Heart fluttering, he hoped Wyatt had decided to stay.

He was greeted by a rumpled, empty bedside, and he frowned disappointedly.

He knew he shouldn't have wanted him to stay, but he did.

He found himself tracing the outline of the place where Wyatt had slept beside him last night, the soft rays of morning sun seeming to suspend him and his heart, which oddly… hurt. Before he could process the feeling, John's phone vibrated on his bedside table and he sat up, scrubbing a hand over his face and wiping away the last dregs of sleep.

It was Sally.

His heart skipped, and he opened it.

Thanks for last night.

He watched as bubbles appeared and disappeared, and John hesitated, writing out his own text: "I think we should talk". His finger hovered over the send button. He pinched the bridge of his nose and sat up a little straighter, reaching for his reading glasses and focusing.

Last night had been the best night he'd had in months, maybe even years. And he didn't know what the hell to do about this situationship they were in.

They couldn't be boyfriends, at least not where the hospital was concerned. It was against their policy for senior residents to date anyone beneath them. Workplace romances were strongly frowned upon. But they were consenting fucking adults and could be together outside of the hospital. And for the first time, John realized that was exactly what he wanted. He wanted Wyatt to be his.

Swallowing the nerves, he was about to push the send button when Wyatt texted.

My friend has an art show tonight. If you're free...would you want to come with me?

The breath in John's chest exhaled in a sigh, and he smiled.

Yes.

Really?

Really.

I should've stayed.

He glanced at the empty pillow and realized that it was not hurt he was experiencing, it was longing. A deep, unshakable thing. It was longing for more. More days in the sunshine with Wyatt. More nights like last night.

John texted back.

Yes, you should've. I planned on making us breakfast.

Shit. I fucked up.

You did. Maybe next time.

Tonight?

John's heart was racing and he swallowed, letting his heart answer for him.

Ok.

Is it tonight yet?

He laughed, a blush forming on his cheeks.

Wyatt started texting again, and then the bubbles stopped. John waited, feeling both nervous and excited.

Can I kiss you at the art show? Would that be ok?

His's chest tightened, and he placed his hand over his heart, rubbing the spot.

Yeah, I would like that.

We should talk, John.

Agreed.

Send me a picture.

He blinked, blushing some more.

I'm with Reyes for the day, cleaning out his garage. And I wouldn't mind thinking of something other than dust bunnies and possibly rats.

John chuckled and snapped a picture of himself, uncaring that he was still wearing his glasses, and sent it.

Wyatt's response was quick.

Jesus. Those slutty glasses make me so fucking hard.

He scrubbed a hand over his red cheeks, giggling like a damned schoolboy.

And your smile… I'm obsessed with the crinkles around your eyes.

Heart doing rollercoaster swoops, John texted, deciding to be as bold as Wyatt.

Send me a picture. I'd like to see you sweaty and covered in dust bunnies.

Yes, sir.

The picture Wyatt sent him had blood shooting to his cock, and he nearly yanked his phone away, as though seeing something he shouldn't. Except it was sent to him—*only* for him. Wyatt had lifted his shirt, revealing the hardened muscles of his torso and the sharp V lines that ran down to the hemline of his jeans, which John was tortuously envious of and infatuated with. He let out a strained breath, staring a little too long at those heavily defined muscles.

The next picture Wyatt sent was of himself, but wearing not his white cowboy hat, but a trucker hat, backward, his hair messily sprouting around the edges of his ears. His playful smile was mischievous, intentionally teasing John.

Feeling utterly reckless, John texted.

Good boys don't tease their daddies.

He reached for the sheet covering his semi-hard on and began stroking it to life, looking at the image of Wyatt in that sexy fucking hat. Deciding to bait back, he snapped a picture of his hand over the sheet and sent it.

A second later, Wyatt was calling him on video. John nearly laughed and answered it.

Wyatt's voice was clipped and low, "Don't say anything."

He watched as Wyatt walked through Reyes's garage and out onto a driveway, his beautiful face illuminated by the sun, his skin sweaty from moving boxes all morning. "Reyes, where's your bathroom?"

"Yeah, man, straight through the dining room and down the hall on the left."

"Thanks."

Wyatt, without looking at the screen, moved quickly through the garage and into the house. John, smiling like an idiot, scrubbed a hand at the back of his neck as Wyatt made it to the bathroom, closing and locking it behind him.

Panting, Wyatt finally looked at the screen—at him, their eyes locked. "Fuck. You kept the glasses on. Thank God."

John, pulse racing, watched as Wyatt set the camera down on the bathroom sink and began unbuckling his jeans. Was he really about to…?

"Seriously?" he asked, astounded, watching Wyatt's fumbling hands over his own jeans, eagerly reaching for himself.

"Seriously," Wyatt husked. "You started this."

"Oh, absolutely not, *you* started this."

"Yeah," Wyatt let out a tight, suppressed groan, hand fisting around his cock. "I may have wanted to see what you'd do."

Oh fuck.

He watched the younger man's primal, unashamed display as he yanked off his hat, followed quickly by his thin white T-shirt, giving John exactly what he wanted.

"Put the hat back on," John croaked, causing Wyatt to smirk, eyes heatedly glancing back at the screen before slipping the hat on and rotating it backward.

"Good?" Wyatt asked in his low, timbered tone.

"Good," he panted, desire trickling down his spine like warm water at how much Wyatt seemed to like—no, need—to please him.

"Let me see you," Wyatt demanded.

John flipped the screen around, pulling back the sheet and revealing his hardening erection.

"No," Wyatt said breathlessly. "I want to see all of you."

He shivered at the sexy drawl in Wyatt's tone, quickly arranging the pillows and sitting back against the headboard, making sure everything could be seen.

"Good?" he asked, settling into the position, refusing to feel self-conscious about how exposed he felt under Wyatt's scrutinizing gaze. He lifted his knee, widening his thighs apart and stroking his thick cock in his hand, already beginning to breathe hard.

"Good..." Wyatt horsed out. "Damned good."

John dropped his head back, eyes low and on Wyatt's, as they both stroked themselves, looking at each other.

"Talk to me," Wyatt murmured. It sounded strained and laced with need.

He realized what he was asking, and he expected to feel that flush of embarrassment, but didn't. Seeing the stark hunger reflected in Wyatt's expression inflamed him.

"Show me," John ordered coolly, indicating with a dip of his chin to his cock. Wyatt obeyed immediately, withdrawing himself from his jeans, revealing his beautiful sex, which was already leaking with precum on that perfect, thick tip.

"Good boy," he hummed, stroking himself in tandem with Wyatt.

"Fuck." Wyatt leaned over the bathroom sink, fingers gripping the smooth marble as he thrusted his cock into his clenched fist.

"But you weren't a good boy this morning, were you, baby?" John growled, bolstered by Wyatt's reactions to him.

"No..."

"You left to move fucking boxes."

"...so... fucking... stupid," Wyatt groaned, pumping himself, back arching.

"You're not stupid, Lawson," John said, shifting into his Dr. Donnelly tone. "You made a mistake, we all do. This feeling is a teachable moment. Remember this for next time, so you know not to leave when you're wanted."

Wyatt's panted, whispered moan rasped through the phone speakers. He was attempting to muffle the sounds he was making for John, and something about that fact aroused him even more.

"You wanted me to stay?" Wyatt's eyes flickered to his.

Impaled by his gaze, John realized that this wasn't part of the dirty talk. Something was telling him that a small part of himself, the sensitive one he had locked down years ago, was demanding to be heard—to speak.

"Always," John admitted in a rush, cheeks burning from the furious blush staining his cheeks, but he didn't want to stop and think about how wrong that had been. How vulnerable. His hand matched Wyatt's pace, mimicking the hard stroking. His thighs and cheeks clenched, feeling the build between his legs and the tightening around his balls.

"Me too," Wyatt replied, his tip leaking over himself. "I want you so fuckin' bad it hurts."

John's heart fluttered like a storm of butterflies through his entire body. His legs widened, body throbbing with pleasure, and something else—something primal, something carnal. "If I were there… I'd be fucking you. God, I wanna fuck you…"

"Yes."

"I'd bend you over that sink and fuck you so hard that you wouldn't be able to bend over without feeling me still inside you."

Wyatt shuddered, his back muscles trembling, gripping his dick. "Yes… fuck yes, daddy."

The word ripped through every muscle in his body, and John's cock nearly spurted too soon.

Daddy!

Fuck, it felt so wrong and yet so goddamned good.

Oh, sweet fuck.

"But I wouldn't give you the pleasure of coming in your ass…" John growled, dragging his hand over himself, barely hanging on. "You'd be on your knees, my cock muffling your moans as I came down your throat."

Wyatt bucked, jerked, and climaxed. His hips arched upward as cum coated his fist and sprayed messily all over Reyes's bathroom sink. His cowboy was panting and cursing, and John hummed, riding his hand, feeling his tip beginning to pulsate with a tingling rush.

Wyatt's eyes were riveted to the screen, lips parted and chest heaving with breath, watching.

"Wyatt..." John's throat worked to swallow, the air constricting in his chest as he was on the verge of climax.

"Say it again," Wyatt said softly, voice strained with something vulnerable.

His orgasm came swiftly and punishingly, unleashing a torrent of hard waves of spine-tingling sensation. "Wyatt...!" He yelled, his tip erupting with such power that his body spasmed.

"That's it," Wyatt cooed darkly. "Say my name when you come for me, daddy."

He cursed, shivers racing all over his flesh at the 'daddy' title, and waited for the shame to override his common fucking sense. And yet, it didn't. He didn't want to shame himself for enjoying how much he liked hearing Wyatt call him that.

"Jesus, you're so sexy," Wyatt murmured. "If I were there, I'd lick up the mess you just made screaming my name."

He smiled bashfully, scrubbing his clean hand over his face beneath his glasses and sighing.

"You're coming with me tonight to this art show, then we're going back to your place to finish this," Wyatt said firmly.

He nodded, "Yeah."

"I don't know how the hell I'm supposed to get through the rest of the day without getting hard thinking about what we just fuckin' did."

John laughed weakly, tears forming at the corners of his eyes for some reason, suddenly grateful that Wyatt's perceptive gaze couldn't see that closely through the phone.

"You okay?" Wyatt asked quietly.

"Yeah, I'm fine."

He stared, eyes narrowing.

"I'm good," John insisted. "Go."

Wyatt hesitated before saying, "I like it when you call me by my first name."

He swallowed the lump in his throat, unable to look away at all the raw, honest vulnerability in the younger man and wishing he could be more like him, more honest with himself and everyone around him. A life without armor, John wondered, marveling at the possibility.

"I like it even better when it's in bed." Wyatt's smile widened into a mischievous grin.

John laughed, feeling content and… "God, I like you."

Wyatt froze, and so did he.

Oh fuck!

"Shit, I—that's not what you meant—I…" John fumbled, panicking, grabbing clumsily at his phone, needing to end the call.

Fuck!

"John."

No.

"John…!"

He managed to hang up, cursing angrily at himself. Flipping off his glasses and pushing his fingers into his eyes, he let out a groan.

What the hell was he thinking? He wasn't. He was in full post-orgasmic glow and admitted to something that had been swirling inside him since—well, since the moment Wyatt had first kissed him.

He liked him. A lot. And he knew it was bad because he told himself that he wouldn't do this. That he wouldn't get involved with someone who would eventually leave, because everyone always did. And Wyatt especially wouldn't want a future with him—how could he? John was old, broken, and… fuck. Wyatt deserved a king. Someone who could take care of him the way he took care of others. Someone like him, adventurous, fun, and full of life. Because he had so much life to live. He couldn't possibly want to settle down with a nearly 50-year-old burnout doctor who looked forward to boring nights sitting out on his patio, drinking wine and looking at the stars.

Wyatt's future was bright and big.

And not with him.

John blindly headed to his shower and heard his phone vibrate, alerting him to a call. He ignored it, knowing it was possibly Wyatt.

Shame ate away at him underneath the hot spray of the shower, and he hated himself for being so vulnerable, so stupid. They both agreed to the terms of this situation, and he had declared that if feelings were caught, it would have to end. But he couldn't give Wyatt up, and it made him feel so weak to admit this to himself.

John scrubbed a hand over his face, lost in conflicted, raging emotions.

He felt like a tiny boat caught in a storm at sea, rolling between two crushing waves. One wave made him feel as if he could touch the clouds and the sky above him, elated and happy because of a very clear emotion that gripped his heart like a vice.

But he couldn't acknowledge that emotion. It was too dangerous. The next wave slammed into him, nearly making him gasp at the drowning fear that plunged into the pit of his stomach.

Finally, after a long scalding shower, he walked back into the bedroom and saw the missed call on his phone. Gritting his back molars, he checked it and saw that it wasn't Wyatt—it was Justine, his sister.

He opened it and saw the text message from her.

"We'll be at the cemetery at 10. See you soon."

A heavy anvil dropped onto his chest and he glanced at the date on his phone. Guilt rippled through him and he cursed himself for forgetting.

Today was his brother's birthday.

Chapter 13

John

The yellow flowers were remarkably bright against the dreary gravestone. He marveled at the bouquet Olivia had picked out for today. Jacob would've loved them, he thought, pushing his aviator sunglasses higher up his nose and smiling softly. Olivia made herself busy with the pile of leaves beneath the oak tree a few yards away from Jacob's gravestone. Sunlight shone brightly over the cemetery's well-manicured, lush green lawn. The brilliant blue sky was clear for the first time in days. He inhaled the cool autumn breeze, trying his best to relax, but it was difficult to do that here.

Justine felt frazzled, her messy, curled hair pulled back into an even messier bun. She sighed, "I swear to God that child is making me gray and likes it."

He smirked, "Olive just knows what buttons to push."

"Because I planted them," Justine grumbled. "She's a mini-me."

"Yes, she is," he concurred, glancing between them. Olivia's dark blue eyes crinkled in a giggle as she dove for her doll and dinosaur in the pile of leaves, curly hair swishing behind her.

"No Chad today?" he asked.

Chad was Justine's husband, who he assumed was with their infant son. Justine had named him after their late brother, but everyone called baby Jacob "Jake."

Justine's eyes flipped restlessly between her daughter, the gravestone, and back to John. "I love my son, but that boy has attachment issues. Won't let me pee without screaming his head off. Chad took him to Mom and Dad's. Mom..." she paused.

John finished her sentence, "couldn't be here today. I know."

"It's too hard with dad."

"Oh, I'm aware," he replied gently, unsure if he could hold both his dad and Jacob in his mind at the same time today.

Justine's fingers brushed his hand, and he exhaled the breath he hadn't realized he was holding. He squeezed her hand in return.

Her face was a reflection of his, just a few years younger. And his face would've been a reflection of Jacob's had he decided to live. The three of them had looked so similar growing up that they were dubbed the Donnelly trio, which always sounded like a garage band name to John. The only difference between them was the hair. Justine inherited their father's curly, messy locks.

Justine had a youthful glow about her today, especially under the sparkling autumn sunlight, the sprinkling of freckles on her nose and cheeks adding to her beauty.

He leaned down and kissed her temple, pulling her beneath his shoulder, his arm draped around her. "Is it your turn or mine?" he asked, as they both squared up before Jacob's gravestone.

"Yours... I think. I dunno, mommy brain."

"It's okay. I'll do it."

She dropped the side of her head onto his chest. "Good. You're better at this than me."

"Whose judging?" he asked teasingly.

"Me."

He chuckled. "Alright..."

He stared down at the black and white picture of their brother, Jacob Donnelly, eternally captured in marble and stone. The picture was taken when he had just turned 21, and the whole family went down to Santa Barbara to celebrate his birthday. He was in college, at the beginning of his life, with a beaming, handsome grin as he stood on the beach. He was so young, so full of spirit and light.

"Happy fiftieth, you old fart," John drawled, causing Justine to let out a snort of laughter, elbowing him in the ribs.

"Serious," she muttered.

"He never was."

"True, but still."

He sighed, "We miss you... Every day." His throat closed, and he cleared it. "We know you miss us too, and one day in this grand universe, we'll all be together again. But until then, thank you for bringing the laughter into every conversation, especially the serious ones. Thanks for being the best big brother we could've ever asked for. I'm sorry we couldn't..." he paused, thinking about his last conversation with Jacob, and how often over the years John had tortured himself for it. But eventually, he had forgiven himself. And deep down, he knew Jacob did, too.

Eyes brimming with tears, he blinked hard, feeling himself resist his emotions.

And then he heard Wyatt's voice in his mind.

"You're a storm that gives and vanishes... Don't vanish..."

For the first time in his life, John gave himself permission to cry.

Justine leaned back to glance up at him, concern etched on her face.

"I'm—" Fine? No. He wasn't, and he wasn't going to say that. "I'm sad."

She nodded, hugging him closer. "Me too."

Heart opening, John began again, this time meaning every word. "In case you can hear us, wherever you are, we forgive you for leaving us. We know you didn't want to. We will always love you no matter what," he whispered, squeezing his sister against him. "Justine could've used an extra uncle to help with the kids…"

She laughed, her tears glinting in the sunlight. "So true."

They stood there a moment longer, holding each other and letting the tears fall.

"It feels weird without mom and dad," Justine confessed.

"They're here in spirit. We can pick up some ice cream or hot chocolate on the way back. I'm sure Olive would like that."

Justine arched her head back, scrutinizing him. "You're being awfully nice today."

"I'm always nice." He sounded peevish even to his own ears.

"Not lately…" she said with a long sigh. "I dunno how to say this to you, but I want to."

"So just say it."

"This last year, you've kinda been a dick."

He snorted and rubbed his knuckles through her hair. She yelped, shoving him away. "You're gonna mess up my mess!"

They both laughed. Olive popped up from the leaves roaring with her dinosaur, the doll's head severed from her plastic neck.

"Doll's gonna need surgical," he commented drily.

"I like you like this," Justine said, a genuine affection in her tone. "Whatever you're doing—keep doing it."

He blinked, averting his gaze and feeling an unexpected blush form on his cheeks, immediately thinking about Wyatt. "Sure thing, captain."

Justine stepped forward, eyes widening, and snatched the sunglasses off his face. "Oh my God, you're dating someone?"

He opened his mouth to reply, then promptly closed it again.

How the hell was he supposed to have this conversation? He had secretly hoped that coming out to his family would involve several bottles of wine. He wasn't ready to have it in front of Jacob's gravestone, and yet he knew Jacob would've loved this. He always loved life's little or big surprises.

And this would certainly be a surprise.

Finding out that her brother, after forty-plus years, was gay. Because he certainly was after all the incredibly dirty, erotic things Wyatt had been doing to him for the past month.

"What the fuck?" Justine stared, incredulously. "You're supposed to tell me everything, that was our deal."

They were both in high school when Jacob committed suicide.

John was a senior, and Justine was a freshman. They took it exceptionally hard and made a pact on the day of their brother's funeral that they would always tell each other if something was going on, no matter what. They would be each other's 'first to know' phone call or conversation. Mom and Dad were relegated to second place from that day on. Not out of distrust or lack of love, but something about losing a sibling had changed their relationship, mostly for the better, bonding them in their shared trauma and going through the waves of grief together.

"You're right," John replied. "I should've told you."

"Who is she?"

His chin jerked back.

She.

Nope. Not a she.

"Is it someone you work with? Tinder? Bumble? Peacock—fuck if I know anything about dating apps these days," Justine rushed out.

"Maybe we can talk about it later…?" he suggested delicately.

Justine balked and then glanced around at the empty cemetery. "Are you serious?"

He shot her a stern look that would normally have medical students running in fear. But unfortunately for him, Justine was made of sterner stuff than that.

She folded her arms defiantly across her chest, waiting, intentionally tapping her fingers on her arm.

"It's complicated," he muttered, trying to stall the inevitable.

"What is?"

"My relationship."

"So, it *is* a relationship?" she asked, gaping.

"Maybe."

"What do you mean, maybe?"

"Justine," he said sternly.

"Johnny," she mimicked in the same tone.

He groaned, raking his fingers through his hair and then the back of his neck.

Just rip the band-aid off.

"Fine, okay, yes, it's a co-worker. No, we're not official because he's still finishing his residency."

Justine's face remained perfectly still, and he held his breath. Her silence felt deafening. He waited for several long heartbeats, wondering how she would react and hoping to hell it didn't hurt too much if she reacted badly.

"Say something," he croaked, his throat aching.

Justine's eyes held his, beginning to water, yet her expression was firm. "He?"

He simply nodded, unable to speak, never realizing how hard this conversation would be.

She blinked rapidly as though downloading and absorbing the information. "How long?"

"How long…?"

"How long have you known you were…" She froze, tears sliding down her freckled cheeks. "Why didn't you tell me? Did you think I wouldn't understand? That I wasn't safe?"

John's heart broke in his chest and he felt his own tears burn behind his eyes again. "That's not it. You know that."

"Then *why*?" she gasped with a sob.

He sucked in a breath, "I dunno why… I just…"

"You don't talk to anyone!" Justine snapped, her emotions breaking over her like a hurricane. "About *anything*, Johnny!"

He suddenly realized this had nothing to do with his sexuality. This was much bigger.

She let out a frustrated grunt and slugged him hard on the arm, making him step back, stunned and yet… not. They were both highly sensitive people. Where John could let his emotions run into a deep well, Justine was more of the flaming campfire that sometimes sparked and crackled when one least expected. It's why they balanced each other so well. Her willingness to show her emotions, without shame and without self-criticism, was always something he envied.

Wyatt also had this ability.

John blinked, wondering if he should stop fighting the emotions pent up in his chest, like a lake bearing against a dam, and just surrender and accept the way his sister could. The way Wyatt did.

Justine jerked a pointed finger to Jacob's gravestone, yanking him out of his thoughts. "Do you know how worried I was about you? How scared I was this past year, wondering if you… If I was gonna lose another brother?"

He stilled, jaw clenching like a steel plate, and realized in that moment that she knew all along how close to the edge he stood. "You know I wouldn't."

"Do I?" she hissed, tears streaming down her face.

"Justine…" he reached for her.

She shoved his hand away. "Why didn't you tell me?"

"I don't know," he admitted roughly. "I didn't know."

She blinked through her tears, "That's not good enough, and you know it."

He glanced toward Olive, heart hammering in his chest, seeing that his niece had stopped playing and was watching them, frowning. John swallowed hard and shook his head, averting his gaze from his sister, the first person in his life he couldn't lie to.

"This last year was hard," his voice tightened. "Really hard. I was drowning. I couldn't breathe. Couldn't sleep. Couldn't function unless I was at work, and even then, it wasn't enough. I didn't realize how far gone I was until Wyatt saw me. And then I saw him…"

John thought about that night at the bar, thinking of how lost he had been, how dark he had gotten. How dark he allowed himself to go. Yet he had been more nervous about Wyatt, shaking like a leaf, and when their gazes met and held, when their lips touched, everything fell away.

The dark edge that John had been standing up against vanished.

Because Wyatt was safe.

And his sister was safe, too. She always had been. But he had forgotten what that felt like because he'd been staring too long into the dark, and it had blinded him. And for some horrible fucking reason, John believed he had to cling to this darkness and push those out who wanted to help.

He supposed that's what darkness did. It made people irrational and difficult. Because the harsh truth was that this was *all* his doing.

It was John who had complicated his relationship with Wyatt.

John, who put up the arbitrary barriers and rules to keep Wyatt away from him.

John, who had become a silo, slipping into an echo chamber of darkness of his own creation.

And it took someone he didn't know, someone he didn't have to worry about or take care of, to see him in that darkness.

God, I'm a fucking idiot.

He scrubbed a hand at the back of his neck, heart sinking, and glanced once more at Olive. "You okay?"

She nodded, her wavy curls bouncing. "Are you okay, Uncle Johnny?"

Tears released, seeing her in a pile of leaves clutching her toys, then seeing his sister, mad as hell and face flushed with it, glaring him down while she cried—and then his brother's gravestone, cold and lifeless.

"Fuck, I'm sorry." The tension in his chest broke, and the cry that came forth was the same one he had in Wyatt's arms. "I'm so sorry, Justine."

Her lips curled into a deep, heartbreaking pout and she grabbed him, hugging him fiercely to her chest. Olive ran to them, flinging herself against them and beginning to cry, feeling her family's emotions.

After several long moments, Justine pulled back, kissing Olive on the top of her head, and looked up at him. "I'm sorry for my big reaction."

"Don't be," he reassured. "You had every right to be concerned. And I should've told you I was struggling. I should've known better."

"You are the kindest, most sensitive man I know," Justine said softly. "But you chose to be more compassionate to everyone else except yourself. I wish you would just take an ounce of what you give to others and give it back to yourself."

He closed his eyes briefly, seeing his last image of Wyatt, grinning like a fool over the phone and John admitting to how much he liked him, and how that brief vulnerability had made him run. Wyatt deserved better, and so did he.

Justine was right.

It was time to make a change. Starting with himself and accepting his feelings, no matter how messy, out of control, or disordered they were or felt. He couldn't be scared anymore. Fear was what drove their brother to the edge, and over it. Fear of never being enough. The shame, blame, and judgment that were universally felt by so many, and crushing to some.

And he was tired of letting that dark shame crush his light.

He was done hiding.

Done judging what he couldn't control—his sensitive, vulnerable heart.

He saw the flash of a white cowboy hat, and with a slow grin, his heart fluttered.

"I'm working on it," he replied, kissing his sister's forehead and then Olive's. "Let's get some ice cream."

Chapter 14

Wyatt

He was so damned nervous he thought he might vomit all over Jin's art gallery floor.

"Oh my God, stop it." Jin materialized out of thin air, holding two glasses of champagne and shoving one into Wyatt's hand. "Drink. You're making me nervous, and it's *my* show."

Wyatt polished off the entire glass in two gulps, letting out a chest growling burp because of the bubbles.

A waitress dressed in a fairy costume and carrying an empty silver tray walked by. He placed his glass on it, voice hoarse as he said, "Two more."

"Please, stat," Jin insisted, before rounding on him. "What's happening? You're sweating. Is this a panic attack in real time?"

"Yes—no," he gasped, sucking down air. "Maybe."

He glanced around at the art pieces, which were image after image of men. All kinds of men: thick, dark, furry, muscular, tattooed, pierced, bald, old, gray. And butt ass naked.

Naked. Naked. Naked.

And he unknowingly invited John to this. On their first official date.

The art show was a collection of photos capturing 'real men in the wild', with themes of exposure and natural masculine beauty. Every wall in the gallery was decorated with massive, blown-up art pieces that towered over them. The men in the photos were all doing something, whether in their kitchen making coffee, at home, or in public places like the library, at work, or at the grocery store.

And all Wyatt saw were the number of fleshy, hard, semi-hard, or deflated dicks.

So many dicks!

Some of the art pieces were over-exposed shots grouped together to make one person, or polaroids decorating a chandelier. One of the models was actually here, standing on a rotating centerpiece, also very naked, and being critiqued openly by viewers passing by. He was well defined, flawlessly built and hung like a horse, with a piercing right through his...

Oh, sweet baby Jesus.

Jin urgently waved down another waiter, who was also dressed in fairy wings and little else. He was carrying what appeared to be water in crystal glasses on his tray, and openly cringed at the sight of Wyatt, who self-consciously raced a hand through his sweaty hair.

"Vodka?" the waiter drawled, his mascara sparkling on his pink eyelashes.

Without answering, Jin plucked the entire platter out of the waiter's hands. "Thanks, honey."

The waiter gawked, looking offended.

"Shoo," Jin snipped, hissing through his teeth, prompting the waiter to dart away.

"Did you just hiss at him?" Wyatt asked, already grabbing two drinks off the tray.

"Yes, I did. She's a prickly bitch. She worked the last show." Jin frowned, watching him gulp down a shot. "I've never seen you this nervous."

"I should call him," Wyatt strained out, the vodka burning his throat, making its way to his chest. "I should warn him. Why didn't you warn me?"

Jin arched a thinly plucked eyebrow. "When would I have done that exactly? You are never home! It's like living with a ghost. I only know you exist because the coffee is rinsed out at night and magically comes back on in the morning."

"It's on a timer," he breathed, reaching for another shot.

Jin tilted his hips, blocking his hand. "Oh no, hon. Give your liver at least five minutes to catch up before you take another." Jin then drank two shots in front of him and handed the empty tray to another passing waiter.

"I don't see what the big deal is," Jin said, glancing around the warehouse space.

Its industrial design matched well with the sleek feel of the show and the people invited, who dripped wealth from their designer clothes, down to their fine, pointed heels. It was an eclectic group tonight. Ranging from reality TV stars to drag queens to CEOs with their trophy husbands or wives, and their mistresses on the other side. These were the type of powerful people who were open with their likes and dislikes, unashamed in how they dressed, who they fucked, or what they said. It was Jin's crowd, and sometimes Wyatt's. But he wasn't sure how John would react. A newly out older man who possibly spent more time in the emergency department than anywhere else.

It would certainly be a shock, Wyatt thought, hands on his hips, fighting the urge to pace. Maybe John wouldn't even come. He had ended their phone call rather abruptly.

Wyatt thought he'd been hit by the sun when he heard John admit his feelings for him. He burned from the inside out with pure, unfiltered joy, followed quickly by fear as he watched John panic and end the call before he could even reply.

John kept closing him out, and he wasn't sure how he felt about it anymore.

He wanted to be patient with John and knew it was the best strategy. But just because he knew he should do something didn't mean he actually wanted to do it.

Oh, and let's not forget the phone sex, because holy hell, Wyatt hadn't expected to come that hard. Maybe because it was rushed. Maybe because John looked so damned sexy, or because it was very taboo to do in his friend's house. Regardless, when he did climax, he momentarily stopped breathing, seeing spots in his vision and coating Reyes' bathroom vanity with his spent, creamy bliss.

It was dirty and hot, and he couldn't stop thinking about those slutty glasses John had worn for him, and his rich chest hair that Wyatt wanted to drag his nails through and take a nap on.

"I think I'm seeing spots right now," Wyatt muttered, mostly to himself, scrubbing a hand over his stubbled jawline.

"It's just a date, right?" Jin asked curiously.

Just a date.

If only.

Wyatt grimaced at his best friend, inhaling a deep breath and feeling the first indicator of alcohol warming his insides. He noted Jin's outfit then and smiled for the first time all evening. "Love the suit, by the way."

Jin beamed, immediately twirling, showing off his sparkling orange-red suit that shone beneath the lights. His tanned, exposed chest was seen through the sharp V-neck of his blazer, adding the sexy flare that Jin always insisted on. His jet-black hair was slicked back and his cheeks were freshly shaved.

"You look good," Wyatt said approvingly. "Do *you* have a date?"

Jin pouted, "I wish. Nope, just mama. She'll be here later. She can drink all these bitches under the table and then some. She's my ride or die now that she's finally accepted her out and proud son."

He chuckled, and his eye caught sight of a tall, attractive man standing with a group of people who were admiring the Polaroid wall. He was staring directly at him in the way a hawk would before pouncing on their prey. And then, as if to show he wasn't that obviously on the hunt, he winked at Wyatt. He knew exactly what kind of wink that meant in this crowd.

Jin suddenly let out a gasp, causing Wyatt to jump. "Oh my God, I think that's a Real Housewife. I need to say hello."

"I don't."

"Then stay here," Jin snapped, darting away and heading toward a group of tall, gorgeous women.

The second Jin left, Wyatt couldn't help but anxiously glance back toward the entrance, where the floor-to-ceiling windows overlooked the busy LA street. No sign of John yet. He pulled out his phone, hoping maybe he would've called or texted…

"Hey," a deep voice said, drawing Wyatt's attention.

He glanced up from his phone and saw that it was the tall guy who had winked at him. He bit back the urge to sigh, sliding his phone into his pocket and suddenly wishing he had a drink in his hand. At that moment, another waitress walked by with drinks, but the cups were darkly mismatched and had an array of decorated straws.

He stopped the waitress, "What are these?"

She smiled, bright green glitter adorning her youthful face. "Mystery drinks."

"With alcohol?"

"Duh."

"Fantastic." He reached for the purple one with the umbrella sticking out of it.

The tall man also took one, the bright green one with a twirly straw.

"I'm Conner," the tall man said as the waitress strolled away, her cat tail swashing behind her.

"Sorry, not interested, Conner," Wyatt said firmly.

Conner, to his surprise, smiled. And Wyatt realized in that moment how attractive the man was. Sharp, almost regal features, with dark black hair and a perfectly cut square jaw with a dimple in the middle. If he wore glasses and a boring suit, he'd be Clark Kent. But he wore a casual yet expensive long-sleeved black shirt and khaki pants with polished leather shoes. He screamed sex and money, and in that order.

"You'd be surprised how often I hear that," Conner said smoothly, taking a drink out of his curly straw.

Wyatt arched an indifferent eyebrow.

He'd been hit on plenty of times since moving to LA and traveling in the same circle as Jin. He blamed it on his boyish good looks, his dark, sandy blond hair, and his cowboy boots. Tonight, however, he left the cowboy side of him at home and wore an all-black finely cut Italian suit that molded to his body like butter. He had to admit, after putting it on, he rather liked dressing up. The blazer fit a bit snugly over his biceps, but everything else was perfect despite not wearing it for a couple of years.

"You related to Glenn Powell? Maybe that Jake-something-actor?" Conner drawled, tonguing his straw.

Wyatt bit his back molars. "Have a good evening, Conner." He clipped out and attempted to leave when Conner snaked a quick hand over his wrist, stopping him.

"Aw, c'mon, I didn't mean to offend, just trying to have a conversation."

"And I already told you I'm not interested. Now, please, if you would, kindly let go."

Conner didn't, and Wyatt was about to yank free when someone cleared their throat loudly, and he glanced toward the sound, recognizing those dark, hauntingly blue eyes instantly.

"Hope I'm interrupting," John said with that half-smile that didn't reach his eyes as he glanced at Conner.

"Let me help," John said in his doctor tone as he casually leaned forward, grasping Conner's wrist and forcing it off Wyatt's, but he didn't let go. "You know, the wrist is a delicate thing, especially the older we get. Usually due to bone density loss or muscle overuse. With the right pressure here and… here." John realigned his fingers over Conner's wrist, bending it backward and tilting up his middle finger as if to demonstrate. "I could snap a few bones, and your pitching season would be over before it's even started, Mr. Hobbs."

Conner Hobbs.

Wyatt's eyes widened in recognition. Hobbs was the pitcher for the LA Dodgers.

Holy shit.

Conner shook off his hold, pretending indifference, though Wyatt caught a glimpse of alarm in the man's expression. "I was just talking…"

"So am I," John said casually. "If you'd like, I could educate you on how easy it is to fracture a nose."

Conner's hand shot up defensively, taking a step back, but not before he glanced arrogantly at Wyatt, "Your loss, handsome."

"Not really," he drawled back, and Conner returned to his gaggle of fangirls and boys.

"Well, that was interesting," John said, amused.

Maybe it was the buzz filtering through his bloodstream, or the adrenaline of watching John literally threatening to break a pro baseball player's wrist for him, but Wyatt couldn't stop the big silly grin that tugged at his lips. "That was hot."

John's chest rumbled with a chuckle, the corner of his eyes crinkling in those deep lines, and Wyatt reached for him, unable to resist.

"Can I kiss you now?" He asked, a mere breath away from the man of his dreams.

John's amusement was replaced with an excited heat that thrummed through Wyatt's entire body.

"Please." The ache in his voice, the plea, had Wyatt nearly launching onto him, kissing him thoroughly, greedily.

John grabbed him by the front of his shirt, dragging him against him, returning the kiss with just as much force. Wyatt's ears roared with the thundering sound of his heartbeat, and he melted into him, fingers clawing through his thick, sexy beard.

A beard, he decided, John could never shave off.

He pulled back, catching his breath and flushed with desire. Those were the kisses they shared in the privacy of the hotel rooms, not in public. When he had asked John for the kiss earlier on the phone, he hadn't anticipated it to be a passionate one, but tame and appropriate for public viewing.

John seemed to be thinking the same thing as he said, "That wasn't the kiss I was expecting."

Wyatt grinned, "I'm marking my territory."

John's laugh lines crinkled once more, and fuck, it was dreamy. He needed to make his man laugh more often.

His man.

"I'm serious," Wyatt said earnestly. "You're a newly gay man at the gayest art show in LA right now. I'm not risking a single person here thinking you're available."

"I'm not, am I?" John asked quietly, eyes locked with his.

"No," he whispered. "Just in case you were wondering, I like you, too."

Emotion flickered across John's face, and he released him, fixing Wyatt's crumpled silk suit shirt and jacket. "Well, that can mean only one thing, Dr. Lawson."

Wyatt watched the transformation to Dr. Donnelly, and his cock thickened between his legs.

"We agree upon treatment and should proceed accordingly."

"Which is?"

John licked his lips, intentionally keeping Wyatt close, as though unable to tolerate the slightest amount of distance. "We date. Go out. Fuck, as often as humanly possible. And we forget the rules. They don't matter anymore."

His heart skipped, lungs constricting with an elation he wasn't anticipating. Did he really mean it? Did he want to date—openly? Without the stupid rules caging them? Hope pierced through his chest, getting far too close to his heart.

John swept an appreciative gaze over his body. "I haven't told you how good you look yet. And fuck..." he drawled out that word, lighting the match to the gasoline in Wyatt's veins. "You look good. Really good."

Wyatt, like a moth to a flame, inched closer, his stomach swooping. "You like what you see, daddy?"

John sucked in a breath, eyes dilating at the title.

Wyatt liked seeing him squirm with desire. He wondered how hard his cock was, because Wyatt's was, and he liked this teasing game a little too much. He glanced heatedly over his body. John wore a light blue suit in a muted shade that perfectly matched his dark brown hair and complexion, paired with an open white V-neck shirt beneath and tanned loafers. He looked like he just walked out of a magazine shoot.

"I like what I see, too," he breathed, fingers itching to take what was his.

John suddenly stepped forward and kissed him hard. "You're killing me, baby," he rasped against his lips. "This is supposed to be our first date. But you make me wanna drag you into the nearest fucking closet and... *fuck...*"

John kissed him again before tearing his lips away, taking a giant step backward. Heart galloping like a stampede, Wyatt shot him a mischievous grin, which John returned, looking rakishly bashful.

He loved John's duality—one moment being strong, confident, and effortlessly masculine, to the next being gentle, modest, and ridiculously cute.

John lifted curious fingers to his lips, his head tilting. "Is that vodka and cranberry juice I'm tasting?"

Heat pooled into Wyatt's veins, liking that John knew what the inside of his mouth tasted like. "Yeah, it was a mystery drink."

Wyatt spotted the waitress with the cat ears and tail and waved her his way. John smiled politely at her, choosing the bright pink drink from her tray.

"That's my favorite," cat-ears said. "Rum, mango blend."

"Wonderful, thank you."

"The pink matches your outfit too, Zaddy," she cooed, biting her lower lip and eyebrows wiggling before sauntering away.

John laughed. It was loud, easy, and so fucking delicious that a few heads turned in their direction, and Wyatt had the absurd urge to throw a blanket over his head.

"Oh God, it's already starting," he moaned, pinching the brim of his nose. "I can't take you anywhere. You'll be eaten alive."

"I don't get out much, if I'm being honest. So far, this is great."

"New rule..." Wyatt declared, resisting the need to flee the den of hornets.

John's eyebrows raised. "I thought we weren't going to have rules anymore?"

"You're right, we aren't," Wyatt replied, using his own official doctor tone, "Complete transparency between us, here on out. Agreed?"

"Agreed," John nodded. "I can live with that."

"Okay, so, here it goes. Truth is, I had no idea that the art show was like *this* when I invited you," he said, cringing slightly.

John unexpectedly chuckled, rubbing the back of his neck. Wyatt decided that this flustered neck rub that Dr. John-Fuck-Me-Please-Donnelly did was his latest obsession.

"I'm fine with it," he said genuinely, glancing around the art gallery.

Surprised, Wyatt stared, "Really?"

"Really."

"So, this doesn't—uh, make you uncomfortable?"

"Why would it? We see all kinds of people all day long. These are just photographed well and not maimed, broken, or bloodied."

"True." Wyatt nodded, realizing that he should have known John would respond so well. He was kind. A trait that many people overlooked. He appreciated John even more for it now.

"I'm glad you're here," he admitted softly.

They stared at one another, and Wyatt wanted to kiss him again.

"Me too," he replied. "I'm sorry for how I ended our call today."

"Don't worry about it."

"I *did* worry about it," John whispered, stepping closer. "A lot, actually. Because even though I didn't mean to say it, I meant it. I like you, Wyatt. I do. And, I'm sorry for the rules. I thought that by making them, it would protect me from getting attached to this," he glanced from his lips to his eyes, "to you."

Wyatt's stomach swirled like a dust tornado.

"The problem is, it didn't work," John admitted. "Now, I think it's time we had fun together, outside the ED and bedroom." His fingers reached for his, grasping and squeezing.

Wyatt realized that John was asking without words to hold his hand.

His heart fluttered and he swallowed, nodding, and together they took a tour around Jin's art gallery. And Wyatt was pretty sure he was walking on clouds, never feeling this light before in his life.

They tilted their heads to the side and slowly backed up, trying to find the right angle for the overexposed portrait of a gymnast doing a back-breaking bend, nude, with a black-and-white studio in the background.

"Double-jointed," John declared. "Gotta be."

"Maybe just really bendy," Wyatt replied, tilting his head to the other side to see how the man managed to arch so deeply. "Or missing a couple of ribs?"

John hummed, considering, looking mildly impressed and amused.

They managed to get through nearly half of the gallery, taking their time, talking and laughing, holding hands, and sneaking glimpses at one another.

Wyatt had never felt giddy before, but he was now, and he couldn't stop smiling. Which he knew was ridiculous, but he didn't care. John was confident and utterly at ease with himself and everything around him. Wyatt had seen glimmers of this version of John when he first started working with him at the hospital, but over the last six months, John had gotten quieter, smiled less, and had become somewhat moody, if not irritable.

Almost as though a darkness had settled over him that he couldn't shake.

He wanted to know what had happened to him, but he knew they'd eventually have that conversation. Right now, he wanted to enjoy this—him.

"I believe at art shows, you're supposed to be looking more at the art than the person you're with," John commented smoothly, bringing Wyatt's hand up and pressing it to his lips, not taking his gaze off the gymnast portrait.

Wyatt flushed, feeling the bearded kiss over his knuckles.

It could be like this.

Just like this—with him.

Always.

Wyatt swallowed, emotion gripping his heart like a vice, wondering if this was...

"Jelly," a voice drawled behind Wyatt, making him jerk and spin, seeing Jin had gathered his art friends and had swarmed them.

Shit.

"Oh, my Daddy," a gorgeous drag queen said in a stunning pink sequin gown with matching high heels, her gaze raking up and down John's form.

Jin stepped forward, eyes darting between them, jaw unhinged.

Wyatt cleared his throat, "Jin—meet Dr. John Donnelly."

The group of art friends swooned over the title, and Wyatt immediately regretted it.

"More like Dr. Daddy," one of Jin's friends hummed.

"You know them both?" another friend from the group asked, amazed. "Jesus, I need to up my game to hang with you, Jin."

"You didn't tell me!" Jin growled angrily at him before shooting John a serene smile, "Hi." Jin then promptly twirled on his heel, hands whipping out in a flourish. "Ladies, do you mind giving us a sec?"

His group of friends sighed longingly and nodded, shooting Wyatt and John lingering glances before strolling away.

"Jin's my best friend and roommate," Wyatt explained to John, who politely held out his hand in greeting.

"Nice to meet you," John said, and they shook hands. "The art show is fantastic. Wyatt told me you curated the pieces. You have excellent taste."

Jin squirmed in delight. "Thank you. Glad you're enjoying it, Dr. Donnelly."

"Please, call me John."

Wyatt tried not to laugh at Jin gushing and could empathize with his bestie. He, too, gushed whenever John stared a little too long.

Jin's gaze cut icily to Wyatt's, narrowing a fraction. "You didn't mention *who* your date was, darling."

"Didn't know I had to, *darling*," Wyatt retorted smoothly.

"You should establish a safe word, right now. We're two hours into this showing, and queens are getting slouched. The daddies are always the first in line to be targeted, like Val Kilmer in jean shorts."

John let out a yelp of laughter and Wyatt rolled his eyes. "Fine, our safe word is…"

"Cardialgia?" John suggested.

Wyatt hummed, nodding. "Excellent suggestion, Dr. Donnelly. We can also consider proctalgia."

"Good physicians always have multiple strategies or possibilities…"

"Stop speaking in tongues!" Jin snapped. "I can only hold them at bay for so long."

"What about the after party?" Wyatt asked teasingly of his bestie.

"You're not serious," Jin shot back.

"Almost always, babe, you know that," Wyatt replied.

Jin's after-party last year had been legendary, mostly due to Wyatt's contribution.

Jin pushed his fingers into his forehead, shaking his head. "I cannot guarantee your safety."

"What's happening?" John asked, eyes bouncing between them.

Wyatt paused, frowning, "*My* safety?"

"I was going to surprise you," Jin sighed. "I booked the Bull Horn."

Fuck yes!

"What's the Bull Horn?" John asked.

Wyatt grinned, raking his fingers through his hair, wishing he had brought his hat.

Jin noted the gesture and crossed his arms over his waist. "Your hat is in my office. And a change of clothes."

He nearly danced in delight and grabbed Jin, bear-hugging him. "You *do* love me."

"I so do. It's awful. Let go," Jin muttered.

"Still don't know what's happening," John commented.

Jin smirked, "You're in for a treat, Dr. Donnelly. Show starts at 10pm, cowboy. Don't be late."

Chapter 15

John

The Bull Horn was a country dive bar with a mechanical bull smack dab in the middle of it, surrounded by a leather-cushioned fence and thick padding beneath. The bar was reserved for the rest of the evening for Jin's art gallery after-party. It was packed to the brim with sparkles, glitter, sequins, wigs, heels, and fans that snapped and flayed to life with wrist flicks and hair sweeps. John was mesmerized by the color and vibrancy of the people crowding around the bar and the bull as he managed to shoulder his way through to the bar.

He hailed the bartender and signaled for two beers.

Wyatt and John had entered the bar together, but once Wyatt was spotted, he was immediately pulled away by a mob of drag queens. Wyatt jumped up above the wave of fans and wigs, yelling out that he'd be right back.

John found an empty barstool and took a seat, turning it to enjoy the view of the crowd that had already begun gathering excitedly around the bull, which was worn and beaten-up. Its horns were worn down, capped, and flat, ensuring no one got stabbed if they went flying off the front end. The bull's hide was real, black, and freshly brushed. The brown leather saddle was strapped securely over its flank.

The colorful strobe lights danced all over the arena, illuminating it as country music roared from the stage speakers, which were decorated with cowboy hats, rope, spurs, and even a couple of pairs of leather chaps.

John arched his eyebrows, knowing Steph and Samuels would love this place. Maybe when Wyatt finally got his doctor's badge and residency finished, he could tell his friends about them and they could all come back here as a group. He smiled at himself, enjoying the idea of eventually telling his friends, even his family, about Wyatt.

He pictured Wyatt at his side during the holidays with his family… saw him move in—living with him, sleeping in his bed, together. He'd never have to come home to an empty house again.

His throat tightened, and he blinked rapidly as the emotion bubbled up.

It's been one date, John. And we're still on it.

Don't mess this up and start thinking too far ahead.

But he couldn't help it. Everything just felt easier being around Wyatt—natural, even. He couldn't remember how long it had been since he laughed this much.

"Ladies and Queens," Jin announced from a microphone on stage, drawing his attention. Jin's wonderful pink glasses framed his face and his confidence oozed from him as he walked the length of the stage that sat behind the bull arena. "Welcome back to the Bull Horn!"

Cheers erupted from the crowd, followed by whistles and shouts.

"I'm so glad everyone could come out and support not only the art, but the artists. This year, we've raised over twenty thousand dollars on behalf of the Queer Love Art Collective!"

Another round of applause broke out, and John caught a glimpse of a familiar white hat emerging from backstage, quickly making his way through the crowd toward the bar where John sat.

Jin kept talking about the art show and the people involved, but he heard none of it. All he saw was his cowboy, white teeth flashing in a grin over his tanned, stupidly gorgeous face, his sandy blond hair tucked beneath his white hat as he emerged from the crowd and spotted John.

He was wearing tight, light-blue jeans, a faded white T-shirt, a sizable golden medallion belt buckle, and… was his skin shining? Wyatt's exposed, muscle-bound arms glistened under the flashing lights of the bar and by the time he finally reached him, Wyatt was practically panting, grabbing the extra beer out of John's hand and taking a long drag.

John traced a finger over Wyatt's forearm and felt the silky oil.

"Body oil," Wyatt explained gruffly, setting his beer down on the bar. "For the fans."

"Fans—what?" John asked, trying hard not to gape like a fish.

"Fans—money, for charity. The better I look straddlin' and ridin' the bull, the more money we make," Wyatt said triumphantly, flashing him a grin.

"How many times have you done this?"

"Once, last year. It was my idea to do this as an after-party," he gestured to the mechanical bull. "Mostly for people like me who weren't interested in purchasing art but still wanted to donate." He edged closer to John, his pale blue eyes sparkling with mischief that licked up his spine. Wyatt slid between his legs on the barstool, invading his space. The smell of liquor, body oil, and musk filtered through his nose.

Jesus fuck, this kid is gonna kill me.

John tipped his head back, heat pooling low in his belly. Wyatt saw something in his gaze and moved closer still, their bodies brushing, and not a single person paid them the slightest attention. Here, they were free to touch, taste, and marvel.

"Last year, they made more doing this with me than they expected. So apparently, Jin and the gallery are making this the official after-party from here on out. They even brought in another guy to ride after me."

"Was it just you last year?" he asked.

Wyatt hummed, and somehow John felt it in his chest. "I can put on quite a show."

Something about the way he said it, about the confidence radiating from him, lit a fire beneath John that he felt in only rare moments in the ED, and now… with Wyatt. John, without thinking, without needing to, reached up and grabbed Wyatt's thin shirt and jerked him down, their eyes colliding and holding.

Wyatt's pupils dilated, capturing John's open mouth, spearing his tongue inside and nearly rocketing John off the stool.

Wyatt's lips peeled back, whispering heatedly against the shell of his ear, "You're the only ride I can't stop thinkin' about."

His cock reared to life and he gasped at the sensation of Wyatt's eager, urgent kisses at his neck, caressing him, sucking, licking.

"I ride first," Wyatt murmured breathlessly. "There's a trailer out back for the cowboys to change and go into if they take a hard fall."

John tensed.

"Which I won't," he reassured, grazing his teeth against his neck. "I do get a little worked up doing this, though…" he husked.

Holy fuck.

John, frozen to the spot, could only stare in wonderment at his sexy cowboy, letting his fingers clutch at his waist and wanting desperately to drag his body against his for friction.

"And if I do this right," Wyatt said between kisses along his jawline. "You'll be just as hard as I am when I'm done."

"I'm hard right now, cowboy," he murmured in a tight groan.

Wyatt cursed and sucked harder on his neck, bruising him, and discreetly slipped his hand between their bodies to feel the proof of John's desire.

"Fuuuck," he groaned into his ear, slipping the lobe into his mouth and biting. "I've never ridden with a fuckin' hard on before."

John gripped the back of Wyatt's neck and dragged him around for another searing kiss.

Someone moaned nearby, and a few others turned and started making squeeing sounds at their very public PDA. John blushed, pulling back, licking his lips nervously and touching the hickey on his neck.

Wyatt looked completely unbothered compared to how nervous he seemed at the art gallery. He wondered if it was the familiar environment of the country bar that gave Wyatt that much more swagger. Wyatt's chest was heaving beneath the thin white T-shirt, his eyes on the fresh hickey at John's neck and a slow grin crawling up his lips.

John's dick shuddered at his possessive, claiming gaze.

Jin's voice boomed out over the PA system, announcing Wyatt's name, and the crowd roared in excitement for their favorite bull riding cowboy. He dragged John off the barstool and led them through the crowd. His heart raced in his chest and his blood thumped in his skull, but he heard and felt none of it, focused only on Wyatt. He positioned John right outside the arena's padded wall, and without a word, slipped off his hat, placed it on top of John's head, then yanked off his shirt and tossed it into the crowd. The crowd yelled hungrily, demanding that he take off more clothing, to which Wyatt replied with a coy wink and a smile. He snagged his hat from John and kissed him hard and fast, before jumping the wall between them.

John raked his fingers through his hair, shouting over the crowd. "You didn't say anything about doing this shirtless?"

Wyatt's smile was pure sin. "Jealous, daddy?"

John's heart swooped into his belly, feeling Wyatt's heated gaze go straight to his cock.

"Good," Wyatt purred and sauntered over to the black mechanical bull, giving the crowd another flashy, handsome smile before climbing onto it.

The strobe lights went out in that instant and everyone grew louder, the lights flashing to life over Wyatt and the bull. His oiled, shirtless torso glistened, his hands firmly grasping the reins and legs locked around the bull, smiling broadly and tipping his hat, looking right at John.

John couldn't help but chuckle, scrubbing a hand over the back of his neck and blushing.

I'm so fucked.

"Well, ladies and queens," Jin drawled over the microphone. "This year, Wyatt won't be the only one on the bull. In fact, he's got some—*stiff*—competition."

Conner Hobbs strolled arrogantly out onto the stage, and the crowd roared again. John arched an unimpressed eyebrow as the young pitcher walked out in all black with a matching cowboy hat.

John, deciding to be petty, booed.

Wyatt noticed this and grinned affectionately at him.

Oh damn, kid, stop.

Stop making this so easy for me to fall for you.

The music began to play, and Wyatt shot Jin a firm look and shook his head.

John realized that Wyatt was protesting the song of choice for his 'show'. Jin rolled his eyes dramatically before hopping off stage, quickly running up to the ledge of the padded wall. It was far too loud for John to hear their conversation. Jin grinned wickedly, his gaze sweeping through the crowd and stopping on John. He winked, raced back upstage, and put on the new song. Apparently, the bar's DJ for the night also controlled the lighting, and when the song started, the lights matched the heavy bass tempo.

The mechanical bull came to life beneath Wyatt's legs.

The song pulsated with the same need that thrummed through the crowd.

It was Nine Inch Nails, *Closer.*

Oh, fuck me.

This wasn't a bull ride—this was for *him.*

Wyatt was showing off.

But he didn't have to. John was already rapidly falling without a parachute, if not already dead on the ground by the impact Wyatt had on him.

Wyatt's hips began rotating and flowing in the slow start of the beast he rode, his muscular body melding and moving seamlessly, effortlessly. The slow pace of the bull matched the song's beat. Wyatt's strong thighs gripped the bull more tightly and the bull began to slowly buck back and forth, the crowd crying out in elated cheers and whistles. John's cock jerked to life, and thank fuck he was standing next to the padded barrier, because he was getting harder by the second.

Jin waved to the digital projector screen behind him and hit the buzzer to begin the donation pool, using a QR code and a link.

"Tell this cowboy how goooood he is," Jin drawled into the microphone. "And donate your cute little asses off for this hunky bull ridin' man!"

John watched in amazement as a flurry of numbers began to rotate on the screen, the pride banner flying in the background and the name of the charity organization in bold letters at the top: *Keep Art Gay! Support LGBTQIA+!*

People beside John were fanning themselves with their snap fans, while others danced provocatively to the song's hard beat, all watching Wyatt. Whistles, cheers, catcalls, and money. It wasn't a charity ride—it was a strip show. He raked his fingers through his hair, wringing the back of his neck and shaking his head. He hoped to God that Wyatt didn't take any more of his clothes off, or John would have to tackle him off that bull.

He pulled out his phone, snapped the QR code, and added funds to the donation pool. Once he finished, hand still clutching the phone, he decided to give in to temptation and take a video of his cowboy, grinding into the bull in a way he could feel all the way down to his toes.

The song's tempo quickened, and the bull did too, which Wyatt anticipated, angling his hips up and down, matching the sway and buck of the mechanical bull. He lifted his hand high into the air and sat back, showing off his entire body in a way that made John's mouth dry.

The money poured in, and so did the cheering.

It was incredible.

He'd never seen anything like it.

Wyatt's grin fell into a sexy, furrowed concentration as the bull picked up speed again, and he continued to ride with one hand, thighs straining against the bucking bull. John was beginning to sweat, feeling the telling tingle between his own legs and imagining his cowboy riding him later.

He watched the primal display of his hard abdominal muscles rolling and tensing, his bicep flexing and arm tightening on the reins, his hat low and ass tight in his jeans.

"Sweet baby Yellowstone," Jin cooed into the microphone. "I think this cowboy likes to put on a show. But you know what he likes a hell of a lot more—praise. Give this boy some love, honey."

John tucked his phone away and listened to the outpouring of love from the crowd. Some were saying the most sexual, outlandish things, which weren't surprising, nor were they offensive, simply adding to the sexual drama of the show.

"Our cowboy Wyatt is spoken for this evening, ladies and loves," Jin announced.

The crowd moaned, and some applauded.

"A certain Zaddy whose praise this cowboy loves."

John gaped and the spotlight swung onto him, illuminating him on the spot, and the crowd went wild. He wanted to duck and run, but he was pinned against the wall, people oohing and aahing all around him.

"Tells us, Zaddy," Jin said, his voice only a subtle drawl, yet everyone in the audience heard him over the PA speakers and music. "Is your cowboy doin' a good job?"

John nodded, breathing hard, trying not to feel embarrassed, knowing he was literally surrounded by people who understood and celebrated them.

"He is for us, too," Jin remarked drily. "We are all envious of you two love boats! Look at y'all, for fuck's sake. This would be a rom-com we would all pay money to watch! We love a bearded daddy with his cute cowboy."

John scrubbed a hand through his beard, fighting back the telling blushes, yet his gaze was locked with Wyatt's, and his focused attention was heightened as the song peaked, coming to an end. The bull bucked wildly now, trying to throw him off. The crowd roared, encouraging him to stay on.

John joined in, clapping and hollering for Wyatt.

The song slowed, and the bull did, too. The digital numbers on the screen kept spinning, and finally stopped when the song did.

Wyatt straightened, waving his hand and beaming that perfect fucking smile of his, blue eyes flashing over the crowd. He slid off the bull, and without hesitating, raced right over to John, the padded barrier between them. Wyatt slipped off his white hat and put it once more on him, followed by a crushing, sweaty kiss.

The crowd screamed its approval, and both men smiled against each other's lips, seeing only each other.

Chapter 16

Wyatt

Jin announced the next bull rider, and the spotlight swung to Conner Hobbs.

Wyatt slipped over the barrier between them and said in a panted rush, "We have maybe five minutes."

John nodded, touching the brim of his white hat and grinning.

Fuck, he looks good in my hat.

He quickly tugged John through the crowd and to the side of the stage, where a backstage bathroom was located.

"What about the trailer?" John asked, noticing where he was being taken.

"I'm not gonna make it."

Which was true. Wyatt was so hard after that kiss and the ride, he was about to nut in his damned jeans like a teen, and he couldn't have that. Not when John was here, wearing his hat and looking like a dream.

He dragged him through the dark backstage and into the personal bathroom stall. It was like an airplane bathroom, with a built-in sink and toilet. Not much, but just big enough for both of them.

Hands shaking with adrenaline and desire, he reached for his belt buckle, needing to get his throbbing cock free. "I wanna suck your cock, but I don't think I can do it in here."

John laughed breathlessly, "It's okay."

"It's not," he grumbled, pushing him roughly around to face him, hand grabbing John's thickening sex and sighing. "I couldn't stop thinking about riding you on that bull. Hearing you moan for me..."

John let out a gasp, arching into his palm, his cock filling it.

"I won't last two minutes inside you," Wyatt admitted.

"I don't care. Just ride me, cowboy," John panted.

And that's all the permission he needed to hear. He spun John around to face the sink. Slipping his leaking cock free and spitting into his hand, he lubed the pulsing flesh, nearly groaning at the sensation of his own fingers. John made quick work of his pants and gave Wyatt his perfect, globe ass. He palmed it roughly, unable to stop himself. John moaned.

He manhandled John's sex, stroking it with a firm jerk, causing John to curse and latch onto the sink.

"I need..." Wyatt whispered into the back of his neck, sliding his slickened tip over John's tight asshole.

"What?" John gasped.

Wyatt spat again, rubbing his fingers over the tight rim and nearly shooting his load at just touching his clenched hole.

"I need to be rough, daddy, is that all right?"

John's head dropped between his shoulders, and he let out a tremulous breath. "Fuck yes."

Wyatt pushed his leaking tip into the rim, slipping inside just enough before driving home. John's moan filled the space between them, and Wyatt felt nothing but the sensation of the tightness gripping his cock like a squeezing fist. It felt so good being back inside him that his knees buckled and he was forced to grip the sink, his hands next to John's. Something about being on stage, the bull ride, and seeing John in the crowd, blushing and *his*, unraveled the hard knot in his chest that had haunted him ever since he left Arizona.

He always thought Arizona was the home he could never return to. And for the first time in seven years, he felt something he thought he had lost.

Home.

And now being sheathed deep inside John, listening to his panted moans and feeling his tight channel clenching around him, he realized he could never leave him.

He was completely, utterly ruined for this man.

"*Fuuuuck*," Wyatt hissed between clenched teeth as John arched his back against him and fucked himself on his cock.

Sweating and slick with body oil, he didn't want to ruin John's sexy blue suit. But John was writhing against him in a way that was impossible to ignore, and he reared back before pounding forward. He was back on the bull, driving his hips into him with that same hard, furious pace. John took it all, gasping and whimpering with need.

"Look at me," Wyatt demanded, dragging his fingers through John's hair and pulling him up, making his back arch deeper into him, hips widening.

John's haunting blue eyes were blown out with lust. Their eyes collided in the mirror, and Wyatt pushed the hat firmly on John's head, slipping his hands down his sides and to his waist, drilling into him with an unstoppable pace. The sounds of their dueling moans and slapping bodies echoed off the bathroom walls.

"Fuck, Wyatt," John whispered, fisting his own cock. "I wanted to be that fucking bull..." his confession shot straight to his cock, and his balls began to tingle. "I wanted your cock stuffing me. Coming in me..."

Wyatt's mind exploded, ingraining every breathy sigh, every word, burning them into his memory as his body responded with its own explosion, climaxing damn near violently. The orgasm was so brutal that he stopped breathing, shooting endless jets of cum into John's tight ass.

John bucked against him and reached behind him to hold Wyatt close to his shoulder, ass cheeks squeezing around him, milking out the last drop as both men gasped for air. They stayed exactly like that until his cock softened inside him, and unexpectedly, John reached further, his shoulder able to bend without pain or stiffness. He captured Wyatt's mouth with his and kissed him hungrily, thoroughly, lovingly.

Yes, yes…

Love me.

Wyatt nearly froze at the thought, and his heart slammed into the bones of his chest. He loved him. He loved John. And nothing scared him more than that reckless, wild emotion thrumming through his entire body, making him tremble.

"Are you okay?" John asked, breaking the kiss and searching his face with his warm blue eyes.

No. I'm fucking ruined.

I love you so goddamned much.

Wyatt slipped out of him, afraid John could see the love written all over his face. Without thinking, he dropped to his knees, shoved John's cheeks apart with his hands, and licked the cum off his tight, leaking entrance.

John jerked against him, reminding him of the bull, and he instinctively caught his hips, sinking his face further into his ass, tonguing him relentlessly now.

"Wyatt… baby… oh fuck… you're so… good."

Wyatt reached between his legs and fondled his balls and hard dick roughly.

"Shit." John grabbed onto the sink once more and sucked in a breath, letting Wyatt squeeze and suck and graze his teeth over him.

"You're gonna shove your cock down my throat and fuck my face after I'm done destroying this tight fucking hole," Wyatt rasped.

"Fuck-fuck-fuck...!"

Wyatt pushed both cheeks wide and licked him up and down the seam before pushing into the tight ring with his tongue, feeling the older man shake under his touch. But he wanted more. He wanted all.

He released him and turned, placing his naked back against the sink and forcing John to straddle his shoulders while standing, precum smearing his thick, red tip.

Wyatt swallowed, looking up at him. "Fuck my face. Use me."

John, breathing hard, nodded. He grabbed a handful of Wyatt's hair and guided his sex into his mouth.

They were impossibly close.

The small confines of the bathroom and its position forced Wyatt to be engulfed by this man. The musky scent of his sex filled his nostrils as he slowly thrusted down his mouth and into his throat. The way his fingers dug and gripped his hair, pulling and yanking. His body shivered. John's arousal and body's reaction to this was stunning. Perfect. Intoxicating.

It was so fucking hot that his own cock was slowly coming back to life. He liked the weight of John practically sitting on his shoulders, spearing his mouth.

Wyatt slapped John's plump ass hard, sucking at the same time. He gasped and bucked forward. Wyatt did it again on the other side, his mouth full to the brim with John's thick, beautiful dick.

He grabbed his globe cheeks roughly and dug his fingers ruthlessly into them, wanting to bruise his fucking ass with his grip, focusing John to thrust deeper down his throat, which he took, relaxing the muscles and gagging only a little.

John cursed heavily and let Wyatt guide him, curling his biceps as he pushed John's entire body forward, thrusting into his mouth over and over, saliva pooling and dripping from his lips.

"That's it, baby," John whispered, eyes intent on the movement of his thick erection sliding in and out of Wyatt's mouth. "You're perfect… you're…" his gaze held his, "Mine. You're mine."

Wyatt groaned, heart hammering, watching John ride his face, humping himself onto him.

"You want that, don't you, baby?" John breathed. "To belong to me… only me…"

Yes! Forever, if you'll let me.

He hummed instead, cock miraculously rehardening between his legs.

"No one else gets to know what your cock feels like but me," John husked, his tone low and edgy. "No one will ever know how good you are at sucking cock…"

Wyatt's grip hardened, sucking ruthlessly, causing John to lean into him, knees buckling.

"I want you all the time," John confessed. "All the fucking time…"

Wyatt finally fisted a hand over his cock and squeezed, unable to stop the building pressure and annihilating feel of this moment.

"Wyatt," he chanted like a prayer, his big, paw-like hands cradling his face as he came.

It wasn't rough like it had been, more like a revelation, exposing John for all his vulnerabilities and accepting it. Wyatt watched tears touch the corner of John's eyes as he unloaded into his mouth. He swallowed, milking him thoroughly and dragging every ounce out of his body. John stared down at him. "God, look at you, baby. So beautiful. So perfect…"

Wyatt shuddered, slowly slipping John's sex out of his mouth and gasping.

John flicked a lazy, gentle thumb over his lips. "I've never done anything like this before."

The affectionate way John was looking at him made him question if he was referring to the heady, frantic bathroom sex or something else…

Wyatt managed to get to his feet and pulled him into his arms, letting him rest against him. He shoved his aching cock back into his jeans, wanting to focus on John.

"You bring me to life in ways I never thought possible," John whispered, kissing his neck, his soft beard stroking him.

Wyatt wanted to hear every whispered confession, but not here. He pulled back from their embrace, fingers pressed against John's lips. "As much as I wanna hear more—and trust me, I do—anything said after an orgasm doesn't count."

John sighed and smiled, "Okay."

He sucked in a breath. "Okay."

"Come home with me."

"Yes, sir."

They stayed to hear which cowboy had won the evening's performance, which was, of course, Wyatt. Jin had intentionally played *Pony* by Ginuwine for Hobbs, and he only got half the amount of donations that Wyatt managed to earn.

"No one cares about *Pony* for Hobbs, because no one can outdo Channing," Wyatt explained before he went onstage to accept the roaring applause for his victory next to Jin, who thanked and applauded the crowd for their generous donations.

The bar gave Wyatt one of their souvenir shirts to wear home, themed for the evening reading: "Gay cowboys love me."

John picked up Mexican food on the way back to his place, and they gratefully demolished their burritos with a couple of glasses of wine, followed by a lovely shower together. After managing another orgasm under the hot spray of the shower, both men were thoroughly exhausted and stumbled into John's massive king-sized bed.

The silk navy blue sheets felt like heaven against Wyatt's naked flesh as they snuggled together. The weighted feeling of John's arm draped over him, the soft inhalation of his breath, and the silence of the house…

Wyatt didn't even remember falling asleep.

He felt the warmth of the sunlight on his skin first as he slowly opened his eyes, squinting initially at the dazzling rays of light peeking through John's blackout curtains that never seemed to be fully closed. He sighed and realized his cheek was resting on a deliciously furry, warm chest.

"Good morning," John hummed.

Unable to resist, he slid his fingers through his chest hair, loving the springy, thick feel of it. "Good morning."

"I haven't slept that good in a long time," John confessed, seeming to marvel at this fact.

"Multiple orgasms will do that to you." Wyatt kissed his chest, inching closer and casually tossing his leg over his, not wanting to leave this bed all day if they could manage it.

"Did you ride bulls as a cowboy?" he asked, his fingers tracing up and down Wyatt's naked back. "I was wondering that last night after watching you."

He shook his head. "I like my neck and skull where they are."

John chuckled.

"I never rode," he explained. "But Mateo took me to a couple of rodeo bars. I couldn't drink, but I could do that. He taught me how to line dance that summer, too."

"He sounds like a good man."

"He was."

"Do you think—had he lived—that you and he…?"

Wyatt knew what he was asking and had often wondered the same thing over the years. "I dunno. Sometimes I think we could've made a go at it. Other days, I'm not so sure. I think it would've been hard for him to leave behind being a ranch hand. It was his whole life. It wasn't mine."

"Have you talked to your father since he kicked you out?" John asked quietly.

"No," he replied with a sigh, knowing John wouldn't judge him for that.

"I have a confession," John said unexpectedly. "I may have spoken to your… um, Aunt Nancy the other day."

Alarm shot through his bloodstream like gasoline and Wyatt quickly sat up, "You what?"

John lifted both hands in a defensive gesture. "I'm sorry, I didn't mean to interfere with your family life, that's not my place. But she called the ED the other day, insisting on talking to you."

"So, you talked to her instead?" he asked, unable to keep the accusatory tone from his voice.

"I had to," Dr. Donnelly replied. "You were in with Samuels on a cardiac patient, and I had no intention of dragging you out to talk to someone who shouldn't have called the ED in the first place if it wasn't an emergency."

Air exhaled from Wyatt's lungs and the panic in his chest tapered off. "So—it wasn't an emergency?"

"No, it was not."

"What did she want?"

"To talk to you." John's eyebrows lifted, "She said you've been ignoring her calls and her texts. She sounded worried. Should I be worried?"

"Is this John or Dr. Donnelly asking?"

John exhaled, scrubbing his hand over the back of his neck. "Sorry, you're right. It's none of my business."

Wyatt folded the sheet over his lap, deciding it *was* his business. Or at least, he wanted it to be. "My dad isn't doing well."

John held his gaze, listening.

Wyatt's throat closed, and he cleared it. This was not how he wanted to spend his lazy day in bed with John. He raked his fingers through his hair, feeling inexplicably nervous. Normally, he was good at talking about his feelings with almost everything, except when the topic was about his father and the *real* reason he left home.

"He was diagnosed with prostate cancer a couple of years ago. The treatment was going well, last I heard, until it wasn't. Then my aunts started callin', askin' me to come back."

John straightened, shifting back against the headboard. "Is he…?"

"Dying?" Frustration swelled in his chest. "Probably."

"You don't want to see him?"

"I dunno," Wyatt breathed. "I dunno…"

He pushed his fingers into his eyes, deciding right then and there to give voice to the hurt that haunted him—the reason he'd been running ever since Mateo had died. He had never really felt settled over the last seven years, like a restless horse trapped in a stable, needing to run.

Just say it.

"I blame him for what happened to Mateo," he admitted. "And… I blame myself. I don't know if I can ever go back there."

John stilled, holding his gaze.

His fists curled into his lap. "My father worked those horses into the ground. Him getting cancer was the best thing for them." He knew it sounded cruel, but he didn't care. His relationship with his father was complicated and layered. He loved the old man, but in some ways, he hated him, too.

He glanced over the slope of John's neck, seeing the bruised hickey he had given him last night, and some of the anger released from his gut. Not at the sight of the bruise, but the shoulder. Seeing him so relaxed, no longer in pain, settled his raging heart.

"It's why I recognized what was happening to you. How burnt out you were," he said. "The horses would get like that sometimes. So beaten down by his grueling fuckin' schedule that they'd lock up—freeze. I spent hours at the barn after the ranch was closed, working those knotted muscles so they could walk pain-free the next day. Mateo knew what I was doin'. Didn't say anything about it. Had the best summer of my life, and then all hell broke loose and I was banned from ever coming back to the ranch—to those horses. I didn't even get a chance to say goodbye."

John reached for him, gently opening his fists and slipping his fingers through Wyatt's. His hand was warm and comforting. Emotion welled in his throat, hating himself still for what had happened all those years ago.

"Then one morning, I got the call about Mateo. That he had to be airlifted to the hospital. His back was broken because a horse fell on him," he gritted out. "But she didn't fall. She didn't get startled on the trail either, because she was the most fucking experienced horse on that ranch. She locked up on Mateo and fell, crushing him and breaking her shoulder. She was *my* responsibility. I should've told my dad she wasn't good to ride. Her shoulder was frozen," he admitted, and John's eyes widened in surprise.

The shame welled up inside him like a crushing avalanche, and he jerked his hand away from John's soothing touch. He didn't deserve it.

Wyatt pushed the palms of his hands into his eyes, refusing to imagine Mateo, strong and sure, broken beneath his favorite horse. Both were so scared and hurt, clinging to each other, neither of them knowing that the fall would be fatal for them both.

"They shot her in the head on the trail. Nothing they could do. They might as well have shot Mateo, too, because he died the second he got on that horse. And that's *my* fault. That's my father's fault. I knew, and I didn't do anything."

John's hands framed his face firmly, shaking his head, eyes intense. "No, you can't think like that."

"I can't *stop* thinking like that," Wyatt croaked out, painful tears finally breaking him. "It's why I can't go back there. I look at that dyin' old man, and it should be me."

"I'm so sorry," John whispered thickly, embracing him.

"It should've been me," he ground out harshly between sobs. "I should've been on that horse. I should've told him…"

"Wyatt, it's not your fault. It's not. Horrible things happen all the time. We see it at work every day. We can't put that on ourselves. We can't, or it will kill us."

Wyatt blinked through his tears, holding to his anchor—his rock. And yet, John wasn't perfect. He struggled, just like Wyatt, and there was something about that fact that calmed and reassured him.

"You're a good man," John whispered. "It's why Mateo loved you. It's why…"

John's words stopped short, and he leaned back, eyes clear despite the emotion reflected in the dark ocean blues. Wyatt stopped breathing, heart hammering so hard he was sure John could hear it.

John slowly wiped his thumb across Wyatt's face, chasing away a tear. "My older brother committed suicide when I was in high school."

Wyatt sucked in a breath, stunned.

"I was the last person he ever talked to," John admitted, grief lining his expression. "He called the house to talk to Mom. She was out with Dad, seeing a movie with our sister that night. I was at home because I was supposed to be studying for a test. But I wasn't. I was waiting for..." he shook his head, and his eyes crinkled with that half-smile. "The version of this story I usually tell is that I was waiting for my friend, James Day, to call. But the real version of events was that I was agonizing over my 'friend' calling. "Because I had a crush. My first ever, and I was so nervous and confused..."

John paused to drop soft, delicate kisses over Wyatt's knuckles. "I've never told anyone that. I was so ashamed of myself because I didn't want to talk to my boring older brother who was away at college. I couldn't wait to get off the phone with him. And Jacob, my brother, was in pain. He was suffering, and I had no idea."

Wyatt opened his hand, dragging John's open palm to his mouth and kissing it, throat aching from the story and unable to imagine the grief—the trauma—the blame he must have felt for a long time, never getting to be fully honest with anyone until now.

He understood now why John was so closed off. Because he felt responsible in some ways for his brother's death, the way Wyatt did with Mateo.

"I hated myself so much, for so long, that I buried that boy deep, deep down until there was nothing left of him." John's tears fell, and yet he wasn't fighting them this time. He accepted them, without shame, and Wyatt had never seen anything so strong, so beautiful in his life. "I thought that I had to do right by Jacob and give back to others, the way I should've given to him. I spent nearly my whole life in blame and shame, Wyatt. And I can tell you one thing that I have learned from it."

John's gaze impaled him. "Nothing. Because the truth is, I got to be the one who talked to my brother on the last day of his life. I got that. Not my parents or my sister—me. And I love the fact that my brother got to hear my voice before he left us. He got to hear someone who loved him, even though he couldn't love himself enough to stay with us. And that day you found me at the bar, I didn't believe anymore that I was enough..."

Wyatt stilled, fingers clenching over John's hand.

"Our minds take us to dark places. The shame will invade your thoughts, your feelings, and your memories if you let it. But you can't let it. I won't let you," John's voice broke. "This last month has changed me. You've changed me. I'm not selfish for wanting to talk to my crush instead of my brother. I'm not selfish for wanting you. And God help me, I want you. No, I need you, Wyatt. I need you here, with me, through all this shit—this pain—this crazy fucking life. So, please don't blame yourself for what you couldn't have stopped. You did what you could, and Mateo knows that."

Wyatt's heart broke and reshaped in that instant. He leaped into John's arms and held him close, the pieces of his heart melding together. His heart took on a new piece—a piece of John.

"How are you so good?" he asked, voice barely above a whisper.

John released a weak laugh, "I have no idea. Just born this way, I guess."

He searched his face, seeing the vulnerability and unease from sharing so much of himself so that he could ease Wyatt's suffering.

"Thank you for telling me," Wyatt whispered. "About your brother."

"I'm glad you told me about what happened. If you need anything…" his voice was a thready, wonderful rasp that reached into his soul and continued to soothe his wrecked, aching heart. "I'm here. I wanna take care of you too, you know."

He hummed, kissing away John's tears. "I wanna spend the day with you."

John smiled, lines crinkling around his eyes. "And how would you like to spend it, baby?"

"I have a few ideas."

"Please tell me it doesn't involve leaving this room?"

Wyatt grinned and they kissed, sinking into one another and saying with their bodies what they couldn't yet say with their hearts.

Chapter 17

John

"I've said this before, and I will keep saying it until you hear me: we need more nurses," John leveled at Tanya with an uncompromising gaze. "My team is working with a skeleton crew. With the nursing shortage and increasing demands from higher-ups, we're losing good people. People who want to help, but are shackled by the politics of this place, and insurance companies dictating what can and can't be done."

John leaned forward, snapping his reading glasses off and tossing the digital tablet filled with her charts and areas of 'improvement' onto the table between them.

Tanya's lips flattened. "That is not the point of this meeting, John."

"Then what is the point? If you want me and the people still willing to do this job to keep giving you more, I don't see how that's feasible. Especially not at the rate we're going. I can't remember if Dr. Walsh has actually taken any time off. He practically lives here because he doesn't have a consistent alternate for the night shift. Mendez, our security officer, is underwater most days, and we need at least two security officers at the door with another in the lobby. You wanna see our performance times go up, you gotta actually participate, not walk around and critique us at every turn. We don't need that. We need a full staff."

Tanya's shoulders straightened under her dull brown blazer. "I understand your concerns, John. I really do." Her placating tone was not helping John's mood.

The fact that he had to sit and endure this meeting first thing Monday morning was bad enough. But the real reason for his shitty mood was Wyatt.

John woke Sunday morning to an empty bed, after they had spent a glorious, mostly naked day in bed on Saturday, talking, making love, and napping. It was the best day he had had in recent memory and he had hoped Wyatt would stay the whole weekend. Maybe he should've just asked, but instead, he woke to an empty house. Not a trace of Wyatt was left, as if he hadn't even been there at all. And that hurt more than being left.

John immediately got dressed and went for a run. He had to get out of the house, to let the storm of the weekend's intensity wash over him. Sex with Wyatt was changing his fucking brain chemistry—hell, Wyatt was changing him, and he had admitted it to him.

John took to the dirt trail behind his home, winding up through the LA hills, absorbed in his thoughts. The pounding of his footsteps vibrated up his legs, reminding him of all the incredible things Wyatt had done to his body. He was sore from sex alone, and yet it thrummed with something else, too—something energetic that sparkled inside his chest and burned to be released.

He sucked in the chilly, misty air, letting the run clear his mind.

When he returned home and checked his phone, sweat dripping down his neck, he heaved a disappointed sigh at the empty screen.

Wyatt hadn't reached out. And he feared he wouldn't until he saw him at work on Monday.

John stepped into the same shower Wyatt had so carefully tended to his shaking, shivering muscles. He sighed, dropping his temple onto the cool tile, a painful constriction forming around his heart. He dug his fingers into his collarbone and down over his upper chest, attempting to release the tightness, but it didn't work. The band around his chest was unshakable.

Had he asked too much of him? Had he given too much? Had he scared him away? Fear and insecurity washed over him, leaving him unsure of what to do. John didn't let people in for this very reason. The pain of losing them was too much. He cared too much.

John had always struggled with his emotional sensitivity throughout his life. He was shamed for it a few times, both at school and at work. He was told to bottle and suppress it. Doctors don't cry, they contain. They're stoic, not vulnerable. They hold back their emotions, no matter how painful it is for them.

And yet Wyatt wanted to see it—feel it—hold him during it.

He wasn't afraid of his big emotions. He was fearless.

John, feeling achingly pathetic, played the commercial of Wyatt on the screen in his living room about a dozen times that lonely Sunday, watching and re-watching him charge ahead, boldly stopping a breath away from the edge of the cliff, and feeling even more ridiculous the more he watched.

Maybe he needed to be more fearless again. John pushed his fingers into his eyes, fighting back a headache.

His phone vibrated in his pocket. Hope flaring in his limbs, John reached for the phone and saw it was his sister. He released his breath and answered it.

"Hey," Justine said in a rush over the phone. "Sorry to bother you. I just wanted to plan Thanksgiving with you."

He paused the commercial, slumping back into the couch. "Yeah, of course."

"Are you working that day?"

"Yeah, of course," he repeated with a slight tease.

She sighed, "Right. Well, maybe next weekend then, instead?"

"Sure, sounds good."

"Your place?"

He paused. He had never hosted in his new home since his divorce—granted, he'd been living in it for over two years now and hadn't done much to it other than the backyard and the living room. His place was bare and needed life.

"With the kids, our house is a mess, and I don't have the energy to clean..."

"Absolutely," he replied, cutting her off. "I'll host, don't worry about it."

"Really?" She asked, unable to hold back the excitement in her tone.

"Really."

"So... how're things?" Justine hinted, changing the topic.

He glanced at the paused image of Wyatt, smiling beneath his black hat, sweat glistening off his perfectly tanned skin. "I'm all right."

"Johnny."

He leaned forward, pinching the brim of his nose, "Okay. Yeah, I'm not all right."

"Spill, now."

"I think..." His throat closed, and he nearly groaned. "I think I'm in love."

"You sound like you're being tortured!"

He chuckled, the tension easing from his chest. "It feels like it."

"How come?" she asked compassionately.

"Because… fuck, there are so many reasons I shouldn't be with him. He works under me—he could lose his position at the hospital, so could I. He might have to repeat his last year of residency. I might have to…"

Stop working in the ED.

The thought gave him pause, and he waited for the anxiety, the remorse of not being the attending at his hospital anymore. But nothing came. He was more concerned about Wyatt's future than his own.

"That's *if* the hospital finds out, right?" Justine asked.

He swallowed. "Yeah."

"Big if."

"I know."

"What about him?"

"What *about* him?" John asked slowly.

"Does he love you, too?"

His eyes flicked back to the screen and his belly tightened. "I…"

I hope so.

Fuck.

He scrubbed his hand over his face, "I don't know."

She sighed, "Well, I think you should invite him to Thanksgiving. Let mom gush and grill him."

"I haven't told her yet." Not about Wyatt, he thought, but that her son is gay.

"So? She's a grown-ass woman. She can handle it. She's handled far worse, Johnny. We all have. Who you love doesn't matter to us. This is your life. We'll love you regardless. You know that."

Emotion welled behind his eyes and he smiled, "It's always good to be reminded."

"I'll remind you every day if I have to because I have to meet the man who swept my brother off his feet." Justine paused, seeming distracted. "Sorry, I gotta run. Olive is trying to feed Jake a potato chip."

"I love you."

Justine's voice was lighter as she replied, "I love you."

He spent the rest of his Sunday organizing, cleaning, and unboxing the last of his boxes. It felt surprisingly good. He ended the day watching a football game, drinking a glass of wine, and thinking of how he was going to ask Wyatt to move in with him.

John's heart skipped in his chest at the mere thought.

This is so crazy.

And it was happening so quickly. But he wasn't sure he cared about social expectations or norms anymore. Not when it came to his happiness. Because Wyatt made him fucking happy, and he reminded him how to take care of himself again. If that wasn't love, he wasn't sure what was.

"...the fact of the matter is, John, that until your performance evaluations improve, we cannot start talking about staffing issues."

John turned his head back to the conversation in Tanya's office, frustration eating away at his patience. "Did you even hear what you just said, Tanya?"

She blinked.

"Did you even listen to what I said?" He asked incredulously. "How can we possibly meet your standards when we're working purely in survival mode? You're lucky Dr. Samuels, Dr. Walsh, and I don't walk out of this hospital and find somewhere else that will treat us like human beings instead of robots and listen to our concerns. We are the best doctors in this city, and you know it. You let us walk out because you refuse to work with us, and that will get around," John said firmly. "No doctor in their right mind would willingly come here and be put under the same pressures you are asking of us. I'm trying really damn hard to get you to wake up and work with me. Because out there…" he pointed to her closed office door, toward the emergency department. "People are going to die because you refuse to see the human element in all of this. You're too focused on arbitrary numbers and your bottom line. That shit doesn't matter. You can't tell me you got into medicine to crush a doctor's ability to save a life."

Tanya parted her thin red lips, about to reply, then sat back, her chin jutting out defiantly.

John sighed, his shoulders tensing, and he intentionally rolled them as he sat forward. "Look, clearly we want the same thing here, but we're trying to go about it in our own way, without consideration for the other. Why don't we try—just for five seconds, each sit in the other person's perspective, and see if we can't collaborate—not compromise—on a way forward."

Tanya's rigidity softened, and the taut lines around her puckered lips released. "All right, I think we can…"

The phone on Tanya's desk rang, and she glanced at it, frowned, and answered it. Her frown drew tight over her face.

"Police are on their way?" Tanya asked. He hesitated and watched as her eyes snapped to his before hanging up the phone. "There's a situation in the ED."

John got to his feet, unfazed, and heard Tanya fumbling with her chair behind him to follow. Emergency medicine never stopped.

He pulled his stethoscope out of his back pocket and slipped it over his neck, jogging down the stairs instead of taking the elevator, knowing it was faster. Steph was already waiting for him at the back door.

"Police are on their way," Steph informed him.

"I heard. Where's Mendez and the others?" John asked, steeling himself and preparing for whatever was waiting for him behind those doors.

"Mendez and his team can't get to him."

"Who?"

The doors from the hallway opened onto chaos.

Lights, sounds, screaming, crying.

Blood.

This was *not* a normal scene for his department.

The long hallway of the thruway that connected the nurse station and adjoining rooms was at a standstill. His eyes found Mendez, his larger body recognizable over his team. He was on his knees, holding his nose in both hands, with Ava at his side, shaking.

Reyes was standing beside a large, beefy man with tattoos covering his exposed arms. He had a shaved head and a Nazi symbol on his chest, which told John everything he needed to know. Reyes had his hands out in a defensive gesture, his upper lip swollen and his eyes focused on the surgical knife in the man's hand, which was pointing directly at...

John's heart stopped.

No.

Wyatt's body was unusually stiff, as though his survival instincts were telling him to freeze at the sight of the predator who had him in his sights. The large bald man with tattoos held a knife to Wyatt's throat, blood already slowly seeping from beneath the blade.

No!

John stepped forward, unable to stay back.

"The police are almost here, John," Steph whispered frantically, grabbing his arm and attempting to stop him.

"We don't want any more violence, sir," Wyatt's voice dropped into that steady, deep octave. The same voice that soothed horses, patients, and John.

The tattooed asshole with the knife snorted angrily through his large nostrils, glaring at Wyatt.

"We're just tryin' to do our jobs," Wyatt reassured. "It's safe here..."

John saw a brief movement from Wyatt's hand. Blood was rapidly descending his arm. His fist was clutched tight as thick wet droplets coated the white tile floor beneath him.

He was hurt. And if he had been cut with a surgical blade, it could be bad—or go bad very quickly, depending on where he was cut.

"Fuck you, faggot," the man with the knife hissed. "Get out of my fuckin' way."

John realized then that Wyatt was braced against a gurney, protecting an elderly woman whose eyes were wide and confused.

"She needs treatment..." Wyatt said gently. "We're not gonna hurt her."

"Fuck you!"

"Hey, hey..." John stepped slowly toward them, hands out. "Whatever is happening here, we can talk about this like rational adults."

The large man lurched forward, doubling down on his attempt to control the situation, but he didn't cut any further into Wyatt's throat—yet. John held out a hand, forcing himself not to react.

Nurses screamed, and Reyes glanced uncertainly at John. He shook his head slightly, indicating for Reyes to stay back. Mendez, upon seeing John, slowly got to his feet, his eyes locked on Wyatt and the man with the knife. Samuels, whom John couldn't see but knew was there, was also probably waiting in the wings, ready to tackle this bastard if they had to.

Wyatt's direct, pale blue eyes never once left the man's face, holding perfectly still.

"Police are almost here," John said calmly. "There is no need for any of this."

The man with the knife was at least a foot taller than John and weighed considerably more.

"Why don't you lower the knife…?" John said in his steady, even tone.

"Fuck off!"

"Is this your mom?" John asked, directing his question only at him.

The man's scowling face turned mutinous. "I told her she's not safe here. I told her not…" The man blinked and shoved Wyatt hard into the gurney. The elderly woman jumped, confused and frightened.

John sidestepped, following the movements like he would an opponent in the ring. It had been years since he boxed, yet he knew that the training had never really left him.

"This is the safest emergency department in all of LA, I can promise you that. Every single person in this room wants nothing more than to help your mom. We're not here to hurt you or her. We're just here to help her the best that we can…" John reassured. "What I cannot guarantee is what will happen when the police arrive."

The man's jaw clenched, sweat beginning to bead on his temple.

"The safest way out of this is to drop the knife."

He saw a flash of wild fear and paranoia in the man's eyes, and the shrinking cage that seemed to be closing in on him.

Wyatt sensed it too, and released his breath, voice thick and laced with emotion… and fear. "John…"

The man with the tattoos twitched.

That's all it took, slicing the surgical knife across Wyatt, who leaped backward to avoid the cut.

John's heart stopped.

And everything moved all at once.

Reyes yelled and Mendez charged, along with Samuels, who appeared out of nowhere.

But John moved first.

He rammed his shoulder hard into the man's torso and they went flying backward, slamming into the tile floor and skidding across it in a heap of limbs. Before the man could move, Samuels, Mendez, and Reyes dogpiled them. John managed to grab the man's wrist and yank the bloodied knife out of his hand. The man reared, attempting to strike him. John saw all the other men pinning him down, and for a split second he thought about putting the knife to this man's throat the way he had done to Wyatt's.

He gripped the knife once before tossing it on the ground toward the nurses' station. Sawyer, another resident, saw it and stopped it with her shoe, shaking as she grabbed it off the floor, her eyes wide.

Police announced themselves then, and with their guns drawn, descended on the chaos.

John's fists were shaking but he managed to hold the man down with a knee to his throat, the other men holding down his flaying limbs. John craned his neck and saw Steph putting pressure on Wyatt's throat. Blood spilled out from beneath her hands, and she was yelling for help.

Wyatt's gaze was locked with his as he sat in Steph's arms on the floor taking slow, measured breaths to slow his heart rate and thus his pulse, slowing the blood loss.

John froze, staring in horror and fear as panic ripped through him.

Samuels was on his feet, grabbing John by the back of the neck, and together they raced to Wyatt. He wrapped his arm around Wyatt's waist, Samuels on the other side, and hauled him onto an open gurney.

A team of nurses descended on him, applying everything they needed to measure his pulse and heart rate.

Reyes appeared at John's side, "Police got the bastard."

John's face remained composed, even though everything inside him was shaking.

"Lawson..." he murmured, voice cracking.

Wyatt's eyes lowered slightly, and his hand fell away. If the blade had been a normal kitchen knife, it wouldn't have done this much damage. A surgical blade could cut through tire rubber if enough pressure was applied.

"His heart rate is dropping."

"It's missed the internal jugular vein. It's superficial at best, but bleeding like a son of a bitch," Samuels cursed. "Is he bleeding somewhere else?"

John grabbed his arm, turning it over, and saw that the bed sheet was already soaked. He was losing blood from a main vein in his arm, and quickly.

"Tourniquet," John ordered, and Samuels squeezed the device over Wyatt's arm, the blood flow immediately stopping.

"We can glue this sucker back together," Samuels said. "Shouldn't be too bad of a scar."

"O negative," John instructed the nurse to replace Wyatt's blood loss.

After a few agonizing moments of waiting for the fluids, pain medicine, and new blood to pump through his system, Wyatt's eyes finally opened and he let out a whooshing breath as he glanced down at his arm, which John was cleaning of excess blood, giving him access to the cut so he could seal it.

"Rise and shine, cowboy," Samuels said jovially, yet his expression was pure relief.

Wyatt blinked and swallowed, his head resting on the white pillow, his skin grayish. "I feel like I got hit by a bus."

"Nope, just a knife-wielding maniac," Steph said from the doorway. "Reyes—Mendez needs someone to look at his nose."

"On it." Reyes glanced at Wyatt. "Fuck, man, that was crazy."

"Yeah," Wyatt murmured, looking dazed.

"Glad you're alive, cowboy," Steph said, eyes brimming with emotion as she and the other nurses stepped out, leaving John, Wyatt, and Samuels in the room alone.

Adrenaline depleted, emotions now slammed into him like a crashing wave, and John's eyes burned with tears. He let them fall, wiping them on his shoulder as he worked on sealing Wyatt's wound. The cut didn't look deep enough to cut through muscle, but it was enough to cause significant blood loss.

"Can you move your fingers?" John asked, his voice rough, unable to look at him.

Wyatt hesitated.

"Move your fucking fingers, Lawson."

He did, wiggling them and then touching the tips together onto his thumb. Good movement, so no muscle damage.

"Can you feel the tips?" John asked.

"Yeah."

No nerve damage.

John released the breath trapped in his lungs, wiping the other side of his cheek on his shoulder.

"John… look at me," Wyatt said softly.

He shook his head, swallowing the lump caught in his throat. "I can't."

He didn't want Wyatt to see his fear—his pain—his love.

Fuck.

He loved him so fucking much. And he knew Wyatt would read it all over his face.

"You're off the rest of the week and next," John bit out. "I don't want to see you in my hospital until you get a call from Steph to come back."

"John..." Wyatt's tone sharpened. "I'm fine."

"Dr. Donnelly to you, young sir," Samuels countered, his eyes flicking back and forth between them.

"I'll have Dr. Samuels finish this up," John said, and Samuels moved around the gurney to start the repair of the wound. "Once Steph clears you, I want you to go home. Tanya will probably reach out tomorrow for a full report on the incident."

"John...!" Wyatt declared, emotion flooding him. "I'm okay. I'm okay... look at me, please."

His shoulders trembled, but finally he did. And then the floodgates opened, breaking him open and ruining every defense he had around his heart. Wyatt practically leaped out of the bed, grabbing John's wrist and yanking him back to him, their eyes colliding.

He felt Wyatt's uninjured hand grab the back of his neck and drag him down for a kiss, yet it wasn't hard—it was reassuring and packed with everything they both wanted to say in that moment.

His heart, his aching, damn heart, was lost. Completely, utterly gone. Wyatt had it now. And he couldn't fucking breathe without him.

Wyatt seemed to sense his pain, pulling back just enough from the kiss to whisper, "I'm okay. I'm okay."

John nearly sobbed, gasping as tears fell relentlessly.

The door opened, and someone let out a squeak.

"Taschen," Samuels barked. "Close the door and stay right fuckin' there."

John's heart dropped into his stomach and he reluctantly released Wyatt.

Fuck. Not Taschen.

Samuels, without missing a beat or stopping his careful patch of Wyatt's exposed vein, glanced briefly at her. "Come here."

Ava, eyes wide and carefully avoiding John and Wyatt, stood ramrod straight next to Samuels.

"Remember that debt you owe me?" Samuels said in an icy tone that John had never heard him use before.

Ava squeaked again and nodded mutely.

"I'm callin' it in, honey." Samuels side-eyed her just as coldly. "You speak a word of this to anyone, and I mean anyone, and you'll be back in first year residency so fast, your head will spin like the goddamned Exorcist. *Capisce?*"

Her big eyes widened in fear and she trembled. "Yeah, yeah, got it."

John watched as Samuels instructed her to leave and she stumbled over her feet, nearly racing out the door, still avoiding looking at them.

"What was that?" John asked Samuels incredulously.

Samuels arched both eyebrows at him. "What was that?" he glanced between them. "Really? At work? Are you fucking kidding me?"

"You knew?" he asked, stunned.

Samuels scoffed, offended. "Of course, I knew. You've been eye-fucking each other for over a month. And don't even get me started on standing idly by having to listen to Lawson's praise kink in real time."

Wyatt barked out a laugh and dropped his head back onto the pillow, still pale yet slowly coming back to life.

"Why didn't you tell me?" John asked.

Samuels shrugged, "I figured you'd tell me when you were ready. I know what it's like to have feelings for someone and not know what the fuck to do about it."

John scrubbed his hand through his beard, unable to stop his eyes from moving back to Wyatt's, who was watching him and reading everything on his face like an open book.

Shit.

He had to have seen the truth.

He knew. He had to.

A few minutes later, Samuels said, "You're done, cowboy." He peeled off his bloodied latex gloves, looking proudly over the stitch job.

John inspected Samuel's work and nodded approvingly. "Looks good."

"You may need to ice your shoulder, slugger," Samuels said with a hitch of his chin.

He glanced down at his shoulder, noticing it was stiff and braced against his body. "Shit. I didn't even realize."

"Other priorities," Samuels said knowingly, and shot a hard look at Wyatt. "You'll need to keep it clean. Probably scar a bit, but it'll look cool."

Wyatt smiled weakly at him, "Thanks." He hesitated before adding, "I don't trust Ava not to say anything."

"Don't you worry about it," Samuels said. "I have her on three HIPAA violations because of that mouth of hers."

"Three? And you didn't think to tell me?" John snapped at his colleague.

"Are you questioning my decision not to report her? Now?" Samuels snapped back. "Seriously?"

He hesitated and instantly shut his mouth. Samuels was helping them out, making sure their secret was safe—for now, at least. It was only a matter of time before the ED found out.

"They were minor ones. Teachable offenses. Except that she wasn't quite learning to curb her tongue. So, I figured I had her," Samuels said with an indifferent shrug. "Let's just say I, myself, can be morally questionable, and I'm okay with that."

"Who are you and what did you do with Samuels?" John asked, shaking his head in stunned wonderment. Samuels was a good man, and yet knowing he was willing to blackmail gave him pause, but not for too long. This time, he was doing it for a good cause.

Samuels smirked, "Your new best friend. And just so you know, I don't have plans for Thanksgiving. I expect a text message for a time and place, John. Now, you kids make it quick. I can give you five before I send Steph in."

"Thanks," Wyatt murmured.

Samuels winked at him and left.

"Come here," Wyatt rasped. "Please…"

He couldn't say no to him, and once more, Wyatt dragged him back down, gripping firmly to the back of John's neck and raking his fingers upward to his hair. He tipped his forehead into his, releasing an unexpected, strangled breath. "Fuck, I was so scared."

The intimacy, the vulnerability, broke him.

He held Wyatt close, framing his face and closing his eyes, unwilling to see the knife back at his throat. All John wanted to do was sink into him and kiss him—touch him, feel his steady heartbeat against his. But he couldn't. He couldn't…

Wyatt almost died. And John could do nothing to stop it.

This was why he didn't get close to people. This was why he gave everything to his job, not to anyone who could actually hurt him—or get close enough to do it.

"Then I saw you…" Wyatt breathed, kissing him softly on the lips. John melted into him. "And I knew I'd be okay. That if something happened to me…"

"Stop," he hissed. "Fuck, stop."

John's throat tightened. He wanted to run, to escape the fear crushing his chest like an anvil. He thought he could do this. He thought that he could move past his fears, but he couldn't...

"John..." Wyatt's voice wavered.

"Do you realize what could've happened out there?" he growled through gritted teeth, feeling gutted and hollow. "How fast that could've all gone south? I can't save everyone, Wyatt. Even if we're standing in the middle of a god damned hospital."

"That's not what I meant," Wyatt replied calmly, too calmly.

He jerked his gaze to him, and Wyatt was staring right through him and into his soul. "I knew that if that man cut my throat, I'd die in the arms of the man I loved."

The world shifted and tilted him off its axis, and his heart was pierced with both elation and fear. He stumbled back, both hands covering his face and dragging his fingers over his eyes.

"I know you feel this, too," Wyatt whispered.

"I'm sorry."

"Don't... just stay. Stay with me."

He couldn't. He had to run—flee—do anything else but stay and feel everything. It was too much. It all was just too fucking much.

John blindly walked to the door, ripping it open and walking past the police, the blood, the noise—he needed air. He needed space. He needed it to fucking stop for one minute.

I just need a minute.

One minute.

John took the stairs two at a time, heading up to the roof. It was the one place in the whole hospital where he could have some privacy. The sunshine blanketed his face the second he rushed out to the helicopter med bay, which was currently empty. He sucked in giant gulps of air, eyes straining upward to the bright blue skies as he walked to the edge of the building that overlooked the sprawling city and feeling small in comparison.

He loved Wyatt.

He loved that cowboy doctor more than anything else.

And he could've lost him. It happened so quickly. One minute, he was thinking about asking him to move in, and the next, he was watching a man hold him at knife point. Life, he realized, would never be in his control. Maybe that was the point. And maybe he wasn't supposed to be perfect, either. Because it was a fucking mess. Life was supposed to be hard, messy, beautiful, wonderful, painful—all of it.

Controlling his heart had been an illusion all along.

It took loving Wyatt for him to finally see it.

John glanced down at the edge he stood close to and once more scrubbed his hands over his face, thinking about Wyatt... his brother... his family...

He somehow could feel Jacob. He could feel the weight of death pressing onto his shoulders and how fragile life could be.

"Johnny," the wind seemed to whisper. He glanced over his shoulder on the ledge and saw him—Jacob. He was dressed the way he remembered him. Casual, loose-fitting jeans, a band T-shirt, and his dark hair brushed back from his strikingly handsome face with the haunted blue eyes that just didn't seem to belong.

Jacob, young and alive, was standing in the sunlight with him on the edge of the world. And then, without hesitation, he stepped off. John sucked in a harsh breath, watching his brother fall. His gut swooped and his heart kicked, but he didn't follow—he couldn't. He had so many reasons to stay.

So many reasons to live.

And one reason was inside, sitting on a hospital gurney, asking him to stay.

John stumbled backward from the ledge, his knees buckling as he sank into himself and cried.

Chapter 18

Wyatt

Jin pushed the dry turkey meat on his plate, a grim line tugging down his mouth. "You're really doing this…?"Wyatt glanced up from his dinner plate and finished the bite of mashed potatoes in his mouth. "Yeah."

"What can I do to make you stay?"

Surprised, Wyatt tilted his chin back. "You care that much?"

"Of course. I may have avoidant attachment tendencies that make it look like I don't care, but I do. According to my therapist, anyway."

Wyatt snorted a laugh. It was the first genuine laugh he had all week since the incident. "Flight's already booked."

"You don't owe them anything."

"It's my decision."

"It's not. It's heartbreak deciding for you. And it's stupid."

"I'll come back," Wyatt reassured, knowing it was true.

After the attack at the hospital, he realized two things. One, he couldn't keep ignoring his father. He needed to confront his past, or else he would never be free from it. And he needed to be, because he felt contentment, peace even, whenever he was with John. Which then led him to the next epiphany, when John had come to his rescue.

His capable, calm captain, ready to protect and defend, had without hesitation been willing to take on the knife-wielding maniac for him.

Wyatt, in that instant, realized that his love was fiercely fucking protective.

Seeing John put himself in just as much danger terrified him because he couldn't imagine a world where John didn't exist. So, Wyatt had done the only thing he could to keep the attention on him. He showed the man with the knife pressed against his throat his fear, and that was enough to snap him, just like he probably snapped with his elderly mother when she showed fear toward him. Predators always responded to fear. But Wyatt hadn't been fast enough and had felt the blade knick his throat as he jumped out of the way. The next thing he had seen was John on top of the man, holding the blade, his expression almost unrecognizable.

He knew John didn't have a violent bone in his body, and yet, he should've. The most sensitive people, the most loving and loyal, could also be the most violent. Their empathy made them understand and feel everything so intensely. It was the reason Wyatt had fallen so fast and hard for him.

Wyatt had breathed a sigh of relief when John tossed the blade aside.

No one had ever come to his defense like that.

No one had ever bothered. Not even Mateo, when his father kicked him out.

Everything happened so quickly that Wyatt didn't remember passing out, only that when he came to, Samuels and John were standing over him. And seeing the emotion beautifully strained on John's handsome face, all Wyatt could feel was love. He had become pure love, motivated and propelled on a single, clear emotion: need. A needy urgency to wrap his arms around the man that he loved, hold him close, and be utterly engulfed by him.

Nothing else mattered.

No one else in the room mattered.

What he hadn't expected was John's reaction…

But maybe he should have. He should've known he'd run. He should've fucking known…

His throat tightened with anger, and he cleared it, refusing to stew in the rejection again.

"Which is code for never," Jin grumbled. "Oh my god, you are the worst version of a Taylor Swift song right now."

The buzzer to their apartment pinged and Jin rolled his eyes, "For Christ's sake, Amazon. Don't you ever stop?"

He pushed the button, answering it, "Yes?"

"Oh, hi—I'm hoping that Lawson is home—Wyatt Lawson."

His eyebrows arched, recognizing the voice over the intercom. "Steph?"

Jin glanced back at him, "Do you want me to let her in?"

He nervously sprang to his feet, hand grazing over his overly whiskered jawline and unkempt hair, wondering if he had time to change his two-day-old shirt.

"Yeah," he finally said with a resigned sigh.

Jin hit the button, letting her in. A few minutes later, there was a knock on their apartment door. Wyatt answered, greeted with a kind, warm smile from the day-shift nurse.

"Hey, kid," Steph said, looking genuinely pleased to see him. "Sorry to burst in on ya, but I heard you're leavin', and I wanted to talk before you left."

The only person he had told was Reyes. And knowing Reyes, he probably told…

"Ava tell you?" he asked irritably.

Ava knew about John and him, which was entirely Wyatt's fault. He blamed it on the rush of adrenaline and crazed-induced love coursing through his veins, polluting his brain. He'd been idiotically careless. But so far, Ava had kept her lips firmly sealed. He only hoped it would stay that way. He didn't care what happened to him. He cared about what happened to John.

"Our talented gossip queen of the ED?" Steph drawled knowingly. "No, not this time."

If Steph had known he was leaving, John might have found out, too.

He had submitted a time-off request with an unknown return date, mostly because he wasn't sure what his father and aunts might need from him once he went back home.

"Come in," Wyatt stepped back, waving her inside. "This is my roommate, Jin."

"Hi," Jin smiled, pushing his sparkling blue glasses up the bridge of his nose.

Steph's smile broadened, "How come I haven't met you sooner? Lawson, you could've brought him to the Hot Dog Palace with us!"

"Oh, I'm also a gossip queen," Jin said with a dismissive wave. "Wyatt doesn't trust me to keep his secrets, especially when liquor is involved."

"Well, we don't have that many secrets in the ED," Steph declared.

"Because of Ava," Wyatt countered.

"Because we're a family. We watch out for each other."

"How did you know where I live?" he asked, realizing he had never told anyone where he lived, not even John.

Steph shrugged off her coat and hung it on the vintage coat stand Jin had picked out on one of his many antique-thrifting adventures. "Oh, honey, when you've been around confidential files long enough, you discover all kinds of things. Just don't tell HIPAA I'm here."

"I like you," Jin remarked. "Drink? We have beer, wine, and pre-made cocktails in a can."

"Huh, that sounds lovely. What do ya got, bartender?"

After several minutes of informing Steph of the value of margaritas in a can, she sat at the dining table with Wyatt while Jin gave them some privacy and sauntered off to his room.

Steph leaned back into the small wooden chair, sipping her canned margarita. "You look… like shit."

He frowned, nodding. He knew exactly how great he looked because Jin mentioned it daily. He hadn't shaved or slept much this week. By day three, he had finally stopped calling and texting John. He was a certified mess, strung out with a broken heart.

He declared his love to the literal man of his dreams and was met with silence.

He wasn't sure what was worse—a Nazi wielding a knife at him or John's refusal to pick up his phone.

"How's the arm?" she asked.

He pulled back the white sleeve of his shirt, revealing the healing wound with the fresh bandage. "Good."

"Good," she nodded. "So, you're leaving us?"

"Yeah. But I'll be back."

She hummed, scrutinizing him. "This doesn't have anything to do with what happened, does it? Cause right after, Tanya and John talked. We now have more security and hired three more nurses. Workin' on a few more doctors, too. Walsh will finally have another consistent night-shift doctor on rotation, and Samuels can put in for vacation, if he ever leaves."

"That's great," he said, attempting to sound enthusiastic.

"So, if it ain't from what happened, how come your paperwork didn't have a return date? You're a good doctor, Lawson. We need you."

Wyatt's heart sank, and then once more, the anger that had been so easily at the surface lately rose in his chest and he glared at her. He had submitted his FMLA paperwork to the hospital through Steph, who insisted on doing it for him when he asked where to submit it. He knew he was running. But he didn't know what else to do. His Aunts were calling daily, and his father probably wouldn't make it to Christmas.

He couldn't control John. He couldn't control his anger these days, either.

But he could control his decision to go home.

Wyatt leaned back, arms folded over his chest. "I just need some time."

She nodded, "Yeah, I get it. The job's intense, but I didn't take you for someone scared of a bit of pain, Lawson."

"I don't think I was scared enough," he admitted, thinking of John.

"What do you mean?"

He shook his head, refusing to elaborate. "You don't have to worry about me."

"Oh, honey, yes, I do. That's what good pseudo mamas do. We notice when things happen to our kids. And I know something's happened. In fact, I know that the day you left the hospital, Dr. Donnelly's good mood also left us."

"Sorry to hear that," he muttered.

"Yeah, me too. Johnny's a good man. Sensitive," her dark brown eyes impaled him from across the table, as though looking for something. "I bet if you asked him, he could tell you the number of lives he's lost, but not the ones he saved."

Wyatt rubbed his temple, fighting the burn in his belly. Steph didn't have to give him more reasons to love John.

"He's never risked getting close to anyone. Even his ex-wife said so the last time I saw her. Johnny pushes people away because he's scared.

He sees the suffering, the grief of his patients and their families, and denies it to himself. But the job can't love him back, no matter how much he pours into it."

"It's never enough," Wyatt said softly.

She nodded. "You are, though."

He stilled.

"I know," Steph said simply. "I blame it entirely on old age that I didn't figure it out sooner."

Jin's voice rang out from the other room, clearly eavesdropping. "Queen, you're gorgeous, and don't look a day over 40!"

She laughed, "Thanks, honey."

"How?" Wyatt asked.

"Johnny told me."

Stunned, he sat back.

"It took about half a bottle of whiskey and Samuels and me berating him, but eventually he folded like laundry and couldn't stop talkin' about ya. I've never heard him talk like that about anyone. Not even Melissa."

"Melissa?"

"His ex-wife."

John never really talked about that past life—the one where he was married to a woman. And yet, he had. He told him that he had buried himself and all that he was after his brother's death, trying to cope and be something that he wasn't.

"I shouldn't have been surprised Samuels already knew," Steph chuckled, "That man was a bit too excited to hear that Johnny and his favorite cowboy were an item. Samuels likes you—so do I. So does Johnny."

Wyatt didn't say anything. He couldn't. His throat had all but clammed up, and his bleeding heart was hemorrhaging in his chest.

John had told his friends about them—whatever they were, he still didn't know because they hadn't talked since the attack at the hospital.

He gritted his teeth, jaw flexing.

Steph took a long sip from her canned cocktail. "You know, I'm a bit disappointed in you, Lawson. I thought you were more of a fighter than this."

He tilted his head back as though she sucker punched him.

"What happened to the fearless cowboy running that horse like the devil was chasing him?"

He exhaled. "He grew up."

"Or, maybe he got cold feet. We all do. But that doesn't mean we don't step back into that arena. You do it every day when you walk into the emergency department. Gladiators is what we are. Johnny gave up for a while there. And every single one of us in that department felt the change in him when you took notice. You're a tough son of a bitch. You took on a knife-wielding asshole and made it out alive."

He leaned forward, baring his soul. "He doesn't want me."

Steph didn't even blink. "Bullshit."

"Doesn't make it any less true."

Steph shook her head, disappointed, eyes flickering to the window over Wyatt's shoulder. "Melissa really did a number on him," she raked her fingers through her thick dark hair, sighing. "They tried for years to have a kid. Painted a nursery and everything. Their therapist told them to create the space as though the baby were coming. And it never did. It devastated them both, but especially him. He couldn't give her what she wanted. And I think..." Steph's eyes watered, but the tears never fell. "I think Johnny lost himself during that. I think he believed that if he gave Melissa a baby, it would be enough. It would be enough to make up for the lack of love in their marriage. Because he didn't love her. If he truly loved that woman, he wouldn't have been working sixty, sometimes eighty hours a week."

Steph drummed her fingers on her can. "The divorce was messy. It took another couple of years for Johnny to come out to me. But he still chose the safety of his job over finding a partner. I don't blame him for it. Any one of us would've done the same thing..."

The swift pang of grief filled him, imagining the pain John must have endured. The loneliness of it.

"I love him," Steph breathed, emotion tightening around her lips. "But he's a fuckin' idiot if he thinks that this job is better than the people around him who care. And maybe, I was hoping, a fearless kid like you would help remind him of that fact."

She abruptly stood and pulled out a piece of paper from her purse, tossing it on the table.

"Sorry, not sorry, Lawson."

He opened it and saw it was his FMLA paperwork, meant for Tanya.

"I gave Johnny—and you—another day. Figure this out, and you'd better be back to work on Monday, or I swear to God, I will drive to Arizona myself and finish what that truck started and drive you off a cliff. Now go save my best friend from his self-destructive bullshit."

Chapter 19

Wyatt

He felt foolish standing on John's doorstep holding a bottle of wine.

What the hell am I doing?

Steph's motivational speech had bolstered him all the way here, but once he got off his motorcycle and walked up the front steps, nerves got the better of him and he hesitated, hand hovering over the buzzer. He still had time to run, to put his helmet back on and walk his stupid, sorry ass out of there before he humiliated himself any further.

C'mon, Wyatt.

You can do this.

He sucked in a fortified breath and nearly jumped when the door swung open, startling him. A little girl, no more than five, stood before him, dressed in a fluffy yellow dress with a golden crown, holding a sparkling plastic scepter.

"Hello!" She flourished her scepter rather sharply at him. "You bow in the presence of a queen."

Wyatt snorted and covered it quickly with a cough, sinking into a bow, "Your majesty."

She patted his shoulder with a snap of the glittering scepter. "Rise, knight." He once more tried not to laugh, as she indicated to his black helmet with narrowed eyes, "Armor?"

"Safety first, your highness," he tapped his knuckles to his head, and she nodded approvingly.

"My mom makes me ride with my helmet, too," she declared loftily. "Says I'll end up in Uncle Johnny's realm if I don't."

He smirked, nodding. "I would have to agree with your mother. I work in Uncle Johnny's realm, and it can be, at times, a treacherous place. Not a place fit for a queen such as yourself."

She sniffed, "What is your name, knight?"

"Wyatt. I'm training to be a doctor like your uncle."

She beamed, "Cool."

"Is your uncle around?"

"Out in the backyard grilling a turkey."

"Do you mind if I come in? Or I can stay out here until you get him."

She hesitated, and then he heard a voice behind her. "Olive, really? How many times do I have to tell you to let an adult answer the door?"

A woman appeared in the doorway, her rich brown hair in a scattered, messy bun. She wore pale blue jeans and a long forest green blouse, with dark blue eyes—John's eyes. This must be his sister, he realized.

"Hi, sorry," she said with a bland yet pretty smile. "Can I help you?"

"I was just stopping by to say hi to Dr. Donnelly. I was in the neighborhood."

"With a bottle of wine?" She asked, her gaze narrowing.

"He did me a favor last week…" He paused, glancing at the little girl named Olive, knowing he needed to keep this story kid-friendly. "He saved me from a mighty troll. I'm here to give him my regards."

She nodded, glancing behind her as though debating on leaving him on the front porch.

"This is Dr. Wyatt. He works with Uncle Johnny," Olive stated, smacking her mom in the butt with her scepter. "There's another doctor here today, too. Dr. Sammy! He's cool."

Wyatt remembered that Samuels practically threatened John for an invite to his Thanksgiving.

Oh shit.

Turkey, Samuels, John's family… they were all here at John's house to celebrate a late Thanksgiving, and Wyatt had just crashed it.

Mortified, he stiffened and tried not to show his panic.

"Ouch," the woman said, snatching the scepter out of her daughter's hand. "I'm Justine, John's sister. And this is my daughter, Olivia."

Wyatt politely held out his hand, and Justine shook it.

She opened the door wide and ushered him inside.

He fought down his nerves, knowing it was too late to retreat now as they walked through John's house. He was unable to stop his thoughts from returning to the last time he was here, of feeling John's slumbering body pressed against his, showering together, playing house, making love. It had been so easy to fantasize about what it would be like to be here all the time. To not just be John's guest, but his partner… his person… *his.*

Emotions tightened in his stomach like a fist, and he noticed the kitchen island and dining table covered with bowls, plates, and food.

"We got lucky with the weather," Justine commented. "Well, my dad did. Insisted on grilling the turkey this year. We're all outside on the patio."

Slipping his fingers through his hair and pushing it out of his face, he stepped out onto the sunny backyard patio.

It was gorgeously designed, with plenty of space for a party. There was a paved walkway with concrete around the house and two fire pits, lit and radiating plenty of heat. Beautifully colored potted plants were covered for the season, and he knew this place would look spectacular in the spring. He noted the four planter boxes alongside the fence line and the jacuzzi.

John's home represented him. Clean, well-maintained, orderly, and...

Lonely.

Wyatt had noticed it the first time he was here. All this space, all these rooms, and no one waiting for him when he came home after a long shift. The thought stayed with him. Yet seeing John's family, laughing and gathered in his home, seemed to breathe life into it.

And apparently into John, too, who was standing by the grill wearing a plastic yellow tiara and a scepter of his own, shoved in his back pocket as he held a baby in his arms. He was cooing lovingly down to the bundle of blankets in his arms as curious, tiny hands reached for his beard, digging into it the way Wyatt loved to do. He couldn't help but feel the tug of a smile on the corner of his lips, getting to witness John so relaxed with his family.

An older man, whom Wyatt assumed was John's dad, kept lifting the grill lid to check on the turkey.

He was momentarily transfixed by the easy, natural smile on John's face.

Wyatt's heart thudded. He loved his smile.

He loved *him.*

Fuck. Knock it off.

He sucked in another breath and felt the snap of something on his butt. Glancing down, he saw Olivia with her golden plastic scepter once more. "This way, knight."

He couldn't help but chuckle, wondering how she had gotten the weapon back already from her mom.

"She's got a thing for smacking people's butts with that, so watch out," Samuels's drawling voice said, and Wyatt glanced up to the older man.

He was dressed in casual dark jeans, a navy-blue undershirt, and a gray plaid long-sleeved flannel shirt over it. Even though he was younger than John by a couple of years, his gray was richer through his brown, slightly curly hair. He was a very handsome man in his own right, but he never paid much attention to it because another ED doctor had Wyatt's full attention.

He saw the heavy bags under Samuels's eyes, and his usual easy smile seemed a little more strained. "I think it's how she keeps her subjects in line," Samuels said, taking a sip from his glass of wine and eyeing him frankly. "Good to see you, man. How's the arm?"

"Good."

He nodded and glanced toward John, who hadn't noticed him yet. "John invited me over cause all my family's back in New York. Didn't want me celebrating Thanksgiving alone. Oh, and I also sorta blackmailed him into it."

Wyatt saw the twinkle of mischief in his eyes as he winked and turned back to the firepit he had been sitting at with another man, who yanked the scepter out of Olive's hand, chastising her. That must be her dad, Wyatt amused.

"Johnny!" Justine said, walking down the few steps and toward her brother. "You got another guest."

John, still cradling the baby, turned, and his smiling face fell slightly in surprise at the sight of Wyatt. He felt a flush begin to creep up his cheeks.

I shouldn't have come.

I've interrupted his family time.

Fuck, I'm an idiot.

Justine slid her arms beneath John's and carefully cradled the baby into her arms. "I'll take over."

He nodded, "Give me a couple of minutes."

"What? Afraid I'll let papa burn the turkey like he did last year?"

John shook his head with that half-hearted smile and quickly walked up the few steps of his patio to Wyatt, who was frozen in place.

"Let's go inside," John said quietly.

Wyatt noticed the tension in his shoulders and nodded, following him back inside the house and closing the heavy slider door behind him, butterflies swirling in his stomach. John walked into the kitchen and glanced over his shoulder at the party outside, seeming to make sure no one followed them.

"What are you doing here?" John asked in a clipped tone, and Wyatt knew John was having a serious moment, but he couldn't take him seriously with that plastic tiara still in his hair.

He set the bottle of wine down with the rest of the food spread out on the kitchen island, placed his helmet on the floor and strode up to John, whose throat bobbed the closer he got, eyes narrowing.

"You've got…" He reached and plucked the tiara from his hair, placing it on the kitchen island.

John snorted a slight laugh, rubbing a hand through his hair and tousling it.

Unable to stop himself, Wyatt stepped a little closer, invading his space.

John wore a sexy beige cashmere sweater that sculpted the contours of his body, the sleeves pushed up to his elbows, paired with navy blue jeans and black designer boots with a hint of beige to match. His beard was a bit overgrown, though, and his hair unkempt. He had the same bags under his eyes as Samuels, and he vaguely wondered how hard the last week he had missed was.

"Steph came by," Wyatt admitted, wanting to touch him but resisting. "Told me some things…"

"Shit," John scrubbed a hand over his face. "I'm sorry. I didn't mean to tell them about..."

Us.

John cleared his throat roughly, "I was drunk. Not an excuse, I know. I shouldn't have done that, I'm sorry."

Wyatt wouldn't reveal that he was thrilled he had told his friends about them. It was one of the reasons he was there. But *what* John had told them, he still didn't fully know. He had also intended to come over and seduce him, intentionally dressing in the same all-black outfit from the commercial and debating on wearing the cowboy hat too, because John seemed to like it so much.

John seemed to realize this and glanced heatedly over his body. He tried to step back, but Wyatt followed, wanting to stay close.

"Steph mentioned you're leaving?" John said gruffly.

"Yeah, gonna head home for a bit."

John's averted gaze swept to his, stiffening.

"Apparently, all it took was a near-death experience for me to finally realize that I need to go home, say my goodbyes." Wyatt, deciding to be honest, said softly, "And you. Everything that you told me about your brother made me realize that I want one more moment with my dad. Even if he doesn't."

Emotion passed over John's face, but before he could decipher it, he turned his back on him, busily checking on something covered in tin foil on the stovetop. "When are you leaving?"

"Flight leaves tomorrow morning."

John's gaze snapped to his, and he saw it—the emotion swirling, on the brink of losing control. He hoped, prayed to the gods in the universe, that it would result in one of those crushing, soul-searing kisses John was so fucking good at.

"Why are you here, then?" John asked, his tone curt.

"I think you know why."

"I do, but I can't talk about that right now."

Wyatt pressed his lips together in frustration, forcing himself to release the constricted breath in his chest. What the hell would it take for John to break and finally pursue what he wanted? To chase the horse, *him*, who had been running after him this entire time. Wyatt thought back to the first night he seduced him and how much he didn't need John to chase him, that he was happy to gallop after him, tail fucking wagging. Now, too much had happened between them, and he needed more.

Because he was tired and angry, needing the storm to come after him.

But John's entire demeanor was standoffish and unyielding, once more closing him out the way he had done countless times before.

"I interrupted your evening," Wyatt stepped back, heart sinking. "Your family's beautiful, John. Olive is a spitfire. You have your hands full with that one."

John, rooted to the spot, watched him with dark eyes. "You're leaving."

He nodded, leaning down to pick up his helmet. "Yeah. Sorry again for interrupting. I'll… I'll see ya."

He made a hasty retreat, too afraid that he wouldn't be able to stand his ground and would fold the second John swayed close enough to him.

Wyatt headed to the front door, wondering if he was making a mistake. If he was putting too much on John. If this stupid game he was playing was even fucking fair. But what choice did he have? He couldn't keep backing John into a corner. That wasn't fair to him, either. John needed to make this decision for himself. And if he truly wanted this to be over, he'd let Wyatt walk out that door and out of his life for good.

He fisted his hand onto his helmet, wanting to crush it when he didn't hear footsteps following. He reached for the door handle, heart breaking in his chest and hating himself for how hard this was.

John's hand slammed the door shut and roughly spun him around.

Wyatt saw the fury in his gaze.

The storm had finally broken, and it was a glorious, raging sight.

"That's it?" John hissed through clenched teeth. "That's it?"

Caught in the lightning strike of John's emotion, Wyatt sucked in a breath, forcing himself to hold to his resolve. "I won't—can't—keep chasing you, John. I fuckin' can't. This horse is tired."

John exhaled, his breath warming the space between them, strain pulling at the lines around his eyes. "Stay," he whispered so low Wyatt almost didn't hear it.

Tonight? Tomorrow? Forever?

He wanted to ask, but instead clamped his jaw down into a tight squeeze.

"Stay."

That wasn't enough, and they both knew it. Wyatt reached for the handle again and John moved, pinning him against the door with an arm and pressing his chest against his.

"I don't know how to do this," John murmured.

"You do," Wyatt drawled softly. "You're just scared."

John swallowed, eyes briefly closing, fighting himself. "I am," he admitted. "I'm terrified of the hold you have on me."

He sucked in a surprised breath.

"I'm terrified that if you walk out this door, I will never fucking recover."

His heart slammed into his chest.

"It's the same feeling I had when I saw that knife at your throat," John rasped. "...when you were losing all that blood..." his hands moved, gripping the front of Wyatt's jacket, clinging to him. "I know I can't stop death, but I'm a coward, and I can't bear to see it and the pain that comes to the people I care about."

The floodgates of John's emotion had finally opened. John's eyes brimmed with unshed tears. "I couldn't save my brother. I can't save my dad from his brain deteriorating. I can't save my mom from watching the love of her life fade away. And for a moment, I thought I was going to lose the only person in my life that made all of that go away..." John released him, tears sliding down his cheeks. He scrubbed his face. "I don't know if I can give you what you need, because all I want to do is take from you. I want to take everything you give me."

Wyatt reached for him, framing his face and raking his fingers through his beard. "Did it ever occur to you that you give me the same thing? It's supposed to be like this—giving and taking. All you have to do is look at me, and I can feel myself calm or spark. You haven't taken anything from me that I didn't want to give. And until recently, I was okay with that. But I need more from you, John. So much fucking more."

John stared at him, uncertain and vulnerable. "Me too. I need you so much. I never felt like this, Wyatt."

Thank fuck!

Relief swelled inside him as something broke and ignited in the space between them, and without another word, they collided like a storm at sea, crashing and fighting together. John pushed him against the door and Wyatt went willingly, their kisses assaulting and powerful. He moaned in the back of his throat as John pinned him with his hands and hips, grinding into him and sending flashing hot sparks down his back to the tips of his toes.

John's hand reached between them, stroking him roughly over the denim of his jeans and causing Wyatt to buck against his hand.

They shouldn't be doing this here. Not with John's entire family a room away.

"John…" Wyatt groaned between his fiery kisses.

John's touches grew more frantic, more powerful. "You're gonna stay here. You're gonna have Thanksgiving with my family. I want them to meet you. And then, you're going to move in with me…"

Wyatt gasped, tilting his head back, shaking. His words struck at his heart like an arrow, slicing away all the final barriers he had attempted to erect against this man in the last week.

"But first," John pressed, drawing his lower lip into his mouth. "You're gonna cum for me."

Wyatt gaped, mouth unhinging as John ruthlessly stroked him over his jeans, his other hand pinning him to the door roughly.

"I have to apologize, baby," John said in the sexiest stern-daddy-doctor tone that sent electrical currents through his entire being. "And the only way for me to do that is to ruin you the way you ruined me."

He suppressed the urge to moan loudly, John's touch unraveling him as he unbuckled his belt, and shoved his hand into his jeans and beneath his briefs, fisting his cock. Wyatt's head thumped back against the wood of the door and he surrendered instantly to him. John growled, watching his body give into his touch, one muscle at a time.

"Good boy," John murmured.

"Ah, fuck," he cursed in a smothered gasp between his lips, precum leaking down his shaft.

John hummed approvingly, dipping his face against the side of his neck now, his beard scratching his neck beneath his collar as he began to kiss and suck, hard. Wyatt jerked against him, not wanting to sport a fresh hickey if he was about to have Thanksgiving with John's family.

"John..." Wyatt protested weakly, hands digging into his shoulder and hips bucking against his unrelenting fist.

John grazed his teeth over his neck, unfazed.

"Don't fuckin' give me a hickey," he whined, sounding pathetic even to his own ears. And on any other occasion, he would love to be marked by John.

John ignored him, ruthlessly sucking on his neck and pressing the pad of his thumb into the tip of his cock, smearing the precum over his fat tip. He released a strained breath, legs tensing.

"I like you like this," John husked gravelly. "I never thought I would like taking so much..."

John pressed his body against him now, humping into his side and letting Wyatt feel the bulge of his own erection. Blinding desire gripped him as he reached for John, kissing him brutally hard. They humped and ground themselves against the door, kissing frantically, knowing time was short.

Wyatt was close, the orgasm overwhelming him.

John sensed it, pumping him, pushing him to the edge. "That's it, baby..." he said in a thready, sexy voice, ravishing his neck some more and sucking the same spot.

Wyatt's cock twitched, "Please..."

"Please, what?" John breathed.

Oh god.

Wyatt nearly came right then and there, but he wanted to see John's face when he said it. "Please, daddy..." he panted out, thrusting into John's hand, letting him feel his cock throb at the word and how it affected him, too.

John's deep, lustful groan echoed low from his chest, "Fuuuck."

His eyes were nearly black as he reached for Wyatt's throat and gripped.

Wyatt's eyes rolled back, "Yes… daddy."

John let out another weak, needy sound.

This went on for several panting moments, finger digging into his neck and cock, John's intent gaze on him, watching it all.

"Do you know how sexy you are right now?" John growled. "Dressed like this? Looking like a fuckin' dream—my dream. God, I want to fuck you, baby…"

Wyatt's legs buckled beneath him, pressing himself against the door to keep himself upright, feeling the sweeping crash of the orgasm build to the tip of his dick.

"I'm gonna…" he whispered frantically.

"Cum in your pants," John commanded. "I want you to feel this. Feel us smeared on your dick all fuckin' night."

Oh Jesus.

He erupted, spewing hot, endless streams of cum into his pants and against John's fist. And John continued to milk his pulsating cock without mercy. "Good boy…"

Wyatt's entire body seized, another wave crashing over him at the feel of John's collaring grip.

"That's it," John panted. "Keep coming, baby."

Wyatt emptied himself until there was nothing left, collapsing into John, chest heaving for oxygen. John pushed him back against the door, forcing him to watch as he dragged his hand out of his pants.

"Open your mouth," he commanded.

"Ah fuck," Wyatt gasped, lips parting instantly.

"So eager," John murmured, smearing his cum over his lips and tongue. Something dark and haunting slid over John's expression, and he kissed him, sliding his tongue into his mouth and tasting him. "You make me want to do the craziest things…" John confessed.

Wyatt smiled, blissed out of his mind and still trying to catch his breath.

"Unbutton your shirt."

Curious and with trembling fingers, he unbuttoned his black flannel, revealing the black undershirt beneath. John wiped the rest of Lawson's climax off his hand and onto the shirt, staining it.

He almost laughed until John's hand proceeded to roughly push upward, palming his pec and pinching the nipple above the shirt. His desire was evident through his possessive touch. He then buttoned Wyatt's jeans and clasped his belt, paralyzing him. John was in full control, touching where he wanted, taking what he wanted. Wyatt had given him permission to be selfish, and John's transformation was fucking incredible.

"I like you like this, too," Wyatt admitted in a rush.

John's dark eyes slid to his.

"Taking control," Wyatt said, relaxing against the door and eyeing the bulge pressed against John's pants. "Using me however you like. The number of times I've imagined you just like this… Dr. Donnelly making me cum in my pants before he bent me over and fucked me raw."

It was John's turn to gasp.

"Collaring me with those big fuckin' hands, riding me until there's nothing left," Wyatt whispered. "I want you unhinged. Wild. I want that storm inside you to break me the fuck apart."

John dropped his forehead into his temple, sucking in a hard breath. "Jesus Christ, Wyatt…"

"We can save all that for later…" Wyatt nipped at his jawline and pushed him backward, sliding off the door, heart fucking glowing. "You have a turkey to cook."

Chapter 20

John

An easy, impossible lightness settled around him like a halo as he kissed his sleeping nephew's forehead in the car seat. Justine handed him Olivia next, and he buckled her into her toddler car seat as she drifted in and out, her yellow queen dress rumpled from play and her tiara tangled in her hair.

"See ya later, sweetheart," he murmured to her, kissing her temple. "I love you."

"I love you too…" she yawned, "Uncle…"

He smiled, closing the car door quietly.

"Thank you for a wonderful evening," he said to his sister, kissing the side of her face.

She hugged him back and wiggled out of his arms, "I'm not used to furry beard kisses."

He and Chad exchanged hugs next. Their parents had already left for the evening. Their dad struggled staying out too late, and their mom wanted him somewhere familiar before bed. Chad climbed into the driver's seat and Justine hesitated, glancing at Wyatt's motorcycle.

John kept his expression carefully neutral, sliding his hands into his pockets and smiling, waiting. Justine was more intuitive and upfront with her feelings than John. He supposed it was a second child thing.

And more than once this evening, she watched Wyatt—and John. Granted, Samuels was also in the mix, but she for some reason paid him absolutely zero attention.

"So, have you figured it out yet?" He asked gently.

Her eyes, surprised, shot to his. He was never the one to bring things up. He blamed this entirely on Wyatt, who somehow, in the span of a month, had reopened the closed door around his heart that he had been so scared of.

Justine glanced uncertainly at the bike again and then at him. "He's young."

John's smile deepened, and he nodded, "That he is."

She stiffened, "I don't..." she exhaled, uncertain. "I don't want you to get hurt again."

"Unfortunately, we all do. Something I'm working on accepting. It must be a Donnelly trait."

Justine's expression softened. "You really love him, don't you?"

"I do," he replied firmly.

She sighed, "We were cursed by being raised by romantics."

He chuckled, "or blessed."

"Yeah, whatever. Well, if he shows up to Christmas, I suppose it'll be official."

John swallowed. The image of Wyatt in his parents' kitchen, in his childhood home, stirred something inside him. "We'll see."

"God—really?"

He raised his hands in a defensive gesture. Justine always bristled when he used his doctor voice on her. "Sorry, you're right. Truth is, I haven't asked him yet."

"Will you?"

"Yes."

"Good. I like him. I caught him dueling with Olive in the backyard with those stupid plastic whipping toys Chad bought her. She needs someone who'll keep her on her toes. We're all too soft with her."

Something inside him warmed, loving that Justine so graciously accepted John's sexuality, and also Wyatt being in his life. It meant a lot to him.

"I liked Samuels, too. He's got a fat chip on his shoulder, though. That man needs a woman who will..."

John cringed and shook his head, "He's not into women, J."

Justine's eyes widened. "Him too?! Your nurses must hate life with all these hot gay doctors walking around."

A burst of laughter rumbled from his chest.

"Or love it?" She said, considering it. "Lawson, especially. Jesus, that kid has an ass you can bounce a quarter—"

"Goodnight, *sister*."

"Okay, okay. Goodnight, *brother*."

He waved them goodbye and made sure they got out of the gate before heading back inside to find Samuels and Wyatt cleaning up the kitchen and dining room.

"You don't have to do that," he said, closing the front door.

"Yes, we do," Samuels retorted. "I haven't had a meal like that since I left home."

Wyatt paused, hands deep in the pile of dirty plates, rinsing and loading them into the dishwasher. "Me either, now that I think about it."

"You and your dad did a good job with the turkey, but damn, that pumpkin pie your mom brought knocked my socks off," Samuels said with a whistle, using a wet rag to wipe down the dining table.

"Who made the stuffing?" Wyatt asked.

"Chad," John replied, heading to the living room to put on some music. "Justine avoids the kitchen like the plague. Always has, even when we were kids."

"Nicely done, Chad," Wyatt said with a teasing smile. "Really knows how to stuff the stuffing."

Samuels shot him a look and both men laughed. John shook his head and felt the easy laughter roll out of him. He picked out his favorite Muddy Waters record, placed it on the turntable, moved the tone arm, and hit play.

He joined Wyatt in the kitchen and pulled out extra Tupperware to pack the leftovers in, and enough for Samuels to take some with him.

"You going back home for Christmas at least, Samuels?" John asked.

He shrugged noncommittally. "Maybe. I dunno. Not much left for me there these days."

"No parents?" Wyatt asked.

"Nah, dad skipped out when I was a kid, and mom… isn't the nicest person to be around voluntarily, especially during the holidays."

"What about friends?" John asked.

Samuels stilled, before quickly shaking his head, his expression closing. "Nah, no one special."

Wyatt glanced at John, exchanging a curious look. Samuels wasn't being forthcoming, and John, knowing when to back off, merely nodded, closing the container full of turkey. "Well, Justine likes you. Both of you. So, this is the official Donnelly invitation to join us for Christmas, if you don't have any other plans. We'd love to have you."

Wyatt stiffened next to him, and John brushed a reassuring hand onto his back as he reached for the plate of stuffing. "Especially you," he whispered lowly, unable to resist kissing his cheek as he returned to the food containers.

"Thanks, man," Samuels said, walking back into the kitchen. "That's very nice of you."

"You're welcome. Steph usually shows up with her husband a bit later for dessert and drinks."

Samuels grinned. "Even more reason to come."

John finished packing two very full containers of food for Samuels and placed them before him, along with an entire uneaten homemade apple pie.

"You're kidding?" Samuels said incredulously down at all the food.

"Nope," John patted his back. "My fridge is full already. Whatever you don't want, I'll take it to work for all the broke med students."

Wyatt rolled his eyes at him, sipping his wine with soap bubbles on his hands and looking deliciously sexy while cleaning the dishes. A few strands of his sandy blond hair draped over his eyes, his long black sleeves rolled up past his elbows and the top button of his black flannel securely fastened, all of which reminded John of what was hidden beneath.

Wyatt saw something in his expression and his gaze lingered over his mouth, taking another slow sip of wine, intentionally tilting his neck upward and exposing the bruising red mark on his neck that he had managed to keep covered with his collar all night.

John's cock twitched.

"All right," Samuels declared. "I think I'll head out." He patted the back of John's shoulder, giving him a genuinely appreciative look. "Thank you for this. I uh…" he cleared his throat. "I didn't realize how much I needed tonight."

John's heart stuttered at the sight of grief tightening his friend's face, and he nodded. "Of course. Anytime. I'm serious about Christmas, too. Please come if you can."

Samuels nodded tightly and winked at Wyatt, hands filled with food. "See ya later, cowboy."

John walked him out to his car, and when he came back, Wyatt was in the living room, sprawled out on his couch, Muddy Waters crooning all over him.

One of his favorite songs clicked on, 'Country Boy'. He shut and locked the door behind him, strolling into the living room and standing over Wyatt, who slowly tilted his chin up, blue eyes heady and needy.

"Come here," John breathed.

Wyatt reached for him. John pulled him to his feet and into his arms, and they began to sway in a slow dance.

Wyatt hummed, dropping his head onto his upper chest, hands traveling over his body freely. He wanted nothing more than to finish what they had started earlier, but he also equally, and maybe more powerfully, wanted to hold his cowboy in his arms.

They swayed, moving to the guitar's rhythm.

"Your family is incredible," Wyatt murmured against him. "Which makes sense, they raised you."

"Thanks. Justine appreciated you playing with Olive at her level of intensity."

Wyatt chuckled, "I think she'd prefer being Zorro more than a queen."

"Yeah, that sounds about right."

"Your mom is really nice. She reminded me of you."

John nuzzled his face into Wyatt's hair. "I haven't seen her this happy in a while. It was good to see her smile."

"Well, yeah, she has one less person to worry about."

He paused mid-sway. "What do you mean?"

Wyatt leaned back, hesitating. "She may have… uh, asked me directly if we were seeing each other."

Startled, John recalled the brief moment he saw Wyatt and his mom setting the dining table together. His mom was intuitive, like Justine, like him. She was a smart woman, too, and had probably known all along that her son was gay.

"And?" he asked quietly.

"I wasn't going to tell her we're just fucking," Wyatt said, exasperated. "So yeah, I told her we're together."

John released him, pulse racing. "How'd she react?"

"She looked happy to me," he reassured. "Then she asked if I was serious about you, and then how old I was. I told her I was serious and that I cared about you a lot."

John suddenly laughed, it was weak with relief. "My sister did the same thing when we were saying goodbye."

His cowboy shifted, looking nervous, "And?"

John studied him, seeing the trace of blush on his cheeks as he whispered, "I said the same thing."

Relief relaxed Wyatt's features, and he swayed into him. "Well, good thing our stories lined up, or that would've been awkward."

Technically, their stories didn't line up. He had told Justine he loved Wyatt twice now, and even Wyatt didn't know this yet. And besides, his parents loved him and would love him no matter who he loved, so it made sense that his mother's reaction was so… unbothered. He smiled.

"I have an idea," he said, kissing the side of Wyatt's stubbled cheek.

Wyatt hummed, their bodies brushing.

"Well, more of a request."

Wyatt's eyes leveled with his. "Go on."

John sucked in a nervous breath. "I know that normally at this point we—well, we have fun." He felt ridiculously self-conscious all of a sudden. "And I know I sorta promised something earlier. But I like this, too. A lot, actually. Could we sit outside and just…?"

"Are you asking to *not* have sex and *talk*?" Wyatt teased, a slight smile tugging at the corner of his lips.

"Yeah."

"I'll open another bottle of wine," he said easily, already heading for the kitchen, and paused. "Do you have a sweater I could borrow?"

John nodded, loving the idea of seeing his sweater on his cowboy.

A few moments later, John joined Wyatt on the patio and noticed that he had grabbed not only a fresh bottle of wine and their glasses, but also a pumpkin pie with two forks.

His chest warmed and he smiled as he handed Wyatt his favorite old sweater from a trip he took to Tahoe a few years back. He slipped it on, the blue sweater fitting him perfectly. Wyatt then promptly patted the spot beside him on the outdoor sofa.

John snuggled close beside him, feeling the heat from the firepit warming him, but not as well as Wyatt.

"Serious question," Wyatt said in that thready, deep voice that turned his insides to goo. "Whipped cream or no whipped cream?" he hitched his chin to the pumpkin pie.

John smirked, "On you or the pie?"

"I thought you said you wanted to chill."

"Oh, I do, but I also love it when your voice drops like that. It's so fucking sexy. It gives me goosebumps almost every time."

A glorious blush sparkled on his cowboy's cheeks. "It's the tone I use with patients when they're scared—or the horses when they need to be calmed. Or…"

John saw the glimmer of mischief in his pale blues.

"Seducing you," Wyatt admitted.

"You've known this whole time?" he asked, surprised but not. Wyatt could read him like an open book, so of course he figured out how his voice set his pulse racing.

Pride flashed on the younger man's face as he murmured, "I figured it out the first night I had you in bed."

His chest tingled and he reached for him, kissing him, blood heating in his veins like lava as he kissed down his jawline to the red hickey on his neck and ravishing him once more.

Wyatt let out a whimpering sigh, "Fuck me."

John closed his eyes, loving how desperate he sounded. How good he felt against him. How perfect his evening had been once he had shown up.

"I think I plan to do exactly that…" he drawled, causing Wyatt to gasp a breathy sigh. "…Later."

Wyatt's next sound was slight disappointment and a pout.

John snorted in surprise, releasing him, "Are you seriously pouting?"

"What?" Wyatt whined. "Just because I like to ride you like the best damn stallion in all of LA doesn't mean this cowboy doesn't like to be taken out for a ride himself every once in a while."

He chuckled, leaning forward to share the pumpkin pie as they sipped their wine.

"Thank you for coming tonight," John said after a few minutes, setting the empty pie tin on the ground. "I liked seeing you here, with my family."

"Thanks for letting me stay. I'm sorry—"

"Don't apologize for anything. You didn't do anything wrong."

"I shouldn't have just shown up tonight."

John sighed, "And I shouldn't have shut you out." He reached for his hand, their fingers tangling. "I shouldn't have done that. I'm the one who's sorry."

Wyatt's fingers wrapped with his, his voice gentle as he said, "You ran."

He tilted his head to the side and acknowledged the truth, knowing what he was referring to: Wyatt's vulnerable confession of love for him after he was attacked.

John didn't want him to take back the words. And a part of him was terrified of hearing it again, because only a few months ago he had been steps away from the black void in his soul. And he wasn't sure he was ready to let love in yet. No matter how much he wanted it—needed it. How much he felt it for Wyatt.

"I ran," John acknowledged in a harsh grate.

Wyatt's pale blue eyes sparkled against the orange light of the fire. "I suppose after life-altering orgasms and almost getting your head cut off aren't exactly the best times to confess anything."

Once more surprised by Wyatt's levity and lightness, John pressed his firm kiss into his knuckles. Or maybe it was the best time, he thought.

"Where did you go?" Wyatt asked quietly.

His eyes searched his, frowning.

"Samuels was worried about you when you left my room. He mentioned he saw you take the stairs."

John swallowed, averting his gaze, unable to hold it. "Outside. Just went to get some air."

Wyatt nodded slowly, knowingly. "On the roof?"

Fuck.

"Only quiet place in the whole damned hospital," John said, noting the defensive armor pushing against his chest, wanting to protect himself.

"Look at me," Wyatt's voice was direct and low.

Something told him not to, to run again—to not let him see how scared he was. Because in this moment, he knew Wyatt would see it again, the love and the fear, meshed together in this horrible fucking knot that he couldn't untangle, that was stuck in the hollow of his throat and in the pit of his soul.

He finally did, sucking in a deep breath and staring head-on into the face of the man he couldn't hide anything from.

Wyatt's gaze was unexpectedly soft, almost tender, as he drew his hands into his lips, kissing each finger one at a time. Not in a sensual way, but an affectionate one. "I'm not worried, just so you know."

"About?"

"You."

The aching pit tightened in his stomach and he trembled. He hadn't expected that. He had learned at a young age that armoring himself, suppressing his emotions with family and friends, was a way to control not only what they saw when they looked at him, but also to protect them from worrying. Especially his parents.

"Why not?" John asked tightly.

"I think you believe that being sensitive makes you weak. It doesn't. It's the strongest thing about you. And you run from it because you have some shit in your head about, I dunno, being a man? A failure? Enough?"

He sucked in a breath, disconcerted at how paper-thin his armor was against Wyatt.

"You don't ever have to hide it from me," his cowboy whispered. "I wish you didn't feel ashamed about the most incredible part of you."

The invisible weight strapped to his shoulders slowly began to slide down his back and off his body.

"Your emotions don't scare me, John." Wyatt reached for the back of his neck, dragging him into a tender kiss. "It's your armor that does."

Speechless, emotion gripping his heart like a fist, Wyatt once more pressed his lips against his before leaning back to begin rubbing his shoulder again, and he let out a hiss of pain.

"When Samuels said you tackled that asshole with your shoulder, I knew you'd be sore."

A weak laugh spilled out and his incredible, sexy, compassionate cowboy rubbed his shoulder down, humming low and throaty, forcing John to relax again.

After several minutes, John was sprawled out on the sofa, shoulder thoroughly taken care of, sipping wine and stroking his fingers through Wyatt's soft hair. He loved the feel of his head on his lap as they gazed into the fire and the dark landscape of his backyard.

"Tell me about your dad," Wyatt asked softly.

Maybe because he was so relaxed, he felt that he could talk about his dad. Or maybe it was because it was Wyatt asking. "He was diagnosed last year with dementia. We had been seeing signs for a while, though. He'd forget small things, telling the same stories, losing his sense of direction in the grocery store he'd been going to for nearly twenty years."

He blinked back the emotion swirling behind his eyes. "My dad and I were pretty close, especially after Jacob died. We've always been a close family. I can't imagine not seeing them as often as we do. Hell, I'd babysit Olive more if I had more free time."

"You're lucky," Wyatt murmured.

John glanced down at the highlighted blond locks curling through his fingers. "Yeah, we are." He took a sip of wine, letting his emotions settle, letting the quiet stillness of the night roll over his body and the warmth of Wyatt against him. "My parents were lucky, too. They fell in love fast and hard. Said 'I love you' after only three months and got engaged within a year. My parents found their soulmates, and it made me and my sister silly romantics too, believing in true love."

"Do you still?" his voice was barely above a whisper, but he heard it.

"The honest answer… I dunno anymore. I spent nearly ten years married to a woman I thought I loved. I eventually realized that it wasn't love—it was people-pleasing and avoidance. She worked a lot. I worked a lot. Whenever we finally were in the same place at the same time, we were too exhausted to do much other than sleep. We didn't do this," he admitted roughly.

"Do what?"

"Cuddle by the fireplace and just talk."

Wyatt's hand reached over and found his, dragging it away from his hair and over his chest. The steady beat of his heart ticked beneath his palm, soothing him.

"My ex and I fought," John heard himself say. "Not enough to divorce, but enough to hurt each other. We tried for a baby, ignorantly thinking that would fix the issues between us. And then she couldn't have kids, and that was it. All that time, putting our energy into hope only to have it be denied, killed whatever was left between us. She left a few months later. The divorce was…" he sighed heavily, "well, it was pretty gruesome even for an ED doctor."

"I'm sorry."

"I want to still believe in soulmates like my parents," he murmured, his hand stroking Wyatt's chest, smelling his faint natural scent mixed with fire and wine. "I do know one thing," he said, voice unexpectedly shaking. "I've never felt like this with someone before."

"Probably because I'm pretty fuckin' incredible," Wyatt teased arrogantly, rolling up to glance at him. The firelight danced over his beautiful face and John, at that moment, was in awe, smiling down at him.

"That you are," he replied, swallowing the emotion.

"You are too, you know."

Something quiet passed between them, and John kissed his shoulder, "Thanks."

"Come with me to Arizona," Wyatt said, surprising him.

He blinked, hesitating.

"Come with me," Wyatt pressed firmly. "And then when we're done, we'll come home."

Emotion, like a gut punch to his stomach, hurdled through his entire body. "Home?"

"Here," Wyatt breathed. "Right here with you."

John closed his eyes briefly, realizing that everything he just said to Wyatt was a lie. That he did believe in soulmates—not just because of his parents—but because of him.

Wyatt sat up, slipping his hands around John's waist and drawing him close, releasing a long sigh. "I don't wanna go anywhere without you. I don't think I can anymore. You've ruined me entirely. I'm addicted to the crinkled laugh lines around your eyes, your half-hearted smile, your fuckin' beardy kisses, and the way you look at me… just me. I would imagine it's the same feeling the moon gets when it looks at the stars. Or when the sun looks at the flowers in spring."

John's eyes watered and he laughed weakly, "Now who's the romantic?"

"I've always been a romantic. You just gave me permission to actually be one." Wyatt kissed him tenderly, lovingly. "Say yes, John."

He nodded, heart aching. "Yes. I'll come with you."

Wyatt kissed him harder then, looking victorious for only a moment before picking up their wine glasses and standing up. "Let's go to bed. We have an early flight tomorrow."

"Tomorrow? Seriously?"

"I booked an extra ticket, hoping you'd say yes."

He opened his mouth to protest when Wyatt cut him off with a firm head shake.

"You know all we gotta do is tell Steph and she'll handle it."

John stiffened, uncomfortable with the idea of—what? Asking for help? This had been his problem the last six months, and it took the people around him to remind him he wasn't supposed to do everything on his own.

"Okay," he released a hard breath. "Samuels isn't going to be thrilled, possibly sharing shift time with Walsh."

Wyatt frowned, "Did you catch what he said earlier about no one special back home?"

John stood and nodded. "You think he was lying?"

"If I had a you back home that I was in love with and couldn't have—I would have to leave."

Goosebumps erupted over his arms and he swallowed, envious of how easy it was for Wyatt to be so vulnerable with his feelings, and how the word "love" continued to roll off his tongue in reference to him.

Wyatt shook his head, "I feel bad for him. Something must have happened that made him move all the way across the country to avoid his, Dr. Donnelly."

He blushed, "You think so?"

Wyatt's pale blue eyes locked with his. "I know so."

They walked back inside the house and Wyatt set their glasses down, slipped his hand into John's, and led him to the bedroom. John was oddly nervous as Wyatt flipped on the bedside lamp and began to pull off his sweater and the shirts beneath, revealing his beautiful chest, all soft skin and hard muscles.

"I want that ride, Dr. Donnelly," Wyatt husked in that seductive voice, and John released the breath in his chest.

Fuck yes.

Wyatt stood before him, slipping off his buckle, eyes heated and low, chest panting already with desire as he stripped before him.

"Do anything you want to do to me," Wyatt said almost pleadingly. "I fuckin' need it, daddy."

John nearly groaned, realizing what he was asking. He was asking for the command—the authority of Dr. Donnelly that was steady and sure, confident and—him.

He went to him, hand collaring the base of his throat and tilting him back, watching the excitement blaze up at him, hungry and needy.

Wyatt wanted to be dominated, and John wanted that, too.

"Undress me," John ordered coolly.

Wyatt's breath exhaled from his nostrils, and he complied instantly, hands trembling as he did so, slipping under his sweater, dragging it off his body and revealing his naked chest as he started to reach for him. He let his cowboy explore his body, trailing grasping hands over his shoulders, pecs, and downward to his jeans, unbuttoning him quickly with an eagerness that was felt all the way down to his toes, filling his cock.

He slipped off his shoes, helping Wyatt with his jeans and briefs, and stood naked before him, his cowboy resting on his knees, hands cupping the backs of his legs and slowly moving upward.

John shook his head, knowing how much Wyatt loved to suck his dick, but not tonight—tonight he was in charge. He moaned at John's denial and defiantly grazed his face against his thickening cock, hands traveling upward to palm his ass. John nearly choked out a gasp at the sight of Wyatt's needy expression as he bypassed his dick, clearly wanting it but reluctantly getting to his feet, pouting.

He reached for his throat again, liking the feel of his leaping pulse beneath his grasp as he glared at him. "Do that again, but don't open your mouth."

Wyatt let out a rush of air and instantly dropped to his knees, brushing and burying his face against John's cock and the hair nestled around it. He'd never seen something so dirty—so sexy. His cock was straining and beginning to leak as Wyatt desperately fought the urge to open his mouth, his lips tightening as he nuzzled and pushed John's cock over his chin and lips, pressing hard and urgent kisses beneath his shaft, against his balls, into the hair. Wyatt continued to push and press. The sensation he was creating was both arousing and frantic, and he liked watching him squirm with desire.

John lifted his leg onto the bed, widening his stance, and Wyatt didn't wait to be told what to do as he pushed his face under him, hands opening his cheeks and kissing his tight entrance.

"Use your tongue," John rasped.

Wyatt moaned and did, burying his face into his ass, tongue spearing hotly into his hole, and he rewarded him with a deep groan. Wyatt instantly reached for his jeans, unbuttoning them and grabbing the bulge that was tenting against the denim.

"Both hands on me, baby," John ordered, and Wyatt didn't protest, hands on his cheeks, widening him again, tongue lapping and thrusting.

John's cock thickened between his legs, slapping against his thigh as he began to rock his hips over Wyatt's tongue. This would've been easier on the bed, but he didn't want to lose his position of power. He wanted Wyatt to be the one on his knees or back.

John reached behind him, grasping Wyatt by the back of his head, and arched into his face, shoving him deeper into his ass. The tantalizing sounds of wet sucking and groans filled the air as John felt nothing but his cowboy's tongue and mouth devouring his entrance.

"Fuck, you do that so fucking good, baby."

Wyatt whimpered.

"You like eating my ass?"

He whimpered again, shaking against him.

"Fuck yes," John moaned. "Give me that fucking tongue."

Wyatt lapped greedily until John's tip was smearing all over himself and he finally couldn't stand it anymore and yanked Wyatt off him. He fell back in a whoosh of breath and let out a stream of curses, grabbing his dick over his jeans, painfully aroused.

"Come here," John commanded, and Wyatt did. "Take off your jeans."

Wyatt nearly stumbled trying to get them off so quickly, and John could've laughed at how adorable he was, but he kept his expression composed, not wanting to break the spell of authority that Wyatt clearly had a raging hard on for. When his dick popped free from the confines of his briefs, he was brutally hard, precum wet against his tip.

John reached for him, moving his hands over his muscled chest and down the sloping V of his hips, to the apex of his cowboy's glorious dick. It was his turn to suck.

He dropped to his knees and Wyatt let out a surprised, breathy moan, followed by a stream of curses as John opened his mouth over him and drew in the thick, straining cock.

He tasted the salt, smelled the musk of his sex, and his cock twitched eagerly as he began to suck up and down the shaft. The feeling of Wyatt moving in and out of his mouth was intoxicating and addicting, and he loved the feel of the thick flesh that filled him, sliding over his lips, nearing his throat.

"John…" Wyatt whispered hoarsely. "I—fuck…!"

John gagged on his dick, throat closing over him, making him shudder and blindly grab him with both hands around his head, fucking his mouth.

"Fuck, daddy," he moaned arching backward, quickly spearing in and out, humping and moving down his throat and mouth as if he were fucking him, and John was so hard he couldn't think, only feel.

But he didn't want Wyatt to climax like this. He wanted to feel him shudder and break beneath him. John pulled back, ruthlessly tonguing his tip and causing Wyatt to buck before he slid off him.

"Get on the bed," John grated out, his throat raw from the intrusive feel of Wyatt's sex.

Wyatt climbed quickly into bed, practically stumbling, his stomach heaving with breath and cock deliciously full, hair tossed and lips parted in want. He, in this very moment, wanted to imprint this image of Wyatt in his mind forever and draw it out as long as he could.

"Touch yourself," he growled.

Wyatt slowly traced his hand over the flat planes of his stomach and down to the apex of his masculinity, grasping it and tugging it upward.

"You're beautiful," John rasped.

Wyatt trembled, stroking himself, and John, unable to resist the visual temptation, took his own meaty cock in his hand, fisting over himself. Their eyes locked and held.

It was incredible.

He was incredible.

Breathtaking.

"Fuck," John sighed. "Beautiful and mine. Aren't you, baby?"

Wyatt swallowed, his throat bobbing, as he pulled his cock root to stem. "Yes, yes." He arched upward, already writhing on the bed.

He slinked onto the bed, crawling over Wyatt's body, ravenous for him in ways he didn't understand and never knew he could be for a person. And yet he was. He wanted to be engulfed, consumed, and completely vanish into him.

With a roughness he didn't anticipate from himself, John gripped Wyatt's thighs and up over his hips, digging his fingers into him, marveling at his big dick and hard body.

"God, I want you," he murmured, releasing him to reach for the lube on his nightstand and slickening it over the tips of his fingers before moving back beneath Wyatt, tilting his hips to give him access and feeling his tight entrance.

Wyatt cursed, gasping and vibrating against him as he slicked his rim, fingering him.

"So tight for me," he whispered.

Wyatt shivered as he pushed a finger into his tight entrance. His other hand fondled his balls, cupping them roughly and watching his young cowboy squirm some more.

He slid another finger into him, causing Wyatt to buck against him, moaning deep in his chest.

"The sounds you make with just my fingers in your ass," John said hoarsely. "I can't wait to hear the sounds you make when it's my dick."

Wyatt whimpered, trying to hump John's fingers, and he let him, enjoying the show of him rutting himself against him.

"That's it, baby," he drawled. "Show me how bad you want it."

Wyatt's eyes seared into his, fully blown out and almost unrecognizable with wanton horny lust. John just discovered Wyatt not only had a praise kink, but a dirty praise kink. The dirtier, the better.

"You're such a good, slutty boy for me..." John praised, and Wyatt's cock pulsed, leaking messily onto his stomach.

"Jesus, fuck..." Wyatt arched. "John...!"

He smiled deliciously down at his cock and sucked it into his lips, fingers deepening inside him, tasting the salty sweetness of his precum. He swirled his tongue around his engorged head before slowly popping off, watching it thump against Wyatt's stomach so hard it looked almost painful.

Heat pooled into his veins at the needy, desperate sight of him as he speared him a few more times, watching him writhe and gasp before finally sliding out of him and pressing the head of his cock into his entrance.

"Are you ready, cowboy?" John asked, breathing constricted and heart hammering.

"Please!"

He bit his inner cheek, ridiculously pleased and turned on, excited to turn this cowboy into a messy, ruined puddle of limbs and bliss. He held himself above Wyatt, hips locking into position as he pushed forward, sinking into his ass, his cock stretching his tight channel, and John nearly choked in pleasure.

"Oh fuck," John panted, feeling the rushing build of his own climax throb to the tip of his sex and the base of his balls. It felt so fucking good as he pushed deeper and deeper until Wyatt let out a torrid cry from the pit of his throat.

He had fucked Wyatt before, but this felt different. This felt like the first time, but better. He couldn't appreciate it before because he was so riddled with shame and armor, unwilling to receive the true pleasure from it. Now, he was fully exposed. Fully unguarded, desperately needing to see how good it was for Wyatt and feel that inside himself—inside his heart. Because Wyatt was seared into his soul.

John pulled slowly out, feeling the tightness of his cheeks clench around his cock, drawing out the ecstasy. He shuddered, and without waiting drove forward into a pounding thrust, hitting the prostate and causing a full back bend from Wyatt, who nearly launched off him. John held him down and did it again and again. The bed rocked against their combined movements.

He thundered into him relentlessly, watching Wyatt take it like the best bull riding champion, not once breaking rhythm. It was hypnotizing and...

"So fucking beautiful," John admitted out loud, watching the tensing of Wyatt's abdomen, his flexing hips, his clenched jaw as he held back the crushing orgasm. "So beautiful…"

John rutted into him, leaning over with both hands on the bed, fucking him with reverence. "My… good… dirty… cowboy. You take dick so fucking good."

Wyatt moaned. It was loud, unhinged, and wild. The sound went straight to his cock. He wasn't sure how much longer he could do this and knew he wanted to see Wyatt crash before him. He had to. John roughly reached between them, palming his throbbing cock as it slapped against his stomach, and tugged. Wyatt squirmed and the tension around his cheeks slammed around John's cock, hips bucking upward, eyes closed, straining—everything straining in glorious display just for him.

Mine.

He's mine forever.

"Fuck, baby!" John groaned.

Wyatt shuddered, cock erupting in his hand, streams of his bliss flying upward to his chest and stomach, coating him with milky, creamy cum.

"Christ, you cum so fuckin' good for me," John rasped, mercilessly tugging another few pulsating jets from Wyatt's cock as he continued to fuck him. His tempo was jerky and wild, losing his sanity with each thrust. Wyatt, breathing hard while being rocked and pounded, reached between them, eyes locked with his. He fingered his bliss and pushed it between John's lips, who sucked his finger down greedily. Tasting his man. Tasting the climax that John fucked out of him.

Tasting what was *his.*

That was his undoing.

He climaxed, breaking into Wyatt, shooting his load deep and hard into his tight ass. Wyatt clenched, milking and drawing him out, "God, yes..."

John shuddered, blinking back the stars behind his eyes.

He finally finished, heart racing as he slowly withdrew from him, body trembling.

Wyatt didn't move or speak, merely looked at him, panting and coated in cum, looking irresistible.

John, taking a page out of Wyatt's book of lovemaking, lowered himself over Wyatt's deflated cock and licked his tongue lovingly over him. His cowboy hummed, reaching for him and scraping through his hair.

"Cleaning up the mess you made, daddy?" Wyatt said hoarsely.

John's cock, impossibly, twitched.

He licked and licked, taking his time and marveling at the hard lines of Wyatt's body with his tongue and lips. Dipping lower, to the place between his legs, Wyatt arched for him, giving him access to the dripping, ruined ass he just annihilated with his cock.

"Please," Wyatt's voice was throaty and rough.

John did what he asked, wanting to. He tilted Wyatt's hips back, legs apart and ass open, pushed his beardy face between his cheeks and licked his puckered hole clean.

"Fuuuuck..." Wyatt gasped.

John tasted his cum leaking from him and pushed it back in with his tongue. Wyatt writhed against his face, slowly rocking his hips against him. It was a dirty sight.

Mine. Forever.

Thank fuck.

He finished cleaning him and sat back, smiling and panting, blood heating every limb of his body.

Wyatt swallowed, eyes at half mast, "You're fucking good at that."

John grinned, got up, and grabbed a towel from his bathroom, cleaning Wyatt and himself off before sliding into bed and spooning the loose-limbed cowboy against him, nuzzling the back of his neck. Wyatt sighed contentedly and pulled him close.

"I love fucking you," John confessed, kissing Wyatt's naked shoulder.

He hummed, "I love being fucked by you."

"Good. Because I'll need to do that at least once a week."

Wyatt relaxed deeper into him and laughed. "Yes, fucking, sir."

John smiled, his heart barely suppressing the words he was so desperate to say, and yet he didn't know why, but he couldn't say it.

Both men drifted off to sleep. And for the first time in their relationship, they knew that whatever tomorrow brought, they would be okay because they had each other.

Chapter 21

Wyatt

The flight to Arizona hadn't been awful because of John, whom Wyatt kept looking over at as though making sure he was still there. When Wyatt had asked him last night, it hadn't been planned, but more of a wish. So, when John said yes, surprised relief had filled him, knowing he could be a little more confident on his journey home because John would be by his side.

When they arrived at the ranch, John let out a low whistle. "It's beautiful. I don't know what I was picturing, but I don't think this was it."

Wyatt grabbed John's hand from across the rental car and kissed his knuckles, unable to speak. It had been years since he'd been back. So much anger and grief came up when he thought about the ranch, his father, and Mateo.

But now, those feelings had finally settled. He pressed his lips into the heartlines of John's hand, love filtering through every fiber of his being for this man.

"Thank you again for this," he said softly.

John's eyes collided with his. "You don't have to thank me."

"I know."

"Do we need to reestablish a safe word?" John teased lightly, breaking the tension in Wyatt's chest.

"God, I hope it doesn't come to that."

"It won't," John's voice was even and firm. "I won't let it."

"My Aunts can be pretty intense. They make CIA interrogators look bad."

"I think I can handle them," he murmured, slipping his hand out of his and cradling his chin, stroking the line of his jaw with his thumb. John could handle anything, Wyatt knew that. He knew that this inner-city emergency department doctor was battle-hardened and tested by years of practice.

But could he handle Wyatt's heart, which felt like a thousand galloping horses stomping on his chest? Because John was here—with him—for him, and he loved him so much it fucking hurt. And he knew he'd never love anyone like he loved John.

"Ready?" John asked gently. "If not, I can drive us to a nearby bar… have a couple drinks… maybe get a hotel…"

"Fuck, that sounds good," Wyatt grated out, staring into the dark blue spark of John's heated gaze. "Kiss me."

John did, it was firm and yet gentle. It was exactly what he needed.

John pulled back, searching his gaze, "Safe word is eructation."

Laughter spilled from Wyatt's chest, "Really?"

John grinned, slipping on his sexy aviator sunglasses. "Wonderful. That was the exact result I was looking for, Dr. Lawson. So, yes, we will need to implement this into our vocabulary for the time being."

Wyatt tried not to melt like hot butter in his seat at the sound of Dr. Donnelly speaking.

"None of that, Dr. Lawson," John instructed firmly, both eyebrows arched as he popped open the car door. "Can't have you looking at me like that the next few hours and not expect me to drag you into an empty bedroom—or horse stall?"

"Only if it's clean," Wyatt drawled longingly and climbed out of the driver's side, inhaling the scent of dust and nature, a calm settling over his body as his boots hit the ground.

Wyatt gazed over the large house, which over the years had transformed from a working ranch into a private estate for tourists to rent. The porch had been re-stained and wrapped around the house, with plenty of cushion seating, fire pits, and overhead fans. The house was painted a cream white color and trimmed in dark brown, with potted plants adding the flare of color that lined the pathway and porch.

John's eyes moved from the house to Wyatt's beneath his sunglasses, and he bit back a sigh just looking at his handsome doctor. He wore a maroon-red button-up that was slightly wrinkled from all the traveling, which he rolled up past his elbows, exposing his thick forearms and wrists. An all-black watch dangled from his wrist, and he wore dark blue jeans and worn hiking boots. His brown, graying hair was ruffled, and his beard was trimmed. He looked relaxed and yet made sure to keep glancing Wyatt's way, checking on him without saying anything, which he appreciated.

He stared at the watch on John's wrist, his gaze traveling to his firm hand and fingers.

He wondered what his hand would look like with a matching black band around his ring finger.

Wyatt's chest swooped, and his heart slammed into his chest.

Oh fuck.

The door to the estate swung open, and Aunt Nancy and Aunt Carol appeared. Wyatt's thoughts were completely muddled by the time the older women made it down the porch steps, their flittering gazes jumping from Wyatt to John, clearly excited.

"Oh my God, Wyatt, honey," Aunt Nancy wrapped her arms around him, hugging him tight against her tall, slender frame. "I thought you were never..."

"Hush," Aunt Carol snipped at her. "We're so glad you're here, hon."

Aunt Carol hugged him next, her fuller build was sturdier and her hug firmer, as she patted his back.

They were married partners, the only gay couple Wyatt had known growing up, until he moved to LA. Aunt Nancy, his father's sister, had the Lawson family's sandy-brown blond hair that naturally waved and pale blue eyes. She wore red cowboy boots and a blue short-sleeved dress. Her skin was well tanned and her hair naturally graying through the blond streaks. He smiled warmly at her, remembering briefly that the last time he had seen her was a few Christmases ago.

Aunt Carol, her wife, had short hair and a round face. She wore jeans, a plain brown T-shirt, and a rodeo buckle. Her boots were black and her smile was contagious. She had been the first one to figure out Wyatt was gay, and he would always appreciate how she talked to him about it when he was a confused teenager.

"This is John," Wyatt motioned them to him. "My—uh..."

Boyfriend?

"Partner," John supplied cooly.

Wyatt's heart kicked again, and he wondered what it would be like to hear him say: *husband.*

What the fuck, Wyatt—knock it off!

Way too soon.

But was it? Because his heart, which he listened to and trusted, wanted to say these things to him now, and he didn't want to ignore it. But he also didn't have time to process it now. Not here.

Aunt Carol shot Wyatt a surprised look before clasping John's hand. Aunt Nancy followed, eyes wide.

"Good to finally meet you both," John said politely, and Nancy stiffened.

"Dr. John Donnelly?" Nancy asked.

John's eyebrows raised, and he nodded. "I believe we spoke on the phone."

She swung her gaze to Wyatt, lips parting in surprise. John had mentioned that one of his aunts had called the hospital trying to get a hold of him and he had intercepted the call, which meant he had probably used his title when answering… which meant she had just figured out where they had met.

"Nope," Carol said flatly. "Not goin' there, they just got here." She glanced at the rental car. "You boys need help unloadin'?"

"We didn't bring much," Wyatt admitted.

Carol pursed her lips, "Short stay?"

"Yeah."

Disappointment reflected on her face, but she hid it well behind a cool nod. "Well, c'mon in then."

The front door opened, decorated with fresh flowers and medical supplies.

Wyatt stopped in his tracks.

John's reassuring hand was on his lower back as he released the breath in his chest and walked through. The house's natural wooden beamed ceiling gave it a wide, open feeling, along with its floor-to-ceiling windows overlooking the ranch. His father had done a lot of the woodworking in the home himself after his mother had left them. He supposed it was his father's way of fixating on something—giving himself a project rather than pursuing the woman who had left him. Wyatt's mother died several years later in her sleep from a brain aneurysm. He was barely ten when he went to her funeral and met his half-brothers and sisters—the family she had built outside of him. He was confused and angry that she had chosen herself, leaving him behind with his cold, unapologetic father.

"He's in his room," Nancy informed him. "The hospice nurse will be back soon..."

"What's his diagnosis?" John asked, slipping his sunglasses off and over the open collar of his shirt. His eyes slid to Wyatt's, held, and then returned to Nancy's.

Wyatt didn't want to walk down the hallway.

He didn't want to see his father.

He wanted to go to the barn, see the horses—be anywhere else.

"Cancer," Nancy said tightly. "Prostate cancer. He stopped treatment two months ago. He was getting too sick with the chemo, too uncomfortable. He made the decision himself to just—you know..."

They did.

His jaw clenched. His father was a stubborn old bastard, and when he had made up his mind about something, he refused to bend. Another family trait, he supposed.

He released another breath and headed down the hall.

"Wyatt," John called softly. "Do you want me to...?"

He shook his head and followed his feet to his father's bedroom. If he didn't go now, he would never go.

His father's door was open, and the heart and oxygen monitor he was hooked up to were silent. Thankfully, the hospice nurse had muted the beeping. His throat bunched, and he finally looked at his father. His once handsomely stoic face was gray and ashen, the skin loose over the planes of his cheeks. The oxygen tube wrapped around his ears and into his nostrils, sustaining what was left of his lungs and body. His hair was patchy and thin, yet Wyatt could still see the streaks of sunlight mixed with the chestnut.

The strong, imposing man his father had once been was gone. He hadn't realized how bad it had gotten, and regret clawed at his insides for waiting this damned long to have the courage to come back. Tears formed at the corners of his eyes but he blinked, refusing to show emotion.

"Water," his father's voice was the barest of whispers.

Wyatt didn't hesitate, always willing to be of use to his father, even if the man never loved him. He loved him for what Wyatt did—but not for who he was. He fetched the glass of water from the bedside table and placed the soft plastic straw against his father's lips. He noted the sheen of lip balm coating his lips, preventing them from cracking.

He watched his father's throat work as he drew in the water and sighed, settling back down into his pillows, already spent from that slight movement. Wyatt carefully placed the water back and glanced back to see a pair of bright blue eyes looking back at him.

"Dad," Wyatt said with a nod.

"You're here," he rasped.

Wyatt was unsure if it was surprise or indifference in his tone.

"Yes, sir, I am."

His father's stare impaled him on the spot, making him feel like a kid all over again. But he wasn't a kid anymore.

"Why are you here?" his father asked.

"I think it's pretty obvious," Wyatt replied, glancing at the oxygen tank.

"You don't need to be here," he said sharply. "I don't need… you… with this."

Wyatt exhaled. His father never needed him, and his mother didn't want him. He was invisible to them both. His father only saw him as another ranch hand who ate at his table and cleaned out shit from the stalls.

Maybe it had been a mistake coming here.

"I'm sorry you feel that way," Wyatt said slowly. "I'm sorry if I was ever a burden to you. I didn't mean to be. I think the only thing we have in common is our stubbornness and love of horses," he choked, clearing his throat. "I… I can bring a horse around, if you want?"

His father's gaze wavered. "I can't ride anymore."

Wyatt nodded, "Can you walk?"

"No."

Wyatt glanced down at the hospice bed, frowning, wondering if it was anything like a hospital gurney and if he could roll it out.

"I got a wheelchair," his father grumbled. "Nancy knows where it is."

"Okay," he turned on his heel, and his father's voice stopped him.

"You don't—you don't have to do this."

Wyatt read his father's face and knew in that instant, he did.

"Yes, I do."

Wyatt strode down the hall to find Nancy, Carol, and John in the kitchen, drinking iced tea and sitting around the table.

"Could I get his wheelchair?" Wyatt asked Nancy.

She jumped up, head nodding. "Yeah, but we were told he shouldn't leave the bed without a nurse…"

"Well, good thing your nephew is a doctor, then," John said, also getting to his feet, his steady warm eyes holding his.

"I'm gonna bring a horse around," Wyatt informed them. "We'll lift him out of the bed when we get back."

Nancy and Carol stayed, and John followed him out the door.

Wyatt blindly followed the trail behind the estate to the massive working horse stable. He heard the birds chirp, felt the heat of the sun on his face, and yet his heart ached. It ached for the parents who couldn't give him the love he deserved. Ached for the father who wanted to see a horse more than his damned son.

"You okay?" John asked.

"Not really," Wyatt muttered. "He doesn't want me here."

"I think we all would like to believe that some of us soften under the eyes of death. But sometimes, the fighters insist on going down swinging."

"You mean the assholes."

"Well, I was trying to be…"

"Nice about it," Wyatt finished, the tension in his back shifting a little. "Because that's what you do. You see the kindness in everyone."

"Don't you?" John asked with a soft challenge in his gaze.

Wyatt shook his head, "Not today."

The two men walked silently into the barn, the scent of animal, hay, and leather filling his nostrils. He finally released the breath his soul seemed to be holding since he arrived.

Wyatt strode through the barn, hoping to recognize one of the horses but knowing it may be unlikely due to the years he'd been gone. His boots stopped at the second-to-last stall. It was Roxanne's best friend, Charity. He grinned, reaching for her snout, stroking up and down her thick brown fur.

"Hey, you…" He drawled. "Damn, it's good to see you."

"Who's this?" John asked, petting her affectionately.

"Charity. She was best friends with… Roxeanne. The horse that…"

Mateo's horse.

His horse.

John grasped his shoulder and nodded in mute understanding. He glanced back at Charity, trying to bring understanding and compassion to the darkness that had settled around Wyatt ever since they arrived. A darkness John held with light.

Because that was who he was.

"Hello, girl," John cooed, a genuine smile dancing on his lips, drawing up the crinkles around his eyes. "You're a looker, aren't ya? Aw, I see some gray. Looks better on you than me."

He gave him a sheepish, bashful smile, and Wyatt blinked.

"I love you."

John's hand stilled on Charity and he turned, dark blue eyes suspending him.

Wyatt had already told him how he felt that day at the hospital and neither of them had brought it up again. But he felt it so powerfully in this moment, the undeniable truth that blazed through his soul like a torch piercing the black.

"I love you so goddamned much that I can't breathe," Wyatt admitted, voice cracking. "I wasted my entire life wishing my dad would just love me. That's all I ever wanted. My mom left me behind and started another family. I never had a parent who loved me the way I needed to be loved. And it took coming back here to realize that I don't need that anymore. I need *you*. I need you to come to me on bad days and on good days. I need you on *my* good days and my bad days. Because I'm fuckin' terrified that I don't matter to anyone. Fuck, I need you to love me, John..."

Tears flooded him and he stepped away, digging his palms into his eyes and breaking apart at the seams.

Fuck.

He knew this would happen. He knew that coming here would hurt.

John's arms were around him, bringing him to his chest, and Wyatt collapsed against him, sobbing into his shoulder and breathing in his scent, embracing him like a life raft, desperate and gasping.

"I want everything from you, John," Wyatt confessed. "And if I can't have that, leave me here. Leave me in this fuckin' place and let me die like that old man, because you're my soulmate. I felt it the first time I kissed you. I think that's why I couldn't let you go. I can't let you go..." He continued to cry, shaking.

John pulled back, tears wetting his cheeks. He kissed him hard and dropped his temple to his. "You matter, Wyatt, don't you ever, *ever* doubt that. You matter so much to me," he rasped, voice threaded with emotion.

"I was too scared to say it, and I should've," John continued. "I fell in love with you on that first damned night. I was so scared because I didn't know it was supposed to be that easy. So, I tried to make it hard, thinking it couldn't be real—that *you* couldn't be real. And you wouldn't stop giving me reasons to love you," John praised, kissing him tenderly. "You were relentless and thank God for that. And when I saw you hurt, it broke me. I ran because it hurt to love you and lose you. I'm so, so sorry for that. I understand now that I can never, ever do that to you again. And I won't. I won't, baby," he said firmly, kissing the tears off his cheek. "I love you."

Wyatt hugged him hard against his body, so hard he could feel his heart beating against his own.

"I need you in my bed, my home, my life. I need you so fucking much." John continued, both men's tears turning into joy. "I think I might even beat my parents' record..." He drew back, capturing Wyatt's hand and tracing his ring finger. Wyatt's heart stopped and his breath sped up. "'Cause I don't think I can wait a year to make you mine forever."

Oh God.

Wyatt roughly grabbed him, pushing him against Charity's stall. John let out a whoosh of breath from the impact as Wyatt devoured him, heart dancing in his chest.

"My answer is yes," he whispered against John's wet lips.

John let out a sigh, and more tears filled his eyes. Wyatt was obsessed with his vulnerability, his sensitivity—knowing he felt everything so deeply, so passionately—and that heart belonged to him now.

"But first, we'll live together," Wyatt said, unable to stop the smile spreading across his face and knowing he probably looked like a fool in love, but it didn't matter because John was looking back at him the same way. "Make sure it works."

"It will," John replied firmly, kissing him.

"It will."

He thought briefly of seducing John in the barn, of feeling their love in the most sensual way possible, with the smell of leather, hay, and animals filtering through his bloodstream, becoming a bit animalistic himself. Because he could do that here. This barn was the only place growing up where he felt truly free. He had lost his virginity to Mateo here on a stormy, hot night, caught up in the turbulence of the storm and each other. Working with the horses here also made it the first place he had understood the value of giving without wanting anything in return. He had found himself here, became the person he is today because of this scared place.

And damn, did he want to drop to his knees right now and give in to the temptation.

But he had unfinished business with his father. Until things felt settled and he could breathe easier here again, all those deliciously naughty things he wanted to do to John would have to wait.

"I know you've got complicated feelings about being back here," John began slowly, fingers reaching for the collar on Wyatt's shirt and stroking the stubble beneath his jaw. "And I certainly don't want to add to it, but..." He glanced over his shoulder at Charity, his eyes crinkling in a warm smile before sliding back to Wyatt and holding it. "I think I would love to see your home through your eyes someday. Me being the student, you being the teacher. Teaching me how to ride a horse, do the whole cowboy thing. I am positive I would love every second of it."

"Even cleaning out a stall?" Wyatt asked, throat clenching.

John scrubbed the back of his neck, bashful and so heart-stoppingly cute. "Yeah. Sign me up, John Wayne."

Emotion welled up inside him and he nodded. "I would love that."

John's smile reflected his love and excitement, and Wyatt couldn't hold back any longer, giving him another thorough, ravishing kiss. John swayed and melded into him. Their embrace wasn't sexual, it was love. Their vulnerability, it was just them. Without barriers, expectations, or shame.

"And just so we're clear," Wyatt rasped between kisses. "This place *was* my home. It's not anymore, John. You are."

He mentally attempted to ingrain the image of John, just like this, in his mind to hold forever. His reaction, his happiness, his glow.

"I want everything from you," Wyatt whispered, dropping his temple to his.

"And I'll always give it," John murmured, trembling against him.

But Wyatt wasn't done. He wanted to rip all the armor off of John and never be pushed away again.

"I want you to give me what you can't—what you won't—because that's what I need," Wyatt framed his face in his hands, forcing him to look at him. "I need all of it, because all of it is *you*, and I love you."

"Yeah, ok," he breathed as tears, fat and heavy, slid down his handsome face. "Fuck, I love you so much. You see me, you see all of me, and that's a gift. You're a gift. You're a good man—a good fuckin' soul. How'd I get so lucky?"

He slowly kissed his tears away, holding him. "That's my line."

They kissed one last time, and then Wyatt showed him how to bridle a horse, and together they led Charity out of the barn. Her pretty mahogany-gray hair shone under the sunlight as she moved with muscular grace across the trail back to the house.

He tethered her to the horse post outside by the porch, and together they helped his father out of bed and into the wheelchair. John carefully maneuvered the oxygen tank as he guided him out onto the porch.

His father didn't say anything, but he sighed when he was settled outside, seeing Charity and the sprawling ranch. Everything his father had built and loved so dearly. Wyatt knew his father's love was reflected not in his words, but in his labor and time. He swallowed his grief and proceeded to brush Charity, teaching John how to do it and how to talk to her. John was an attentive, easy student, taking his instruction effortlessly.

The Arizona sun was glowing in an orange haze, illuminating his father's pale skin as he leaned back, taking it in.

They spent a long time out there.

Carol brought out a bottle of wine and Nancy made a simple pasta dish that they enjoyed for dinner on the porch. Wyatt's father didn't say much as he watched the sunset and the horse. He didn't eat, didn't drink. Wyatt had glanced at the oxygen monitor, knowing his father's heart rate was steadily declining throughout the day. Nancy had called the hospice nurse, and she was on her way to be with the family.

"She needs to be bedded," His father ordered gruffly, indicating to Charity.

"Yes, sir," Wyatt said automatically, getting to his feet and noticing how the sun was tucking itself behind the distant horizon, taking him back to countless times his father had given this order around this time.

"Can it wait?" John asked quietly, checking his father's monitors, a grim line flattening his lips.

"Yeah." Wyatt noticed his father's eyes were barely open, but just enough to focus on John. "You my doctor?"

John smiled politely, "At the moment, yes."

"My boy's trainin' to be a doctor."

John hummed and nodded, sliding his hands into his jeans pockets, so casually attuned and listening the way he would with a patient, or with him.

"Is that right?" John asked.

"Workin' in the city," his father rasped. "Big city doctor."

"Impressive."

"Damn right," his father said, surprising him. "He's—he's a good kid."

John nodded, "I couldn't agree more."

Wyatt's father's gaze studied John's. "You know him?"

"I do," John murmured. "I happen to love him very much."

Wyatt stilled, eyes darting to his father's, waiting for the reaction.

His father nodded weakly. "Good."

Wyatt's heart broke, tears racing down his face.

Forgiveness was complicated. Hard. And yet, also so fucking soft and fragile, like a warm tear on a cheek, or like the drifting of new snow through the air. He had a choice at that moment: keep holding on to his anger and hurt, or accept his father. Accept that this man did the best he could with what he was capable of, and maybe that was enough. Because the forgiveness wasn't for his father… it was for himself.

He shuddered and knelt down to his father's side, emotion clogging his throat as he reached for his frail fingers. "I'm here, Dad."

He sighed. "I'm sorry."

"It's okay," Wyatt managed to say through his tears.

"It's not," he muttered. "I didn't—I failed you. I shouldn't have hurt you. I shouldn't have kicked you out—denied the only good thing in my whole fuckin' little life."

"Stop."

"I..." he sighed again, guilt pinching around his lips. "I should've done better by you."

His heart broke even more, remorse eating away at him and feeling like he, too, should've done more than just run—that he should've done more than just a phone call here or there. That maybe...

No, no regrets.

Not now.

Don't let our last moments be like this.

John gave Wyatt a silent look full of compassion and tenderness. He thought of the first time he lost a patient at the ED and how John had been there, holding him with simply a look.

"Your last words aren't allowed to be an apology, Dad," Wyatt whispered, kissing his forehead.

"Love you, son," his father whispered, gurgled and strained, and his eyes were wet with tears.

"I love you, too."

The next few days happened in a blur. His father passed in his sleep that night, with Wyatt by his bedside. Nancy and Carol had already made funeral arrangements, and the lawyer came by with the deed to the ranch, which Wyatt signed over to his aunts, who sobbed upon receiving it from him.

This wasn't his life anymore.

The funeral was small, yet he was surprised to see Mateo's pregnant sister had come to pay her respects wearing a pretty floral coral dress, her husband by her side. He greeted her with a hug and a kiss, they exchanged pleasantries, and then he introduced John to her. It felt good to see the warmth in her bright brown eyes as she shook John's hand, and tears unexpectedly swelled in his throat.

He never knew what closure was until that moment.

Mateo had been his first love.

And John was his last love. His true love.

Everything had come full circle.

The plane ride was short, but he was exhausted by the time they made it back to John's place the following day.

John called the hospital and requested another week off for both of them, as well as a meeting with Tanya when he got back to inform them of their relationship, which Wyatt agreed to. He wasn't worried and was ready to take whatever consequences they might face, and so was John.

They spent the next few days moving Wyatt into John's place. He was still adjusting to this being his home, but was slowly getting used to it, especially now that his things were there. Jin was excited for him. They agreed to make time for each other and planned brunch for the following week to fill him in on all the details.

Wyatt finished breaking down the last box and stuffed it into the recycle bin. He headed back inside and closed the front door, pausing at the sight of his cowboy boots next to John's shoes.

I belong here.

I'm loved here.

His thoughts stilled him. John had truly worked hard on making this place feel like his. Feel like home. Wyatt's grief had rolled in waves the last few days, but every time he needed comfort, John was there. He knew it would take time to move through the grief and he was okay with that, because he was okay. He was more than okay.

He was home.

He was loved.

And he couldn't wait to start this next phase of his life with the man of his dreams by his side.

"I'm too tired to cook. How does pizza sound?" John asked from the kitchen, pulling out two beers from the fridge.

He tore his gaze away from the shoes and strolled into the kitchen, taking the cold beer John handed him. "Sounds good." He cracked the can open and took a sip, letting the carbonated flavor pop on his tongue. "So… now that I'm moved in, do you prefer summer or fall weddings?"

John choked on his beer and came up laughing. "Easy, cowboy, we've got time."

"I prefer fall," Wyatt continued, smirking. "Cooler weather, and if we wanna have it outside, which I think we should—"

"Wyatt—"

"We should probably plan for early next fall, because I want your dad to be there."

John's tone softened, "Wyatt…"

"Because he needs to see his son happy," he pressed on determinedly. "He needs to know you're taken care of."

John's throat bobbed, and he reached for him. "We don't have to be married for him to see that."

"He does. He's a romantic, just like his son."

He tilted his head into Wyatt's, sighing. "I love you so damn much."

"I love you more," he murmured back. "We should host Christmas."

John kissed him. "My parents usually host, it's sorta their thing."

"Okay," Wyatt kissed him back, nipping his lower lip. "*We* can host New Year's."

"Yes, *we* can."

"And I'll propose in front of everyone there. Champagne, ring in the bubbles, make it a whole big thing."

John laughed, blushing, scrubbing a hand over the back of his neck. "You're not gonna let this go, are you?"

Wyatt shook his head, smiling. "Never when it comes to you."

John stared right through him and into his soul. "Good. I love you."

"I love you."

Chapter 22

John

Christmas night

"I'm surprised you didn't go back home," John said to Samuels, who was unlocking his locker.

"Yeah, well, been busy here," he said with an indifferent shoulder shrug.

John's gaze narrowed. Maybe he was spending too much time with Wyatt, but he had been noticing body language far more often lately. And he was noticing that Samuels seemed *off* this week.

"Not to push the subject…" John began.

Samuels's chin hitched to the side, green eyes fixed on his. "Something tells me you're about to push anyway."

"Well, yeah. I care about you, man. And you've been distant this past week. Wanna talk about it?"

Samuels scratched his whiskered cheeks, debating. "Now?"

John nodded, glancing around the empty hallway. They were off the clock, both heading home, and it was the holidays. Mostly everyone was in a good mood, unless they were coming in as a patient.

"Yeah, now."

Samuels's hands stiffened on the sweater before tugging it on, ruffling his hair. "It's…"

"Complicated?"

"Yeah."

"Aren't we all?"

Samuels arched an eyebrow, "Have you started therapy, or is that Wyatt talkin'?"

"Both," John admitted, unable to stop the warmth spreading through his entire body at the casual reference to Wyatt's influence on him.

Once they had returned to work, both men disclosed their relationship to their higher-ups. After several lengthy conversations, Tanya agreed to let Wyatt stay, but only on different shifts until he was fully accredited and licensed, after which they could work together. So for now, Wyatt worked with Walsh on the night shift. The other agreement he came to with Tanya was that Wyatt and he would have the same days off.

Being passing ships during the workweek was hard, but having the same days off together made it more bearable.

They also planned to travel, taking much-needed vacations and seeing the world together. John hadn't taken a proper vacation in years, but now he had a reason to. And he may have impulsively decided to go ring shopping with Justine and his mom last week, so… there was that.

John had also rebooked a session with Miles, the therapist he saw a few months ago, and was giving it a real shot this time. He knew his job was challenging and he knew Wyatt could handle almost anything, but therapy was more for John, and what he appreciated most about his sessions with Miles was the emotional processing component. It was a safe place to just let everything out and begin to understand himself better. He learned that dark thoughts were normal, and physicians often need a lot of support due to the trauma that occurs while working in emergency medicine.

John was working on accepting help, and it felt good, most of the time. But there were some days when he still wanted to hide. Maybe that's why he was so focused on Samuels, because he understood his friend far more than he realized. Selfishly, too, John wanted to see him happy. So yeah, if he had to stand here all night, he would.

"Don't evade the question," John said, relaxing against the lockers and folding his arms across his chest.

Samuels sighed, "All right, fine. I'm avoiding home because of a certain… friend."

"Just friends?"

"Unfortunately," Samuels grumbled.

"For…?"

"Me," Samuels said it casually, yet John heard the faint trace of emotion laced in his tone.

Wyatt had been right. Samuels had run from love, just like Wyatt said *he* would've done if John hadn't loved him back.

"Mostly me," Samuels continued, clearing his throat. "Though he'd probably argue that he loved me, but as a brother."

"And that isn't enough?" John asked knowingly.

Samuels looked uncharacteristically defeated. "Fifteen years is a long time to hold out hope for something that will never happen."

"Jesus, Samuels, I'm sorry. That's rough." John stared at his friend, searching his face and knowing he was in pain. "Wanna talk about it?"

"Don't you have somewhere to be?"

John kicked his feet out to the side, getting even more comfortable against the metal lockers, "Nope."

Samuels huffed, shoving his hands into his jeans pockets, his body tense in comparison. Clearly, this conversation made his friend uncomfortable, but much like Samuels, he seemed to bear it well. He wondered how much he could tolerate, and if that was a good thing—or not.

"So, what happened?" John asked. "Something must have happened for you to be here."

"I kissed him," Samuels stated simply, without the slightest remorse.

John arched his eyebrows, impressed, and then thought about Wyatt, knowing what it was like to be on the receiving end of one of those surprisingly passionate kisses. And if Samuels had fifteen years of pent-up emotions, he could only imagine what kind of explosive kiss that was for his "friend".

"That's it?" John teased.

Samuels glowered. "It was a *kiss* kiss."

Yeah, he thought, he knew exactly what he meant. It was the kind of kiss that ruined a person. Destroyed them for the next person. And Samuels had done it to his best friend.

"And it was at the worst fuckin' moment possible. It was at my grandpa's funeral," Samuels admitted.

John blinked, "Okay, so... what'd he do? Hit you?"

Samuels let out a huff through his nostrils. "No, unfortunately. Instead, I somehow induced paralysis, which, thinking back, makes sense. He couldn't exactly slug me at my grandpa's funeral. And I haven't seen him since."

"LA's pretty far from Boston, from what I hear."

"Yeah, it is." Samuels shifted, yanking his backpack out of his locker. "Are we done with the interrogation?"

John smiled, hands shooting up defensively. "Yes, we are. Sorry. Dinner's at six. My mother likes roses, any color, and my dad likes whiskey, any kind."

Samuels smirked and nodded, "See you later."

John turned to him, "Can I just say something?"

"Sure…?"

"It's Christmas, Samuels. You know, the time of year for forgiveness…"

Samuels's hand fisted his backpack. "It's not like that. I already know he's forgiven me."

Curious, John's eyebrows furrowed. "So, what's the problem?"

"I haven't forgiven myself."

John felt the stab in his gut, recognizing that pain. No wonder he liked Samuels so much—they were very similar. "Why not? You were vulnerable—grieving…"

Samuels shook his head, "No, I don't regret the kiss. I regret that it took me that long to finally do it."

A deep sadness passed over Samuels's face, his lips tightening before releasing an almost strained breath. "Let go or be dragged. I spent fifteen years hanging on to someone who could never love me back, and it's not his fault. It was self-imposed. Very likely due to my lack of self-worth, with a heavy sprinkling of childhood trauma and mommy issues."

John nearly laughed at how casually he said it, but resisted.

Samuels scrubbed a hand over his mustache. "I will always love him, and I know he will always love me. The difference is… *how* we love each other."

John's chest tightened, and he nodded. He couldn't imagine being in love with Wyatt and him not loving him back. He empathized, feeling incredibly helpless for his friend. He wished he could do more.

"Thanks," Samuels said, surprising him.

"For the interrogation?" John asked.

"Yeah, actually. Felt good to talk about it."

"My therapist is teaching me the importance of talking about hard stuff," he said lightly. "I can send you his number if you'd like?"

Samuels's throat bobbed and he nodded, "Yeah, okay."

"Good." John straightened, slipping his hands into the front of his sweater pockets. "See ya later tonight, Dr. Samuels."

"Yeah, text me if you guys need anything else besides flowers and whiskey."

"Will do."

John zipped up his hoodie and headed out the front lobby, busy as always, but the staff had decorated it with Christmas lights and hung white paper snowflakes made by the patients in the pediatric ward. The cold night air was refreshingly cool in his lungs as he headed toward the employee parking lot, excited to make it home and celebrate his first Christmas with Wyatt and his family.

He heard the revving of an engine and glanced up in surprise.

Wyatt, dressed in his sexy all-black cowboy getup, was straddling his bike and waiting for him.

His pulse stuttered and he hummed in approval. Wyatt slipped off his helmet, heat dancing in his bright blue eyes. "Wanna ride?"

Fuck. Yes.

"I certainly do, cowboy."

Wyatt smiled, handing him his spare helmet.

"You gonna dress like that to my parents' house?" John asked, raking his gaze over his body.

"No, I wore this hoping I'd get lucky before we went."

He bit his lower lip, excitement pooling in his belly. "Oh, so this is a seduction tactic?"

"Fuck, I love the doctor tone."

"Well, Dr. Lawson, I'm sure I could accommodate your needs tonight. But if we show up late to my parents' house, I will be very displeased."

Wyatt grinned mischievously, "We wouldn't want that, would we, Dr. Donnelly?"

Damn, this is already turning out to be the best Christmas ever.

All because of this very sexy, very generous cowboy of mine.

The end

Note from the Author

The inspiration for this story came to me during a difficult time in my career working as a mental health professional. I felt very unseen and was doing a tremendous amount of giving that led to over-functioning, burnout, and depression. Meanwhile, I felt like the universe was trying to tell me something. The Heated Rivalry TV show debuted alongside my other favorite show of the year, The Pitt, and my debut MM romance/thriller book, *I'd Find You In The Dark*, was finding its audience and fans.

I realized that the need for more MM romances with happily-ever-afters was being sought after in ways I could never have anticipated, but had always personally wanted. I felt like MM authors had been given true societal permission and acceptance of the genre in a *big* way. Meanwhile, on a personal level, I was experiencing my own mental health crisis, and this story came to me—well, Dr. Donnelly came to me. Because, in many ways, he is me. I needed a character to *hold* what I was carrying, so I created Wyatt to *see* the weight of the burden.

The universe listens even when we think it isn't.

Soon after I wrote this story, my life shifted again, and with the help of my husband, family, friends, and fans, I was able to come back to myself.

Being seen is such a gift and a power.

This book is an intimate portal not only into a love story but also a love note to those in the healing professions (or personal givers) who struggle to ask for help, hence the title: *Give Me What You Can't.* For many of us givers, it feels impossible to let go of what we carry because we *know* what it feels like, and we would rather do it ourselves than let someone else struggle.

I hope you enjoyed John and Wyatt's love story as much as I enjoyed writing it. And that maybe it gives you permission to love yourself a little bit more and to take a moment to truly rest, however that looks for you.

Lots of love,

Arielle

Acknowledgments

To my incredible husband, Paul. Your unwavering support, love, and encouragement got me to the next step and the step after that. I love you so damn much. Thank you for everything!

To my mom, thank you for your continued support and enthusiasm for my work, even when it surprises you. You are my rock in so, so many ways. You're the kind of mom people wish they had, and lucky me—you're mine! Forever! MUHAHA!

To Justine, you were an inspiration throughout this book for me. Your strength, endurance, and resilience are marvelous fucking things—just like you. I love you with all my heart and can't wait to keep geeking out over romances with you until we're old and gray and cackling with laughter in a bookstore or restaurant somewhere.

To Mandy—my editor! DUDE! *Dude.* You are an angel for reading SO much of my work in the last few months and working your butt off for me. Seriously. I cannot express my love and heartfelt gratitude for all that you have done and continue to do to support my author journey. I hope to one day repay the favor and cannot thank you enough for everything.

Thank YOU!

To those who have supported my writing online and in person, words cannot express my deepest love and gratitude! Being an indie author is, at times, grinding work, so whenever a fan reaches out to me, it reminds me to keep going and not give up on my dreams. So, thank you.

Thank you to the incredible people and fans who have reposted my social media content, reviewed my books, and spread the word about them. It has meant the world to me to be accepted into the book community and your hearts! I deeply love hearing about, seeing, and being a part of how my characters and stories have touched your lives.

Special shout-out to: Ash @badbacon101, Eve @bookishevelynn, Aly @alyoop270, Ariel @chapternchaosfounder, Blanca @books_n_me, Jenny @jam.readsalot, P. Grayce @p..grayce, Tonya @novel.tea_books, Jessica @jessie_dooyle, Stephen @neonatal_steeb, Kylie @kylies_bookaddiction, Gaby @purple.monsta, Hannah @hannah_ashen, Jor Chad @neoncherrybookshelf

About the Author

Arielle Bitetti is an indie romance author. On paper, her life is conventional, but in her mind, it's a sweeping epic with vast worlds and stories yet to be told. She lives in California with her loving husband and her young, adorably cute son whose boundless energy and love sustains her soul.

Join her Newsletter for all the fun goodies and major news direct to your email inbox at www.ariellebitetti.com. With exclusive giveaways, first look at character art/inspo, bonus chapters, and more!

Leave a Review

If you enjoyed this book, please consider leaving a review (even if it's in the form of stars). Anything, even a few words, can help the next reader find *Give Me What You Can't.*

Thank you so much for reading!

www.ariellebitetti.com

Follow me on TikTok & Instagram, where you can stay updated with new book announcements, sneak peeks, and bonus content.

@ariellebitettiauthor

*Not ready to leave our handsome ED doctors yet? Well, I think you're ready for Dr. Samuels's shift to start. And trust me, darling, you're not gonna wanna miss all the things he has to say to a certain best friend...

Give Me What You Will

"Why does the day shift get the new cleaning crew? They should be on the night shift. We need the ones they get in NASCAR, or Formula 1, that clean a floor in like five seconds and move on," Dr. Samuels complained, surveying the massive wet spot on his ED floor. "Someone's gonna slip."

Steph, the day-shift charge nurse and central-hub mom, snorted along with her replacement, night-shift nurse, Nicole. The two older women were reviewing the charts and notes for the night-shift patients in the lobby, ready to hand them over.

"Hey, we all gotta start somewhere," Steph chided him. "And Tanya likes you so much for your charming personality that *you* get the new pit cleaning crew instead of Johnny."

Sam muttered a curse under his breath, clicking the computer screen alive with the wave of the mouse, clocking in to his shift. "When is John coming back? I thought they were supposed to be back by now."

They—meaning John and the younger, newly licensed Dr. Wyatt Lawson, whom John started seeing a few months ago.

Steph side-eyed him, sipping her coffee out of her pink Stanley steel mug. He'd been complaining all week that John and Wyatt were gone. Probably because he had to deal with the night-shift psycho, Dr. Walsh, who was a certified asshole.

"Another week, Dr. Samuels. Need me to write it down on your forehead?" Steph drawled.

He smirked, preferring the sassy Steph over the parental one. He was a grown ass man that already had a mom. Granted, his biological mom was crazier than shit on toast, but still.

"Maybe. I prefer sticky notes, though," he retorted with a lazy smirk.

"Great. I'll tack it onto your forehead, then."

He chuckled, clocked on, and straightened, tossing his stethoscope around his neck and tucking his golden necklace beneath his dark gray scrubs. It was his grandfather's military dog tag, and ever since Papi passed away eight months ago, it had never left his neck. Papi had only one tag on his necklace when Sam had found it among his belongings, and he didn't know where the second tag was. It had been one of the many mysteries surrounding his grandpa that still bothered him, adding another reason to return to Boston and look through the boxes his mom had kept of Papi's. Except that would mean going *back* to Boston, and he wasn't doing that if he could help it.

"Wanna see the pictures Wyatt sent me?" Steph asked, already pulling out her phone from her pocket.

Sam glanced down at the screen, inwardly keeping his expression composed as he glimpsed the romantic, dark blue water canals of Venice, and Wyatt pressing a smooch on John's graying, bearded cheek for a selfie on a gondola.

Christ, they were cheesy.

Sam swallowed the envy bubbling up in his throat like acid and managed to say, "Cool," and felt like a total jackass.

Ever since John and Wyatt had become an official couple, they had been taking a ton of time off. This recent vacation was to celebrate Wyatt's graduation from his last year as a resident, officially becoming

Dr. Lawson, the ED Cowboy. Sam loved them like his own family, and while he wasn't jealous of them, he was envious of what they had.

A loving relationship that fucking worked.

Sam bit back a sigh, reaching for his Papi's tag beneath his scrubs and wondering if he was cursed to be alone like him for the rest of his miserable life. And if so, maybe being a workaholic was a better route than slowly drinking himself into a lonely grave. The irony was that Sam didn't drink that much or smoke. Probably because he spent all of med school working in a bar and his mother smoked like a chimney, so those vices were definitely ruined.

He preferred ignoring all his problems until a cancerous tumor appeared in his body, and then maybe he'd deal with it by getting it surgically removed.

Sam glanced up at the evening patient board that was shifting into the day-shift one. The hustle and bustle of the ED calmed his frayed nerves. He liked the storm of the weekend shift. It was usually busier, messier, and more interesting in his opinion.

His Papi used to say, "It's in the Samuels blood to be adrenaline junkies. If we aren't pursuing the thrill of the chase, we're boring men."

Grief twisted in his gut.

I miss you, you cranky old bastard.

"Hey!" someone shouted from the lobby.

Mendez, the ED's security guard, appeared at the doorway, blocking whoever was trying to come back.

"Hey! Sammy! You in there?"

Sam's heart stuttered to an unexpected halt.

He recognized that voice—that stupidly sexy Boston accent.

No. Fucking. Way.

The hospital door was shoved open, and a broad-shouldered, thick Irish-Italian man with jet-black hair and stubbled whiskers on his cheeks strode through the doors and back into Sam's life. Just like that.

No…

Mendez was hot on his heels, trying to stop him.

Frankie, Sam's former best friend, with his ridiculously handsome face and very punchable Italian nose, was grinning like a buffoon and striding through the ED like he owned the place. Sam had the inexplicable urge to hit something.

Mendez jumped in front of Frankie now, and Sam sighed, watching Frankie duck and slide past smoothly, maintaining his smile and completely undaunted. Mendez spun, looking thoroughly agitated. Yeah, his former best friend had that effect on people.

"Frankie…" Sam growled irritably under his breath.

Frankie wore a black T-shirt and a collared blue-and-black plaid overshirt, with the sleeves pushed up over his thick forearms, revealing his tattoos. His dark jeans looked new, and the fancy black-and-white sneakers certainly were, with how bright they were. His shoulders were rolled back, spine straightened, and he walked without the slightest indication that he had a bum knee.

Sam couldn't help but sweep his gaze up and down Frankie's body and inwardly sigh. It had been eight months. Eight months since he'd seen this man, and he still fucking ached at the sight of him.

Damn it.

Frankie was broad where Sam was tall, and he was thicker, too, which Sam knew was all carefully curated muscle that Frankie had developed over years of training as a mixed martial arts fighter, even going pro a few years back, until a fight shattered his knee and his dreams.

And to his utmost irritation, Frankie Casavani looked good.

Too good.

Fuck.

Eight months wasn't long enough. Maybe a couple of years between them would have been better, Sam thought grimly, scrubbing a weary hand over his face.

When their eyes finally met and held, Frankie's face split into that slow grin that always sent heat ricocheting down his back like a bullet.

"Sir!" Mendez shouted briskly. "You can't be back here."

"Hey, man, I'm just here visitn' a friend. Isn't that right, Sammy?" Frankie shouted, forcing Sam to fucking acknowledge him.

Goddammit, son-of-a-bitch.

Sam maneuvered around the workstation and stopped abruptly at the pool of mop water and…

"Frankie—stop!" Sam held out his hand and watched in horror as Frankie's expensive sneakers slipped out from beneath him, his feet flew into the air, and he crashed backward onto the floor, smacking the back of his head on the wet tile.

"Shit!" Sam muttered, racing over to Frankie's side, getting down onto his knee and seeing the blood pool beneath his head. "I need a gurney, now!"

Frankie blinked, disoriented, cringing and reaching for the back of his head. Black thick hair mixed with blood on the white tile floor.

"Frankie," Sam said in his calm, reassuring tone. "You fell and hit the back of your head. We're gonna lift you onto a gurney and check for a possible concussion and look at the injury."

"I—what?"

"You slipped like a fuckin' cartoon character, Frankie."

Frankie's eyes opened, seeking him, and when their eyes met, he visibly relaxed, that slow grin of his coming back despite the clear pain he was in. "Eh, there you are…"

Sam's throat tightened. "You hit your head pretty hard, man."

Frankie reached for him, grabbing him by the face with his large pawlike hand and patting him affectionately. He was always so damned touchy.

It took everything in Sam not to react to Frankie's casual, affectionate display, and he grabbed his hand, placing it on his chest as the gurney appeared and he, Mendez, and another nurse lifted Frankie onto it.

"Room 4 is open," Nicole, the night nurse, said from behind him, and he nodded.

"Can you get this cleaned up? And tell whoever did this that I wanna see them later," Sam said in a clipped tone as he wheeled Frankie into the open room.

"When'd you grow a stash, man?" Frankie asked, reaching for him again to touch his mustache. "Jesus, when did you get old? You have more gray in that thing than Nona did."

Sam couldn't help but smirk. Frankie always liked to wind him up and spin him out. Nona was Frankie's gray pittie that liked getting into as much trouble as Frankie did.

He pushed the gurney into the room, giving the nurse and student doctors instructions on the tests he wanted to run and then paused, glancing back at Frankie, suddenly distracted. "What do you mean Nona *did*?"

"Is the room supposed to be spinnin'?" Frankie asked, ignoring his question.

"Yeah," Sam replied coolly, snapping on his gloves. "This is our carnival room. We also have a room where the walls talk. But it's padded."

Frankie snorted a laugh and cringed, "Fuck, Sammy, I missed you."

Sam hesitated, stomach swooping as he maneuvered to the side of the bed. "Sit up."

"Oh, doctor-serious now."

Sam brushed his fingers through Frankie's hair, finding the wound and checking it. "One of us has to be," he murmured, "Doesn't look too deep. Superficial at best. We should check for a concussion, though."

Frankie sighed, "My favorite word."

Concussion.

"You're probably fine, Frank. Nothin' to worry about."

Frankie's silence, however brief, told Sam everything he needed to know. He sighed, placing gauze over the wound. "How's the pain?"

"I'm fine. Nothin' I can't handle."

"I can get you some Tylenol."

"Nah."

"What about your…?" He glanced down at Frankie's knee and asked without words. Frankie's lips flattened, nostrils flaring, and he gave a firm shake of his head, indicating that his knee was fine.

His bum left knee had never fully recovered from being broken during one of his MMA fights, and on some days, he walked with a limp. Whenever Sam asked about it before, he dismissed him, telling him he was "fine". Nothing's changed. Sam bit back a curse, refusing to challenge him about it.

Sam pressed his hand to the back of Frankie's head and cradled it, trying hard not to notice how Frankie relaxed into his touch. He hated how much he liked it—how sensitive he was to every little thing this man did, and how his heart raced despite knowing better.

Frankie leaned back to look at him, his dark brown eyes suspending him. "You look good, Sammy."

"Thanks. You too."

"I know," Frankie said with a charming smirk.

"I never thought you'd leave Boston."

"Me either," Frankie retorted. "Funny thing is, I had to. 'Cause apparently my best friend decided to go AWOL on me and stop replyin' to my text messages. Hell, wouldn't even bother to pick up his damned phone."

"Yeah, sorry, man. Life's been busy here."

"Busy," Frankie said flatly. "Busy? That's all I get?"

Sam cleared his throat and stepped back, gauging the blood and seeing that it had already decreased enough to stop applying pressure.

"What do you want me to say...?" Sam heard himself say out loud and immediately sighed in frustration.

Frankie's eyes flicked to his lips and back up. "I dunno. Maybe I've taken one too many blows to the fuckin' head, but how 'bout you start with, 'I miss you too, you handsome son-of-a-bitch'."

Sam averted his gaze, making busy work with a fresh strip of gauze and one more check of the wound. His stomach tightened into coiled knots, thinking about the last time they saw each other and how he had ruined the best thing he had in his life. But it took blowing up the best thing in his life to finally be free of it—of *him*. To give Sam enough space to rebuild a life without Frankie in it.

"No stitches needed, that's good," Sam said in a clipped tone, instructing the other nurses to leave, knowing he could handle this without help.

Once the room was empty, Sam paused. The last time he was in an empty room with Frankie...

"Sammy," Frankie drawled, exasperated.

"We should get you a CT scan, make sure—"

"No."

"Okay... well, if you experience a headache later—"

"I know the drill, doc," Frankie snapped. "You don't gotta tell me what to do with a head injury."

Sam nodded, glancing at the door to the ED. "I'll have Steph, our discharge nurse, come in and..."

"You gonna fuckin' look at me at any point today?"

Sam stilled. "I prefer not to."

"And why the hell not?" Frankie growled.

"I think you know why."

He snorted, "No, man, I don't. What happened is water under the bridge. Papi died. You were upset—I was upset. I get it."

Sam jerked his gaze to his, seeing the steel glint of denial to go back to that moment that ruined their friendship forever. Because it did, whether Frankie wanted to acknowledge it or not.

"So, that's how you rationalized it?" Sam challenged, feeling an icy chill sweep through his bloodstream.

"We've been best friends nearly fifteen fuckin' years, Sammy. We're gonna fuck up now and again. We all make mistakes."

"Mistakes…" Sam drawled the word, rolling it on his tongue and deciding that was not the word he would've used for what happened.

"Yeah."

"So, me slipping my tongue down your throat was a mistake?" Sam whispered.

Frankie's eyes sharpened, and then, impossibly, his lips tilted upward in a soft, insolent smirk. "You didn't get that far."

Sam stared, stunned, opening his mouth to reply, but nothing came out.

"Honestly, Sammy, eight months over that—? Really? You've done far worse to me over the years." Frankie continued to smile up at him from the gurney, folding his hands over his chest and looking completely unfazed by this conversation. "And I mean, it was inevitable. My best friend is gay, I'm incredibly fuckin' sexy. It's bound to happen. You finally couldn't fuckin' resist me."

Sam's cheeks flushed, and he attempted to cover it by pinching the brim of his nose. "Christ, your ego is the size of Mount Everest."

Frankie cocked his chin to the side, grinning, "That's why you love me."

Yeah, he did love him. That was the problem.

"We're family, Sammy."

They weren't family. Hell, Sam wasn't even from Boston like Frankie was. They met at Frankie's dad's bar, and like a moth to a flame, Sam was captured by Frankie's easy charm and sexy smile, and the intensity behind his gaze that felt inescapable.

Because that's who he was.

Irresistible. And apparently, Frankie actually was inescapable.

The distance Sam put between them felt right, necessary even, and the only damned way he could move on. Because Frankie was as straight as they came. The epitome of a ladies' man. Sam had watched the conga line of girls cling around Frankie's neck for the past fifteen years. And he'd had enough. It took losing Pappi for him to finally choose himself for once.

"Look," Frankie pressed, eyebrows lifting high. "I didn't fly all this way to sit in the damned hospital lobby. Let me buy you a beer—some food. Let's catch up."

One evening in Frankie's company wouldn't kill him, and then he'd fly back home and Sam could maybe go another eight months, maybe even a year, without having to see him again.

"Fine," Sam muttered.

"Don't look so enthusiastic, Sammy. I might take it personally."

He shot him a hard look. "You're lucky you didn't need stitches. I would've enjoyed sticking a needle into that thick fuckin' skull of yours."

"There he is," Frankie crooned victoriously. "Good. So, what time you pickin' me up and where we goin'?"

Sam chuckled, feeling the weight on his shoulders shift a little. Frankie was a determined bulldog and wouldn't let this go. And he couldn't blame him. Sam had left abruptly, without a word, and deep down, he knew that it was wrong. Frankie deserved more than that.

He could handle a couple of hours with Frankie, because the truth was, he missed the hell outta him, too. And when the night was over, he'd say goodbye for good. Because once Sam had moved to LA and away from Frankie, he realized something.

He couldn't ignore the truth anymore.

That kiss—that stolen kiss—changed *everything* for him.

Sam no longer had any interest in being just friends with his best friend.

He couldn't. Not when he knew what his lips tasted like after all these damned years. He wasted so much of his life pining for what could never be. It was time to move the fuck on, because he couldn't go backward, and he wouldn't. He had protected Frankie from the truth of his feelings for too long. Maybe it was time to tell him the truth, and then he'd finally leave Sam alone for good.

And if words weren't enough to convince Frankie that this was for the best, then…

I'll kiss his ass again and force him to let me go.

Coming Fall 2026

Book Tropes:

Best Friends

Bi-Awakening

Dirty Talk

Fight to Fuck

Possessiveness

They like it rough

Made in the USA
Coppell, TX
21 June 2026

82617108R00218